The Manor is set in Poland in the latter part of the nineteenth century when the country was emerging from medievalism, and railways, roads and modern cities were being built everywhere. Calman Jacoby, a pious and conservative Jew, in one sense understood the times in which he was living. Having been able to lease the manor lands of a treasonous count, Calman laid the basis of his fortune by selling timber for railway sleepers. But in another sense Calman belonged to the world which was passing away: his innate conservatism made him suspicious of the new revolutionary ideas rising everywhere around him. Although it is the impact of this new secular civilization upon Calman and his family which forms the core of *The Manor,* this is more than a novel about a family, detailing as it does the conflicts and ideas which gave birth to the modern era.

Isaac Bashevis Singer
THE MANOR

SECKER AND WARBURG · LONDON

Printed in Great Britain by
Fletcher & Son Ltd, Norwich

TO MY WIFE ALMA WITH LOVE

AUTHOR'S NOTE

The Manor was written between 1953 and 1955. As with many of my stories and all my novels (with the exception of *Satan in Goray*, which I wrote while still in Warsaw), it was first serialized in the *Jewish Daily Forward*. Although *The Manor* is being published many years after *The Family Moskat*, it portrays an earlier period—the epoch between the Polish insurrection of 1863 and the end of the nineteenth century. It was the era of gas lamps, the time when the Poles had finally become resigned to their loss of independence and turned to a kind of national positivism. Poland now began to emerge as an industrial country; railroads were built, factories were opened, and the cities grew rapidly. The Jews, who until 1863 for the most part still lived in a ghetto atmosphere, now began to play an important role in Polish industry, commerce, the arts and sciences. All the spiritual and intellectual ideas that triumphed in the modern era had their roots in the world of that time—socialism and nationalism, Zionism and assimilationism, nihilism and anarchism, suffragettism, atheism, the weakening of the family bond, free love, and even the beginnings of Fascism.

This volume, although it stands as an independent story, constitutes Part One of the complete saga of *The Manor*. Part Two is now in the process of being prepared for the English-speaking reader.

The Manor was translated by my nephew, Joseph Singer, and by Elaine Gottlieb, the wife of my unforgettable friend Cecil Hemley. The book was edited by Cecil Hemley, Elizabeth Shub, and Robert Giroux, to whom I wish to express my deepest gratitude.

I wish also to thank the National Foundation on the Arts for the grant awarded me in connection with this work.

I.B.S.

ONE

I

After the unsuccessful rebellion of 1863, many Polish noblemen were hanged; others—Count Wladislaw Jampolski among
them—were banished to Siberia. The Czar's soldiers led the
Count in chains through the streets of Jampol, the town
which bore his name.

Though it was dangerous to have anything to do with an
insurrectionist, the priest appeared to administer a farewell
blessing, wearing his vestments and holding a crucifix. Peasants removed their caps; women wept.

There was great excitement when the Count passed the
cluster of huts on the outskirts of the town, where the Jews
had only recently formed a community of their own, known
locally as The Sands. Since Jampol was still under the jurisdic-
tion of the Church, Jews were not permitted to live in the city
itself and had to pay a toll for the privilege of entering it.

The residents of The Sands were astonished by the bearing
of the aristocratic prisoner. The Count with his wind-blown
white hair and mustache, his jaunty stride, flushed face, and
unbuttoned fur coat, with his hat at a rakish angle, seemed as
unconcerned as though he were going off to a party.

Some weeks later the town crier, after summoning the people of Jampol with his drum, read out an edict that had come
from St. Petersburg. The Imperial decree announced the total

confiscation of Count Jampolski's estate except for the land already divided among his former serfs. Countess Maria Jampolska was given six months to vacate the ancestral manor. Eventually it became known that Czar Alexander had deeded the Count's possessions to a duke who was one of his generals.

The Jews shrugged their shoulders: such was the way of the Gentile, where might was right. Calman Jacoby, a Jew of some standing who dealt in wheat and traded with the manor, obtained from the village officials the name of the new lord of the Jampolski manor. Paying a clerk eighteen groschen, he dictated a letter to the duke in St. Petersburg, stating that whereas he, Calman Jacoby, was a trustworthy, God-fearing man and a warden of his community, he ventured respectfully to beg his Excellency to grant him a lease on the manor and all that went with it. Calman concluded with the offer of a generous annual rental.

There was no word from St. Petersburg for some time. Then one day the duke arrived unannounced in Jampol and, settling down at the manor, sent a Cossack to bring Jacoby to him. The Cossack, riding bareback on a small horse, wore a cylindrical cap, a single earring, and carried a leather thong instead of a whip. He led the way at a slow trot, while Calman walked behind. The Sands' inhabitants were close to panic. They feared that false accusations had been leveled against the community and expected retribution, disaster, and bloodshed. Calman's wife Zelda, accompanied by the children, escorted Calman part of the way, wailing as if he had already died. It was rumored a gallows had been erected in the manor courtyard; Calman was to pay for having traded with the rebels.

When Calman entered the manor hall and saw the new master, he prostrated himself to kiss his gleaming boots and plead for mercy. The duke was young, with curly hair and luxuriant side whiskers, and he was wearing civilian clothes. He ordered Calman to his feet. Calman, who could speak some Russian, answered the duke's innumerable questions and the next day returned home with the lease to the manor. Soon afterward the duke departed, leaving Calman Jacoby in charge of the Jampolski estate.

Calman Jacoby's first move was a judicious one. He informed the Countess Maria that she was free to remain at the manor for the rest of her life. Furthermore, he would provide her with horses for her coach and milch cows for her household. He also promised to keep her supplied with wheat, barley, potatoes, groats, and other staples. Calman then came to terms with the bailiff and stewards, though they were known to be drunkards and thieves. Nevertheless, the Jampol peasants resented this Jew, an infidel, who lorded it over Polish soil in the name of an alien oppressor. But at least he did not put on airs. Poland had fought and lost once again. Her finest sons were now being driven into the dismal icy tundras, where the survivors of the 1831 revolt still languished. What did it matter who ruled in the meantime?

Calman Jacoby moved into a cottage formerly inhabited by the manor blacksmith. After nailing mezuzahs on the doorposts he had all his household effects brought in: two sideboards, one for meat and the other for dairy products; the Passover dishes; the everyday crockery; the wardrobes, beds, benches. Calman also had an oak chest, covered in cowhide and braced with brass bands, where he kept his money, articles that were pawned with him, and his silver candlesticks. Since God had denied his Zelda the blessing of a male child, Calman had to save for the dowries of their four daughters.

It was soon apparent that Calman's new venture was a fortunate one. The harvest that year was abundant. After the emancipation of the serfs, much of Count Jampolski's land had been distributed among the peasants, who now had permission to graze their cattle on manorial pastures and cut timber in the Count's forest. However, there were too many hands to work the small individual holdings. Only yesterday these peasants had been slaves who were whipped for their efforts; now Calman Jacoby paid them cash for their work and did not expect his hand to be kissed. He consulted the elder peasants on where to sow seasonal crops, where to plant potatoes, beets, cabbages. From the neighboring gentry he learned of the new threshing machines that were replacing flails. He installed a machine for chopping straw used in cattle fodder. He opened a tavern and a general store in Jampol where one could buy cloth, kerchiefs, shawls, furs, leather, trimmings, iron sauce-pans, pickled herring, lubricating oil, as well as scythes, sickles, hammers, saws, files, nails. The peasants who shopped at Calman's store or drank in his tavern received a discount. Some paid in Calman's private currency—slips of paper printed in Yiddish and bearing his stamped signature. He granted credit to those who qualified for it, and paid more than the market price for flax, calves, oxen, honey, hides, and other surplus produce, which he exported to Warsaw.

Calman had infringed on the law by opening his shop in Jampol, but the Russian officials looked the other way. The entry toll for Jews was abolished. Jampol was no purer than other Polish cities. Wherever Poles settled, the Jews were sure to follow. Other Jews from The Sands began to acquire sites in and about the Jampol marketplace. Jewish tanners, cobblers, coopers, tailors opened workshops. Polish merchandise now moved freely into Russia. Only on the Sabbath did the Jews of Jampol pray collectively, making up a minyan, or quorum of ten, at a private home; but a synagogue was being planned. A cemetery was needed also, for the Jewish dead still had to be carted to the town of Skarshew, where the burial society charged exorbitant fees.

Calman Jacoby prospered rapidly. Though not yet forty, he was already wealthy. No great scholar, he could just about manage to find his way through some of the simpler parts of the Talmud. Nevertheless, he was esteemed for his piety, honesty, and shrewdness.

He was a man of medium stature, broad-shouldered and straight-backed, with calloused hands like those of a peasant. He had a broad, pitch-black beard, a narrow forehead, beetling eyebrows over a large nose, and a thick bullish neck. Yet his dark eyes were spiritual and kind. Like all pious Jews, he wore long sidelocks and close-cropped hair; his neck, ears, and nostrils were tufted with hair. On the High Holy Days his sonorous voice led the congregation in the afternoon prayer. On weekdays he prayed at the first sign of dawn. His breakfast consisted of bread, herring, and cottage cheese, followed by a long draught of water.

Although Calman employed modern methods in business, he refused to have his household tainted by current fashions. He forbade Zelda to use tea or coffee, and at night he lighted his room with a solitary tallow candle or a wick in a saucer of oil. He dressed like other Jewish merchants, wearing a high-crowned hat and an ankle-length caftan. His trousers were held up by a piece of string.

Zelda, who came from a genteel family in Krashnik, longed for brass doorknobs, carved wooden beds, chairs with cane seats, and other signs of affluence. She would have loved to see copper saucepans and basins hanging on the kitchen wall. But Calman insisted that such luxuries, merely decorative at first, would soon become indispensable. And if it should happen that they could no longer be afforded, debts would accumulate until a man would end up bankrupt.

The women in and around Jampol envied Zelda. But she was dissatisfied. Her father, Reb Uri Joseph, had been a scribe, and her family was noted for its men of learning. Her husband, for all his wealth, lacked refinement. His strength made him clumsy, and he had no idea how to handle a woman as delicate as she. He was stingy about consulting doctors. He wouldn't believe that she was not always up to his carnal demands. In the first years of their marriage there had been frequent quarrels and even talk of divorce. But Calman was not a man to relinquish a woman easily.

It had been difficult to raise the children with Zelda constantly ailing. But, thank heavens, the worst was over. She had help now.

All the daughters assisted in the housekeeping, especially

Jochebed, the eldest, who was already of marriageable age. Zelda also had a maid, Faigel, and a man-of-all-work, Getz. On summer days, she could now sit on a chair on the lawn and have a footstool brought to her, while she read the Yiddish version of some sacred book.

Zelda was gaunt, with a pointed chin, a red, bony nose, and pouches under her bleary eyes. She had withered prematurely. As she read, her bonnet kept bobbing, and she was constantly brushing away the bees that mistook the artificial flowers adorning her hat for real ones. Though she was thankful to the Lord for His mercies, Zelda could not accustom herself to sitting in the fields, in the midst of nowhere. There was no place here where women could worship, no butcher shop, no friendly porch where neighbors gathered. The stream purled on its way, trees rustled, cows lowed; shepherds roasted potatoes over bonfires, sang ribald songs.

Zelda thought about her daughters: they should have friends their own age; they should be getting married—she wanted Torah-studying sons-in-law in the house. She longed for grandchildren. One's own children were born of pain, but grandchildren were sheer profit. With God's help, she would one day be a mother-in-law and a grandmother.

II

The estate adjoining Calman's property belonged to a nobleman named Jan Pawlowski. Before the liberation of the peasants, he had owned three hundred serfs. A widower, he lived alone. Closeting himself in his room, behind locked shutters, he sipped brandy through a straw from a carafe on the table, and occupied himself with an endless game of solitaire.

In his youth, Pawlowski had been involved in lawsuits all of which he had lost. He had been married to a famous beauty who had died of consumption while still young. The abolition of serfdom had left Pawlowski with only fifty acres of arable land, a tract of forest, and a low hill said to contain limestone.

Pawlowski sent his steward, Krol, to Calman with an offer to sell the hill. Calman replied that he had no use for it. What should he, a mere leaseholder, do with a hump of earth wedged between the estates of two strangers? But Pawlowski, who was in debt and desperately in need of money, had persisted. After considerable haggling, Calman bought the hill for a small sum.

It developed that Calman had stumbled on a treasure, for the hill was actually composed of the highest grade of limestone. Calman hired laborers and an expert to supervise the quarrying. A kiln was erected, the lime was dug, baked, and then carted to Jampol. The furnace blazed day and night. The spiraling smoke from the chimney was a sulfurous yellow, which at times turned red with shooting flames, and reminded Calman of Sodom and Gomorrah. The Jews believed that if the fire continued for seven years it would surely bring forth a salamander.

The peasants complained that the Jew was contaminating the Polish countryside, putrefying the air, but the authorities ignored them. Poland, after the insurrection, was full of activity, as if awakened from a long slumber. Workshops sprang up, mines were dug, forests cut down, and railroads built. Polish products, textiles, leather goods, brushes, sieves, sheepskin coats, glassware appeared on the world market. As soon as the Jews were granted permission to reside freely in the cities, the country began to grow.

It was said that Calman had been blessed by a holy man. A building boom was in progress, and his lime quarry yielded immense profits. Scores of Jews and Gentiles earned their livelihood from it. Calman purchased horses and wagons and built a smithy. As if all this were not enough, the Russian government decided to build a railway line through Jampol. The contract was awarded to the Warsaw magnate Wallenberg, a Jewish convert to Catholicism. Since steel rails needed wooden ties, Calman had one of his clerks write a letter for him to Wallenberg offering to provide ties at a cheaper price than anyone else. Wallenberg asked Calman to come to Warsaw to discuss the matter.

On the morning of his departure, Calman brushed his beard, put on his Sabbath gaberdine, polished his boots, and climbed into his carriage. Getz sat in the driver's seat. Calman leaned out of the window to say goodbye to Zelda and the four girls. "Godspeed!" exclaimed Zelda, bursting into tears. So much good fortune had begun to alarm her. She feared the Evil Eye and, from the holy volumes she had read, knew that riches might portend disaster. She would prefer to live in the poorhouse rather than have the slightest harm befall any of her children, even the chipping of a fingernail.

Faigel, the maid, came out with a chicken, which she had roasted and wrapped in cabbage leaves, to give to Getz. He sat on the box wearing a peaked leather cap and high boots. His little tufts of yellow beard were trimmed. A small mustache sprouted on his upper lip. He had watery eyes, tawny eyebrows, and a nose shaped like a ram's horn. He waved his whip at Faigel familiarly.

"Behave yourself!" Faigel admonished him.

Calman's daughter Jochebed was blond like her mother, with the same narrow face, pointed chin, prominent nose, and freckles down to her neck. Though already eighteen, she was still not engaged to be married. Calman had been so preoccupied with business that he had neglected to find a husband for her. This was another matter he intended to take care of in Warsaw. Her sisters had nicknamed her "the young spinster." It was not easy for Jochebed to think of herself as a rich man's daughter. She still wore frowzy clothes, worked hard, and tended her sisters. On weekday evenings she helped Faigel the maid pluck poultry. On Sabbath afternoons, after the cholent dinner, she read the Yiddish version of the Pentateuch at her mother's side. A fortuneteller had once told Jochebed she would die young and she had never forgotten it. Now, standing back with her mother, she likewise called out, "Godspeed!" and dabbed a tear with her apron.

Shaindel, "the Gypsy," a year younger, stood on the carriage step, to embrace and kiss her father. She had sparkling black eyes, jet-black hair, and a dusky complexion. Shorter than her older sister, she had rounded hips and a large bosom. She loved costume jewelry, earrings, bracelets, and flowers to twine in her hair. Now that her father was becoming rich, Shaindel made a list of things she wanted him to bring back from Warsaw: a necklace, shoes with buckles, hair ribbons, canvas and thread for embroidery, scented soap. Calman promised everything she asked. This daughter brightened his life with her vivacity; she pampered him as if he were a favorite uncle, not her father. Having gone over the list, she added, winking at him, "And don't forget a handsome bridegroom!"

Miriam Lieba, at fifteen, was already half a head taller than Jochebed. With her blond hair in two plaits, her slenderness, her blue eyes, her graceful neck and straight nose, she did not look Jewish. The ways of a wealthy young lady seemed to come naturally to her. She yearned for fashionable clothes, read Polish books, and even had had a tutor from Jampol to instruct her. Rather than share her sisters' bedroom, she preferred a small attic room of her own. Coming forward, Miriam Lieba presented her father with a list of the Polish books she wanted from Warsaw, and kissed his forehead. She affected a remote and pensive air, for she was in the midst of a Polish novel about a countess who had left her castle and eloped to Paris with a violinist.

Tsipele, the youngest, eight years old, with diminutive pigtails, was dark like Shaindel. A pious woman came regularly from Jampol to instruct her in prayers and penmanship. The warmhearted Tsipele could not resist beggars, and whenever one came to the house she parted with all the pocket money she had. Her father, mother, sisters, and even the peasant women were always kissing her. Tsipele asked her father to buy her a doll in Warsaw and a miniature prayer book like one she had seen at a friend's house in Jampol.

On the way to Warsaw, Calman realized for the first time

that he was a man of consequence. Innkeepers fussed over him; salesmen trailed after him. Peasants whom he had never seen before called him "squire" and raised their caps to him. Even the dogs seemed to be in awe of him. It was as it is said in the Book of Proverbs: "When a man's ways please the Lord, He maketh even his enemies to be at peace with him."

Warsaw was so changed that Calman, who had not visited it since before the rebellion, barely recognized it. Streets which formerly had been forbidden to Jews now had many Jewish residents. The town had expanded, buildings crowded each other, and the shops were full of people. The courtyard of the inn where Calman was staying was so jammed with wagons that Getz could scarcely find room for the horses. Everywhere, the wooden sidewalks were being replaced by flagstone, gutters deepened, and new lampposts erected. Across the Vistula, in the suburb of Praga, the sky was filled with writhing smoke from the factory chimneys.

Calman proceeded to Wallenberg's office. Wallenberg was short and stout, had a huge head, mutton-chop whiskers, a crooked nose, dark Jewish eyes. He was dressed in a black jacket, checked trousers, a high collar and broad cravat. Calman presented his credentials. He was the leaseholder of a manor and the proprietor of a lime quarry; he also had a letter from the magistrate at Jampol attesting his honesty. Calman, who spoke the Polish of the peasants, frequently broke into Yiddish. Wallenberg, just as the Russian duke had been, was favorably impressed with Calman. He offered him a cigar, and after detailed negotiations, Calman obtained a contract to supply ties for the Imperial railway, as well as a substantial payment in advance. When they parted, Wallenberg shook Calman's hand and wished him luck—in Yiddish.

On the street, Calman was besieged by a host of beggars—deaf-mutes, cripples, hunchbacks. He distributed alms and was blessed in return. At a kosher restaurant, he and Getz had a city meal: noodle soup, meatballs, applesauce, brandy with egg cake. After dinner, since he was in a hurry and did not know his way about, Calman hailed a droshky, which clattered over the cobblestones among pedestrians who scarcely bothered to step aside. How they escaped being knocked down was a mystery. Porters crowded the streets hauling all kinds of loads; women venders squatted on the sidewalks in front of their wares; students strolled about with elegant young ladies. Mounted police armed with lances patrolled the streets, on the alert for any new signs of rebellion.

Reb Ezekiel Wiener, whom Calman had in mind as a father-in-law for Jochebed, was a follower of the Hassidic Rabbi of Marshinov. He lived in a fine house on Mead Street, and Calman, seeing his brass nameplate at the entrance, was awed by it. The maid who opened the door gave him an insolent glance and told him to wipe his feet on the mat.

The family was expecting him. Reb Ezekiel Wiener, a small, red-faced man with a broad silvery-white beard, introduced his wife, who wore a wig fastened with combs. She was all smiles and her fancy Yiddish was incomprehensible to Calman. The matchmaker was there too, drinking tea and nibbling cake. The prospective bridegroom, Mayer Joel, was a tall, dark-complexioned young man, wearing kid boots, a cloth gaberdine, and a silken vest from which a watch chain dangled. He smiled slyly, twirled his sidelocks, and made witty comments. Taking a sheet of paper from a drawer, he signed his name in Hebrew, Polish, and Russian.

"You may examine him to see how much he knows," Reb Ezekiel observed.

"I'm no scholar."

"Then get an examiner. In Talmudic studies, you'll find him very advanced."

But Calman did not want to waste time in further discussion. At his insistence, a preliminary agreement was drawn up whereby he contracted to provide a dowry of three thousand rubles, all the wedding gifts, and in addition to support the newlyweds for the first ten years of their marriage. The ceremony formalizing the engagement of the young couple would take place at Jampol. Mayer Joel gave Calman a letter for his future bride, which he had copied word for word from a manual of model letters.

The following morning, at dawn, Calman said his prayers and left for home. He found the city and its constant din oppressive. In the chaos and babble, amid such towering structures, a man could easily forsake God and be forsaken by Him. Getz lashed the horses. Once out of the city, Calman sat back comfortably, reflecting. His wealth was increasing, his enterprises expanding—the Lord preserve him from the Evil Eye. Did he deserve it? Perhaps his rewards on earth would be paid for by damnation later. Calman vowed that he would never become like the rich men of Warsaw, inflated with their own importance; he would always remain a humble, unaffected Jew.

The news of Calman's contract preceded him to Jampol. Lumbermen, brokers, job applicants surrounded him the minute he arrived. Fellow merchants suggested that he employ a bookkeeper and a cashier, since he could no longer keep his money in his pocket or in a chest. His business ventures now involved millions of rubles.

While in Warsaw, Calman had been advised by the lime merchants to build a branch line linking his quarry to the railway. This would, of course, cost a fortune, but the banks would not deny him credit.

Locking himself in the back of his store, Calman took out a pencil and wrote down columns of figures. He was no expert at mathematics, but he could add, subtract, multiply, and divide. And he never forgot the old saying: He who lives without reckoning dies without grace.

2

Calman soon discovered that it is as difficult for a rich man to be parsimonious as it is for a poor one to be extravagant. The house would have to be refurbished for the visit of the future in-laws, for how could such refined people be expected to eat with tin spoons and sit on wooden benches? With a zeal that astounded him, Zelda and the girls began to redecorate the house. Zelda purchased wardrobes, tables, sideboards, chairs, beds, vases, and bric-a-brac from Countess Jampolska, since many rooms at the manor were no longer in use. A craftsman from Skarshew repapered the walls, painters stained the floors. New clothes were needed too, and tailors and dressmakers made coats, gowns, and underclothes for Zelda and her daughters. A fox-lined overcoat with little tails dangling from the inner seams was tailored for Calman, as well as new caftans and breeches. New boots were ordered from Warsaw.

Calman scarcely had time to reproach his family for their prodigality, however, for he went to bed late and was up at cockcrow. He had to supervise reapers and threshers, make sure the meadows were mowed in season, the hay gathered and stacked properly for drying. The peasants needed careful watching, for some of them stole. Innumerable disputes, arguments, and lawsuits developed. Calman was obliged to bribe the court assessor as well as the local chief of police, and to distribute gifts among their subordinates. He was swamped with proposals of various kinds: a Jewish bailiff recommended that Calman distill brandy and brew beer, since the Jampol countryside was especially suited to the cultivation of hops; a sugar refiner wanted him to plant beets. The merchants supplying the builders clamored for more lime than the kiln could produce. Calman now understood the meaning of the Talmudic saying: The more property, the more anxiety.

Nevertheless, Calman had signed a contract, and there was no question of his not honoring it. The railway demanded its wooden ties. To supply them, Calman had bought a tract of nearby forest and the trees were now being cut down. The work went slowly because the lumbermen, a hard-drinking crew, were forever going off on sprees and had to be driven back while in a state of drunken stupor. Moreover, the watchmen were incompetent and timber vanished in large quantities. Calman had to assert himself everywhere. He built a hut in the middle of the forest and took two dogs and a gun along for protection, although he loathed firearms. A man alone in the forest had no other alternative. Ever since the insurrection, gangs of bandits roamed the countryside. Calman also began to ride horseback in order to cover the great distances, and since a long gaberdine was awkward, he adopted a short jacket. To keep house for him in the forest, he was compelled to hire a Gentile maidservant, Antosia, since no Jewish girl would trust herself alone in the wilderness.

The blows of axes, the grating of saws echoed through the woods. The finished ties were carted and stacked along the track of the future railroad. Discarded logs, wooden chips were taken to the lime kiln to be used as fuel. Wherever possible, the pine trees were tapped for turpentine. At night Calman returned to his cabin so exhausted that he slumped onto his crude bunk in his clothes, and Antosia had to come and pull off his boots. On several occasions he missed his twilight prayers, but made up for his dereliction by repeating the Eighteen Benedictions during the evening prayer, first throwing a coat over his gun, so as not to utter hallowed words in sight of a weapon. He stood in a corner, facing east toward Jerusalem, with his forehead resting against a plank, and prayed with deliberation, inwardly translating the words from Hebrew to Yiddish:

"Make us lie down in quietude, O Lord our God, and cause us to rise up to life, and spread out the tent of Thy peace. And ward off Satan before and behind us, and envelop us in the shadow of Thy wings."

While Calman mumbled and sighed, Antosia prepared dinner, boiling water and milk, cooking dumplings, millet, or potatoes, depending on the day's menu. Calman ate no meat on weekdays. He had to watch Antosia closely, and even supervised the milking of the cow, for how could one trust a Gentile to observe the dietary laws? His appetite, stimulated by the forest air, was always ravenous. After washing his hands and saying the appropriate benediction, he sat down, eating slowly and abundantly, swallowing the brimming bowl of milk that Antosia set before him. The chirping of grasshoppers, the cries of birds settling down for the night came through the tiny window. Midges, butterflies, and moths circled the single candle, casting weird shadows and singeing their wings in the flame.

Antosia hovered close by, bringing the saltcellar, more bread, serving cheese or honey. She came from a village near Jampol, and her husband had disappeared while serving in the army. Though still in her twenties, she looked almost forty, had a snub nose, green eyes, a stubby chin, freckles, and ash-blond hair. With no one else to talk to, she told Calman all the details of her past: how her poor dear father had died of consumption; how her sweet mother had introduced a stepfather into the home; how her stepfather had beaten her every evening with a wet rod which she herself had been forced to soak in slops for the purpose. Sitting on the floor near Calman, scouring a pot with cinders, she would relate her story in a plaintive, singsong voice.

"He beat me unmercifully, he did. There was I, kissing his feet, while he kept on whacking me as if I had no more feeling than a cabbage. He was like that—when he started whipping, he couldn't stop. If my dear mother tried to stop him, she got it too. The beast had no pity!"

"Just a murderer," murmured Calman, between mouthfuls.

"Ah, but he could be sweet as an angel, too. When the devil left him, he was as tender as my own father. He'd call me to the table, pinch my cheek, feed me from his own plate. And then he'd smile so lovingly. I forgot all the beatings when he smiled."

"Is he still alive?"

"No. Dead."

"That's how it all ends," muttered Calman to himself. It was futile to offend God; and of what use were earthly riches? What did the Holy Book say? Money is a temptation and a chastisement. Getting up from the table, Calman washed, said the concluding grace, and then, without a pause, began to recite his bedtime prayers. Antosia, shaking up his straw pallet to make it more comfortable, always found a few grains of wheat in the straw and popped them into her mouth. In some ways she was like an animal. Every evening, circling about Calman, baring her teeth in an endless grin, she found things to do to keep her in the cabin, although her bed was in the stable. Night after night, Calman had to endure Joseph's temptation in the presence of Potiphar's wife. But he would not expose himself to damnation. Had not God blessed him with fine daughters and wealth? It was true that Zelda, after each childbirth, had been unapproachable for months on end, that she lived on medicines, had undergone her change of life at an early age, and had long since become frigid. But where is it written that all must go well with a man? Men more pious than he had fared even worse. Calman resolved to assume no further commitments. The manor and the lime quarries were more than enough for him and would support all his children after his death. The forest was fit for wolves, not men.

Soon his meditations ceased. His eyelids grew heavy and closed. A single snore issued from the depths of his body. The next thing he knew, the sun and the twittering birds had awakened him.

11

In Jampol not only Calman but the whole Jewish community was prospering. As the Jews moved out of The Sands, Gentiles moved in. Land for a synagogue had been acquired and the foundations laid, a burial ground had been purchased, and a rabbi had come. Calman had contributed liberally for everything.

Though Calman had sworn not to embark on new business ventures, he became involved in a scheme to revive a half-ruined brickworks that lay on the outskirts of Jampol. The owner had fled to Krakow to avoid paying his sons' ruinous debts. With his assets and cash reserves, Calman could always borrow money at low interest rates, and by acquiring the brickworks he was able to supply not only timber and lime but bricks as well for the new communal projects.

That year Calman and his family stayed in Jampol for the High Holy Days, the New Year and the Day of Atonement. After the services on Simhath Torah, followed by the parade of scroll bearers, Calman invited the worshippers to his tavern. He set out food and opened a cask of beer, a barrel of wine, and a keg of mead. Even the rabbi, Reb Menachem Mendel himself, joined in.

As the feast was ending, Calman pledged himself to build a poorhouse, whereupon four husky, inebriated men hoisted him on their shoulders and bore him in triumph to the site of the synagogue, the rest of the crowd trailing behind. Once there, the men formed a ring and danced, with the children in the center frisking about. The women stood on the sidelines, clapping and laughing gleefully. Members of the Ladies Aid Society of the new Burial Association had brought along a hollowed gourd with candles in it, which they now lit. They tried to place the gourd on Calman's head as a crown, but he refused such a tribute. Zelda protested that it was a pagan custom learned from the peasants, who crowned their newly appointed headmen in that way. Shaindel took the gourd and mischievously placed it on her own head. Immediately, a cluster of young women led her off in state to the rabbi's wife, but it was the rabbi's son, Ezriel, who came to the door. Shaindel, intoxicated by a goblet of wine and crying, "I am the queen of Jampol!" tugged one of his sidelocks.

The next day it began to rain and the rain continued for four days. The foundation of the synagogue became a pool; houses were flooded; the stream that drove the Jampol mill submerged the sluices, and the dam burst. Weeks of freezing rain and snow followed.

Reb Ezekiel Wiener, the future father-in-law, sent a letter from Warsaw to say that it would be a great strain upon himself and his family to travel to Jampol twice, once for the betrothal, and again for the wedding. He therefore suggested an early wedding, to be held on the Sabbath of Hanukkah, and Calman agreed. Jochebed was about to turn nineteen, the age of spinsterhood, and Shaindel was only one year her junior. Calman had inherited from his forebears the principle that the sooner one's daughters are married off, the better.

Zelda hastened the preparations for Jochebed's trousseau. A Warsaw merchant supplied silk and velvet, wool and lace, but the local dressmakers complained that Jochebed was hard to fit. Gaunt and small-bosomed, she had no hips worth mentioning and her hands were rough. Despite the help of the maid, she had continued to knead dough, carry pails of water, bend over the washtub, bake bread, and fuss around with brooms and mops. Jochebed could not outgrow the period of Calman's poverty.

The wedding was a noisy event in Jampol. The bridegroom's family arrived from Warsaw in three covered wagons. The men wore coats lined with fox and squirrel. They walked about puffing cigars and pipes, humming Hassidic melodies, or else were absorbed in abstruse theological discussions. The women were dressed gaily in satin bonnets and fancy wigs, headbands, fur-lined coats, capes, and all sorts of fur stoles and muffs. They smelled of almonds and honey cake, and exuded an air of cosmopolitan vanity. As Calman's small house could not accommodate all the visitors, beds had to be set up in the barn. Soon after he arrived, Mayer Joel, the bridegroom, who was not particularly reticent, went to inspect the cattle in their stalls. Accompanied by his brother, he then set off on a long stroll through the fields, now sown with winter wheat. On their return, the two reported having glimpsed a deer.

The girls in the Warsaw party included not only the bridegroom's sisters, but also first and second cousins, and these young ladies assumed a lofty attitude toward the unsophisticated girls of Jampol. Assembled for the wedding, they strutted about in dainty shoes with singularly high heels, and wore snug-waisted gowns with pleats. Their faces were unblemished and their coiffures in the very latest style. Constantly nibbling cakes and other delicacies, they made sly gibes at the bride and mimicked the country girls. When the dancing started, they paired off, followed the most intricate steps, and called to the musicians for special tunes. The Jampol girls, afraid to display themselves, looked on, astonished. Shaindel, Calman's daughter, was furious at the insolent Warsaw coquettes. Light on her feet, and knowing she danced well, she asked Mirale, the rabbi's daughter, to be her partner. Mirale blushed.

"I don't know the steps."

"You don't have to know them. Come on!"

Placing one hand on Mirale's shoulder, Shaindel encircled her waist with the other arm, and they whirled round and round, their feet drumming the floor.

"Why hasn't Ezriel come?" asked Shaindel.

"Because his gaberdine is torn."

"Then why didn't you mend it?"

Mirale was at a loss for an answer.

"If I had a brother, I'd look after him," said Shaindel. "A litter of girls was all that my mother could produce," she added and laughed uproariously.

The marriage canopy was set up outdoors, on the frozen snow. The younger women, carrying twisted candles, ranged themselves in two rows before it. The frosty air was still. Calman and Reb Ezekiel escorted the bridegroom, who towered above them, out of the house. Striding rapidly along, he glanced furtively right and left. A beard already sprouted on his chin. His eyes were dusky and his velvet cap was perched roguishly on his head. His sidelocks were twisted into tight little horns. The tops of his high kid boots gleamed from beneath the hem of his overcoat. Though a Hassid, he had the powerful physique of a Cossack, and the girls whispered among themselves that he could easily tuck Jochebed away in his belt.

Next Jochebed was led out by her mother and her mother-in-law. Zelda could scarcely walk, her legs were so swollen. The doctors said that, among other ailments, she suffered from diabetes.

Under the canopy the bridegroom stepped on Jochebed's shoe to signify that he was to be the master, and crushed a wineglass as an omen of good luck.

At the wedding dinner, after the "golden soup" course, Mayer Joel expounded briefly on the Talmud, and throughout the feast, while doing full justice to the various dishes and the wine, he recounted miracles attributed to the Hassidic Rabbi of Marshinov. He even managed to discuss a little business on the side. The local guests admitted that Calman had picked a winner. But was that surprising? Money will buy anything—even a seat in Paradise!

3

In the shed which served as a temporary house of worship while the synagogue and study house were being built, Ezriel, the rabbi's son, each day studied the Talmud, reciting and interpreting the text to himself in a singsong chant. His father wanted him to follow in the family tradition and become a rabbi, and was already instructing him in the finer points of Judaic law. Ezriel wore full Hassidic dress: skullcap, gaberdine, sash, and trousers tucked into high boots. His sidelocks were shaggy and short. Nevertheless, because of his straight nose, blue eyes, thin lips, and longish chin, he did not look like a typical Hassid. His flaxen hair was streaked with gold. Only his high forehead suggested the Jewish intellectual.

Reb Menachem Mendel had long been concerned about the erratic behavior of this slender boy, who was fond of sitting on roofs and climbing up ladders, who liked to chop wood, dig ditches, and who often wandered off for long tramps in the fields. As a child, he had set snares for birds, carved whistles from reeds as shepherds do, and brought home not only cats and dogs, but frogs and other unclean reptiles.

Worst of all, he had begun a long time ago to ask questions that reeked of heresy. Does a live carp suffer agonies when it is scaled and cut to pieces for the Sabbath meal? Why are some people poor and others rich? What was there before the universe? Does a goat have a soul? Was Adam a Jew? Did Eve wear a bonnet? And he was constantly finding contradictions in the Holy Writ, pointing out that in one place it is stated that a man is punished only for his own sins, but in another, that the third and fourth generations must suffer for them; and first the Lord is said to be invisible, then it is written that the elders while they ate and drank saw the Lord. For another thing, Ezriel criticized the prophet Elisha for causing the children to be attacked by bears; the boy felt bitterly reproachful toward King David for slaying Uriah the Hittite, and he wept and blasphemed when he read how Abraham sent his concubine Hagar into the desert with nothing but a jug of water, and how she almost perished of thirst.

Reb Menachem Mendel, descendant of a long line of wise men, could not understand how he had fathered this misfit. He blamed it all on his wife Tirza Perl, whose father, Reb Abraham Hamburg, warden of the Jewish community of Turbin, was an inveterate opponent of Hassidism. Whenever Ezriel misbehaved, Reb Menachem Mendel rebuked his wife, saying, "It's that heathen blood of yours!"

In Turbin, his father-in-law's home town, where Reb Menachem Mendel had held his first rabbinical post, Ezriel had utterly disgraced himself. At cheder he had been unable to get along with other boys, mimicking the teachers, telling fantastic yarns, and playing with girls. It was partly Ezriel's fault that Reb Menachem Mendel had gotten into difficulties with his congregation and had had to leave.

Following his stay in Turbin, Reb Menachem Mendel had spent several years in Lublin as an assistant rabbi. There, though Ezriel had gradually acquired studious habits, he nevertheless had been unable to remain settled in any one yeshiva for long. He would be absorbed in his books for days, but then suddenly he would want to be out, touring all the inns and markets, or exploring Piask, the thieves' quarter. Moreover, the read depraved works, reports of scientific observations and experiments, descriptions of natural marvels, guidebooks to big cities and foreign lands, and accounts of life among savages. He would utter such preposterous statements as that the earth revolved around the sun and not the sun around the earth; that the moon is inhabited by human beings; that stones called meteors drop out of the skies. Once Ezriel brought home a magnet to demonstrate its attraction for nails; another time, he lit a candle, covered it with an upturned tumbler, and explained that the reason the flame went out was lack of oxygen.

His mother, Tirza Perl, though alarmed by his antics, delighted in his knowledge, but Reb Menachem Mendel frowned upon it. Reb Mendel knew the ways of temptation. One began with questions, then one adopted modern styles of dress, and next there was loss of faith, even apostasy. Consequently, Reb Menachem Mendel had accepted with alacrity the rabbinate at Jampol. Enlightened individuals could not possibly inhabit so small a community. Baubles such as magnifying glasses, compasses, and maps would hardly be found there. He observed with relief that, once in Jampol, Ezriel again seemed engrossed in his Talmudic studies. Reb Menachem Mendel was anxious now to have him marry without delay, for when a youth finally has a wife, a dowry, a father-in-law to support him, and children of his own, he settles down.

"We'll be proud of him yet, God willing," he remarked to Tirza Perl. "Jampol is not a den of infamy, like Lublin."

Ezriel, seated at the table, had for several hours been immersed in a chapter concerning forbidden impurities. Now he glanced up, resting his gaze on the curtain embroidered with red eagles and blue deer, on the Holy Ark, decorated with the tablets of the Ten Commandments and flanked by two gilded lions standing with tails up and tongues protruding. Crowding the bookcase were the Talmud, volumes of exegesis, the Cabala, law digests, ethical treatises, and other religious books. No matter how defaced the titles on the backs had become, Ezriel could distinguish one from the other by their bindings. Through the window, he saw a sky full of low-hanging clouds. It was snowing heavily. In the direction of his gaze lay Calman Jacoby's manor, beyond it fields, forests, hills, and still farther Germany, France, and Spain. Then came the ocean, where ships sailed to America. On the other side of the New World was the Pacific Ocean, in which, according to ancient belief, the fiery sun each night immersed itself. Further on were Japan, China, Siberia—and so home again!

The earth is spherical, Ezriel had read, one and a half million times smaller than the sun, which is itself no more than a star among millions of others. But in the Bible the sun and moon are presented as two lamps, and the stars merely as lesser lights. The author of the Pentateuch obviously had not the remotest conception of natural science. That being the case, how could he presume to know the truth about other matters? One must assume, therefore, that the Bible was nothing but a collection of legends and old wives' tales. That being so, why study the books of Holy Writ? On the other hand, how had the universe come into being? Could it have created itself? How had the atoms arranged themselves in order, with summer, winter, day, night, men, women, thoughts, feelings? The worldly books Ezriel had read in Lublin, though they revealed many facts, explained nothing. What was magnetism or electricity? According to the authors, things just happened by themselves. The universe was ruled by chance. But what then was chance? And how did it work?

Ezriel yawned, stood up, slowly raised one arm and then the other, flexing his muscles. Where had he come from? Or his thoughts? How could a sperm cell without will or soul turn into a human being with a mind, heart, joys, sorrows, dreams, love? What a riddle!

The door opened and his sister Mirale stood on the threshold, a shawl covering her head, the toes of her shoes caked with snow. Something must have gone wrong at home because as a rule girls did not enter the men's house of worship.

"What is it?" he cried.

"You're wanted at home. Your future father-in-law is waiting."

"Who?"

"Reb Calman Jacoby. And he's brought a Talmud examiner. You're engaged to Shaindel!"

Ezriel's heart began to pound. He slowly closed his book in an effort to calm himself, resolving not to be too hasty, or distressed if nothing came of the interview. Strangely enough, ever since Simhath Torah, when Shaindel had tugged his sidelock, her face had been in his mind; he had even dreamed of her. Their marriage must have been predestined. Yes, a divine eye keeps watch and a divine hand gives guidance. Slipping into his coat, he made a gesture as if to apologize to the Holy Ark for having profaned it with his doubts.

"After you," he commanded Mirale, since it was considered unseemly for a marriageable young man to be seen in the company of a girl, even his own sister.

I I

Calman Jacoby and the Rabbi of Jampol, eager to see their children married, set the wedding date for the Sabbath following Pentecost. Meanwhile Calman invited the prospective in-laws to the manor for the Feast of the New Year of the Trees.

Ezriel and Shaindel, who had exchanged only diffident glances at the betrothal ceremony, by now felt more at ease with each other. It was a family party. At the men's table Mayer Joel asked Calman and Ezriel to accompany him on his next visit to the Hassidic Rabbi of Marshinov. The conversation veered from holy men to Moses Montefiore, from the Rothschild fortune to the bags of gold which certain Polish noblemen had purportedly left in Jewish custody before taking to the forests to fight the Russians.

Reb Menachem Mendel told the story of a dibbuk at Turbin. One night, when a girl went outdoors to fetch a pail of water from a well, an evil spirit took possession of her body. A weird male voice came from her throat. The wandering soul had been a man, a Talmudist of perverse character, who had recited prayers and portions of the Torah backward, starting at the end and finishing at the beginning. He would also wrangle with the sages on difficult points of Judaic law. The bewitched young woman, though ordinarily frail, lifted a rock that three strong men together could not budge. She juggled it as though it were a pebble.

This reminded Calman of his native village, where a corpse had once been summoned to appear before a rabbinical tribunal. The corpse had made a habit of haunting and tormenting his former business partner. The beadle went to the cemetery to summon the ghost by rapping thrice on his tombstone with the rabbi's walking stick. At the tribunal, a corner of the room, partitioned by a sheet, was set aside for the dead man. The judges ruled that the dead man's partner should pay an indemnity of several hundred gulden to the heirs of the deceased, and the haunting stopped.

Mayer Joel, plucking at his fledgling beard with one hand, while with the other he drummed on the table, exclaimed: "What would the skeptics say to that?"

"They'd say it was nonsense!" Ezriel announced, much to his own amazement.

"But people saw it . . . with their own eyes!"

"Saw what? A sheet?"

"The soul is not visible—"

"Science concerns itself only with the visible, with things that can be weighed and measured," said Ezriel, feeling as though he too were possessed.

Reb Menachem Mendel paled and clutched his red beard. Mayer Joel gave his father-in-law a mocking glance. Calman lowered his head.

"Don't you believe in dibbuks?" Calman asked.

"One can't accept the ridiculous."

"Do you believe in God?"

"Of course."

"Well, that's something. At least you believe in God," Calman said.

Shaindel was alarmed. Aided by her younger sister Miriam Lieba, she had been bringing in refreshments, figs, dates, raisins, almonds, cake, various sweetmeats, and mead. With her hair in a chignon, wearing a new dress and a golden necklace, a betrothal gift from Ezriel's mother, she was standing near the table, holding a tray, and listening, delighted that her fiancé held advanced views and was bold enough to express them. He sat there pale, his lips quivering, his ears fiery, his blue eyes fixed upon her. It was she alone who had induced Calman to approach Ezriel through the matchmaker. Every night as she lay in bed she marveled at her infatuation for this young man whom she scarcely knew. Unobserved, she would take the betrothal document from her father's chest of drawers and pore over the signature: Ezriel Babad. It had none of the flourishes of Mayer Joel's hand; there was an austerity about it. His signature seemed to bestride her own. There in the betrothal document, with its ornate border, its gold-embossed *Mazel Tov*, and its Hebrew text, incomprehensible to Shaindel, he and she seemed already united, practically man and wife. Now that Mayer Joel was trying to confuse Ezriel, Shaindel thrust herself forward with the tray.

"Well, daughter, put it down," said Calman. "Don't be shy."

But Shaindel took her time as she set the table with the plates, cups, and saucers handed to her by Miriam Lieba. Let the hot tempers cool! When everything was on the table, the girls still hovered within hearing.

"So you don't believe in the transmigration of souls?" inquired Mayer Joel.

"There's no reference to it either in the Bible or in the Talmud," answered Ezriel.

"Will you accept the authority of Ari the Saint on the subject?"

"Maimonides dissented."

29

"That's the battle cry of the Maskilim—emancipator's talk!"

Reb Menachem Mendel unclasped his beard. "He's really a good boy, but something of a show-off and nonconformist—takes after my father-in-law, Reb Abraham Hamburg. And he's not behaving maturely."

"Marriage will alter him, please God," said Calman, soothingly.

"The truth is all I care about," Ezriel insisted.

"It is absolutely certain that transmigrating souls exist. The world is full of them," Reb Menachem Mendel reaffirmed hoarsely. "In Izhbitsa, a six-months-old infant fell ill, God help us, and as it died cried out in a voice that made the walls tremble, 'Hear O Israel, the Lord our God!' The doctor, a debauched unbeliever, did penance after hearing that cry. He gave up his medical practice and went to live with a holy man. In time he became a saint!"

Reb Menachem Mendel stopped short. His voice was choked. His right hand tingled with an almost irresistible desire to strike Ezriel. Not only was the young fool mocking the Lord and His works, but he was wrecking the match! Calman would call off the engagement. Reb Menachem Mendel saw himself being forced out of Jampol by an infuriated mob. Recalling the passage, "Thy undoing and thy ruin shall from thyself come forth," he mopped his brow and began to fan himself with his skullcap. Even his sidelocks were moist. Calman suddenly noticed Shaindel and Miriam Lieba.

"You still here? Back to the women's table with you!"

"I haven't brought the jelly yet," said Shaindel.

As the girls withdrew, Shaindel gripped Miriam Lieba's wrist. The engagement was as good as broken, all because that overrighteous Mayer Joel had set himself up as God's own policeman. Shaindel was overcome by sympathy for Ezriel, who had let himself be carried away by his passion for the truth. But she would be on his side. She would plead for him with her father: "I marry Ezriel or no one else—ever!"

In the kitchen she burst into tears. Then she washed her face in the basin and examined herself in a mirror. Climbing a stool, she got a long-forgotten jar of currant jelly from the top shelf and returned to the men's table. A Talmudic debate was in progress. Ezriel held forth on the Torah, but managed to gaze directly at Shaindel above the heads of the others. She glanced at him, blushing as she did so from her neck to the roots of her hair.

III

Mayer Joel tried to induce his father-in-law to call off the engagement, but Calman did not want to humiliate Ezriel or his father, the Rabbi of Jampol. Aware of Shaindel's feelings toward Ezriel, Calman made excuses for him. "Who doesn't speak rashly in the heat of debate?" he argued. Zelda sympathized with Mayer Joel, but Calman reminded her of the saying: "Rather slash parchment than rip paper." Better to have a divorce than a broken betrothal. Calman had accordingly presented his gifts to Ezriel, including two hundred rubles for the purchase of a complete set of the Talmud, the works of Maimonides, law digests, and commentaries. Ezriel was to buy the books in Warsaw himself.

The following day he boarded a sled bound for the capital. His father still would not speak to him, but his mother and sister had provided him with food, a change of underclothes, and other travel necessities. In Warsaw he was to stay with Mayer Joel's father, Reb Ezekiel Wiener. Despite the campaign of denunciation that Mayer Joel was conducting, he had presented Ezriel with a letter of introduction to his father requesting that everything possible be done to assure Ezriel's comfort, and adding a postscript, half a page long, of greetings to every member of the large family.

The day was a cold one. The sled traveled swiftly on the hard-packed snow. Icy trees and frozen wastes rushed past, fields flew by. The thatched roofs of the village houses looked like white featherbeds. Toward dusk, icy gusts of wind churned up eddies of snowdust. The sky was overcast, but the setting sun filtered through in purple streaks, like blood streaming from some celestial holocaust. The snow turned red. Heaven and earth seemed one, and, looking out, Ezriel was reminded of a description he had once read of the Arctic Ocean. The sled carried three other passengers in addition to Ezriel. Zelig, a glazier, was going to Warsaw to buy a diamond for glass-cutting; a woman named Blooma was traveling to see a doctor about an abscess in her ear; and a girl, Dvosha, an orphan, hoped to find work in the city. Zelig had on a sheepskin cap, a padded jacket, and straw overshoes such as the peasants wear. With his unkempt beard, now encrusted with icicles, and his bristly iron-gray eyebrows, he resembled a hedgehog.

Taking a pinch of snuff from a horn box, he croaked hoarsely: "Call this winter? In the old days we had real winters! Bears froze to death in their lairs. Packs of wolves slunk about the villages, their eyes glittering like candles. One winter, when I was living at Radoshitz, hailstones fell that were as big as goose eggs! They shattered half the windows of Poland, and the peasants screamed that the world was coming to an end.

"Reb Zelig, can you hear that noise?" Blooma broke in, her head swathed in a blanket over her shawl.

"What noise?"

"A rumbling, in my ear, like wheels. I thought it might be the wind. It doesn't stop—like the gnat in the head of the tyrant Titus, curse him!"

"Don't worry, you'll get better. But if you'll take my advice, you'll keep away from the doctors. When you get to Warsaw, go see Feivele Konskelwoler. He has some magic copper coins blessed by the holy preacher of Kozhenitz. Place one of those next to your ear, and the pain will vanish. You know these doctors—they're all too quick with the knife!"

32

"You don't have to tell me! One doctor thrust a needle into my ulcer! One tells you cold compresses, another tells you hot. But my head begins to tick like a clock the minute I lie down."

"My little brother once pushed a pea into his ear, and did we have trouble getting it out again," chimed in the orphan Dvosha, a thickset young woman who wore a fur vest, and a wool kerchief on her head.

"Are you going to work as a domestic?" asked Blooma.

"That's right."

"Can you cook?"

"I can try."

"Take a tip. Never talk back, just do as your mistress bids. In Warsaw the ladies are always eating, and each meal has a lot of courses. They'll give you plenty of work at the stove. They get their husbands to fuss over them. And they'll wake a maid up in the middle of the night to do the washing."

"Where? At the river?"

"At the river? In Warsaw? Don't be silly! You'll bend over a washtub in the kitchen until you ache. But remember one thing—eat. Eat them out of house and home! My grandmother used to say there was once a wise man who lay face downward three days and nights wondering what keeps people alive, until at last he stumbled on the fact that it was food."

"It doesn't take a wise man to figure that out."

"They'll make you sleep in the kitchen. You'll empty the family's chamber pots. But don't forget to keep a jug of water at your bedside. You'll find it useful if there's a grown son in the house. If he tries to get into bed with you, tell him nicely to go away. If he won't, douse him with water. He'll keep his distance after that. In the morning say it was the cat who overturned the jug."

"You know all the answers."

"Live and learn. I was poor, too, when I was young, and in those days Jews weren't allowed in Warsaw—they turned us

33

back at the gates. Those who entered had to pay a special tax. There was one informer, a Jew himself, who betrayed everyone, but the butchers finally took care of him. When I was a baby, my father died, and my mother didn't last much longer. I stayed with an aunt who was worse than any stranger. On Yom Kippur she'd bless me, but next day the torture began all over again. They married me off to a cobbler who promised me the moon, but he spat blood, poor fellow. When he lost his temper, he beat and kicked me. I bore him three children, but they died young. The last one didn't have a stomach, woe is me. Finally my husband died, and I've remained a widow. Nowadays we have Reb Calman, who never turns anyone away. When it comes to charity, he's almost as good as God. Do you realize, young man, how lucky you are? Your Shaindel has both her head and her heart in the right place—and what a beauty! Dazzling! Yes, I went to your future father-in-law and told him my troubles. He gave me money for the trip and for the doctor's fee, too. What a match—the rabbi's son and Reb Calman's daughter! But why are you going to Warsaw?"

"To buy books."

"Is that so? Very nice! It's your sort, studying holy books, that redeems this wicked world! What good is a woman except to comfort a man? Is it true you don't believe in dibbuks?"

"Who says so?"

"Why, everybody with a tongue in his head, may all their mouths wither. Envy, that's what it is. They want to devour you alive. May the worms get them!"

"Hey, where do you think you're going?" Zelig suddenly bellowed at the driver.

Itcha, the coachman, woke with a start and tugged at the reins.

"Whoa! Back! Back! Where the devil are those nags heading?"

"Caught you napping, eh?"

"Just nodding. You'd better get out, all of you."

"Oh Lord, my legs have gone to sleep," chanted Blooma. "They won't budge!"

Ezriel jumped down and helped the woman out. Under her weight, he sank to his calves in the snow. "The emancipationists are right," he thought. "The fanaticism of Polish Jews is too preposterous for words. While the rest of Europe is learning, creating, making progress, they remain bogged in ignorance. What do these people know of magnetism, electricity, the microscope and the telescope? Who among them has ever heard of Voltaire, Jean-Jacques Rousseau, Kepler, Newton? And what do I know of their theories? Surely not enough. I must study. I must help these people emerge from darkness. Shaindel will assist me." Ezriel scooped up a handful of snow, molded it into a hard ball, and hurled it at the twilight sky.

IV

In Warsaw, Ezriel preferred to stay at an inn, rather than with Reb Ezekiel Wiener. He walked first to Mr. Wallenberg's offices in Krolewska Street to deliver a folder of invoices from Calman. The weather was freezing. Sleds creaked on the icy streets, while their drivers clucked and cracked their whips. Roofs and balconies were laden with snow. Boys in braid-trimmed caps and brass-buttoned coats hurried home, schoolbags over their shoulders. A nun led a file of uniformed girls wearing heavy woolen socks over their stockings. Elegant men and women in fur coats and sable caps promenaded their dogs. A beggar played a hurdy-gurdy. All the shops were crowded despite the cold. Horses dropped manure, which steamed in the cold air; chimneys coughed smoke; carts laden with firewood rumbled into courtyards. For the first time in his life, Ezriel saw coal. At Saxony Park, he stopped to look in through the railing. Boys and girls with multicolored

35

scarves, caps, jackets, skirts, and gloves wove dazzling patterns as they skated on the frozen lake, while those who fell scrambled up, laughing hilariously.

Mr. Wallenberg was in conference and Ezriel waited patiently, hat in hand, in a large office watching the bookkeepers work over huge ledgers. Their steel pens glided over the broad pages as they wrote, blotted, figured, manipulating the beads of their abacuses at an uncanny speed. A maid came in with a tray full of glasses of tea for them. Suddenly the door of Wallenberg's private office opened, and a stout, red-bearded general in spurred boots and golden epaulettes stepped out. His unbuttoned coat revealed elegant braided breeches, and a bulging chest loaded with medals. One gloved hand rested on the hilt of his sword. A liveried attendant opened the front door and stood reverently at attention. Wallenberg escorted his visitor to the threshold, bowed, and waited while the general settled himself in his sled. Wallenberg, with his round shoulders, lofty brow, crooked nose, and flabby ears, looked very Jewish. A short, stocky man, he had a head like a pumpkin, dark glowing eyes, black mutton-chop whiskers that, like the curly hair at his temples, were threaded with white. A stiff collar encased his neck, and he wore a medal on his lapel. Turning around, he caught sight of Ezriel and asked in Polish, "Who is he?"

"He's from Jampol, sent by Calman Jacoby."

Ezriel was awed by the splendor of Wallenberg's office with its elegant draperies and parquet floor, so slippery that he could scarcely walk on it. On the walls hung portraits of gentlemen and ladies, and gilt-framed embossed documents bearing impressive signatures and wax seals. The mahogany desk, with its reading lamp and bronze statuette, was covered with papers. The aroma assailing Ezriel's nostrils was a mixture of cigar smoke, leather, and something unidentifiable.

"What is your connection with Calman Jacoby? Are you his son?" Wallenberg inquired in Polish.

"His daughter's fiancé."

"I see. Be seated."

"Thank you."

"Relax. We won't eat you."

Ezriel sat down.

"Now tell me about yourself. Do you study the Talmud?"

"Yes. And other books, too."

"I see you understand Polish—a rare accomplishment for a Polish Jew. Six hundred years in the country and the Jews haven't bothered to learn the language. What will you do after you're married? Go into business?"

"I'm not sure."

"The Jews are an odd lot." Wallenberg's voice boomed. "Time passes them by. Mankind progresses, but they remain as static as the Chinese behind the Great Wall. Of course, I'm talking about the Polish Jews only, not those of Western Europe."

"Naturally."

"I'll be candid with you, young man. I can see you're no fool. I'm no longer a Jew, I've been baptized. But blood is thicker than water and I can't stand seeing the Jews suffer. How can anyone move into someone else's home, live there in total isolation, and expect not to suffer by it? When you despise your host's god as a tin image, shun his wine as forbidden, condemn his daughter as unclean, aren't you asking to be treated as an unwelcome outsider? It's as simple as that."

"Well, what can we do about it?"

"I won't preach, I'm no missionary. But what will be the end of it? Our assimilationists, who call themselves Poles of Moses' faith, believe neither in Moses nor in Jesus. They appear at the synagogue only once a year, on Yom Kippur. Why do they remain isolated? True, they pray to God for the restoration of Jerusalem, but Palestine is a wilderness; the Messiah coming on his white ass, a pretty legend. Contrary to biblical teachings, modern science holds that the earth was created millions of years ago."

"I know. Kant and Laplace."

Mr. Wallenberg raised his eyebrows.

"Now where did you ever hear of them?"

"I've read about their theories."

"At Jampol?"

"No. Lublin."

"And is your future father-in-law aware that you read such books?"

"I don't think so."

"Well, that's interesting. The ice must be breaking after all. What is your father, a merchant?"

"No. A rabbi."

"That is amazing! A rabbi's son! And how do you account for your blue eyes and fair hair? You didn't get those from your Jewish ancestors! We are all products of Europe. What brings you to Warsaw? It can't be this bundle of papers."

"I've come to buy books."

"The Talmud?"

"Yes. But I also want some scientific works."

"On what subjects?"

"Physics, mathematics, geography . . ."

"Go to Swietokrzyska Street. That's where the Jewish booksellers are, and those Jews in their long caftans are the finest bibliographers in Poland. But, on second thought, why waste money? My house is full of textbooks that are not being used. My children have all completed their studies. Isn't it strange that the Lithuanian Jews should have gone in for education, but the Polish Jews have little interest in secular knowledge? The Hassidic movement is to blame for that. The first thing you must do is master Polish grammar. It is absurd to live in Poland and jabber away in a German jargon, and it is even more ridiculous to live in the second half of the nineteenth century and behave as if you belonged to antiquity. The Poles have a religion too, but they aren't totally immersed in it. If I go to one church service on Sunday, I am considered a good Christian, and I don't have to strap little boxes to my arms and forehead every morning or pray all day long. I've traveled through Turkey and Egypt, and even the Bedouin aren't half as savage as our Hassidim. The sons of Ishmael are at least good horsemen. And let me tell you—the ritual baths are unhygienic. We had a rabbi here who delivered his sermons in Polish. What a sensation! But I don't believe in half measures. The Jews must become one hundred percent Polish. Otherwise they will be driven out as in the days of Pharaoh."

"The Poles are themselves enslaved."

"That's another story."

"The strong want to consume the weak," said Ezriel, a little hazy about the relevance of his remark.

"True, I'm afraid. There's a recently published English book that is causing a furor in the world of science. Its theory seems to be that all life is a struggle for survival and that the strongest species win out. . . . Well, drop in again tomorrow and the cashier will have a load of books for you—bring a suitcase if you can. I'm busy today, but next time you're in Warsaw, look me up."

Wallenberg picked up a small bell and rang it. He wore both a wedding ring and a signet ring. Offering his left hand to Ezriel, he remarked, "Courage, young man! We live in a world of progress."

4

Despite the neighboring squires' advice to the contrary, Countess Maria Jampolska petitioned Czar Alexander to pardon her husband, Count Wladislaw Jampolski. Her plea was that the Count had been carried away by his headstrong nature and that he now regretted what he had done. She, his wife, was ill and humbly begged his Majesty to accede to the Christian charity in his noble heart, and bestow forgiveness on his erring subject. The petition was supported by the governor of Lublin province, to whom the Countess had obtained a letter of introduction. Daily, Maria Jampolska knelt and wept in her private chapel before the image of the Holy Virgin.

In her passionate eagerness, she did something that astounded the Jews of Jampol. She drove to the house of their rabbi, Reb Menachem Mendel, and implored him to pray to God for the liberation of her husband, Wladislaw, son of Wladislaw. A neighbor interpreted, since the rabbi understood no Polish. The Countess then donated eighteen rubles for candles for the synagogue and a small sum to be distributed among the poor.

"All things rest with the Lord," the rabbi told her. But he agreed to offer up a prayer.

And it seemed as though he had actually worked a miracle.

A communiqué arrived from St. Petersburg announcing that his Majesty had graciously consented to issue an amnesty to the banished Count Wladislaw Jampolski, and that the governor of Archangelsk province had been instructed to free the Count and facilitate his journey home. Afterward it was discovered that the Count too had addressed a penitential letter to the Czar, and that the Archangelsk governor had interceded in his behalf.

When the news arrived by mail, the Countess fainted. Her daughter, Felicia, revived her with eau de cologne and brandy, while the nurse, Barbara, a relic with milk-white hair and a red, pock-marked face, unlaced the Countess's corset. After the Countess had dozed off, Felicia decided to write a letter to her brother Josef, who had fled to London after the uprising, and to her sister Helena, who was staying with an aunt in Zamosc. Her younger brother, Lucian, was either still in hiding somewhere in Poland or had perished. A Russian tribunal had condemned him to death *in absentia*, and nothing had been heard of him since.

The cuffs of her sleeves turned back to keep them from being stained, Felicia wrote in an ornate script, a flourish at the end of each word. She rejoiced at the prospect of her father's return; she had lit many a candle before the altar, dropped numerous coins into the charity box, and prayed constantly to God that He might free the exiled Count. Yet her joy was not unmixed, and Felicia felt ashamed before the Lord, who knew one's secret thoughts. Her father had been unkind to her, had called her an old maid, mocked and mimicked her. Felicia feared that after his appalling experiences in Siberia in the coarse company of criminals and Russians, he might prove even more untractable than before. Nevertheless, she implored God to grant her father a safe return, reconciling herself to the indignities he would probably inflict upon her, and forgiving his meanness in advance. Felicia had written only a paragraph or two when she tore up the letter, unable to decide whether she wanted to call Josef "dear" or "my dear." Nothing was as painful for Felicia as making a decision—one reason, no doubt, why she had remained a spinster.

Her father and Lucian were patriots who had risked their lives for Poland, whereas Josef had fled to London. He thought of himself as a philosopher, preached positivism and maintained in each of his letters that only through industry and science, not idle dreams, would Poland be restored. Such ideas, worthy only of tradesmen, had cooled Felicia's feelings toward her elder brother, whom she had worshipped in childhood. Helena, too, was constantly visiting relatives, close and distant, imposing on them, and forming indiscriminate friendships. A new generation had grown up, godless, impudent, selfish. After the 1863 disaster, the nobility had slowly resumed its old way of life. Receptions and balls were being held again, but Felicia was no longer invited to them. The years had passed; her suitors had all become husbands; her friends and her relatives had become distant, acting like strangers. Even the bread she ate was not her own, but the condescending gift of a Jew, Calman Jacoby.

Her father's exile to Siberia, Josef's escape and flight, the death sentence against Lucian had given a tragic significance to Felicia's life. She dressed in mourning, grieved over Lucian, her father, and the lost fatherland. For years now she had nursed her ailing mother and assumed complete charge of the manor house. Though their land had been confiscated, there still remained in the Countess's jewel box strings of pearls, heavy gold chains, diamond-studded combs, golden hairpins. Among the vestiges of their former opulence were delicate pieces of porcelain, silverware, a gold dinner service, a harness encrusted with precious stones. The wardrobes were still packed with furs, silk and satin gowns, petticoats, jackets, capes. Books bound in velvet and silk lined the library shelves. Felicia, not entirely resigned to her fate, felt that, at thirty-three, romance was still a possibility for her. Her luck would surely turn. A "gallant knight mounted on a white horse" might still appear, a touch of gray at his temples, gravity in his gaze, a mature smile beneath his mustache; and at a glance he would perceive her noble heart, the modesty of her soul, her untapped love. A son of the old aristocracy, he would adore poetry and prefer a cottage, a stream, the rustling of the forest, the wisdom of silence. And there would still be time to present him with a son, whom she would name Lucian Juljusz after her vanished brother and her favorite poet, Juljusz Slowacki, who wrote that wonderful song, "I am sad, O God!"

The return of the Count would upset the realities as well as the dreams . . .

Felicia began another letter, then rose and studied herself in the mirror. Her hair, which she wore in a bun, had once been a honey blond, but now it had darkened. Her face was white and narrow and there were bluish shadows under her hazel eyes. She wore black, a high-necked blouse and trailing velvet skirt, onyx earrings, and on her left hand an onyx ring which bore the inscription of the fateful year: 1863.

She went back to her writing. She had childish caprices, sometimes unendurable even to herself. Certain letters of the alphabet appeared sympathetic to her, others odious. Even among the fowl in the poultry yard, she had her loves and hates. It was her tragedy to be incapable of indifference.

Barbara, the old nurse, knocked at the door.

"My dear, your mother's asking for you."

"I'll come right away."

Felicia found her mother with her head propped up on two pillows in the four-poster bed. Two gray strands escaped from her nightcap; her flushed cheeks were crisscrossed with tiny purple veins. Her small nose and thin lips were bloodless above a pasty double chin. Only an extremely perceptive person could have discerned in her the traces of former beauty. The Countess's eyes flickered open as her daughter approached the bed.

"I haven't a thing to wear for your father's arrival, Felicia. You'll have to see Nissen, the tailor."

Felicia was astonished.

"Why, how can you say that, Mama? Your wardrobes are bulging with clothes."

"What clothes? Rags!"

"Father won't be here for weeks yet."

"I don't want to look frightful when he returns. See how gray I am!"

Felicia made no comment. Who would have thought that her mother, old and ill, would still cling to feminine vanity?

"What do you want me to tell Nissen?"

"Bring him here. I shall order new things for you, too. We won't look like paupers when your father arrives."

Felicia's eyes filled with tears.

"I'll do as you say, Mother dear."

11

In the month of March, the quiet of Jampol was upset by the news of the Count's return from Siberia. He had arrived driving a low sleigh, wearing a peasant's sheepskin coat, felt boots, and a broad-brimmed fur hat. He had grown perceptibly stouter. His face was flushed, his eyes glowed with mirth, and his walrus mustache sparkled with icicles. In the sleigh sat a woman in a squirrel coat, with a man's black fur cap on her head, and rugs wrapped around her shoulders and knees. Halting before Calman's tavern, the Count helped his companion down. He removed his fur coat, draping it over the horse, and entered the tavern boisterously, as though already drunk.

Getz, the manservant, happened to be behind the bar when the new arrival called out: "Hey, Jew, how about some vodka?"

The woman, meanwhile, had taken off her fur coat and hat. She seemed to be in her thirties, a brunette with black eyes, dazzling teeth, and a beauty spot on her left cheek. She walked mincingly on high-heeled boots. The townspeople, who had gathered to welcome the Count, stared as the woman rolled a cigarette of thin paper and tobacco, lit it, and began to exhale smoke through her nostrils. She lifted her drink, clinked glasses with the Count, and the two exchanged remarks in Russian.

"Idiots! What are you staring at?" the Count finally shouted at the spectators. "Do you think this is a circus?"

The Count stood up, whispered something to Getz, escorted the woman to Itche Braine's inn, and proceeded on his way to the manor. The Count's family were not expecting him for several days. His wife was asleep; Felicia was reading poetry in the library; Helena, who had just returned from Zamosc, was at the pianoforte in the drawing room. The gate stood open. As the sleigh pulled into the yard, the Count's two hounds, Wilk and Piorun, rushed toward it, yelping frantically. Wojciech, the family coachman, whose duties now included those of butler and valet, came out. Mumbling and damp-eyed, he advanced, cap in hand, toward his master. The old nurse appeared, giggled nervously, clapped her hands, and then broke into loud wails, like a peasant mourning the dead. Helena stopped her music and rushed out in her negligee. Her father, measuring her at a glance, remarked that she had become a beauty. The two embraced. Felicia joined them, and her father kissed her cheeks. She paled: the squire had come home drunk.

"Well, where's your mother?" the Count demanded impatiently.

"Mother's in bed ill."

"What's wrong with her? I'll go and see her."

Still in his hat and coat, tracking carpets with mud, he strode toward the Countess's room. Aroused by the commotion, she was sitting up in bed, flustered, clutching the silver handle of a mirror. The Count halted at the door, momentarily confused. Was that his wife or her mother? In the excitement, he had forgotten for a second that his mother-in-law was dead.

"Maria!" he shouted.

45

"It is really you," the Countess cried. "Now I can die in peace!"

"Why die? You're not that old!"

Drawing near, he kissed her hair, brow, and cheeks. She grew limp and her face flushed. During the ten minutes the Count spent with his wife, Wojciech unharnessed the horse; Magda, the cook, caught a goose and unearthed a clay-covered bottle from the wine cellar, a relic of the old days. The Count emerged from his wife's room, having removed his overclothes and changed his felt boots for high leather ones. Opening doors, he came upon Felicia.

"Why are you wearing black? No one has died."

"I'll change soon."

"What's that you're reading—more sentimental nonsense?"

"Please, Father, don't speak like that. The author is a distinguished poet, a prophet."

"A prophet, eh? You'd better find yourself a man and get married. Hook the first fool that comes along."

The tears instantly welled up in Felicia's eyes. Her father had indeed grown coarser in exile. Even his boots had a vulgar squeak. He wore a rough black shirt, and a brass watch chain spread across his vest. He resembled one of the Russian secret police who had ransacked the manor in their search for Lucian.

"God in heaven, please forgive him," she mumbled.

"Don't you ever crave a man?" The Count propped one foot on the upholstered seat of a chair. "What do you have in your veins: blood or sour milk?"

"Father dear, please don't start teasing right away. We were praying to God for you all the time."

"It wasn't God but the Czar who granted me an amnesty."

"Please, Father, have pity. Don't spoil the joy of your homecoming."

"An honest-to-goodness old maid, that's what you are. There's no God, and Jesus was nothing but a lousy Jew. The

46

Apostles made religion a business. Haven't you ever heard of Darwin? Answer me!"

"Father, let me be."

"Don't run away. Man is descended from the ape. For your information, one of our forebears was nothing but an orangutan." The Count laughed uproariously. "Our ancestors perched in trees and caught fleas. That's the undiluted truth. There's more progress in frozen Siberia than in all of your Poland. Vanity. Stupidity. Bah!"

The Count stalked out, leaving Felicia stunned. He still enjoyed shocking her. He had become thoroughly brutal. He drank; he blasphemed; he no longer had any respect for his own soul.

Entering her mother's bedroom, Felicia observed the Countess standing in lacy underwear, while Barbara struggled to fit her into a corset. Felicia quickly closed the door. She turned another knob and found Helena, also primping.

"I beg your pardon."

"Not at all. Come right in. What do you think of him? Isn't he marvelous?"

How Helena's body has matured, thought Felicia. Only yesterday she was a child. How boldly she stands, half naked, without a trace of shame. What breasts, what shoulders, what a complexion, what hair! She will have her fill of happiness—including the share I missed. She is blessed with everything—except a soul!

After exchanging a few words with her sister, Felicia left. Should she discard her mourning? She had vowed to wear black as long as Poland remained subjugated. She was no longer a child. No one could order her about. Though still undecided, Felicia proceeded to her own room, where the new gray gown made by Nissen the tailor hung in an oak wardrobe. Opening her door, Felicia recoiled. Her father lay sprawled on her bed, his boots on, one foot hanging over the edge. He was snoring. Felicia caught her breath and stared at him. What sort of a person was he? What iron nerves! Was

47

she really his daughter? Why hadn't she inherited any of his strength and will?

"Father!"

The Count opened an eye.

"Oh. It's you. I'm exhausted. Starved, too. I've crossed half of Russia. Take off all that black. The Middle Ages have passed. Too much idealism, too much poetry, too much easy patriotism. Smokestacks are what we need in Poland, towering smokestacks spewing smoke; and fertilizer for the fields— mountains of artificial manure!"

5

Jampol was filled with activity as the railroad line approached. Engineers came from Warsaw with cases of instruments and other equipment. A government inspector with a retinue of minor functionaries arrived and had to be banqueted and toasted with champagne. Calman Jacoby had been granted a loan by the Bank of Commerce in Warsaw and was having the ground surveyed for the spur to the lime quarries. Wallenberg, angered over delays caused by a shortage of ties for the Imperial railroad, wired Calman, threatening to sue for damages and revoke the contract. Calman, besides employing engineers and other skilled workmen, now had the job of procuring rails and freight cars. He had already established an office in Jampol and, because he needed clerks who spoke Russian, had found it necessary to hire Jews from Lithuania.

These strangers, who were beardless and wore Gentile clothes, considered themselves enlightened, but the town found them heretical. One of them, David Sorkess, who had graduated from the Zhitomir Rabbinical Seminary, quoted the Talmud irreverently, smoked on the Sabbath, and wrote poetry in Hebrew. The wife of Shalit, another employee, who came from Vilna, went bareheaded, flaunting orthodox ritual. Ignace Herman, a native Pole who had been an army officer at the time of the insurrection, was rumored to have fought with the Polish aristocrats and was no better than a heathen. They had all become friendly with Grain, the Jampol pharmacist, and spent their evenings at his house drinking tea from the samovar and playing whist. Calman was disturbed because he had to associate with these nonconformists who, the towns-people complained, demoralized the young. Even though he kept accounts himself in the old way, recording in pencil his income and expenses, assets and obligations, the services of clerks and auditors familiar with the Russian language and laws were indispensable to him. Strangely enough, he found that, as a man of wealth, he was now deeply in debt, while as a poor man he had not owed a cent.

During all this turmoil, elaborate preparations for Shaindel's wedding were in progress. Set for the Sabbath after the Feast of Pentecost, it had to be delayed until the Sabbath of Consolation, because her trousseau could not be completed in time for the earlier date. Shaindel, hearing she would have to wait two months longer, wept. Her father, to placate her, held out a ten-ruble note.

"Here, darling, go buy yourself a present."

"Papa, I'm not a child any more."

"Obviously not."

Calman shrugged. His recent wealth seemed to have brought him only complaints. He was forever justifying himself, apologizing, offering bribes, and making promises. Frequently, at night, Zelda woke him to complain of a headache and cramps, insisting he light a candle, apply a heated stove lid to her abdomen, or massage her with vinegar or alcohol. Sitting up with her scrawny neck and wizened face lost beneath an outsized nightcap, she stared into the night, her deeply lined eyes widened by anxiety.

"What good is your money to me?" she would wail. "It won't bring me comfort on earth or grace later. People curse me from envy. If only the children are spared the Evil Eye— may I atone for their sins! God grant them a longer life than mine. What wrong have they done, I ask you."

"What wrong have I done?" Calman countered. "Should I throw our fortune away? It is God's will! What I throw out, others will pick up."

"You think you're a husband? Are you ever here? You're always away. You spend weeks in the forest, night after night. The Lord knows what you do there. You're only flesh and blood, after all."

"You're being silly, Zelda."

"You always were a little coarse. I could have married a scholar. But my mother—may she rest in peace—favored you. What did she see in you? Don't be offended—but you did look oafish. Calman," Zelda suddenly changed her tone, "I don't think I'll last much longer. I get weaker every day."

"Go to the mineral baths—you know I've been trying to persuade you to go. Why suffer here? I want to do all I can for you, but you won't let me."

"Warm springs aren't what I need. I don't want to die away from home. I want to recite my last prayer here. I want my children to cry at my funeral."

Yes, Zelda was sick. Jochebed, who was pregnant, was also not well. Her belly had expanded to the size of a drum; her face had grown yellow and blotched. She feared ghosts, longed to eat chalk and eggshells, and still brooded over the fact that a fortuneteller had predicted she would die young. Mayer Joel had hung amulets inscribed with psalms about her room. He had the Book of Raziel ready to place under her pillow when her labor began, and he had written to the Rabbi of Marshinov, enclosing an offering of twenty-five rubles and requesting his help through prayer. Zelda, despite her ill health, had made a pilgrimage to another miracle-working rabbi and brought back a talisman and an amber charm, both said to be potent in the easing of childbirth. In addition to Dr. Lipinski, she had hired a midwife from Skarshew.

Calman was also upset over his daughter Miriam Lieba. Polish books engrossed her. She objected to women wearing wigs after marriage, disapproved of the Sabbath dishes, cholent and kugel, and was forever at odds with her mother. Once when she combed her hair on a Sabbath and Mayer Joel had scolded her for transgressing, she had said rudely, "It's I who'll roast in hell, not you!" Now neither would speak to the other.

Calman's associates and employees were full of complaints. Every office clerk, middleman, and menial laborer had a grievance. Wrangling among themselves, each denounced the other as a swindler. The forest wardens either neglected their duties or were in league with the thieves. Timber vanished; Calman's grain and potatoes were pilfered by the peasants, who also pastured their cattle on his meadows; the millers helped themselves to his flour; the wholesalers falsified weights and measures and padded his bills. Everyone's palm itched. And how could he, Calman, be everywhere at once?

The more Calman thought about it, the more he came to believe that he was the captive and not the master of his fortune. Actually, his wife was right. What good did his wealth do him? His supper still consisted, as it had when he was a peddler, of a dish of buckwheat grits, and he still slept on a bed of feathers, not of gold. The main difference was that while once he had eaten at a leisurely pace, chewing his food thoroughly, now he bolted it down. His afternoon meal had occasionally been followed by a nap but now, try as he might, he could never fall asleep in the daytime. Fortunately the Almighty, blessed be His name, had given the Jews the Sabbath. Business matters were put aside as Friday evening approached. Carrying fresh underwear and socks, provided by Zelda, and the fringed ritual undergarment, he and Mayer Joel would go to the nearest stream to bathe, or sometimes Getz would drive them to the hot baths in Jampol. Returning, Shaindel would welcome Calman with a freshly baked bun and a saucer of cooked prunes. Then, slipping into his Sabbath gaberdine, he would sit down and begin the recitation of the Song of Songs. Praise God, the demons of drudgery had no power over the Sabbath. Zelda and Jochebed would perform the benediction over the lighted candles in the silver and brass candlesticks, in the presence of all the girls, washed, combed, and dressed in their best. Mayer Joel complained that he could not get used to praying without a quorum. Calman vowed that he would erect a small synagogue on the estate, subsidize a quorum of ten pious Jews, provide a Torah scroll, the Talmud, order a Holy Ark and a lectern as well as a laver, menorahs, and an embroidered curtain for the Ark. He would even build a ritual bath, if only Jochebed came safely through childbirth, Shaindel were married, and Miriam Lieba betrothed. Calman did not intend to live his life without purpose, or arrive in the afterworld with nothing but a sack of sins.

11

Calman finally yielded to Mayer Joel's urging that they make a pilgrimage to the Rabbi of Marshinov for the Feast of Weeks. Reb Menachem Mendel and Ezriel were to accompany them, though Ezriel was not particularly eager to make the trip. He would have preferred to spend his time reading the textbooks given him by Wallenberg. He had begun to study algebra, geometry, Latin, physics, chemistry, and geography, all at once. He had also acquired some dictionaries and an atlas in Warsaw. It seemed a waste of time to neglect this store of knowledge in order to visit a Hassidic rabbi, but he could not easily snub his prospective father-in-law.

Calman had ordered a generous supply of butter cakes and buckwheat wafers for the journey, as well as several bottles of wine for the Marshinov rabbi's table. The coach was to start early the next morning, the day before Pentecost. Ezriel, who had scarcely slept that night, packed a geography book and a compass along with his prayer book and phylacteries.

Dawn came early. Calman and Mayer Joel were to stop for Reb Menachem Mendel and Ezriel. Reb Menachem sighed as he dressed. The Rabbi of Marshinov was, no doubt, a great sage, he reflected, but he himself felt more drawn to a different rabbi, the Preacher of Turisk. Unfortunately, Turisk was a great distance from Jampol, and Reb Menachem had gradually drifted from his spiritual home.

The stars were fading. A cock crowed. Despite the unseasonable warmth of the spring, Ezriel felt chilled. Like a shadow, his mother, Tirza Perl, moved about in bathrobe and slippers. His sister Mirale, hair disheveled, lay in bed, lost in a daydream.

"Watch your manners in Marshinov," Tirza Perl warned Ezriel. "What did your grandfather accomplish? One can't defy the world! Thank God you're lucky in your betrothed —don't spoil everything."

"You like to preach, Mother, don't you?" Mirale observed.

"And I thought she was sleeping! Wash up and have a cup of chicory. Don't be jealous, dear, your turn will come, God willing. What do I have left now? Just two darling doves."

Rumbling wheels approached, then halted near the house. Ezriel carried out their suitcases. The horizon glowed and dew glittered on the grass. A solitary worshipper, hugging the bag that contained his prayer shawl, stumbled like a sleepwalker toward the synagogue. Mists rose from the river. The horses stood with heads obediently bowed, as though whispering together. Mayer Joel, his hat set jauntily on his head, was evidently in high spirits. He had had his way. Calman helped Reb Menachem Mendel into the carriage; Getz, chewing a bit of straw, waved his whip. The two older men sat opposite Mayer Joel and Ezriel.

"Please keep an eye on him, Reb Calman," Tirza Perl called out from the doorway.

"Don't worry," Mayer Joel reassured her. "There aren't any bears running loose in Marshinov."

Getz tugged at the reins and the coach started. It passed the marketplace, the church, and Calman's tightly shuttered store. The road to Marshinov skirted Calman's estate. As though undecided whether to ripen or fall early, the green stalks drooped in the fields. A bird, hovering over a grove, flapped its wings.

54

Shaindel stood, pale and sleepy, near the road, and at her signal Getz reined in the horses. She held out two parcels, one tied with string, the other with green ribbon.

"What's that you're holding, dear? You should be sleeping," Calman said, surprised.

"This is for you, Papa, for the journey."

"Thank you."

"And that's yours," she told Ezriel. They both blushed.

"A good trip!"

"Goodbye."

The coach rolled on. Shaindel's figure receded. Ezriel wanted to wave to her, but felt shy. Calman ran his fingers through his beard.

"What's in those packages, I wonder," Mayer Joel remarked.

"Delicacies, no doubt," Calman said.

"Well, father-in-law, they'll come in handy at Marshinov. There, it's share and share alike. A man may be comfortably asleep at the inn—suddenly some poor traveler will appear to share his bed. That's Marshinov! The rabbi once declared: 'It's easy to profess love for the Lord, but it's not so easy to love a crippled tanner.' One time a Litvak, a skeptic who came only to mock, appeared in Marshinov. The rabbi gesticulates as he prays and this Litvak stood nearby, imitating every gesture. Some of the younger worshippers wanted to strike him, but the rabbi, who knew what was going on, prevented it. Very often petitioners waited days to see the rabbi, but this Litvak was admitted with scarcely any delay, and, strangely, he spent a whole hour with the rabbi. To make a long story short—he became a devotee, and Marshinov, to this day, is his spiritual home. Luckily he settled in Warsaw, or else Marshinov would have become swamped with Litvaks."

"Aren't Litvak Jews like the rest of us?" Reb Menachem Mendel interrupted. "All Jewish souls were assembled on Mount Sinai."

"Yet—"

55

"At Beltz," Reb Menachem continued, "you see Hassidim from remote parts of Hungary who recite the Gemara in a Hungarian dialect—yet have sidelocks reaching to their shoulders."

"Amazing!"

"The Talmud maintains that the ministering angels do not understand Aramaic. Hebrew is their language," Reb Menachem explained for Calman's benefit. "But the Almighty knows all tongues. Even the Sh'ma can be recited in dialects other than Hebrew."

"Wouldn't the Sh'ma sound a little odd in Turkish?"

Ezriel had felt impelled to raise his voice. He had wanted to break in earlier, to say that the man asleep in his bed might be contaminated by the poor stranger with whom he was suddenly forced to share it; that no one had ever conversed with angels, or ascertained their linguistic gifts—but he had restrained himself. Mayer Joel was always on the alert to embarrass him, probably annoyed that he had been duped into marrying Jochebed, while Ezriel was getting Shaindel. Ezriel turned his gaze to the heavens.

A blazing chariot streamed westward. In the east, the sun rose like a bloody head; birds flocked to greet it. Purple shadows lingered on the plains. It was odd to remember that even while the coach rolled toward Marshinov, the earth rotated on its axis from west to east, revolving about the sun as it had for centuries. Ezriel thought of the laws of gravitation. What caused them? Why must one body attract another? The physics textbook he had received from Wallenberg did not answer these questions. He would have to find a more advanced text.

III

Marshinov swarmed with crowds. Even in Lublin, Ezriel had not seen so many people. Hassidic pilgrims were everywhere, in the House of Worship, in the rabbi's courtyard and garden, and throughout the sprawling marketplace. The inns were jammed and guests slept on straw pallets, or even on the bare floor. Calman just managed to find one room for himself, Reb Menachem Mendel, and Ezriel. Getz found lodging with a local teamster. Mayer Joel found his father, Reb Ezekiel Wiener, with his brother, two brothers-in-law, and an uncle from Lodz, and became one of their party. Reb Menachem Mendel and Calman hastened to the ritual baths. Although Ezriel was urged by his father to join them, he managed to escape. He did not intend to bathe in a pool already used by so many others. He made a tour of the town instead.

The windows of the houses of Marshinov were decorated with cut-outs of doves and flowers, with twigs made of silver and gold paper, on which perched small birds, their heads modeled from dough. And placed at the corners of the windows were always some water flags or reeds symbolizing the granting of the Torah on Mount Sinai. Children ran about everywhere, blowing on their reed whistles. Since Pentecost was a dairy festival, the town was redolent of coffee, chicory, milk, and pastry.

Ezriel visited the synagogue of the non-Hassidic congregation. He wandered about the streets and alleys. Girls promenaded in their best clothes; the men were returning home after visits to the baths. The stores remained open for the poorer customers, who the last minute had managed to scrape together or borrow a few coins to make purchases for the festival.

The aimlessness of Ezriel's tour reflected his unrest and impatience. What's wrong with me? he thought. Why do I feel a stranger here? Were people really so blind to the obvious inconsistencies of their faith? God was Master of the World, and in that world the poor were starving. Although He was presumed to be merciful, He allowed the strong to overcome the weak. How had Wallenberg described it? Yes—the struggle for survival. There was certainly no Gehenna to punish whales who devour small fish. Christian nations, praying to Jesus, devastated their weaker neighbors, and though they preached turning the other cheek, their rulers sent political opponents into exile. And the Jews? God's chosen people remained oppressed and forever exiled. Once it was Chmielnicki, then Gonta or Czar Nicholas; it was either mass murder or harsh decrees. Were those victimized Jews supposed to be atoning for the theoretical sins of their ancestors? Hadn't their prayers and Talmud study been fervent enough? The Messiah had not yet appeared. Would he ever? The Book of Daniel had been ransacked by sages seeking clues for the Messiah's coming in *nutrakon*, the interpretation of initials, and through *gematria*, the study of the mathematical value of letters. It was all a lie. They had based all their hopes on a single book, the product of mortals!

It was time to return to the inn; the sun was setting—he had to get into his holiday clothes. But Ezriel had lost his way. He couldn't even recall the name of the inn. Reversing his direction, he strode past a tailor's shop where a garment was hastily being ironed, past an occasional woman still scrubbing the stoop of her house. Wearing satin gaberdines with wide sashes, fur-trimmed velvet hats, slippers, and white stockings, pious Jews were already approaching the synagogue. What would his father and Calman say if he failed to arrive in time? Mayer Joel would, no doubt, have a great deal to say. Calman might become so angry he would break the engagement. Ezriel stood still, looking to the right and left. The inn must be somewhere nearby, but where? He tried to stop some passersby, but not one paused or answered. Didn't they see him? Were they angry at him? He was hot and sweaty. His eyes had begun to blur. It's my nerves—just like my mother. Everyone thought him healthy, but in reality he was sick, half mad. Ezriel became enraged at his father, at Calman, and at Mayer Joel. Why did they drag him to these wonder rabbis? He didn't believe in them, he was not even sure he believed in God. He again inquired the way to the inn, describing it. This time a man replied, but Ezriel could not hear what he was saying, and the man pointed, first in one direction, then in another, as if to mock him. I don't want to live, Ezriel's mind screamed. I don't want to get married and bring more Jews into the world. Wallenberg is right, it's all madness, all this piety and martyrdom! Perhaps I should run away right now. But where? And what would Shaindel do?

A familiar grief overcame Ezriel, a grief he could remember feeling as far back as the first grades of cheder. All the boys except Ezriel had formed a group. He had remained an outsider. Even the teacher had been suspicious of him. The boys had ridiculed him, called him names, hit him, and at the same time had tried to woo his friendship. The pattern had repeated itself everywhere, in Turbin, in Lublin, in Jampol. Here, even in Marshinov, people were reacting to him with hostility. . . . It must be something in me, he thought. But what—my face, my eyes? Do I seem crazy? He pitied Shaindel. She didn't know the kind of man she was marrying. She had arisen at dawn to give him a package of butter cookies.

"Ezriel!" someone called. He stopped short. It was Mayer Joel.

"Where are you going? Have you been to the baths?"

"Yes."

"I didn't see you there."

"Nevertheless, I was there."

"All right, so you were. Where are you going now?"

"Just walking."

"Have you forgotten? It's time for the evening prayer."

"I must change my clothes."

"There's barely time, it's sundown."

Only then did Ezriel notice that Mayer Joel was already dressed.

"By the way," he asked, unsteadily, "where is the inn?"

"Lost, are you? I thought so. Just like a philosopher."

Oddly enough, Ezriel was almost directly behind the hotel. There was the well next to it, there the steps. How could he have missed seeing it? Still confused, he opened a door leading into a kitchen and was greeted by the screams of a young

c

woman in the midst of dressing. He walked up and down the corridors, trying to locate his room. Finally he caught sight of Reb Menachem Mendel.

"Father!"

"Where have you been? I've been looking everywhere. You shame me!"

"Which is our room?"

"This one."

Ezriel entered the cubicle crowded with three cots. Groping in the dark, he changed his clothes as quickly as he could, and with his father and Calman set out for the rabbi's synagogue.

Services had begun by the time they arrived. The candles in the menorahs were already bent with the heat. A multitude of voices, rising from a forest of satin and velvet gaberdines, issuing out of a wilderness of beards and sidelocks, chanted in refrain: "For He is our life, and the span of our days, and by Him shall we be led day and night."

Ezriel stood apart near the entrance. How familiar these surroundings were to him, yet how remote. Some hidden and hostile force seemed to separate him from the others. He no longer felt himself to be among them; it was their holiday, not his.

He could not stand the heat in the synagogue. He left and joined a group of young men praying outside. The evening air was invigorating. Glowworms sparkled at his feet, above his head stars twinkled and a crescent moon sailed along. I get lost in a small town, he mused, but the stars, racing along for millions of miles, never deviate from their orbits. One comet describes a circuit in seventy years!

Ezriel, who had begun to recite the Eighteen Benedictions, could not continue. God might exist, but these words expressed nothing but a faith in a revelation that never took place and a belief in God's love for the Jews which was their own invention.

"Reb Calman of Jampol, please be seated."

Calman was astounded. How was it that he, an ordinary Jew in a coat of common cloth, had been singled out for such a distinction with a study house suffocatingly full of the rabbi's disciples, many of them venerable ancients, dressed in satin, and with long sidelocks? Inclining his head, he followed the two synagogue wardens to a seat of honor. The chief rabbi sat in an armchair at the head of the table. Short, stocky, round-faced, with a silvery-white fan-shaped beard, he wore a white silk gaberdine embroidered with lilac leaves, and a wide hat trimmed with fur. One sexton brought the rabbi a copper jug, basin, and towel, while another poured water over his hands, after which the rabbi chanted the appropriate prayer. To his right sat his eldest son, Reb Shimmon, whose jet-black beard and dark shining eyes were in vivid contrast to his father's white robe and hair. A younger son, Reb Moshe, known as the Rabbi of Chmielev, a tall, lanky man with a beard scarcely covering the tip of his chin and girlishly long sidelocks, also attended the rabbi. Hassidic devotees surged about the rabbi's table, those in front pressing forward as those behind pushed against them. Calman, who was perspiring heavily, found himself unable to reach his handkerchief to wipe his brow.

The rabbi sliced a white loaf, using a knife with a mother-of-pearl handle. After he had taken a single bite, his followers vied for the rest, crust and crumbs, as the loaf was now sanctified. The rabbi merely tasted each course, taking a sliver of fish, a bite of meat, a spoonful of soup, one stewed prune. Throughout the feast, the rabbi's associates broke into Hassidic songs, the crowd joining in the refrains.

Calman, though he had at first gasped for air and felt that he would perish from the heat, gradually became used to the stifling atmosphere. He marveled at the rabbi's radiance. It was as if the Divine Presence had enveloped this seer. Everywhere around him were wet, clinging gaberdines, black, yellow, and gray beards, eyes glowing with fervor. A spirit of unalloyed rejoicing prevailed. Calman, though the local Hassidic chants were unfamiliar to him, joined in the choruses. He was not alone here, but among fellow Jews united in worship of the Lord. Across the table sat an old man with a furrowed brow. He wore a frayed velvet hat and worn coat. Next to him sat a young man, his head bowed so low that his sidelocks brushed the tablecloth. Piping young voices blended with asthmatic wheezing. All sang one hymn. Together they praised the Almighty for His mercies, prayed not for earthly well-being but for the coming of the Messiah and the abolition of evil, slavery, exile, and that heavenly joy and salvation should exalt the world.

Ah, this is the place for a Jew. It's wonderful here, Calman reflected. One's spirit grows younger. During recent years, Calman had become withdrawn. He had met so many swindlers, usurers, parasites. Now all rancor subsided in him, and brotherly love replaced it. Who am I, compared to these pious men? Just another fellow who happens to have made money, he thought. I'll come back here, God willing. Here is where one finds true rejoicing.

Silence was ordered and there was a sudden hush. The rabbi began his discourse on Holy Writ, his voice at first scarcely audible. The men behind Calman pressed forward, breathing on his neck, tickling him with their beards. Soon the speaker's voice gained volume. The rabbi took his text from the Talmud, which states that even before the people knew the nature of the Ten Commandments, they were prepared to obey them.

"Why should this be considered a virtue?" the rabbi continued. "Isn't is more commendable to listen and consider before plunging ahead blindly? Doesn't the Talmud say elsewhere that the evil servant acts first and asks questions later? There seems to be some contradiction here. According to common sense, is not inaction preferable to deeds whose consequences are unknown? The truth of the matter is that in certain cases action does come before thought. The need for a pilgrimage cannot be explained, for it will not be understood until it has been experienced. Philosophy inevitably begins with, doubt, with chaos and emptiness. Thus it is unable to create anything, for what was void to begin with will remain void to the end. Therefore it is written: 'In the beginning God created the heaven and the earth. The earth was without form, and void.' *In the beginning God created*—and only then did He perceive the void. If He had beheld it first, there might have been no creation. When the Almighty gave the Torah to the Jews, He feared that they might first wish to know what it was—for if you argue and think about anything long enough, doubt is sure to arise. This was exactly what happened in the case of Esau and Ishmael, who according to the sages were offered the Torah first, and refused it. But the Jews followed the Lord's way when He created heaven and earth. With them, action preceded deliberation. In the deed, all misgivings were resolved.

"Yet how and when is this principle to be applied? Only in the fulfillment of holy duties. In secular matters and those pertaining to the flesh, it is the opposite course one must follow; one must consider and deliberate first, and only then perform one's duty. It is the evil-doer who first inflicts harm and then asks questions. For wickedness awakens endless questions in man. All doubts vanish in the performance of virtuous deeds. Yet how can one recognize the true spirit of virtue? The answer is: through joy. The man who injures someone is disturbed and full of conflicts. But a good deed is succeeded by inner happiness. For a man who is uplifted, all questions are resolved."

Parts of the rabbi's speech were too abstruse for Calman, but one message in particular seemed meant for him: one must do good and confer benefits without thinking, regardless of motive; but exercise restraint and judgment before injuring someone. "God in Heaven, how true and wonderful!" Calman murmured. The holy man had divined his most secret thought. From now on I shall perform good deeds, be more charitable, assist those who need my assistance, and spend two hours each day studying the Torah. I will be malicious toward no one, and will esteem everyone. Yes. Yes.

After the speech, Mendel the beadle climbed on the table in his stocking feet and began to pour wine for everyone, for the privileged who sat at the table, as well as for those who were standing, and there were no exceptions, not even among the very young men. Calman heard a sexton call out the names of Reb Ezekiel Wiener, Mayer Joel, his son-in-law, and the latter's younger brother. Then suddenly Calman heard, "Wine for Ezriel, son of Reb Menachem Mendel of Jampol."

Calman looked around for Ezriel. The goblet of wine, given by the sexton to the nearest man, passed from hand to hand until it reached Ezriel, standing at the doorway. What a prodigious memory the Rabbi of Marshinov had, thought Calman. He himself was always absentmindedly forgetting the names of his employees, sometimes even those of his daughters, but the rabbi personally honored every man under his roof, young or old. Yet one question still baffled Calman. Why had he been selected for a place of honor? What had he done to deserve it? Was it his wealth? If this were the case, it was probably the work of the rabbi's wardens, not of the rabbi himself. Why should the rabbi need money? An aging man, he was closer to heaven than to earth.

v

During the holiday two young men were proposed to Calman as eligible matches for his daughter Miriam Lieba. One was Jochanan, son of the rabbi's widowed daughter, Temerel; the other was the son of Reb David Gombiner, a wealthy man from Plock. Jochanan's father, Reb Zadock, had been a saint. Even while a very young man, he had fasted two days a week and risen at midnight to pray, and it had been generally pre-

64

dicted that he would one day succeed the Rabbi of Marshinov, whose two sons, Reb Shimmon and Reb Moshe, would be left without a following. But Reb Zadock had died of consumption, which the doctors ascribed to the chilly ritual baths. His widow Temerel, left with two daughters and a son, had never remarried. Like his father, Jochanan had begun at eleven to observe all the fast days, and to perform his ablutions in an icy pool at dawn. His grandfather, the old sage Reb Shmaryah Gad, had once admitted that the sanctity of his grandson surpassed his own. Now sixteen, dark-eyed, with a narrow face, Jochanan was much too small and gaunt for his age. His cheeks were sunken, his sidelocks reached his shoulders, his neck was scrawny, and his Adam's apple prominent. Observers at the ritual bath reported him all skin and bones. On the other hand, scholars called him a prodigy who had memorized the six rounds of Mishnah, and it was even maintained by some that he was already a Cabalist.

Reb Shimmon, who had for many years feared that his brother-in-law, Reb Zadock, might succeed the rabbi, now feared his nephew, Jochanan. And though it was Reb Ezekiel Wiener who was trying to forward the match between Jochanan and Miriam Lieba, it was generally understood that it was Reb Shimmon who was behind it. Jochanan, if he became a rich man's son-in-law, would be less ambitious about the Marshinov rabbinical post, reasoned Reb Shimmon, and also, since Miriam Lieba was rumored to be something of a heretic, she would probably not be too sympathetic toward her husband's becoming Marshinov's spiritual leader.

"Calman, do you realize what a prize Jochanan is?" Reb Ezekiel Wiener asked him. "A jewel! In all Poland you won't find another like him!"

Calman had difficulty accustoming himself to the idea that he might become a relative of the Rabbi of Marshinov. He did not deserve such an honor. It was too much, and he was full of doubts. Fate might be playing a trick on him, raising him up, as the saying went, before knocking him down. He also thought that Miriam Lieba would not care much for this match. She read all kinds of secular books, loved to wear pretty clothing, and Jochanan's religious erudition would mean nothing to her. Who could tell whether they would get along together? Calman feared too that in Jampol men would scorn him for trying to buy his way into the Marshinov court.

He answered Reb Ezekiel humbly: "What should I say? Who am I? A simple Jew, an ignoramus . . ."

"Don't be so modest! Everyone knows Reb Calman Jacoby. Will you call on Temerel?"

"Call on the rabbi's daughter? What am I to do there?"

"She's very anxious to see you. Come, let's go."

To reach Temerel's house, they passed through an orchard where lilac bushes grew among the apple and pear trees. The Hassidim plucked the fruit early in summer, when it was still unripe. The air was fragrant, birds sang, and blossoms drifted to the ground. In the middle of the orchard was an arbor, where the rabbi sometimes sat and instructed his grandchildren. The house—or, as some young wits called it, "Paris"—was two-storied. Reb Shimmon's wife Menuche, herself a rabbi's daughter, managed the household, although the half-paralyzed, aged wife of the old Rabbi of Marshinov was still in command. The wealthy second daughter-in-law, Binneleh, visited Marshinov only for the holidays. Among the women, Temerel passed as a scholar; she received Hassidic visitors and wrote letters in Hebrew.

Calman walked up the red-painted stairs with Reb Ezekiel. Long mezuzahs in carved cases were nailed to the doorposts of the high brass-knobbed doors they passed. When Reb Ezekiel pushed one open. Calman stepped onto the gleaming parquet floor of a drawing room; leather-bound books with gilt edges stood on shelves behind glass, together with goblets, trays, spice boxes, citron holders, and various silver and gold-plated objects. Brocaded draperies hung over the windows, and along the walls stood chairs with purple-tasseled covers.

66

At a little table, in an upholstered chair, sat Temerel, hook-nosed, with high cheekbones and round birdlike eyes. She wore a silk stole and black bonnet. An open book with a fine linen handkerchief beside it lay on the table, which held a carafe of wine and three glasses.

"A good holiday to you," said Calman, flustered and shy as a schoolboy.

"And to you, Reb Calman, and you, Reb Ezekiel," the hostess replied. "What a hot day! Do sit down."

"Have some wine," Temerel said, half inquiring, half commanding. With long, dainty fingers she reached for the carafe, lace dangling from her sleeve, and out of a drawer took three honey cakes.

"*L'hayim!*" Reb Ezekiel raised his glass.

"*L'hayim!*" Calman repeated.

"To your health, and peace! May salvation come to us and all our brethren. May our wanderings cease; may we be found worthy of welcoming the Messiah! We have waited long enough."

Calman murmured a benediction over the wine. He had never heard a woman use such phrases and so many Hebrew words. An aroma of almonds and spices emanated from her. The wine was sweet but strong. The hostess sipped hers, while Reb Ezekiel drank half a glass and set it aside. Calman drank his down.

"Have some more, Reb Calman. It comes directly from Hungary. Let me have your glass."

"Thank you kindly, rebbetzin."

"Good wine won't affect you."

"What are you reading?" asked Calman, and could have bitten his tongue.

"A *B'nai Issacher*. No doubt you are amazed to find a woman reading the sacred writings. Of course there's the old saying that a man who teaches the Torah to his daughter spreads heresy. But in our family all the girls are educated. My aunt, the wife of the Rabbi of Tzozmir, is very learned."

"You don't say!"

"Even my grandmother, may she rest in peace, was versed in the Talmud." Temerel blew her nose emphatically into her fine handkerchief. "But the real scholar of our family is Jochanan. A genius without an equal! The elders wanted to ordain him, but he declined the honor. Such a treasure is rare these days, a gift from heaven. There is only one thing I ask of God: that my son may live long and enjoy good health. Father in heaven, if I may only live to rejoice in his virtues!" Raising her glass to her lips, Temerel sniffed at it and then put it down again.

"And where did you say Jampol was?" she asked.

6

Though Calman had planned to leave for Jampol immediately after Pentecost, he decided at the last moment to remain in Marshinov until after the Sabbath. It was agreed that Temerel and Jochanan were to attend Shaindel's wedding on the Sabbath following the Fast of the Ninth of Ab, and the betrothal, God willing, would take place then. Calman had promised to send his coach for the honored guests. Despite Reb Ezekiel Wiener's insistence that the betrothal be formalized at Marshinov, Calman was determined to wait for Miriam Lieba's consent. Times had changed; people no longer forced their daughters into marriage.

At the end of an hour's session with the Rabbi of Marshinov, Calman had given his host two hundred rubles to pray for his, Calman's, soul. Reb Shimmon then took Calman to his rooms. The rabbi's wife soon joined them and both addressed Calman as though he were already a relative. Calman had also received from Reb Moshe, the Rabbi of Chmielev, a piece of amber which had been blessed by his grandfather and was said to have the power to stop bleeding.

Once the Sabbath was over, Getz hastened to harness the coach, and Calman hurried him along. He was already worrying about his affairs back in Jampol, about all the things he had left unfinished. Moreover, any day now, Jochebed was due to give birth.

On the way back Mayer Joel and Reb Menachem Mendel discussed the Hassidic movement. Reb Mendel insisted that despite its virtues, Marshinov and its rabbi could scarcely be compared with Turisk and the holiness of its rabbi. All the holy men were different, he remarked. Reb Mendeleh Rimanover, for example, accepted substantial donations from his followers, and carried a golden snuffbox, but other Hassidic rabbis lived in poverty. To one spiritual leader it was the study of the Torah that mattered most; to another it was prayer; to a third, charity; each according to his preference. Mayer Joel nodded assent, but at the same time he was annoyed by this praise of Turisk. How could Turisk possibly be compared with Marshinov? He had heard that in Turisk the spiritual leader was given to homiletic interpretations. And what did they amount to?

Actually it was Ezriel who irritated Mayer Joel most. Such irreverence! He had scarcely shown his face at the rabbi's, and at the study house had retreated to the anteroom among the loafers and young scamps. He had even boasted of not having listened to the rabbi. Mayer Joel had spoken to his father-in-law of Ezriel's disrespect, but Calman had replied, "What if he isn't a genuine Hassid? He can still be a Jew," implying some pettiness in Mayer Joel. It was clear Calman had no intention of breaking off the match.

Mayer Joel sulked. What was the old proverb? You can't make a silk purse out of a sow's ear. His father-in-law was not a bad sort, he was simply common. Eager to have Jochanan as a brother-in-law, Mayer Joel felt that Calman was the one who did not quite belong. The situation was demeaning. When Jochebed gave birth, he would ask for the dowry still due him, and they would leave the estate, even if they got no farther than Jampol. He would persuade his father-in-law to make a cash settlement for the years of maintenance still owing. Mayer Joel longed to be on his own; a certain watermill interested him. He did not intend to lose his father-in-law's legacy, but neither did he plan to spend his life among such rustics.

As the night wore on, the carriage grew silent. Calman dozed, thinking of his fields of grain, of the railroad ties, of the lime quarries and the spur line he had ordered laid. His financial obligations were enormous; even the government was impatiently waiting for the rail connection. Now one of his daughters was about to be married to none other than the grandson of the Rabbi of Marshinov. A few years ago he would have laughed scornfully at anyone who had either prophesied his present position or suggested he would ever incur such liabilities. He was most certainly in need of divine guidance to keep him from stumbling now.

Reb Menachem Mendel was engrossed in his concern for Ezriel, his only son. The young man had behaved irresponsibly in Marshinov. What if Calman were to break off the match? The young man would be humiliated. He might even be conscripted—God forbid! Why couldn't he at least control his evil inclinations until after the marriage? For the honored memory of his holy ancestors, rather than for the sake of his son, Reb Menachem Mendel implored the Lord's indulgence.

Ezriel, who in Marshinov on the first day of Pentecost had met a young man named Aaron Asher Lipman, also had much to think about. He and his new friend had both been standing in the anteroom, prayer books in hand but not praying. After eyeing each other a while, they had begun to talk. Aaron Asher was undersized, with a huge head and meager body, a few hairs on his chin, bushy sidelocks, dark eyes. Ezriel, noting his narrow sash, highly polished boots, buttoned shirt collar, and above all the look in his eyes, had assumed him to be enlightened.

"Why must God have new angels every day?" Aaron Asher had asked flippantly, approaching Ezriel and referring to the special verses for Shabuoth recited by the reader from a passage in the *Akdamoth*.

"Perhaps the old ones turn sour," Ezriel had answered jestingly.

By the time the services had ended, Aaron Asher had told Ezriel all about himself. He had a wife and three children; his father-in-law, who had a dry-goods store, still supported him, but he occasionally helped out by traveling to Warsaw to buy merchandise for the store. In the big city he came in contact with enlightened people. He would have liked to go to Vilna or Königsberg to study secular subjects, but his wife was a religious zealot, and his mother-in-law dominated the household. If he had been able to scrape together the fare, he would have run off long ago, but then too he hated to leave his children. He talked on and on: the Rabbi of Marshinov was senile; the self-seeking Reb Shimmon was jockeying for leadership; Jochanan was a fool; Reb Moshe, a hypocrite. In Poland, the life of the Jews had become precarious. The storekeepers outnumbered the customers. The Jews had reached a dead end. Self-righteous Jews had dissuaded Czar Nicholas from allotting land to them at the time he had been inclined to do so, and now it was too late. There was no true language in use, simply jargon. Dressing like Asiatics, the Jews here belonged to the period of King Sobjeski. Such a state of affairs could not continue.

"Do you have a solution?" Ezriel had asked.

"We must extricate ourselves."

"But how?"

The congregation had at that point stood up for the Eighteen Benedictions and the conversation had ceased.

Later the two young men had strolled along the road lined with oaks that lead out of Marshinov. Aaron Asher, seven years older than Ezriel, had read extensively in forbidden books and periodicals. He spoke in a singsong, and with his forefinger wound in the fringe of his sash poked Ezriel's ribs for emphasis. "Our educational methods must be reformed. The Jews must master German as well as Russian and Polish. The children must be taught trades, the long caftans abolished, and the beards shaved off or trimmed. Perhaps some-where—Palestine or the Crimea—land can be obtained for colonies. The world moves ahead, not backward. Even Joshua halted the sun for only a few hours," he had concluded, wink-ing mischievously.

II

A week before Shaindel's wedding, Calman sent Getz with the coach to Marshinov, and it returned bringing Temerel, Jo-chanan, and a servant girl named Kaila. Over the summer, Cal-man had added eight rooms to his house and was now able to put up his guests more comfortably. Miriam Lieba, when he had spoken with her about Jochanan, had protested that she was not the type to be a rabbi's daughter-in-law, but she did consent to look at the young man. If she liked him, well and good; if not, her father was to drop the matter entirely. Cal-man found this plan a good one, although others might have thought it ill-advised.

Miriam Lieba, from behind the curtains of her garret win-dow, peeped out as the visitors dismounted from the coach. Calman, Mayer Joel, Zelda, Shaindel, and Faigel the maid were on hand to welcome them. First to alight, bundle in hand, was Kaila, a tall woman with masculine features. Then came Temerel, whom the maid almost had to lift down from the seat, which seemed to be holding her fast. Prayer book in one hand and handkerchief in the other, wearing a black bon-net, a long-fringed silk scarf, and a black silk dress with a train, she looked about her and made a wry face; the odor of cow dung brought on an attack of sneezing. Last to dismount was Jochanan, stoop-shouldered, pasty-faced, puny, with overlong sidelocks, wearing a velvet hat and a ground-length gaberdine tied with a broad sash. Like his mother, he carried a handkerchief and some sort of sacred book. Miriam Lieba wanted to laugh and cry at once.

"Miriam Lieba, where are you?" Zelda called.

Miriam Lieba, without knowing why, had taken an immediate dislike to Temerel and pretended not to hear her mother for a while. Her cheeks were burning and she wanted to remain hidden. Even her own sister made her feel embarrassed. She seemed to take the entire visit as a joke. Shaindel's eyes were so merry . . .

Miriam Lieba threw a scarf over her shoulders, only to tear it off the next moment. I don't have to put on airs for those idiots, I'll spit at them! She was ashamed of her timidity and at the same time annoyed by her own irascibility. After all, these people had not wronged her. Her father would not marry her off at gun point. She started down the stairs carrying a Polish book: let them see that she did as she pleased. But seconds later she reconsidered: why vex her parents? Yet some inner force was compelling her to spite these people who had come to size her up as if she were some kind of livestock. Only when she had almost crossed the threshold did she become aware of the stupidity of her action. Turning back, she hastily shoved the volume into the larder, upset a pot of sour cream, and had to jump aside to avoid being splashed.

"Yes, Mother." Miriam Lieba finally appeared.

"Where have you been hiding?" Zelda introduced her daughter. "This is the rabbi's daughter—my younger daughter, Miriam Lieba."

Miriam Lieba knew that she was expected to greet the guests or at least nod on being introduced, but she simply stood still, looking at the shrewd-eyed Temerel.

"A beautiful girl!"

"Thank you."

"And tall. May she escape the Evil Eye."

Jochanan, deep in thought, frowned and suddenly averted his eyes: he had almost looked at a female! Shaindel, noting his embarrassment, began to laugh.

"Let me show you the house," Calman suggested to Temerel. "We have no drawing room, just a roof over our heads."

74

"Who needs drawing rooms? I have—may you be spared the same—a headache."

"A glass of milk, perhaps?"

"Not before prayers."

Zelda led Temerel to the room prepared for her, where she immediately washed her hands while her own maid held a towel in readiness. Then she surveyed the room: it looked spotless, and the wooden floor, freshly painted, smelled of pine. Three pillows were piled one on top of the other at the head of the bed, with a bolster of the kind popular among wealthy peasants.

"Which is the east wall?"

"That one," Zelda pointed.

Jochanan, shown to his room by Calman, asked the same question: "Which is the east wall?"

"That one."

"Is there really no quorum for prayer?"

"How could there be? We're outside the town."

"In that case, one is allowed to pray alone."

Jochanan washed his hands and began to murmur his prayers, facing the southeast corner rather than east. After finishing the preliminary morning prayers, he put on his phylacteries. He felt strained after the journey; his thoughts had been disrupted. Rumors had reached him that he was to be married to one of Calman's daughters. But why had it been necessary for him to come here? He had endured the journey by concentrating on the sacred book he carried and by reciting the Psalms from memory, while imploring the Lord to protect him from evil thoughts. But he had been unable to avoid glimpses of meadows, fields, peasants, cattle, extraneous objects that he did not care to observe, lest they deter him from proper service to the Creator. One must surmount all obstacles with fortitude. He recalled the precept that one should recite one's prayer as slowly as one counts gold pieces. And weren't the sacred words more precious than any number of coins? "The Lord is righteous in all His ways, and gracious in all His works. The Lord is with all those who call upon Him, with all who call upon Him in truth. He will fulfill the desire of those that fear Him; He will also hear their cry and save them." What words! God is near all who call him. One only need implore, and He responds. How pale are the follies of the world before truth! Jochanan was conscious of calling upon the Almighty with his mind, heart, and every part of him: "Help me, O Lord! I wish only to serve Thee, devoutly, and to my last breath. I ask nothing more!"

Mayer Joel, coming to look for Jochanan and assuming that he must have completed his prayers, opened the door. But the young worshipper took no notice of him as he continued murmuring the Eighteen Benedictions.

III

The day of Shaindel's wedding, Calman had a serious talk with Miriam Lieba. Fifteen minutes later she left him, her pale cheeks stinging red, her nostrils quivering. She went into the kitchen to tell her mother that Calman wished to see her. The aroma of honey cake and fresh loaves baked with saffron filled the kitchen. The fowl and beef had already been made kosher. Wiping her hands on her apron, Zelda left the room. Soon she returned, smiling but with tear-stained cheeks. Little Tsipele came in; though not quite eleven, she was almost as tall as Shaindel, and her hair hung in long braids: yet she still acted like a child. The cook had baked a special patty for her, marked with a *T*, and had wrapped it in gold paper. Snatching up the hot cookie, she tossed it from hand to hand, complaining that it was too hot.

Zelda, pulling the child to her, hugged and kissed her, tears streaming from her eyes, while she blurted out, "Ah, my poor child!"

"But, mistress, this is a wedding!" one of the kitchen help remarked.

"Go to your father, dear; he wants to talk to you," Zelda said.

"To me?"

"Yes, little chick."

"Look, Papa," Tsipele greeted her father, showing him the cake. "It has my initial on it."

"I'm sure it's delicious, too. Come here, darling."

Sitting at the head of the table, Calman asked his daughter to sit down. She could hardly believe it; he had never before asked her to sit down. She must be growing up.

"Tsipele, have you seen Jochanan?" Calman asked, taking her hand.

"The son of the rebbetzin? I saw him."

"How does he strike you?"

"He has such lovely sidelocks!"

"Would you like him as a bridegroom?"

Tsipele grew serious. "Isn't he going to be betrothed to Miriam Lieba?"

"Miriam Lieba doesn't want him."

"Why not?"

"I don't think she knows herself. Tsipele, I would like you to be betrothed to Jochanan."

Blushing, the girl replied, "I'm too young!"

"Not really. In earlier times, eight-year-old girls were given in marriage. And the actual marriage will not take place for several years. You'll receive fine gifts as a bride. The young man is a prodigy; his grandfather is the Sage of Marshinov. It will be a great honor."

"And what about Miriam Lieba?"

"She won't be a spinster, God willing. She'll find a mate. What do you say, Tsipele?"

"As you wish."

"Remember, Tsipele, this isn't child's play. Jochanan is a great scholar, and an orphan too. He must not be humiliated. You'll marry him, God willing. You won't remain a calf forever."

77

"I know."

"So—you want him?"

"Why not?"

"Well, I don't want to act without your consent. You agree, so it's all right. With God's help, fortune will favor you. You'll be my pride and joy."

"May I go now?"

"What's the rush? Your cookie won't run away. A betrothed girl must be calm. You'll get a watch and chain as a present, and a dowry and a trousseau. Jochanan is older than you, but not so much."

"How old?"

"Sixteen."

"Oh!"

"That's not so old."

"He's a young man already."

"Naturally. So what? You're a young girl."

"I know that."

"Before you realize it, with God's help you'll be grown up. Time doesn't stand still, darling. How long ago do you think I was your age? It seems like yesterday."

"But you already have such a long beard!" Tsipele laughed.

"What of it? Jochanan's beard will grow, too. When, God willing, you're a married woman, you'll wear a bonnet. With God's help, you'll have children."

"I—a mother?"

"Your mother was a little girl too at one time. I remember her at your age. Your grandfather—may his soul rest in peace —was a scribe of sacred writings, a poor but saintly Jew. Every time, before he sat down to write, he would perform ablutions; your grandmother was a virtuous woman. They have both already joined their ancestors."

"Why?"

"Nobody lives forever. Without making due provision in this world, one enters the next one empty-handed. By marrying a sage, you'll find delight in both worlds."

78

"Do you think he'll want me?"

"Jochanan? He doesn't look at girls; he'll obey his mother. You are—may the Evil Eye spare you—a beautiful girl. Your hair is black and your face is fair. He'll be pleased. You'll be a virtuous Jewish daughter. And faithful. Isn't that true?"

"Yes."

"Wait. I have something for you."

Fumbling in his pocket, Calman found a silver ruble. "Here, take this."

"Really?"

"Of course."

"Oh, thank you."

"Buy something for yourself. But now, come here."

Tsipele ran to her father; they embraced and kissed. She combed his beard with her fingers. Calman would have liked to lift her up and give her a ride on his knee as he had done only a year ago, but he restrained his impulse.

"Well, that's all," he remarked.

"May I tell everyone?"

"No. At the moment, it's a secret."

"All right."

Picking up her cake, Tsipele walked out, but turned around to look back. Her mother was waiting with open arms.

"I've heard everything, dear. I have only one wish before the Lord, to live to see your wedding—first Miriam Lieba's, then yours."

"Mother . . ."

Mother and daughter kissed fervently, the former weeping. Calman went to Temerel's room, and his wife followed soon afterward. When they left, Temerel sent her maid for Jochanan. Tsipele remained indoors for a while and then went to the barn, where she crawled into a shed with a little sloping roof which was her hiding place. Nearby was a willow tree and a warped block used for wood-chopping. Tsipele sat there contemplating the silver coin while she consumed her cake.

When the maid came to call Jochanan, he was engrossed in

Holy Writ. From all the whispering, he judged that something was going on. Once or twice, while standing at the window, he had seen some girls passing, one of whom, he assumed, was his bride-to-be. Laughter and conversation had reached him from adjacent rooms. Although all was predestined, he implored the Lord that his wife be quiet and virtuous, not a giggler. What was there to laugh about? If man realized how many demons lurked around him, how easily he could stumble and forfeit the world to come, his fears would keep him from laughing.

Marking the place he had reached in the annotation to the Talmud, Jochanan apologized silently to the authors for having interrupted his communion with them. His heart was beating faster than usual. He halted in the anteroom to adjust his sidelocks. Perhaps his future in-laws might want to look him over. . . .

7

Count Jampolski and his family attended Shaindel's wedding, and it was there that Miriam Lieba met the young Countess Helena. Miriam Lieba, who spoke Polish more fluently than her sisters, was liked by the Gentiles. The two girls were only a few months apart in age. As soon as the marriage ceremony was over, the Count and Countess, accompanied by Felicia, returned to the castle, but Helena insisted on remaining. Taking a seat next to Miriam Lieba at the girls' table, she took a sip of the festive chicken broth, a bite of carp, a white roll. Various women too shy to approach her mother came to Helena and made conversation in a mixture of Polish and Yiddish. When the band struck up and the girls paired off with each other for dancing, Helena, requesting a mazurka from the musicians, threw a coin onto the drum as was the custom, bowed like a gallant before Miriam Lieba, and asked her to dance. The company watched, with a good deal of laughter, chatter, and clapping, the unusual spectacle of a Polish countess dancing with a Jewess. The two girls had similar figures, though Helena's bosom was higher. Helena wore silver slippers with high slender heels and a white gown cut low in front and in back, with puffed sleeves. A medallion hung around her throat, and her hair was combed high in the French fashion. A crowd from Jampol stood in the doorway, watching and jostling each other. "If you live long enough, you see everything," one woman remarked to another.

Before the evening was over, Miriam Lieba received an invitation to visit Helena. But it was not until the day of Tsipele's betrothal—when the Hassidim were celebrating noisily on the grounds of the manor, even urinating on the trees, trampling the grass, and tearing off leaves to use as toilet paper—that Miriam Lieba finally put on her new dress, and carrying the bouquet of flowers she had picked in the fields, started off for the manor house.

Helena, turning the bouquet over to a maid to put into water, took Miriam Lieba to greet her family. The Countess assured her young visitor that she did not look at all Jewish and, having said this, retired to her room. Felicia was annoyed that a daughter of Calman's had to be received at all, but at the same time chided herself for breaking her vow to live humbly and without false pride. Only the day before, she had written in her diary: "If I can't do as Jesus demanded, I prefer to die." So she smiled at Miriam Lieba and complimented her on her dress, one that Nissen the tailor had made—a compliment that was promptly returned.

The Count, wearing riding breeches and an English plaid jacket, both purchased recently, received Miriam Lieba with democratic affability. Sitting down opposite the girls on a bench in the arbor, he chatted about the terrible winters in northern Russia, about the government officials with whom the prisoners fraternized, about the considerable freedom he had enjoyed in exile, having been permitted to ride, hunt, skate. The Siberian peasants went out on bear hunts armed only with clubs. And the natives were tormented by bedbugs. When the Count began to describe how the bugs nested in the moss between the roofbeams of the dwellings and hurled themselves down from the ceiling in the dark to suck blood from their victims, Helena let out a peal of laughter and Miriam Lieba smiled. But Felicia, who stood at a distance and

82

seemed to be scarcely listening, spat into her lace handkerchief.

"How can you talk like that, Father?"

"If the bedbugs don't care, why should I? We're all made of the same protoplasm."

Felicia walked off in disgust. Her father talked of nothing but lice, bedbugs, garbage, rags, anything that was revolting. Even when he ate, his mind was occupied with filth. It was enough to turn anyone's stomach, and Felicia knew that he did it to spite her. During his exile the Russians had infected him with nihilistic notions and their Godless materialism. In his pipe he smoked coarse peasant tobacco, which stank up the house. And that Russian woman—everyone knew about the woman he had brought back, who occupied a cottage in The Sands, where the Jews had once lived. Everything had happened as Felicia had foreseen. Her father drank, used coarse language, and dishonored an ancient and noble family by living openly with a slut. If she had not recognized it as her Christian duty to accept suffering with humility, and if she had not loved her unhappy mother so much, she would have fled the house or killed herself.

Felicia's departure did not annoy the Count, who merely shrugged his shoulders. Presently the conversation turned to the Jews.

"We Poles should learn from you people," the Count said. "We turn gold into mud; you turn mud into gold."

Miriam Lieba reddened.

"There are plenty of poor Jews, too."

"I know, I know, but all of you spend your time plotting how to get rich."

Helena took Miriam Lieba on a tour of the manor, covering her mouth with her fan when a yawn interrupted her talk, pointing out the blue room, the gold room, her own boudoir, the library. Miriam Lieba had been in the manor only once, many years before, when as a child she had accompanied Cal-

83

man on one of his visits. Since then, the building had undergone great changes. Leaks in the roof had damaged the interior. Windows had become crooked, walls had sunk. In the damp library the books, mostly biographies of saints and genealogical histories, were covered with mildew. Helena, motioning Miriam Lieba to a high-backed chair, seated herself on a bench.

"It's so lonely here—sometimes I think I might as well be dead. I don't meet a decent-looking man from one end of the year to the next," she confided. "But what will become of you? Will you marry a Jew?"

"Only if he's attractive to me."

"You're right. I could never marry a man I didn't love. Just recently, in Zamosc, my aunt introduced me to the son of one of her friends. He and I went for a stroll and right away he started to prattle about love. As we were crossing a bridge, he remarked, 'There are a vast number of small fish down there, extremely small ones.' The moment he said 'small fish,' he became loathsome to me. I thought, you're nothing but a small fish yourself. Isn't that odd?"

"I understand you perfectly."

11

That evening it snowed and continued snowing throughout the night, the flakes heavy, dense, and dry as salt. In the morning the temperature dropped and a frost set in. The manor regained its former glory: the roof lost its patches; the balconies and carved moldings became opulent once more. Crystal spears hung from the window frames and patterns of frost blossoms coated the panes. Even the smoke that drifted from the chimney to the clear sky spiraled elegantly. The dogs, Wilk and Piorun, barked constantly; the cow in the barn scraped at the door with her horns; roosters crowed; crows cawed. The fields, sown with winter grain which had already begun to sprout, were enveloped in a whiteness without beginning or end. When a young rabbit scurried from some bushes and gazed at the rejuvenated manor house, the Count seized his gun and fired. The rabbit vanished, leaving behind only the barest trace of footprints.

The Count had risen while it was still dark. Though he had lost everything—his wealth, his son Lucian—his appetite for life had not abated. Thrusting his feet immediately into boots, rather than slippers, he strode through the houschold, slamming doors and waking everyone. Hungry and thirsty, he went outdoors to the well to wash. He would have loved to go hunting if only he had had some pointers or retrievers.

In the kitchen Barbara the nurse ground coffee beans in the hand mill. She prided herself on having inherited from her grandmothers and great-grandmothers the art of brewing coffee. The Count ate voraciously, black bread and butter, and swallowed the dark unsweetened brew. Although he knew it was bad manners, after every gulp he emitted an "ah" like a famished peasant. When a crumb clung to his mustache, he licked it off with his tongue. During his exile, Jampolski had come to the conclusion that etiquette wasn't worth a groschen. He had reread Rousseau. Poland was the victim of too much foppery.

After eating, the Count went to his wife's bedroom. The Countess, who slept so lightly that the faintest rustle woke her, had lit the candle which stood on the night table.

"Mother, get up and take a look at the snow. It's two feet deep."

"Jan, I've asked you repeatedly not to call me Mother."

"Don't you want any breakfast? Something hot to drink?"

"Thank you, nothing."

"You're all bones. Nothing produces nothing. I'll be going into town."

"Why must you always be going to town?"

"To talk to the Jews."

"Why the Jews?"

"Who else is there? All the Poles know how to do well is

85

weep. They bore me. A Jew will cheat you out of your last ruble, but he's not dead on his feet, or forever bragging about some stupid pedigree."

"May God forgive you for such blasphemy."

"What would you like from town? I'll bring you an orange."

"I don't want an orange."

Wojciech tried to help the Count hitch up the small sleigh —the large one was too heavy and took four horses—but the Count would not let him. The Countess, hearing her husband drive off, took the Bible from the night table. She knew to whom he was running. Opening to the Book of Psalms, she began to murmur the sacred words. When she came to the verses about the God-fearing poor man on whom the wicked sharpen their teeth, surrounding him like a bevy of dogs ready to swallow him, she paused. Wasn't her situation like that man's? Wasn't she, Maria, beset by evil? Of her two sons, Lucian was dead and Josef in exile in distant England; her oldest daughter, Felicia, was a spinster; the estate was confiscated; and her husband betrayed her. When she reached the passage, "My mother and father have forsaken me, and God will take me to himself," she began to sob. Her breast ached. Yes, God Almighty remained after everything was lost. After weeping, the Countess usually felt better, but this time she did not. Closing the Holy Book, she kissed the cross engraved on its binding, and rang a little silver bell until Barbara entered.

"Send in Felicia."

"Yes, your Excellency."

When her daughter came, the Countess asked her to sit in a chair next to the bed.

"Felicia, I must talk to you plainly," the Countess began. "You're not a child any more. Your mother won't live forever. And you know you can't rely on your father. I had hoped the ordeal of Siberia would purify him, but if anything his soul has become even blacker. What will happen after my death? I'm afraid he'll bring shame on himself and on you."

86

"Mother, you'll get better."

"Perhaps. . . . Open my handbag. There's a key in it. That's it."

"Why?"

"Do as you're told. Now, open the bottom drawer of my bureau. At the very bottom, to the right, you'll find a jewel case. Take it out. Yes, that's it. Now bring it to me."

Felicia, carefully lifting the ebony box decorated with ivory, carried it to the Countess, who opened it. Inside lay strands of pearls, pins, bracelets, earrings, and all sorts of rings, most of them set with diamonds.

"These belong to me alone, Felicia. They're all I possess— my own, brought from my father's house. I don't want them to fall into your father's hands. He'll only waste what they bring. I want you to have them all, with the exception of the smaller strand of pearls. Give that to Helena at her wedding, but not before. She's more like your father and not so helpless as you are. You're more like me. I pray God you will still find a suitable husband. But in case of need, you'll have these. I want you to take them now."

"Mother, it's not necessary."

"I've thought it over. I don't know how much these are worth, forty thousand gulden at least, perhaps much more. If, God forbid, you should be forced to sell, don't go to a cheap jeweler. Go to Warsaw: on Krakow Boulevard is a jeweler named Adam Nosek. You can trust him."

"Mother, you still have years . . ."

"I make one last request to you."

"What is it, Mother?"

"I know Lucian is not alive. If he were, he would have found some way of communicating with us. He is in heaven among the angels, and I shall soon meet him there. After my death, on my tombstone, I want his name engraved as well as mine."

"Mother, you're tearing my heart."

"I want you to be prepared. It's better. The earth is a vale of misery. What did your father give me? A lot of sorrow, a little joy. My soul no longer wants to stay in my body. Look how thin I am, wasted away. I no longer recognize myself. If I could only see you happy! Find a husband, Felicia, and don't be so choosy. He doesn't have to be rich. As long as he's noble and a man of faith. What happened to our fortune? Well, enough. Take the box and hide it with your things. Where will you put it?"

"In my vanity table."

"You keep it locked, don't you? Good. I want to die without any possessions. God loves the poor. Well, you may go."

Felicia hesitated. "You want me to take it now?"

"Yes. How many times do you have to be told?"

"But, Mama . . ." Felicia, bending over her mother, began to kiss her hands, her forehead. She was weeping in a thin mewling voice like a kitten.

The Countess became impatient. "Please go now," she said sharply.

Felicia, sniffling, took the jewel box and left the room, walking with a swaying gait. Of what use were all these diamonds to her? She locked the box in the vanity table in her boudoir. After a while, her tears dried. She stood at the window and looked out. The upper panes were covered with frost, the lower ones had cleared. Outside, the sun was shining. She could see the tracks made by her father's sleigh and the horses' hooves. Two crows picked at the oats in the horse dung, airing their wings. Suddenly, Felicia noticed Helena with Calman's daughter Miriam Lieba, who wore a knitted jacket and a heavy gray wool skirt, while Helena had on a dark green costume, its lapels decorated with laurel leaves. Both carried skates and were on their way to the lake. Felicia turned her eyes away. Her father was the friend of a Muscovite, and her sister the friend of a rich Jewess. All they cared about was pleasure. Mother was ill and Helena went off skating. She had no heart at all.

At that moment, Felicia knew what she would do when her

mother died. She would enter a convent, bring the jewelry as her dowry, and have it made into a crown for the Blessed Virgin. She, Felicia, needed no worldly treasure. Once and for all she would tear from her breast all earthly hopes, all dreams of material happiness. Bread and water and a hard bench were all she needed.

8

In Wola, a Warsaw suburb, there was a furniture factory that employed about forty men. It was located in a loft which was filled with sawdust and shavings. There Wacek Pracz worked at cutting out holes in a thick board with a hammer and chisel. Nearby, another man sawed lumber, a second planed, a third hammered nails, a fourth drilled with a gimlet. The air was filled with the pungent odors of varnish and glue. Since it was winter, the windows were shut, but some air came in through an occasional broken pane. The building reverberated with the noises of lathes, hammers, and saws. From the yard below came the shouts of teamsters loading furniture and unloading lumber. At one o'clock precisely, the factory stopped work, and the wives, mothers, and sisters of the laborers, their heads covered with shawls, entered the courtyard, bringing hot food, pots of soup, loaves of bread. Seating themselves on logs and boards in the yard, the men spooned up groats, chewed bread and sausage, or tilted bottles of vodka. The air smelled of fried onions and domesticity.

Wacek Pracz sat on a crate near the fence, with his mistress Stachowa. He was above medium height, with a pale, youthful face, light blue eyes, and a blond beard but no mustache. His nose was turned up, his lips narrow, his forehead high. Like the other workmen, he was dressed in a cotton-padded jacket, a shirt open at the neck, patched pants, and heavy shoes. Though Pracz was a peasant name and this man claimed a village near Wloclawek as his home, there were those who whispered that he belonged to the aristocracy. His speech was unlike that of his fellow workers; his curses and vulgarities seemed out of place. After work, he did not accompany the others to the taverns, but went his own way. It was thought that he had probably participated in the 1863 Insurrection, but this was never discussed openly. Everyone knew that "walls had ears and the Russkis had spies planted everywhere." Wacek Pracz was nicknamed the "Squire."

Stachowa came from the people. Before her marriage, she had been a domestic. Her husband, Stach, had died shortly after their wedding, and her daughter Kasia, now eleven, had been born out of wedlock. Stachowa and Wacek lived together without benefit of clergy. The women were curious about Wacek and often questioned her about his habits, his behavior, whether or not he associated with aristocrats, whether he had a family, read books . . . But Stachowa only smiled fatuously. "Do I know? He leaves for work early, and when he comes home, he's dead tired. Sometimes he comes late, but he won't say where he's been. What can a mere woman know of a man? Maybe he has a dozen other women . . ."

"Does he ever beat you?"

"When he's drunk."

Stachowa, a sickly woman whom some claimed was consumptive, had sunken, red-splotched cheeks. She wore her sparse, faded blond hair in a bun, and her pale blue eyes were always tearing, though she constantly smiled. The women did not understand what the "Squire" saw in such a wreck, though it might be simply that she had taken him in when he had been ill and starving, and he had stayed on, becoming attached to Kasia also. "A man is like a dog"—they commented. "Feed him, give him a place to sleep, and he won't leave his kennel."

D

Stachowa, in apron and shawl, sat beside Wacek, eyes on his mouth as he ate. She had brought him a pound of bread, but he hadn't eaten half of it, or finished the soup. She knew the truth, that his name wasn't Wacek Pracz, and that he was not from a village near Wloclawek. He was Lucian, Count Jampolski, of the Jampol manor. But she would never betray his identity—not even if her flesh were cut open and acid poured into the wounds. He might be a nobleman, but what difference did that make when he had no money and carried a false passport? He acted like anyone else: if he was angry, he cursed her or beat her; often too, after drawing his pay on Saturday, he returned drunk and with empty pockets. If she, Stachowa, hadn't washed laundry for the Jews, the three of them would have perished. But one thing she could say in his favor: he was good to her daughter Kasia, bought marmalade for her and was teaching her to read from a primer. They would have gotten by if so much money had not gone for medicines and leeches.

He handed Stachowa the half-full dish.

"Is that all you're going to eat? I'll be taking half of it home again."

"That's all. My stomach is bloated."

"A few more spoonfuls—please!"

"I said no. Do you want me to have cramps?"

"All right. All right."

"What's Kasia doing?"

"Playing in bed with the kitten."

"Well . . . so . . . you can go now."

"Wacek—come home early today. Look how pale you are —paler than anyone else. You know how tired you were this morning—you could hardly wake up."

Wacek stood up. "Go—for heaven's sake, go."

Stachowa tucked the pot under her shawl. That's how men were—they didn't want your love.

Stachowa's room was small. The bed she and Lucian shared was on a gallery reached by a ladder. Below, Kasia sat on the straw mattress of her narrow bench-bed. Her face was small, her hair flaxen, her eyes gray, her skin porcelain white, like that of a doll. She read aloud from her primer:

> "*Tell me, Darling,*
> *Where is the apple,*
> *The coffee-grinder?*
> *And where is the parrot,*
> *Or the cage where*
> *The bird sings?*"

Stachowa paused to listen. What odd things were printed in books! She herself could neither read nor write and signed her name with three X's. But it was fortunate that Kasia was getting an education. The Russians had forbidden the use of Polish—the scum, carrion, boors, accursed Muscovites!

"*He* was here," Kasia said.

"*He?*"

"You know, the other father."

Stachowa grimaced. Her eyes blazed. "I've warned him plenty of times not to set foot in here. The tramp! The beggar! The no-good drunk! What did he want?"

"He said he'd come back later."

"And I'll have the broom ready to greet him with."

She went to the corner and got out the broom. Kasia closed her book.

"Don't do it, Mama."

"You feel sorry for him? After he ruined my life? He left me with a child in my belly and ran off to his whores. Who knocked out four of my teeth? He's a leech, a thief, a leper, a murderer. I don't want him in the house . . ."

"Mama!"

Stachowa stood leaning on the broom. She heard a mouse scratching and, after a while, steps approaching. She cocked her ears. Could it be Wacek? No, Wacek walked like a man, but this was like the creeping of a skunk about to strangle a chicken. She knew it was her first lover, coming to persuade her to give herself to him. Pushing him away a thousand times was not enough. He probably couldn't even get a whore, the wretch; probably had the clap too.

Antek, Kasia's father, opened the door. Seeing Stachowa armed with the broom, he stayed where he was. Short, large-boned, cross-eyed, with a broad nose sprinkled with warts, he wore a cap with a broken visor and a sleeveless sheepskin jacket.

Stachowa glared. "You here again? Haven't I warned you to stay away? Why do you hang on like the plague? Get out! Out! I'll scream for help! I'll call the police."

"Shut up! I'm not trying to kill you. I have a right to see my daughter."

"You haven't. A man who deserts his baby is no father. She's not your daughter."

"Yes, she is—mine and not that escaped convict's you sleep with: that nobody of a bearded young lord."

"Pig! Dog! Hyena! What are you raving about? May God in heaven punish you! May you drop dead on the spot!"

"Be still. Why is she in bed?"

"Because she has no shoes. Now crawl back where you came from!"

"There's something I have to tell you."

"Well, if you must—say it."

"No, it's a secret. Come into the hall."

"No! Sausage is not for dogs, ah no."

"So you won't come?"

"Never."

"And yet you loved me once."

"What used to be, used to be. Now get out!"

94

"Jadzia, don't be so mean."

"What should I do, kiss you? My enemy! You sucked my last drop of blood. What more do you want? I've nothing left for you. No love. No respect . . ."

Suddenly she burst into tears, her mouth twisting strangely. The kitten came forward from behind a box, staring with its green eyes, and began to mewl.

"Antek, go!"

He went, quietly closing the door behind him.

III

That night, Lucian did not return home after work, but stopped at a tavern on Kercelak Place. Having earned several additional groschen from an extra chore, he ordered a glass of vodka, a pork sausage, and a beer chaser. A single groschen remained, and tossing it in his palm, he sought answers to his fate in the way it fell. Would he, Lucian, die a natural or an unnatural death? The indication was unnatural. Would he be shot or hanged? The groschen seemed to deliberate for a moment, then landed on the side which he had designated "hanged." "Well, let them hang me," he laughed, and again spun the groschen on the table. He belched from the garlic in the sausage, and the beer and vodka began to seep through his head. He was not drunk but his brain seemed to be whirling. "I'll do it! I'll do it!" he mumbled to himself. "Every night I dream about it. It has to happen. What's the difference when?"

At Lucian's feet lay a bundle of wood, tied with rope, which he had brought from the factory. He now picked it up and walked out, carrying it on his shoulders. It would keep their room warm tonight. There was more smoke than light from the street lamps. Other laborers were also returning from their workshops and factories, with bundles of kindling wood, bags of potatoes. Woodchoppers were trudging along with axes and saws; peddlers with baskets of frozen apples, onions, radishes, pans of roasted beans. Streetwalkers loitered at gates and fences. A drunk stood near an unhitched wagon and vomited. A forsaken dog walked slowly along, sniffing at the mud. Madmen and beggars sat around the store stoops, unable to find lodgings in the poorhouses. The frost had let up, but the cold was penetrating. An icy wind blew in from the Vistula.

Stachowa lived on Leshno Street, on the other side of Iron Street, in a building set back behind a fence. Refuse littered the banks of snow. Lucian pushed open the gate and walked into the courtyard, passed the stable with horses and, kicking open the door of a dark hallway, stepped in.

He smelled kindling, rags, washing soda, and had to avoid falling over a washtub. Nothing disgusted him more than the filthy Jewish linen. He pulled open another door and saw Stachowa and Kasia by the light of a wick flickering in a container of oil. Stachowa stood in the middle of the room, her shawl over her head, apparently ready to go out. Kasia sat on her bench-bed.

"Late again," Stachowa said.

"Yes, late again," Lucian replied.

"Well, put down the wood."

He dropped it. "You going out?"

"I have to deliver some laundry. The groats are on the stove."

"Yes . . ."

"The liver is probably overdone."

"You have liver? That's good."

"I bought it because you like it."

"Well, thanks."

Stachowa wrapped the shawl closer about her. At the door she said loudly: "I'll be gone a couple of hours." Then Lucian heard her fumbling in the hall. What is she doing there? he asked himself, though he knew she wasn't doing anything but was only waiting to see if he would call her back. There was silence in the hall. She must be holding her breath. Finally he heard the door slam. Maybe she's still there? he thought.

Lately she had been behaving as if she read his mind. He walked over to the stove and lifted the lid of the pot. Ordinarily, he was fond of liver, but the sausage he had eaten at the tavern had spoiled his appetite.

"Well, Kasia, what are you doing?"

"Nothing."

"Did you memorize the poem?"

"Yes, I did."

"I'll listen to it soon."

Lucian ladled some groats and liver into a tin plate, walked past the table, and sat down near Kasia, balancing the plate on his lap. His appetite revived as soon as he began to eat.

"Want some, Kasia?"

"No."

"Why not?"

"Because it's all for you. I've eaten my share already."

"Have some more."

"No. It's all for you. You work and I lie in bed all day."

"Was anyone here today?"

"*He* was here, the other father."

"Ha."

"Mama chased him away."

"What did he want?"

"To tell a secret."

"Oh? Who else was here?"

"Only that old hag from across the yard, Lisakowa."

"What did she want?"

"Well, she has something bad to say about everybody. This one is stingy, that one is dirty. It's the women she talks about. She thinks I don't know what's going on but I do. When she leaves our house, she goes to someone else's and gossips about us. She comes, sniffs around, and says: 'It smells like liver.' Oh, how I hate her!"

"And whom do you love?"

"Only two people in the whole world. Mama and you. Sometimes I love her more and sometimes I love you more. A hundred times a day she'll say to me: 'You're worse off than an orphan.' Lisakowa comes in and Mama blurts out that I have no shoes, no this and that. Lisakowa says: 'Didn't you just buy her shoes for Christmas? She runs around too much and wears out the soles.' And she always says: 'Why don't you send her out to service? She'll be fed and clothed.' "

"One day I'll break every bone in her body."

"I wish you would."

"What will you give me if I do—a kiss?"

"A thousand kisses. But the police will get you."

"I wouldn't wait for the police. How about a game of tick-tack-toe?"

"Yes."

"First let me hear the poem. You must become an educated lady."

Kasia began to recite. Lucian stopped eating. He listened, holding his spoon in mid-air. How beautiful she was! How gloriously her hair cascaded over her shoulders! How round her brow, how bright her eyes, and what a fair skin! Marble. No—a thousand times more delicate than marble. What an odd shape her lips were. If only she were two or three years older—he thought—I would happily kill that Lisakowa for just one smile from Kasia.

"Well, do I know the poem?"

"Yes, you know it. And I love you. I love you terribly."

"I love you too."

"Remember when you were small how you used to say you would marry me?"

"I remember everything."

Lucian and Kasia began to play tick-tack-toe, writing on a board with a piece of chalk. Kasia grimaced and pouted because she lost every game. Lucian kept looking at her and asking himself if this could really be Antek's daughter. What a great stew the world was! God, the chef, stirred and out came wars, revolutions, migrations. Someday He would strain the whole mess through a sieve. What crazy ideas I get, thought Lucian. Well, it's now or never. He rose to his feet.

"Kasia, I want to tell you something."

"What?"

"I'm going away, Kasia."

"Where?"

"If it hadn't been for you, I would have gone long before. I'm talking to you now as if you were a grownup. I want you to understand."

"Yes . . ."

"I love you. You understand what that means, don't you?"

"I understand."

"I love you, even though you are still a child. But I've wasted too many years here already. Your mother is a good woman and she saved my life. But it's a debt that I can't repay. Since I've been here, I've been neither dead nor alive. Do you understand what I'm saying?"

"Yes."

"I can't tell your mother these things. I hate tears. I'm leaving tonight."

"Where are you going?"

"Abroad."

"Where's that?"

"To another country on the other side of the border."

"Do you have money?"

"Exactly one groschen—but this cross that I wear around my neck is valuable. Tell your mother that I will always think of her with affection. I'll write, and if I get any money, I'll send some. In two or three years I'll come back to marry you."

"Ah."

"Will you wait for me?"

"Yes."

"How long?"

"A hundred years."

"You won't have to wait that long. You're still just a child. What if you forget me?"

"I'll never forget you."

"Tell your mother I've gone but you don't know where. Wait three days, then tell her the truth. Now, do you know what to do?"

"Yes. Today is Tuesday. I'll tell her Friday."

"Yes, that's right. But don't mention my marrying you."

"I won't."

"Kasia, in a few years you'll be grown up—and I won't be so old then either. If they try to make you marry someone else, say no. Pray to God for me. That's all. Each night when you say your prayers, mention my name. Say: 'Father Who art in Heaven, have mercy on Thy son Lucian and his wandering soul.' If my letters should be delayed, don't lose heart. Have patience and faith. I wanted to buy you a present but I had no money. Here is my last groschen. Keep it to remember me by. Don't lose it."

"I'll always keep it."

"Hold on to your primer and study hard every day. If you get the opportunity to go to school, go. . . . Well, I'd better collect my rags now."

Lucian climbed the ladder to the gallery. From under the bed he drew a satchel with a copper lock and side pocket. This bag had been his constant companion all through his months of fighting during the Polish rebellion. For years it had lain under Stachowa's bed. He knelt and dusted it off with a rag, then opened it and took out a bronze-handled pistol and a cartridge case containing six bullets. Inanimate objects are so still, Lucian murmured, holding one of the bullets in his hand. A little thing like this lies around for a hundred years and finishes off someone whose grandfather wasn't even born when it was made. From a basket near the bed, Lucian collected a shirt, a suit of underwear, a woolen scarf, and a vest that his mother had knitted for him. The sum of my earthly possessions, as they say in books. The ceiling was too low for him to stand upright. Still on his knees, he backed his way to the ladder.

"Kasia, what are you doing?"

"Nothing. Just watching."

"Will you miss me?"

"Yes."

Lucian climbed down from the gallery. He surveyed the room sternly, as if suspicious that someone lay in ambush in one of the corners.

"What did I forget? No, nothing. Wait. I want another look at you under the light."

He picked up the improvised oil lamp and brought it close to Kasia's face. She was smiling in a frightened way. Seeing the plate of groats still on the blanket, Lucian removed it with his left hand and placed it on the floor.

"Your hand is shaking," Kasia said.

"Yes, a little."

Lucian gazed at the smoking flame. He thought a moment, then extinguished the lamp.

9

Helena and Miriam Lieba were skating on the manor pond one afternoon when suddenly a man emerged from among the trees. Young, with a round beard, he wore a sheepskin jacket, his cap was covered with snow, and he carried a satchel in one hand. Helena gripped Miriam Lieba's arm.

"Look!"

"Don't be afraid, girls," the intruder called, coming toward them. "Stand still and let me have a look at you. Obviously, you're Helena. But who is she?" And he nodded toward Miriam Lieba.

"The question is—who are you?" said Helena. But suddenly she knew. In the manor there was a portrait of her father as a young man—looking like this young man.

"You're Lucian. Is it possible?"

"You haven't yet told me who she is," Lucian said.

"My friend, Miriam Lieba—the daughter of the man who leases the manor."

"I'm sorry I startled you." Lucian turned to Miriam Lieba. "Helena was only a child when I left. Now she's a grown-up young woman. Beautiful, too. Don't either of you say a thing about my being here." His tone changed, and he ran his fingers around his neck. "If I'm found, I'll hang."

"Good God, it is you!" Helena exclaimed. "Yes, I remember you . . ." Helena, in her excitement, took hold of Miriam Lieba, and both girls lost their balance and sat down on the ice. Lucian, attempting to assist them, almost lost his own footing. But finally they were on their feet again. Lucian brushed off Miriam Lieba's jacket and dress, and she thanked him. Helena made a move as if to embrace Lucian, but then stopped.

"Yes, I remember you," she said again, in a solemn voice.

"Our mother?" Lucian asked.

"She's sick. Very sick."

"Yes, I know. There was an item in the newspaper about Father coming home. What's the matter with her?"

"Oh, weakness . . . her nerves . . . her heart . . ."

"And Felicia?"

"She's home."

"Well, thank God. But no one must suspect that I'm here. I came halfway on foot, not by the main road, but through the villages. An old peasant gave me a lift in his sled. What shall I do?"

"Come to the house."

"Won't I be seen going in?"

"No. It's safe. Father's in Jampol—he spends most of his time there. Wojciech sleeps all day—besides, he's drunk. Barbara is half blind. Magda keeps to the kitchen. Go straight to the third floor. No one ever goes up there. It's not heated, but . . ."

"When does Father come?"

"At night . . . sometimes, not even then."

"May I go in now? I must get some sleep."

"There's a bed up there. Wait, I'll go and see."

Helena started off without remembering that she still had her skates on, then sat down to take them off. Miriam Lieba hobbled to the edge of the pond, where she leaned on a mound of frozen snow. Her fingers were numb inside her gloves and she could hardly turn the skate screw. Lucian picked up his satchel.

"I was already written off as dead, eh?"

"Why didn't you let us know? Mother is sick because of you."

"I couldn't . . . couldn't. I still can't believe I'm here. I used to skate on this pond myself once. God, how far back all that is. It seems like a hundred years."

He turned to Miriam Lieba. "Who is your father?"

"His name is Calman Jacoby."

"Jacoby, eh? That means Jacob—Jacob's grandchildren. The Jacob who cheated Esau out of his birthright."

Miriam Lieba was silent.

"I studied once . . . studied. But I haven't opened a Bible for a long time. I don't know how long it is since I've been in a church. For men like me, life is finished. We've become isolated from everything. We live amidst gloom and despair."

"The Count will find his way."

"How? I am hounded like a beast. The police have posters out with my name on them. The Czar wants to exterminate us all, the last pockets of Polish resistance. I didn't want to leave Polish soil. But now I must go into exile."

Helena had taken her skates off. "I'll have a look. You wait here."

Going toward the house, she scanned the fields carefully on both sides, cocking her head like a huntress stalking her quarry.

"Have you known each other long?" Lucian asked Miriam Lieba.

"Only since summer. Countess Helena came to my sister's wedding."

"Did she? Things are changing then. Not so long ago, that would have been impossible. My father always felt sympathy for the Jews, but other landowners ridiculed them, even set their dogs on them. At balls, the court Jew was forced to disguise himself as a bear to entertain the guests. Now we're the victims. Where did you learn Polish?"

"From a teacher. From reading."

"You don't look like a Jewess."

"But I am one."

"Of course, but . . . I stand here and think that I'm dreaming. I tell myself I must be dead. I actually was dead, not in body but in spirit. Seeing familiar places revived me somewhat. Yet I know the sun will never shine again—not on us, not for me."

"The Count should not talk that way. The Count will still enjoy much happiness."

"Happiness? I? Well, thank you, it's been some time since I've heard the word. Where will this happiness come from?"

Miriam Lieba was unable to reply. Her throat had tightened and she was shuddering with cold. Looking toward the manor house, she saw Helena signaling to them and told Lucian. Lucian quickly extended his hand to Miriam Lieba and tipped his cap, revealing brown hair and a high forehead. "I hope we meet again," he said.

Confused, Miriam Lieba mumbled: "Yes, thank you."

II

In the evening Calman, home for supper, sat at the head of the table in a chair with a caned back. He dipped meat in horseradish, and crumbs from the bread he was eating scattered over his beard. To his right sat Mayer Joel, Zelda, Jochebed, and Miriam Lieba; to his left, Ezriel, Shaindel, and Tsipele. Jochebed's baby slept in its cradle. Calman had brought a naphtha lamp with a bronze base from Warsaw, and Miriam Lieba did not lift her gaze from it. She stared at the lamp, the burner, the chimney, the glass. A whitish light surrounded the flame and every corner of the room was illuminated. It was difficult to understand how they could ever have managed with tallow candles. Everyone else was already on the meat course, but Miriam Lieba still toyed with her noodles. She put a spoonful of them into her mouth and forgot to swallow them. She squinted at the lamp and it seemed to cast off golden rays. Mayer Joel and Ezriel were, as usual, embroiled in an argument. Mayer Joel was insisting that Egypt was in Asia, and Ezriel that it was in Africa. "How can it be in Africa," Mayer Joel pointed out, "when it's so near Palestine?" Ezriel jumped up to get the map, but Shaindel stopped him.

"What's the rush? Egypt won't get cold."

"I'm afraid that this time Mayer Joel is right," Calman interjected after some hesitation. "The black people live in Africa. Egypt is near the land of the Philistines—"

"Does Father-in-law want to see it in black and white?"

"Don't run. Finish your supper. You're always rushing, Ezriel. The night is long."

"Three continents meet at the land of Palestine: Asia, Africa, and Europe. The Sinai Peninsula—"

"Do you mean Mount Sinai, where the Torah was given?"

"The entire peninsula is called Sinai. The mountain is actually in the Sinai Desert."

"What's that you're saying, Mayer Joel?" Calman asked.

"Who cares about the lies of heretics? Everything is described in the Pentateuch."

"Not everything is in the Pentateuch," Ezriel contradicted. "Where is America mentioned in the Pentateuch? America was only discovered by Columbus."

"Everything is in the Torah! It mentions lands whose locations even the greatest scholars don't know. Where is Hodu or Cush? One sage claims that they are far off; another that they are near. Have you studied the *Gemara Megillah?*"

"Yes, I have. Hodu is India and Cush is Ethiopia. They're far enough away."

"Then, according to you, the Talmudist who claimed they are near was wrong?"

"The Talmudists did not know geography. In those days they had no knowledge of America or Australia. Those countries were discovered afterward. . . ."

"That means the heretics are wiser than the Torah!"

Mayer Joel slammed his fist on the table. The dishes rattled. The flame in the lamp leaped. Zelda had kept quiet but she sided with Mayer Joel. From beneath her bonnet trimmed with pearl beads, she gazed askance at Ezriel. Zelda was unable to eat the same cut of beef as the rest of the family. She was toothless. Faigel had baked a meatloaf for her mistress and Zelda swallowed small bits of it.

"Are you bickering again? I have asked you over and over to eat your meals in peace. Who ever heard of two young men quarreling so much? One says summer, the other winter. It's day for one, and night for the other. The children of some people kiss each other; here we have nothing but arguments. What's the difference where Egypt is? Just be decent Jews. People who write books try to turn everything upside down to make us forget God Almighty and listen to the Devil."

"Mother-in-law, this has nothing to do with God," Ezriel said.

"I don't know. I didn't go to school. But no good comes of such wrangling. Believe me, I know what I'm saying. Asia here, Asia there. Meanwhile you forget to be Jews. As long as I live, I want my sons-in-law—"

"Mama, you always stand up for him!" Shaindel interrupted, indicating Mayer Joel. "If he told you he'd seen a cow fly over the roof and lay brass eggs, you'd believe him!"

"Children, enough! No more battling at the table. Shaindel, don't be so insolent." Calman's voice became stern. "Mother is speaking to all of you. What she says also happens to be the truth. Today one book is popular, tomorrow another. What made Wallenberg become a convert? His father was a decent Jew, a teacher. It was worldly knowledge that started everything. Don't be angry, Ezriel. I don't want to embarrass you, God forbid. You are as dear to me as my own son. But I want you to follow in the footsteps of your father. What does he lack?"

"What does he have?"

"He will have salvation. He will come to the other world—may he live to be a hundred and twenty—with a sackful of Torah. He isn't, God forbid, starving in this world either. Nor are all heretics wallowing in gold. If I need a bookkeeper or clerk, there are ten for every job. There used to be too few. Now we have too many."

There was a sudden silence. They could hear the wick sucking up naphtha. Zelda glanced at Miriam Lieba, who sat with eyes closed, her head bent over her plate, her lips moving. She appeared pale and drawn.

"Miriam Lieba!"

The girl started and the spoon fell from her hand.

"Why do you sit like a dummy? Are you asleep? Why don't you eat?" said Zelda. "Just look at her! Thin as a straw. Have you got a pain, God forbid? Does something hurt?"

"No, Mama. Nothing hurts."

"She's dreaming of a knight on a white charger," Shaindel joked.

"What knight? What charger? Calman, look at your daughter's face. She looks like an invalid. Her mother-in-law-to-be is due any day: she'll take one look and run off to where the black pepper grows. I, myself, would fear such an apparition if I had a son to marry off."

Calman raised his brows. "Why are you so quiet, Miriam Lieba? Why don't you eat?"

"I'm eating, but I'm not hungry."

"You know your future mother-in-law is coming soon from Lublin to meet you. You'll have to fatten up a bit. I won't have Tsipele marry before you."

Everyone grew silent. Faigel brought in the applesauce and tea. Miriam Lieba stirred the food in her dish. Beneath her hair, her ears burned, although her face was white. A strange warmth overcame her. She was not consciously thinking, but her mind seemed full of thoughts. They pressed against her skull. Within her, words were being uttered, scenes enacted. She dared not even meet Tsipele's eyes. Miriam Lieba was generally shy with strangers, but this time she felt bashful in her own family. What's wrong with me? Am I getting sick? she wondered. She rose, went into the hall, and climbed the

108

stairs to her attic room. For a while she remained standing in the dark; everything that had happened that afternoon re-enacted itself vividly. Lucian appeared as if stepping out of the frame of a painting. He looked at her, smiled, and said something she did not hear. He was bathed in an ethereal light, like the visions of saints described in books by Christian mystics.

Why am I so happy? Miriam Lieba wondered. Only a moment ago I was in torment. Suddenly she knew: what she had been awaiting for so many years was happening. Why hadn't she realized it before? She wanted to laugh, to cry. God in heaven, what would come of it? Miriam Lieba locked and chained her door. She felt the same as she had on Passover night after the Seder, when she had gone to bed after drinking four cups of wine. Walking unsteadily to her bed, she lay down, feeling as though an illness were coming on. Miriam Lieba lay there for a long time, fully clothed, half asleep, in a state of intoxication such as she had never known before. The cold woke her. A midnight moon was shining upon the snow. The trees facing her window seemed to her to be covered with blossoms.

III

Miriam Lieba took the path to the lime quarries rather than the one that led to the manor house. The sky was overcast. Even the smoke from the lime kilns seemed heavy as clouds. Snowflakes slowly began to fall. Miriam Lieba idled along, stopping, looking around her. Yesterday she had made her way without lingering. But today, as in her childhood, the huge house with its balconies and cornices seemed enchanted. In it there lived counts and countesses, proud as ever, despite the recent changes. Surrounded by gold, silver, books, paintings, carriages, servants, they spoke French and played their pianofortes. And behind one of those cornices, a warrior was hiding from his enemies, disguised as a peasant, armed like a knight—a living hero of Polish history. What was he doing at this moment? Was he still asleep? Or standing at the window, gazing out over the snow? Could he see her? Was he thinking of her? What foolishness! Why would he think of a Jewish girl? He could have any woman he wanted. No, it was madness! She mustn't think such things. She would probably marry some storekeeper from Lublin. . . . Miriam Lieba stopped to rub her hands with snow. The fields, sown with winter wheat, extended on both sides. How strange! She felt that what she was experiencing was something familiar that she had known for years, or been through in another existence—yet it was only yesterday that she had met Lucian. Even the name sounded as if she had always known it. Was it possible? She recalled that she used to etch "Lucian" on the frosted windowpanes with her fingernail. Had she once read about a Lucian, or dreamed of him? Or did she actually remember Lucian from her childhood? Could a child fall in love with an adult?

The snowfall thickened. It chilled Miriam Lieba's face, melting in the part of her hair, settling like an ornamental trim on her shoulders, sleeves, buttons, and the edges of her fur collar. She could no longer see the manor. Across the plowed fields, swirling snowdrifts seemed to jump like imps. From somewhere she heard a shot. Was there a hunter out in such a snowstorm, or had war begun? Miriam Lieba imagined that she heard the blaring of a trumpet. Someone was blowing the New Year ram's horn in the middle of winter. Miriam Lieba turned back. She was afraid the path home would be blocked by snow. There were wolves in the nearby forest. Perhaps it would be simpler if they tore her to bits. Then Lucian would remember forever the girl he had met one day, and who had been devoured by wolves the following morning.

As Miriam Lieba walked she hummed to herself:

> "Fall, snow, fall
> Cover all,

My soul is lost
In ice and frost."

The verses in Polish described a soul's wish to be hidden in snow, like a bear in its den, or a seed in the earth. Sleepless the night before, she had been full of happy fantasies; but with dawn her melancholy had returned. Perhaps she should remain where she was. She would be covered by the snow, which would form a mound over her icy grave. Summer? Perhaps spring would never come again. Hadn't Ezriel said that one day the entire globe would freeze over, all creatures die, the oceans vanish, and winter never end? Perhaps the time had come. Miriam Lieba stood for a long while. The whirling wind spun the snow into sheets. Twin snowflakes chased each other. One seemed to change its mind in mid-course and flew away. How beautiful the world was, how vast, mysterious!

Miriam Lieba turned her face up and opened her mouth. A snowflake fell on her tongue and melted against her palate. She shivered. "It's a dream, a dream," she murmured. "Nothing will come of it. . . ." How odd that Shaindel was already married, and even Tsipele was betrothed, while she, Miriam Lieba, daydreamed.

IV

Calman had been gone since daybreak. Zelda had an attack of stomach cramps. Getz, quickly hitching up the sleigh, drove to Skarshew and returned with Dr. Lipinski, who relieved Zelda's pain and prescribed some new medicine. Since he was in the neighborhood, though the sun was already setting, he drove on to the manor. After the snowfall, the temperature had fallen and everything had frozen. The branches of the trees resembled crystal menorahs. Candles were ignited in them by the setting sun and then extinguished. The blue snow sparkled with diamonds. Early stars twinkled in the sky. Somewhere, a dog bayed.

Miriam Lieba stepped outdoors to look toward the manor house. There, downstairs, the rooms would be lit, but upstairs everything would remain in darkness. Between there and here lay a secret known only to God and herself. Breaking the crust of the snow, she rolled a snowball and flung it as far as she could in the direction of the enchanted manor house. A crow, waking, began to caw.

Zelda stayed in bed. Calman and Mayer Joel did not return for supper. Ezriel was the only male present. Shaindel poured gravy over his groats, adding pieces of meat. In the household it was rumored that she was pregnant. Ezriel began telling the girls about the North Pole, where the aurora borealis shone in the sky. For six months of the year it was night; the temperature fell to ninety degrees below; alcohol and quicksilver froze; ice extended over hundreds of miles. At night explorers crawled into sleeping bags made of pelts. Tsipele was dumfounded. Ezriel knew everything!

"I would like to snuggle into one of those sleeping bags myself," Miriam Lieba remarked.

"All by yourself?" Ezriel joked.

Shaindel blushed. "Shame on you for saying such things!"

Miriam Lieba flushed also and her eyes seemed bluer. Uncomprehendingly, Tsipele laughed. Jochebed waddled in from the kitchen.

"What's all the commotion about? Mother is sick."

As soon as Ezriel had washed his hands and said the concluding grace, Miriam Lieba went up to her room. Everything was a vast mystery: the world, mankind, the North Pole, she herself. She seemed to be seething inside, elated one moment, depressed the next, burning hot and cold like the sinners in Gehenna. Ezriel's joke had aroused her. She was eighteen, an age at which her mother not only had been married but had already had children. Standing at her window in the pale evening, she examined the exotic plants that the frost had traced on her windowpanes: palms, cedars, desert shrubs that grew only in Israel—a mirage that must come from the Holy Land, she thought.

Having lit a candle, she threw herself down on her bed and opened a novel that Helena had lent her. The scene was Paris at dusk, and the Marquise, getting into her carriage, directed her coachman to drive to the park. The sunset shed a violet radiance on the Marquise's face and was reflected in the pearls that hung at her throat. The carriage halted. The Marquise stepped out and sauntered down a path. Suddenly her lover was there, rushing toward her and clasping her in his arms. Miriam Lieba's pupils grew large. That was love, that was life! Her lids closed and she imagined what Paris must be like: museums, theaters, towers, castles, brightly lit windows, boulevards jammed with carriages, the odor of flowers everywhere, music, dancing ladies, and champagne corks popping. "Your health, chérie." "Darling, I cannot live without you. Swear that you'll be mine!" "Later, later! Oh, my poor Jean." "Rest in my arms. Kiss me!"

Suddenly she herself was in Paris. She sat in a carriage and Lucian embraced her—simultaneously she was in a carriage, a boudoir, a salon. She was wearing an evening gown, and carried a fan. He wanted to kiss her, but she averted her face. "No, Lucian, I am promised to a storekeeper in Lublin."

Miriam Lieba opened her eyes. The flickering candle had burned low. She blew it out and returned to her dreams. She dozed, awoke, dozed again. She slept fitfully as if she had a fever. Lucian kept appearing before her in different guises, as a civilian, as a soldier in helmet and cape riding horseback, as a traveler on shipboard. They were eloping but there was an obstacle. The sea had been blockaded. An enemy armada approached. A courier had been dispatched. All conspired against her: her father, her mother, Jochebed, Shaindel. Ezriel had cut off his sidelocks and wore German clothes. He whispered in her ear, "Convert!"

She awoke, trembling. She was cold, and the moon was

shining on her. She shifted out of danger, as it was believed that moonlight on a sleeper caused seizures. She sat up, hugging her knees. Outside, it was as light as day. She was hungry, thirsty. She wanted Lucian. What if I went to him right now? she thought. I will run through the fields, tiptoe quietly up the stairs, open his door, and say, "Do with me as you will . . ."

It was daybreak before Miriam Lieba fell asleep. It had begun to snow heavily again. Toward midmorning, voices on the stairs woke her; someone began knocking on her door. She opened her eyes sleepily. The sun was shining and the snow glittered outside. The door opened and in walked Helena. Miriam Lieba stared at her in astonishment.

"Weren't you awake? I'm sorry, but I had to talk to someone . . . and you're the only one who knows . . . outside of Felicia, that is. My father didn't come home last night or the night before either. Mother is too ill to tell. Felicia is no use at all. And Lucian's very nervous. Why didn't you come yesterday? We thought you would. He's been asking about you . . . I thought you were an early riser."

Gradually, Miriam Lieba returned to her senses and began to stammer apologies. "It's a great honor to have you visit . . . but to find me in bed . . . and my clothes are strewn all over . . ."

"Who cares? Yesterday afternoon Lucian was in such a strange mood. Demanded vodka. Suddenly he wanted to rush back to Warsaw. Felicia gave him a necklace and some brooches, part of Mother's jewelry, but he must have money. He has to get across the border. The necklace can only be sold to one jeweler, Mr. Nosek, in Warsaw. But the trip is dangerous. Lucian is afraid to stay here. Someone is sure to find out. And Mother still doesn't know. It's all so strange. Do you suppose we could pawn the jewels with your father?"

"My father is in Warsaw."

"Oh. Perhaps your brother-in-law has money?"

"Ezriel? No."

"I thought Jews always had money on hand. But come, Lucian wants to talk to you. You must convince him to stay for a while. Maybe we can hide him somewhere else. He's afraid of a police search."

"God forbid!"

"Why don't you get up, get dressed—oh, you're bashful? All right, I'll wait downstairs. Don't take long."

"A minute. Thank you. Thank you a thousand times . . ."

Helena shut the door and went downstairs. Miriam Lieba sprang out of bed, poured water from the pitcher into the washbasin, then, after bolting her door, began to wash herself with the cold water. She was trembling with excitement. Wasn't this her fate: to be constantly enmeshed in difficulties and complications? Helena had come to get her. He had asked about her! He loved her!

v

On the way to the manor house, Helena explained the situation to Miriam Lieba. Lucian could not stay at home for long: he risked his life every moment he remained. The Count must be informed; but how could anyone at the manor be sent to the house of that Russian woman, Yevdotya? Besides, the Count had taken the small sleigh and there were no horses to pull the large one. Perhaps Miriam Lieba had someone she trusted who could be sent? Everything must be kept secret.

"Could we borrow a sleigh from the peasants?" asked Helena. "Or what about getting horses from the lime quarry?"

Miriam Lieba did not know what to reply. The quarry would be hard to get to in this storm; but even if they could get there, how could she command the men to lend them horses? The girls pushed slowly on. Helena had boots on, but Miriam Lieba had put on her high-heeled shoes. She had even neglected to wear warm stockings. The path had only been partially cleared. The snow came slanting down, its crystals stinging the girls' cheeks, covering their eyelashes, and encrusting their brows and foreheads. "I'll catch pneumonia," Miriam Lieba thought with a kind of reckless satisfaction. The storm half blinded her. Helena mumbled that the snow was getting into her boots. The girls had intended to take a path that circled around to the back of the manor house so that they could enter from the rear and go straight up a back staircase, but the path was impassable. When they reached the front door, the dogs rushed at Miriam Lieba, jumping and barking, and Helena barely managed to drive them away.

In the front entry, Helena jigged and stamped her feet, dislodging the snow, but Miriam Lieba was too cold. She felt half frozen as, moving stiffly, she trailed Helena up to the attic. She knew she was white as chalk. All the fussing and primping before the mirror had been wasted. The thistles had snagged her stockings and the bottom of her dress. Helena knocked and opened a door. Through a mist, Miriam Lieba saw a different Lucian. He appeared much handsomer and more graceful than he had the other day. He had shaved off his beard and was wearing a green jacket, riding breeches, and German-style leather boots with flexible tops. His hair was parted in the center. Books, a corked bottle, and a glass were on a table. The bed was unmade. Lucian stepped forward. He had been standing in the middle of the room, as if impatiently awaiting them.

"Come in, come in! You probably don't recognize me. I don't recognize myself."

"We nearly froze," Helena said. "Just look at us—half dead!"

"You'll warm up in here. I couldn't imagine where you were. Won't you ladies take your jackets off." He moved toward Miriam Lieba. "If the young lady will permit me? So! Perhaps you'd care for a drink? It's cherry wine, a ladies' drink. That's all I could get . . . But the young lady is completely frozen."

"The wind . . ."

"Perhaps you'd like something to eat?"

"Is she allowed to eat? We don't have anything kosher," Helena interrupted.

"What? Oh . . . kosher, yes. Warsaw is full of Jews. But the lieutenant in our company ate pork, even though he was Jewish. Won't the young lady have a seat? Here, on this chair. May I remove your gloves?"

"Yes—be a cavalier," Helena said. "Where is Felicia? I'll go get something. You are allowed to drink milk, aren't you?"

Miriam Lieba made no reply. Helena went out, shutting the door behind her. Lucian leaned over Miriam Lieba and pulled off her gloves.

"The young lady is frozen. But completely. What cold little hands! Jesus and Mary!"

He held Miriam Lieba's hands in his own for a time, stroked and warmed them. Looming over her, he smelled of cherry wine and of something else—masculine and foreign. Miriam Lieba sat there, knowing that if she had not been so cold, she would have died of shame. Her dress was sodden, her stockings wet through. A puddle was forming beneath her on the floor.

"The young lady should really have a drink. Cherry wine is not forbidden." Lucian poured half a glassful for her and handed it to her. She accepted it, and lifting it with stiff fingers, took a sip, not knowing whether it was kosher or not. She wanted to say something but was unable to speak.

"The young lady should take off her shoes!"

"No, no." Miriam Lieba drew in her feet.

"Ah, bashful! Campaigning in the forests, we had to forget about shame. In the beginning it wasn't pleasant, but one grew accustomed to it . . ."

"Perhaps we should put something on the floor . . . I'm dripping . . ."

"That doesn't matter. What is snow? Water. I expected you to come yesterday. I am in a strange predicament here: I can't stay and I can't leave. I need money. And I want at least to show myself to my parents. I've decided to cross the border—I don't know exactly where, though I've been told one can steal across the frontier in the village of Ojcow. But where is Ojcow? There isn't a map in the whole house."

"My brother-in-law has maps."

"Local maps? I'll have to walk from village to village. It's too dangerous to go directly to the border, or to travel by stagecoach. The drivers themselves inform for the police. Drink some more: you're terribly pale."

"Thank you."

"My mother saved all my clothes. Only the shoes pinch a little. I've shaved off my beard and I'm a country bumpkin again. It's odd how a beard gives one's face a more spiritual expression. Do you know what a beauty you are?"

Miriam Lieba lowered her eyes.

"I do hope the young lady will forgive me. I've lost my manners, grown completely coarse. My father, I hear, has let himself go too. All of us who went through that terrible campaign are disoriented. Some of us have taken to the bottle, others to mysticism. I drink, but I don't get drunk. Everyone knew we were doomed. We were led like sheep to the slaughter, offered up as a sacrifice. Some races enjoy bleeding, and with the Poles it is a sort of passion. We were beaten and we begged for more . . . Our leaders simply led us into ambushes. My one desire is to forget it all. In Warsaw I had already forgotten, but here it all comes back again. Why do you look so sad? You must have a noble soul . . ."

"The Count must not laugh at me."

"I'm not laughing at you. I mean it seriously. I've hit bottom and now it seems to me as if I'm in the clouds. I drank a little to give me courage. . . . Do you have a young man yet?"

"No."

"What will become of you here in Jampol? May I tell you something?"

"Yes."

"I prayed to God—and when I saw you, I knew that He'd heard my prayers. Do you understand?"

"Yes."

"I can scarcely believe it myself. . . ."

Lucian made a move as if to come closer. Helena opened the door, carrying a pitcher, and looked at them laughingly. But then her face changed.

"Felicia's sick too."

10

1

On Purim, the Book of Esther was read aloud. Tsipele, although already betrothed, rattled a noisemaker, cursing Haman, the villain. Shaindel helped Faigel bake poppy-seed cakes, butter cookies, and a saffron loaf braided top and bottom, which was then sliced lengthwise. Faigel also cooked sweet and sour fish. Zelda, convalescent but still weak, was watched over carefully by Jochebed. Ezriel busied himself making spears, swords, helmets, and masks out of cardboard and colored paper; for the beards, he used flax. Before dinner, the young people dressed themselves in their costumes. Mayer Joel played Ahasuerus, Ezriel was Vajezatha, Getz was Haman, Shaindel was Vashti, and Tsipele was Queen Esther, a role originally assigned to Miriam Lieba. But Miriam Lieba refused to participate, and stood apart. Her gaze fell on the two thick candles burning in the twin silver candlesticks, passed in turn to the naphtha lamp shining in the corner, then to the many Purim presents Calman had received from his employees—oranges, holiday loaves, poppy-seed cakes, gingerbread, bottles of wine and mead—and finally reached the window. Outside, a fiery band of color glowed in the sky, the last vestige of the sunset and the first herald of spring.

This Purim the weather was exceptionally mild. A warm, fragrant breeze blew in through the open window. The fields were soggy, the streams already brimming with the melting snows. Miriam Lieba knew that Ezriel was annoyed because she wasn't watching the play. But even if she did look, she wouldn't understand a thing. Her mind was in a turmoil. Had only six weeks passed? Everything was incredible, and there was no one she could talk to. A month ago Helena, without a word, had gone off to her aunt's house in Zamosc. In the week that Lucian had been in hiding at the manor, Miriam Lieba had seen him only twice more. Then he had gone, leaving her with a kiss on her lips and a promise to write. God, how wildly he had behaved, and what fantastic things he had said. How quickly his plans and moods had changed. When he left, he had intended to cross the Prussian border, but Helena had received a message that he had gone back to Warsaw. And he had behaved very strangely to his parents. Two days before his departure, in the evening, he had gone into Jampol on foot, broken into the house of that Russian Yevdotya, quarreled with his father, and even drawn a pistol. The following evening he had walked into his mother's bedroom without warning. The Countess had managed to stay calm, but the old nurse Barbara had screamed and wailed until Helena and Felicia had dragged her out. Lucian had spent the night in his mother's room, and had left the manor at dawn. Two weeks later, Helena had left for Zamosc. He had not written to Miriam Lieba.

Lucian and Helena had departed, but Mrs. Daiches of Lublin, Miriam Lieba's prospective mother-in-law, had arrived. She had taken one look at Miriam Lieba and sung out: "Yes, you will be my daughter-in-law."

How swiftly the sky was changing now: the reds and purples turned to violet, then the violet faded to a soft gray. The moon floated from behind a group of clouds that resembled a flock of goats. The stars burned like lanterns in mid-air. Mayer Joel had taken off his crown and false beard and laid his golden scepter on the sideboard. Ezriel wanted to continue the performance, but Zelda complained that this nonsense had been going on long enough. Miriam Lieba closed her eyes—not until shards were laid on them would she forget this winter, or this particular Purim feast. Would life bring her any happiness? Would she ever love anyone but Lucian? Was it possible that some day she would be a wife, a mother, even a grandmother? God forbid. She didn't want to live that long. Her sort of person died young. This might be her last Purim. She thought of Lucian's words: "If all else fails, one can always put a bullet through one's brain."

"Miriam Lieba!"

She started. Her mother was calling her. All the others had gone in to the supper table.

"What are you thinking about? Horses have big heads—let them do the thinking."

"Miriam Lieba is afraid the moon will fall," Mayer Joel said banteringly.

"Dreaming of her husband-to-be," Shaindel guessed.

Suddenly, Tsipele burst out laughing.

"What is it, Tsipele?" Calman asked.

"Papa, is it true Lekish the Fool has a gold watch?"

The table shook from the laughter and stamping of feet at Tsipele's odd question. Even Miriam Lieba smiled.

"What made you think of that?"

"Ezriel said so."

"Why do you fill her head with such nonsense?" Calman asked. "She's already betrothed."

"I don't know what she is prattling about. She must have dreamed it."

"He did say it."

"Well, enough," said Calman. "Just because it's Purim we needn't make fools of ourselves. In Shebreshin there was once a tailor who believed that on Purim everyone was so busy feasting that no one remembered King David's psalms. And so each year he went to the synagogue alone and mournfully recited the whole Book of Psalms. There was a time when Jews remembered God."

"Jews always remember God," said Ezriel, "but God forgets the Jews."

"Fie, don't say such things!" Calman said, placing his fist on the table. "If God hadn't watched over the Jews, the Hamans would have annihilated us long ago."

Zelda grumbled under her breath against this young man who had trimmed his sidelocks and was corrupting the children. She wanted to chastise him but restrained herself in view of the holiday. Also Shaindel—luck be with her—was pregnant, and if anyone dared say anything against the apple of her eye she would flare up immediately.

Miriam Lieba got up to get a glass of water.

"Are we ready for the grace?" asked Calman.

"Yes, Father-in-law," responded Mayer Joel.

"Then suppose you begin."

"My lords, let us say grace. Blessed be the name of God henceforth and forever . . ."

Calman narrowed his eyes, nodding his agreement. God had been good to him. He had married off two of his daughters. Tsipele was betrothed. Miriam Lieba's prospective in-laws were coming next month for the betrothal ceremony. Ah, he had had his troubles, but he had prospered and with God's help would continue to do so. Calman lifted his hands, and rolled his eyes heavenward. Mayer Joel intoned the words: "Lord our God, oh, make us not dependent on gifts and loans of men but rather on Thy full, open, holy and generous hand."

Mayer Joel's thoughts strayed as he recited the prayer. He had decided to buy the mill in Jampol. Soon he would build a house for himself there. The one drawback in becoming a businessman was that he would have less time for study and for Hassidism. He was already anticipating Pentecost, when he would go to Marshinov. Now that Jochanan was Tsipele's intended groom, he, Mayer Joel, would be received as a member of the rabbi's family. . . .

Ezriel was thinking about Miriam Lieba and kept stealing

E

glances at her. Something had happened to the girl, she was going through some sort of crisis. She seemed to hear nothing that was said to her, constantly gazed into the distance, and was growing thinner, paler, more distracted every day. Had she fallen in love? But with whom? What could be bothering her? Ezriel had tried to find out, but she wouldn't be questioned. Sometimes she herself came to the room he had taken for himself in the attic—knocking before she entered, in the big-city manner. But as soon as she began to talk, she turned red, lost her tongue; her lips trembled, her eyes filled with tears, and she was unable to finish a sentence. If he questioned her, she would run out—embarrassed or insulted, he never knew which. Had she fallen in love with him? From reading Slowacki and other poets, Ezriel knew that love obeys no laws. The writers of the Torah completely ignored human emotion, man's nervous system. He himself had already deceived Shaindel in his thoughts. Shaindel was always interrupting him in his studies, coming to show him what she was embroidering, or to ask his advice on household matters. She just wanted to be near him. Calman demanded that he supervise the account books. And Mayer Joel came to discuss Hassidism, even though he reproached him at every opportunity with being anti-Hassid. Ezriel was making some progress in his studies, but not enough. He had set up a timetable, using the books Wallenberg had given him, to teach himself algebra, Latin, Greek, history, physics. But he never quite managed to keep to his schedule. He was attacked by such passions and fantasies that if he had told anyone about them, he surely would have been considered a criminal or a madman. It seemed that the brain could be both sane and insane at the same time. Ezriel shook his head and murmured:

> "O Fear the Lord, ye His holy ones.
> For there is no want to them that fear Him.
> Young lions do lack and suffer hunger:
> But they that seek the Lord shall not want any good."

An hour after the celebration was over, Miriam Lieba went outside. She stood beside the house, staring up at the moon. Ezriel had remarked that in exactly four weeks it would be the first night of Passover. The wind blowing from the fields was both acrid and balmy. Aimlessly, Miriam Lieba strolled down a path widened by the comings and goings of the family.

Suddenly a figure stood beside her as if risen from the ground. She recoiled and then recognized Lucian. He seemed tall and unfamiliar, dressed in a fur jacket, plush cap, and high fitted boots. His bony fingers caught her by the wrist. She was so taken aback that she forgot she might be seen from the house.

"Miriam," he said, calmly and firmly. "You must come away with me."

"Where?" Miriam Lieba felt her whole body trembling.

"Out of this God-forsaken country. I have money and a passport too."

"But . . . Lucian . . ." She could not control her jaw and her teeth began chattering. "Mother . . ."

"Yes or no. You have to answer me."

"Where have you been?" Miriam Lieba raised her eyes. Fear and pleading were in her voice. He had accosted her like a highwayman.

"I've been in Warsaw. I sold the jewelry. We'll go to Lemberg, and then on to Paris. That's where we'll be married."

Miriam Lieba looked around, fearful that someone might have come out of the house.

"Have you told your parents?"

"I've told no one."

"I must change my clothes," she said, without quite knowing what she meant. Lucian let go of her wrist. He was taller than she and was standing on higher ground. Her throat tightened; her scalp prickled. Only once before had she felt such a

125

sensation when, as a child, she'd been playing hide-and-seek with her shadow on the wall and the shadow had come down and boxed her ears. Lucian took a few steps backward and she realized that he must have been waiting, concealed by the willow near the barn. She moved toward the gate, scarcely able to keep from screaming. She entered the dark hall and began to climb the stairs, halting after each step. Fiery specks appeared before her eyes. Her ears rang. She was sure she was going to faint. She heard Jochebed's baby crying, and Jochebed soothing him. Shaindel and Ezriel were in their bedroom, apparently having an argument but keeping their voices muffled. It wasn't possible that she could leave home and all of them. It will certainly kill Mother, she thought, and Father, too. She reached the door to her room and stood before it. No, I won't go, she said to herself. A rebelliousness seized her and a kind of hatred for Lucian, for whom only an hour before she had been longing.

In the dark she could not find the doorknob, and groped for it blindly. Her room was bathed in moonlight. In the middle of the bed lay a sheet of paper on which, that afternoon, she had written a love poem for Lucian, inspired by what had seemed to her unbearable yearning. How could that be? she wondered. I was almost dying of love. Suddenly she remembered the woman from Lublin who had said, "You will be my daughter-in-law." "No, I will not," Miriam Lieba announced defiantly. "They won't haul me off to market and sell me like a cow!"

For a moment she ceased thinking and stood by the window staring out at the night, the snow, and the moon. "He won't drag me off by force. Oh, I'm such a coward." The life that she would lead if she stayed flashed before her eyes. She saw her future the way a person who is drowning is said to see the past. She would marry the young man who had bribed his way out of military service. The stocky woman with the crease in her brow would be her mother-in-law. They'd shave her head, fit her with a wig, insist that she attend the ritual

126

bath. She'd bear children, wrangle with her mother-in-law, grow old before her time. The life of the Jews was narrow and stagnant. Her mother had had nothing. Jochebed had nothing. The world outside was huge, brilliant. If she went, she would become a countess and have Lucian; she would reside in Paris among its rich boulevards and amorous women. Her mother would die in any case. The doctor no longer held out any hope for her recovery. If she did not go with Lucian now, Miriam Lieba knew that she would always regret it.

But what should she do? Why hadn't he written her even a line in six weeks? How could she trust him? Perhaps it wasn't Lucian at all, but a demon in his shape. She glanced toward her door. Should she bolt it? Should she scream for help? No, she would go down and talk to him. Not now, but when everyone had gone to sleep. Gazing out of the window, Miriam Lieba was overcome with astonishment at her strange destiny, at how swiftly she had fallen in love with Lucian, and Lucian with her. Why must it be me? I'll have to convert. . . . Suddenly she thought of the night of Yom Kippur and remembered a story she had heard of a Jewish girl who had eloped with a Christian youth on the eve of the Day of Atonement. Now on Purim she was about to do the same. . . . The fear that had temporarily receded seized her again. She would lose everything: father, mother, Shaindel, Ezriel, Tsipele . . . she would have to bow down to idols. She, Miriam Lieba?

"No, no. I would rather die," she murmured. She went to her door and chained it, then moved a bench against it. She opened her closet and leaned into its musty darkness. Perhaps it was all a hallucination. Maybe I'm going mad, like Uncle Chaim Yoneh, who hanged himself with his belt. Miriam Lieba stretched out her hand and touched a dress. Then she went to her bed and sat down. Her heart was pounding. She felt nauseous. "I'm going to faint," she mumbled. She fell across the bed, awake, yet as if in a dream. Thoughts came to her; her lips opened and whispered strange words; she saw faces, figures, eyes. Through it all, she knew that Lucian was waiting for her below and that she must come to a decision.

She dozed and dreamed. In her dream, the family was still living in The Sands and it was the Sabbath. Her father was snoring after the holiday meal, her mother was catnapping, Jochebed and Shaindel had gone for a walk, Tsipele was asleep in her cradle. She, Miriam Lieba, had been left with no one to play with.

"Mama, I want to play."

"What do you want to play?"

"I want to play with the shards."

"No, that's not allowed on the Sabbath."

"Well, what can I do?"

"Rock the baby."

"She's already asleep."

"She's apt to wake up. Rock her some more."

"May I write with my chalk?"

"Write with chalk? You shikse!"

"I want to play school."

"Not on the Sabbath."

"I want to go out."

"The door is locked."

"Mama."

"I'll tear your hair out if you don't let me sleep, you little devil. I'll teach you." As her mother leaped from bed, her wig slipped off, revealing her small head with its unevenly shorn scalp. "Calman, where's the cat-o'-nine-tails? I'll teach her. I'll whip her."

Miriam Lieba broke out of her dream. He's freezing out there in the cold, she thought. It seemed to her that she had been sleeping for hours. There was a midnight quiet in the house. Her body felt stiff. She limped to the closet, took out a woolen dress and her fur jacket. Shoes too, she thought, taking off her slippers. And I had better take my shawl. She searched in the dresser for warm underclothes. What else? A kerchief for her head. Her mother had given her a bracelet for Shaindel's wedding. There it was. She had on her earrings.

Could she really be doing what she was doing? Wasn't it all an illusion? Her fear had evaporated, and she had begun to feel almost reckless. "Yes, I'll go away with him. I'll convert—": the mocking voice seemed to come from deep within her, as if it had been lying in wait in some demonic spiderweb. She moved the bench, opened her door carefully to keep it from squeaking, and started downstairs on tiptoe. "They're asleep, they're asleep"—laughter choked in her throat—"I'm as quiet as a burglar. Anyway, he's gone by now . . ." Someone had chained the front door. Miriam Lieba undid the chain, lowering it slowly to avoid making a sound. She opened the door and was slapped by a cold night wind. She was fully awake now, wild, joyous. Suddenly she saw him. He began to run toward her and she placed her finger to her lips.

III

At daybreak someone opened the door of Calman's bedroom. Can it be the wind, he wondered, only half waking. Zelda slept on, undisturbed.

"Papa, papa . . ." He recognized Shaindel's voice. She approached, saying, "Papa, come out. Don't wake Mother."

He got out of bed quietly, put on a bathrobe and slippers, and went into the hall. Shaindel stood shivering in the darkness.

"Papa, Miriam Lieba isn't here," she whispered.

Calman tasted a bitterness in his mouth.

"Where is she?"

"I don't know. The front door is open. She isn't in her bed."

Calman was momentarily silent.

"Did you look in the outhouse?"

"No."

He promptly headed for the privy, located behind the house near the pit where the refuse was dumped. He slipped in the mud, bumped against the shaft of a wagon. Miriam Lieba was not in either of the compartments. Calman turned back. He was wearing only his skullcap, bathrobe, and wet slippers, and the cold cut through him. The wind fluttered his beard. He walked with the measured step of one who knows that he won't find what he is searching for. Shaindel was waiting at the threshold.

"She isn't there?"

"No."

"Papa, God forbid, you'll catch a cold."

"Come, let's take another look upstairs."

Calman and Shaindel ascended the stairs. Miriam Lieba's door stood ajar. Night still clung to the room, but the sunrise had already begun to touch it. The closet stood open, the drawers were pulled out. On the floor lay a jacket and a pair of slippers. As Calman and Shaindel searched, their faces acquired a purple tint; Calman's beard seemed bloodied; a red stain appeared on Shaindel's head-kerchief. On the table lay a sheet of paper. Shaindel tried to read it, but in the twilight the letters were indistinguishable. One could not even say whether they were Yiddish or Polish. Calman closed the door.

"She has run away," he said.

"I'm afraid so."

A verse from the Scriptures came to his mind, but he could not recall the exact words. He had the quotation on the tip of his tongue. His legs almost buckled under him and he sat down on Miriam Lieba's bed. Suddenly he remembered: "The Lord hath given, and the Lord hath taken away."

T W O

II

Two years passed. Jochanan married Tsipele at a sumptuous wedding that cost Calman a fortune. After the seven nuptial days, the couple went to live at the court of the Marshinov rabbi. Temerel could not exist without her son. Besides, Calman's house was soon left without a mistress, for three weeks after Tsipele's wedding, Zelda died. She was buried in the Jampol cemetery, and the engraver was ordered to inscribe a tombstone for her. Jochebed and Mayer Joel moved to a house of their own. Now that Mayer Joel had become the proprietor of the Jampol flour mill, he maintained two residences, one in town and one at the mill.

Only one daughter, Shaindel, lived at home with Calman. Shaindel had borne a son, named Uri Joseph after his great-grandfather the scribe. The baby had already cut his teeth and begun to talk. But even Shaindel did not bring Calman contentment. Ezriel refused to accept the board that had been offered him and had gone off to Warsaw to study. Calman's reproofs and pleas in vain, and only after much insistence on his father-in-law's part did Ezriel promise that he would not shave his beard, would conduct himself as a proper Jew, and spend all the holidays and his summer vacation in Jampol. In return, Calman sent him eight rubles a week.

After the completion of the railroad, Calman's lumber business declined. He was forced to discharge many of his employees, and they became his enemies. A competitor opened a new shop near Calman's general store, and a price war followed. Since Calman could not be everywhere at once, he had to hire a manager. This raised his overhead, and his competitor, who worked alone, could undersell him. Calman had long since abandoned the tavern. Only the manor and the lime quarries remained. With each passing year, the liberated peasants demanded higher wages for their labor in the fields, regardless of the two years' drought that had caused Calman heavy losses. Nor was there any safeguard against theft. Each day incidents occurred; the peasants drove their cattle over Calman's pasture and felled the best trees in the manor's forest. The same peasants who only a few years before had felt the lash and hastened to kiss the hands of every squire, bailiff, and overseer were now bloated with arrogance and ranted against the Jews. In addition, the renewal time for Calman's lease was near and he knew that the rent the duke would ask would be so exorbitant that he would be unable to pay it. Those who envied Calman had maligned him to the duke and spread rumors that Calman had embezzled amounts ten times the value of the entire manor.

The lime quarries, thank God, were still profitable, but what good would the quarries be if Calman no longer had the use of the strip of land on which the railway spur lay? When he had built the private line, Calman had leased the strip from the duke for the same period as the estate. Now the duke was threatening to deprive Calman of his right of way, thus isolating the quarries.

In the past, Calman had enjoyed untroubled sleep; only Zelda, may she rest in peace, had kept him awake. Now Zelda's bed was always made and Calman, alone in the room, longed for the days when she had nagged him. He would fall asleep and waken, his thoughts giving him no rest. Miriam Lieba, may her memory be blotted out, was an apostate. All the facts had reached Calman: she had yoked herself to that

Lucian, the Count's rascal, who was thought to have perished in the insurrection (if only he had!). She not only wandered about with him but already had a child. How Calman had endured this blow he would never understand. Each time he thought of the disgrace, his eyes flooded with tears. What good was his wealth if every lout could sneer at him as "Lucian's father-in-law!"

Calman no longer led the noon services at the synagogue on the Day of Atonement. He had withdrawn voluntarily, and the Jampol Jews had not protested. However, since Calman still controlled the manor, his enemies' wrath fell upon the Rabbi of Jampol, Reb Menachem Mendel, Shaindel's father-in-law. Influential citizens complained that the rabbi was responsible for his son Ezriel's straying from the path of righteousness— that this young man exerted a bad influence on the common people, that he came home for the holidays with forbidden books and poisoned the children's minds. They also claimed that the rabbi's daughter, Mirale, had not conducted herself properly. Engaged to marry a yeshiva student from Skarshew, a man named Jonah, she had returned the engagement contract. Jonah's relatives in Jampol had broken the rabbi's windowpanes. They had hammered nails into his seat in the house of prayer so that his clothes would be torn. Even the almshouse paupers whom Calman supplied with firewood, beets, and potatoes agitated against the rabbi and against Calman himself.

In Marshinov, the old rabbi was ill again. Reb Shimmon, his first-born, harangued Jochanan and urged him either to divorce Tsipele, the sister of a convert, or to leave the court altogether. Temerel, Tsipele's mother-in-law, sent Calman lengthy messages written in a shaky hand and stained with tears, bewailing the situation.

Calman tossed in his bed. What justice was there? Jews, who wouldn't for all the money in the world pluck a blade of grass on the Sabbath or eat an egg with a bloodspot, heaped shame upon a rabbi, a devout Jew, a saint. Calman's competitors stopped at nothing, they dampened his sacks of flour and denounced him to the tax collector and the commissary of police. Besides, a new form of fraud had cropped up among the merchants. They would declare bankruptcy, then make a settlement. To safeguard themselves, the Lodz manufacturers raised their prices in order to be assured of a profit regardless of such bankruptcies.

Calman sighed. He heard his grandson, Shaindel's Uri-Joseph-Yosele, awake and cry. Burek, the dog, barked. The cows in the stall rubbed their horns against the door. The spring was a warm one, and after two years of drought there were signs that the coming harvest would be fruitful. The winter crops had sprouted early, rain and sunshine had been plentiful: the life of the soil was as unpredictable as the life of man. Scarcity followed plenty. When the earth seemed to have grown barren, the juices of life flowed through her again and she blossomed once more. Who could tell? Perhaps God would still grant Calman some comfort. He knew that he could not remain without a wife for very long. Sooner or later he would have to remarry. He had had only daughters with Zelda, but now that Miriam Lieba had committed such a deed, Calman more than ever longed for a son to perpetuate his name.

11

It was decided in St. Petersburg to station several infantry regiments in Jampol, and barracks had to be built to quarter the troops. It was taken for granted that Calman would not only supply the lumber for the buildings but undertake their construction. Yet, when the bids were opened, Calman's bid, for the first time in his career, was not the lowest. The contract was awarded to a builder from Polish Lithuania by the name of Daniel Kaminer. The soldiers also had to be supplied with flour, beef, and groats, cloth for their greatcoats, and leather for their boots. The enterprise was vast, and even after the payment of various bribes and pay-offs, it meant doubling one's investment. Nevertheless, Calman was not too distressed that this contract had slipped through his fingers. He was not anxious to have further dealings with the authorities. Daniel Kaminer had moved to Jampol from Lomza; he lived in The Sands among the Gentiles. He was a short, thin man, with a pock-marked face and a trimmed beard the color of pepper. His teeth were blackish, his nose red and covered with pimples. Kaminer was fond of vodka and spoke Russian like a native. Apparently he had once studied the Torah, for he was constantly citing quotations from the Scriptures and the Talmud to add point to his crude jokes. He wore a frock coat, a stiff collar, and a velvet waistcoat across which dangled a chain of five-ruble gold pieces. On his head he wore a cap with a leather visor.

Kaminer was a widower and had brought with him to Jampol his twenty-seven-year-old daughter, Clara, a widow, whose husband had died of consumption. Clara had studied at a Russian school, spoke Russian and Polish fluently, and hardly ever spoke Yiddish. She was of medium build, dark, with black burning eyes, sensuous lips, a high bosom, and a small waist. There was a beauty mark on her left cheek; she walked boldly, her head uncovered. Clara played the piano, was clever at cards, rode in a phaeton like a Russian landowner, and promptly became friends with David Sorkess and Morris Shalit, who came fron Vilna. Both men had worked for Calman. Her circle also included Sorkess's and Shalit's wives, Sonya and Tamara respectively; Ignace Herman, a bachelor; Grain, the apothecary; and Itka, Grain's wife, who had been nicknamed Grainicha. Evenings, Clara liked to entertain, serving tea from a samovar while she and her guests played poker or whist. Itka and the other women reciprocated by inviting Clara and her father to their homes, and for a while the gossip was that Ignace Herman had fallen in love with her and that they would get married. Clara herself scotched that rumor by declaring that she would not think of marrying a man who had remained a bachelor until he was well over thirty and barely made a living as a bookkeeper.

Although the two men were competitors, Kaminer depended on Calman, since he could obtain lumber, grain, potatoes, cabbage, beets, cattle, and lime at rock-bottom prices only from Calman. Furthermore, Mayer Joel owned the watermill. Kaminer invited Calman to dinner, but Calman was reluctant to go. He knew that Kaminer employed a Jewess in the kitchen, but one couldn't be sure that such people observed the dietary laws. Instead, Calman said he would come after dinner. Kaminer talked like a heretic, though he did have a mezuzah nailed to the doorpost. He lived like a lord: tapestries on the walls of his house; lamps, divans, and paintings everywhere. The maid had been late with her preparations and dinner hadn't yet been served when Calman arrived. The maid, a Jampol divorcee, was summoned and swore solemnly that she had not deviated in the slightest from the dietary laws. She had personally seen to it that the stove and utensils had been made kosher. Though Calman had already eaten, the odors of borscht and roasting meat that came from the kitchen made him hungry again. Clara did not come in until after Calman had arrived. Passover had ended; it was a rainy day. Clara burst in wearing a silk cape, elbow-length gloves, and a flowered hat. She carried a bouquet of flowers that she had picked. She smelled of perfume. Removing her glove, she extended a pale hand to the guest. Though Calman was not used to shaking a woman's hand, particularly that of a Jewess, he forgot himself. Clara smiled, flashing her teeth, and poured him a glass of brandy. As she chatted with Calman, her pet dog nipped at her ankles. Daniel Kaminer gulped down his drink, grimaced, and wiped his mustache. A few minutes later he left the room. The two were alone together.

"Do make yourself at home," Clara said. "I expect you'll be a frequent visitor here."

"I'm a busy man."

"Nevertheless, you'll find time to come." Clara winked and

laughed. She mentioned how clever and attractive Shaindel was; in St. Petersburg, a woman like that would be the toast of the town. Calman asked her if she'd ever been to St. Petersburg and she replied that she had a cousin there with whom she had roomed at boarding school and who was now the wife of a doctor. Clara introduced Russian expressions into her Yiddish, let out peals of laughter, leaned close to Calman, and even took the lapels of his coat in her hands.

Dinner was a banquet. Clara herself ladled out soup for Calman from the tureen. She helped him to all sorts of vegetables. It irked her to see him eat so little. "That's not enough food for a man," she complained.

When dinner was over, Calman, who had never seen a Jewish woman smoke before, was amazed to see her light a cigarette. She offered him one, and forced him to light it with hers. As he did so, she warned: "Be careful that your beard doesn't catch fire."

Finally the men retired to the study to discuss business. Kaminer did not bargain over prices. He insisted instead that Calman falsify the accounts he presented to the quartermaster.

"That's absolutely out of the question," Calman said.

"It's true, then, you really are simple-minded. There's no one who doesn't steal from the Russians, the Czar included. Russia is based on thievery, the whole world . . ."

"I just don't believe that."

"Don't be an idiot and you'll get along better. The colonel gets his share, and the general too. I send gifts not only to their wives but to their mistresses . . ."

"I give too, but I won't engage in false accounts."

"They wouldn't recognize a true one. When working with pigs, act like one."

After they had argued for some time, Kaminer suggested a compromise. He personally would keep the accounts and append his signature to them. If any questions were asked, Calman would be in the clear. Clara knocked on the door and brought in tea.

"Well, gentlemen, have you reached an agreement?"

"Calman's a trifle squeamish. Nowadays one doesn't come across many such saints."

"A saint? How odd! I always thought that saints slept away their lives next to the stove. My aunt used to say, 'An honest man feeds on grass.'"

"God be praised. I've cheated no man yet and I've made a living."

"Oh, come now, whom do you think you're fooling? One doesn't make a fortune praying. If it's the future world you're after, donate a scroll to the synagogue as my Aunt Sprintza did. In business, one can't afford a tender conscience."

III

Calman was aware that not only he but the Count too considered himself disgraced by Miriam Lieba's marriage to Lucian. As for the Countess, she had died without ever having been told what her son had done. After his wife's death, Jampolski went to visit Helena in Zamosc. It was rumored that he would not return to Jampol, but he was away only briefly. Felicia, now that her mother was dead, was thinking of entering a convent, and had even begun correspondence with the mother superior of a cloister. In the end, nothing came of it. Felicia wasn't really prepared to take the veil. She had not entirely given up hope of marrying and having children. In addition, she realized that in a nunnery she would be constantly surrounded by other women. If her life was to be lived in isolation, she wanted to have her thoughts as her sole companions, and in the manor she had both a chapel and a library that were completely her own. Furthermore, it would be a sin to desert her father, and though he most certainly did not conduct himself like a Christian, she knew it was not the place of his daughter to pass judgment on him.

So both she and the Count stayed where they were. His conduct continued to be the talk of the neighborhood. He openly consorted with his Siberian mistress, Yevdotya, announced that he was planning to go into the fur business, that all he needed was a partner with a little capital; while in exile, he had come to know a host of trappers. The Jampol Jews shrugged their shoulders. They had neither sufficient money nor the confidence in the Count that was needed to back such a commercial undertaking. At length Yevdotya deserted her house in The Sands and left town. Barbara, the old nurse, died. The cook Magda found a more lucrative job at another manor, and only the coachman, Wojciech, stayed on. He was of no value. As soon as he'd saved up a few groschen, he spent them on drink. Cataracts formed on both his eyes and he became half blind. Felicia would have willingly kept house for her father, but the Count managed to find himself a servant, none other than Antosia, the soldier's wife who had taken care of Calman when he had lived alone in the forest. Felicia did not want to allow Antosia, who had a bad reputation, into the house, but the Count insisted that he needed her and that if Felicia didn't like it she was old enough to pack up and leave. Once again he insulted his daughter, calling her an old maid who had sour milk in her veins instead of blood. Felicia, as always, suffered in silence.

Both the neighboring gentry and the Jews of Jampol and Skarshew insisted that the reason the Count stayed locked up in his house all day was that he was ashamed to meet Calman. An attic room whose windows faced to the rear became the Count's sanctum; he almost never opened the shutters. He spent his time drinking and reading, and for months on end was seen by no one. Even Felicia saw him only rarely. The only one for whom he would unlock the door was Antosia. Although the Countess's jewelry had been divided among her children (the largest share had been given to Lucian by Felicia), other assets were still controlled by the Count. He sold a valuable harness for next to nothing. Whenever he needed money, he sent Antosia off to Jampol to pawn various articles. He poured himself whisky by the glass but didn't get drunk.

Fully clothed, in bed, he browsed through old books or worked out various gambits on a chessboard. Three times a day Antosia brought him his meals, but he ate little. If he did go out during the day, he walked through the woods, avoiding the path that led into town. For the most part he left the house only at night, and then he practiced calisthenics in the dark, raised and lowered his arms, breathed in deeply, letting out the air with a roar. When Calman saw him one summer evening astride an old mare, both horse and rider seemed to be half asleep.

But though the Count did not seek the world, the world sought him. Josef, his oldest son, wrote him regularly from London. Jampolski never answered the letters. Josef got news of his father from Felicia, who also corresponded with Helena in Zamosc and even exchanged letters with Lucian and Miriam Lieba in Paris. Whenever Felicia knocked on her father's door, the Count would shout, "Leave me alone. Go away." Once, becoming worried, she demanded that Antosia open the door for her.

"Father," she said, "you mustn't neglect yourself like this."

"How am I neglecting myself? I'm healthier than you are."

For once Felicia lost her temper. "You must see that you're making us both look ridiculous."

"You're ashamed of me? A skeleton like you?"

He made no secret of the fact that he was cohabiting with Antosia, and Felicia heard the maid on her way to him each night. In his old age her father had turned into an animal. He did not go to church on Sundays, observed no Christian holidays, seldom changed his clothes, slept in his jacket and boots. Antosia, rather than the barber, trimmed his beard. His mustache became ragged. His language grew as coarse as a dogcatcher's. He never went near a religious book, but read the works of Voltaire, Diderot, Byron, Heine, and George Sand, as well as a huge history of Freemasonry and books about the French Revolution and the Italian Mafia.

Gradually Felicia realized that the longer she lived with this uncouth man, the more she would deteriorate physically and spiritually. She no longer slept at night. Though she ate, she kept growing thinner. The mother she grieved for had been exchanged by her father for a slovenly, almost idiotic peasant. He blasphemed against God, ranted against the Pope. The news that Helena had married a cousin in Zamosc left her father indifferent, and when she gave birth to a son, the grandfather did not even congratulate her.

One Sunday in April, as Felicia left church (Wojciech was waiting outside in the britska), someone overtook her, bowed to her, and introduced himself. He was a man of about forty, small, thin, with a sallow face, sharp eyes, and a pointed mustache. He wore a scanty summer coat and a derby. A colored scarf covered his throat. For some reason, Felicia assumed he was a foreigner. He removed his hat, revealing curly, chestnut hair already graying at the temples. His tone was familiar, as if he knew her. He said that his name was Dr. Marian Zawacki and that he had come from Paris. Lucian had asked him to convey regards to his sister. Zawacki also mentioned that Lucian was in need of financial help, that he was in danger of being deported as a public charge. Felicia, unaccustomed to standing in the street with a strange man, was afraid people would laugh at her. After some hesitation, she invited Zawacki to join her in the britska and accompany her to the manor. It was the first time the Countess Felicia had ever been seen in the company of a man. Everyone looked and snickered, even the Jews.

IV

Although the old Count did not generally come downstairs for dinner, he informed his daughter through Antosia that this time he would dine with their guest. Felicia was apprehensive, for her father had forgotten his manners completely. Not only was he liable to come to the table in a housecoat and slippers, but he might appear simply for the purpose of insulting Zawacki. Felicia therefore warned the doctor beforehand that her father was not entirely well. "I know, I know," Zawacki replied. "Lucian takes after him. Your mother was the normal member of the family."

Felicia had never heard a total stranger·speak this way before. But who knew what the world was coming to? Zawacki had admitted without embarrassment that his father was a Warsaw cobbler and that his maternal grandfather had been a blacksmith in Pultusk. While finishing medical school in Paris, Marian had supported himself as a tourist guide and for a short time had managed a soup kitchen for Polish refugees. It was at the soup kitchen that he had met Lucian and Marisia, as he called Miriam Lieba. Felicia shuddered at every word he spoke. He related how the people of Paris had eaten mice at the time of the Prussian siege of 1870 and how he himself had caught a cat and skinned and roasted it.

It made Felicia feel sick and she said, "I would rather die than eat anything so disgusting."

"What's disgusting about it? We're all made of the same stuff."

"You don't believe that man's soul is divine?"

"Absolutely not," Zawacki replied.

The Count, though generally impatient with people, took to Zawacki immediately. Felicia, who had helped prepare the Sunday dinner, had covered the table with an elegant cloth and the finest china and silverware. But the conversation during the meal revolted her. The men began with a discussion of shoemaking and tanning, the Count wanting to know how leather was tanned, why oak bark was needed, which hides were used for soft leather and which for hard. When they had finished with the manufacture of shoes, the Count's curiosity turned to autopsy. Zawacki described the methods used in opening abdomens and skulls. Anatomy, he explained, had always been his specialty. Moreover, he had a steady hand and wasn't in the least sentimental. When Zawacki described in detail how, after having first removed the fetus from her womb, he had cut open a pregnant woman who had drowned herself in the Seine, Felicia turned white and had to be excused. Zawacki didn't bother to apologize. "After a while you get used to such things," he said. "Why, I sometimes had to boil human heads on my own stove."

He brought regards from Lucian—if Lucian's bitter message could be considered a greeting. Lucian, he said, was a drunken idler and a psychopath to boot. His wife and the child were starving. Lucian's latest plan was either to enlist in the Foreign Legion or to go off to America. When dinner was finished, the Count brought out his chessboard and lost three games in a row to the doctor. As they played, the men rocked back and forth in their chairs, smoking pipes and cursing. Every third word they uttered was "*psiakrew*"—dog's blood. Felicia could scarcely endure being in the presence of this coarse little man in whom all the defects of her father were duplicated. She wanted to get rid of him as soon as possible, but the Count had other ideas and invited Zawacki to stay on for a day or two.

After the Count had gone to bed, Felicia walked out into the night; suddenly she found herself confronted by Zawacki. The doctor was carrying a crooked cane.

"Oh, it's you." Without further ado, he joined her as if they were the oldest of friends. He had gone to school in Krakow, he told her, but had found himself at odds with the other students. Unlike them, he had been opposed to the 1863 uprisings, which he had regarded as nothing less than lunacy. He had known even then that General Mieroslawski was the worst of charlatans and Prince Lubomirski nothing but a pickpocket. As for Mickiewicz's son, what could one say of him other than that great man had sired a midget? According to Zawacki, not even Prince Czartoryski was worth much, the truth being that the whole bloody business had been nothing but a filthy adventure led by a group of sentimental idiots, irresponsible parasites, and barbaric women. Felicia was appalled. The Count himself was not so disrespectful. Finally

145

Zawacki left the subject of politics and began to discuss his own affairs. His medical career had started late because he had had to move from university to university. Then, too, Napoleon III's insane war with Prussia and the crazy antics of the Paris Commune had intervened. Thank God, he was at last a certified physician. As he spoke, he constantly shifted from Polish to French and back to Polish again.

"What's going to happen to you, living here among these ruins?" he asked. "A person could easily lose his mind in such an atmosphere."

Felicia defended herself, although she scarcely knew why. "I can't leave my father."

"Let's face it, your father's senile and slightly degenerate besides."

Although it was not her nature to be rude, Felicia found it difficult to control her temper. "You're speaking about my father."

"What's a father? I hadn't seen my father in years; I went home on a visit, kissed him, and then I didn't have three words to say to him."

"Is there anyone who doesn't bore you?"

"Frankly no. Some people are absolutely mad about dogs, but I hate the animals. A dog is nothing but a flatterer, a sycophant. I prefer canaries or parrots. Monkeys are interesting, too."

"All animals are interesting."

"Well, at any rate, they don't talk nonsense, And they die more gracefully than men. People cling to life as if it were all marzipan and rose water."

"What an odd comparison."

"How is it that you've never married?" Zawacki asked suddenly.

The blood rushed to Felicia's face. "No one wants me."

"I'd want you."

Felicia paled. "I'm afraid you're making fun of me."

"Not at all. It's true you're not young, but neither are you

146

old. Besides, you're a good-looking woman. Lucian showed me the photograph you sent him. He also told me about your eccentricities."

"What eccentricities?"

"Oh, your piety and all that. I can't stand women who are too clever—the cunning ones, I mean. Now don't be offended. It's just my way of speaking."

"I see."

"I want to open an office and I need a wife."

Felicia lowered her head. She realized that the man was in earnest. She had received her first proposal.

v

Although Count Wladislaw Jampolski constantly stressed the bankruptcy of the Polish nobility, proclaiming their inferiority to the merchant class and even to the Jewish storekeepers, he was unwilling to have the wedding of his daughter Felicia to Dr. Marian Zawacki take place at the castle. The Count stated it plainly: it was no concern of his that Felicia was marrying the son of a shoemaker—he even regarded it as an honor —but it was impossible for him to meet the shoemaker and his family at the manor or to dine or spend time with them. To Felicia he said: "I'll give you my blessing; go with him where you wish. But I'm not in the mood for any shoemaker parties!"

There was nothing for Felicia to do but weep. Her tears soaked the earth at her mother's grave. She had already knelt for a long time in the chapel before the picture of the Holy Mother, prayed, crossed herself, murmured her supplications. Felicia had no illusions about her coming marriage: Zawacki was a despot, kneaded from the same dough as her father; he would insult her and deride her in the true manner of a plebeian, and he would bring her and his boorish family together. Yet though she would suffer in this milieu, it was preferable to remaining alone with a half-demented father on a manor that belonged to a Jew. If she must submit to a tyrant, why not one of her own age? Who could tell? He might even be good to her, perhaps she could still have children. Her father maintained that sour milk ran in her veins, but it was far from the truth. More than once, at night, Felicia had felt that the blood within her was his.

Lying in bed until dawn, Felicia took stock of herself. She could not become a nun, even if she forced herself to enter a convent. She would be in danger of breaking her vows, and instead of pleasing God she would anger Him. But she could not remain at home. Clearly heaven had destined her to marry. If she was meant to suffer, this marriage would be her cross. During sleepless nights, Felicia vowed to be faithful to Marian Zawacki, to love him like a wife and sister, to try to soften his bitterness, and to show him and his relatives an example of Christian devotion. Why run away from temptation?

But it was not entirely convenient to marry without a mother, a sister or brother. Felicia certainly must have a trousseau, but she had no idea what she needed or how to prepare it. Her father's refusal to attend the wedding was an insult both to Felicia and to Marian's family. Marian wanted to get it all over with quickly, his impatience and contempt for ceremony were similar to her father's. Nevertheless, Felicia could not allow her wedding to turn into a farce. Meditating long and uncertainly, she decided to ask help from others. She wrote a long letter to her sister Helena, asked advice of the Jampol priest and his housekeeper, made inquiries of her Aunt Eugenia and her cousin Stephanie. Felicia could not go to her husband like a pauper without a wardrobe.

The anxiety, nocturnal weeping spells, and lack of sleep undermined her health. She lost her appetite. Instead of gaining weight, she grew thinner, was perpetually constipated. Her periods became irregular. Every few minutes she washed her hands. At night she was tormented by feelings of doubt, turned in her bed, tossed, sighed: would she be able to satisfy a man? Would Marian be disappointed with her the very first night? Would his relatives conspire against her, ridicule her, would she have to return in shame to her father? There were moments when Felicia wanted to scream and tear her hair. But her belief in God, in His Providence and His absolute goodness, kept her from acting desperately.

Felicia discovered that when one seeks help, there are always those who will respond. Old noblewomen, former friends of the Countess, began to show up at the manor, bringing daughters and daughters-in-law. These friends from the past recommended tailors, seamstresses. Nissen, the Jampol tailor, again came to the manor, took Felicia's measurements, fitted her, wished her luck. At every opportunity he mentioned the goodness and generosity of the late Countess. Felicia's decision to marry Dr. Zawacki had in some mysterious way brought her closer to people, even to those who had never known her before.

VI

Her fiancé's father, the shoemaker, Antony Zawacki, had an old house on Bugay Street in Warsaw. It wasn't easy for Felicia to enter a shoemaker's shop and see her future father-in-law, the cobbler, sitting at his bench in a leather apron, sewing a shoe with a swine-bristle needle, surrounded by his five helpers. One bored holes with an awl, one pounded in tacks with a hammer; another rubbed a heel with a piece of glass, and a fourth trimmed a sole with a curved shoemaker's knife. Antony Zawacki, in his sixties, seemed younger than his years. His thick black mustaches coiled up at the ends, and though the comparison embarrassed Felicia, his eyes had the gleam of polished shoes. His hands were hairy, his fingers short, the square nails ringed with dirt. He did not even rise when Felicia entered. Measuring her with an experienced gaze, he called to his wife in the kitchen, "Hey, Katarzyna, we've got a visitor!"

Katarzyna was a small, thin woman with sharp limbs and angry eyes who resembled her son. Seeing Felicia, she quickly wiped her fingers on her apron, executed something like a curtsy, and extended a dirty hand. Felicia had come alone. Marian had not wanted to be present when Felicia met his parents.

"The gracious Countess!"

Felicia walked past a kitchen where large pots boiled on the stove. The helpers received food in addition to their wages. On the table there was a loaf of black bread larger than any Felicia had ever seen. In the living room there was a dresser with a mirror and a vase full of artificial flowers. A roll of flypaper dangled from the lamp. Two framed photographs of husband and wife together and a photograph of Marian in the uniform of a high-school student hung on the wall. Although it was midsummer, the windows were nailed shut, and for a moment the smell of dust and leather nauseated Felicia. She sat on the sofa upholstered in some shiny material, and green wheels spun before her eyes.

"Would it inconvenience you terribly to open the window?" Felicia asked.

"Window? What for? It's still nailed up for the winter."

"My wife is afraid of fresh air," Antony Zawacki said, accusingly. "Excuse my language, Countess, but it stinks here!"

He leaped to the window and, tearing it open, pulled out the length of straw that had sealed it against the wind. A mild breeze smelling of refuse and pitch blew in from the courtyard.

"Well, why are you so quiet?" Antony asked his wife. "Offer the Countess something!"

"I don't need you to teach me manners, Antony! I wasn't brought up in the gutter."

"The Countess must be thirsty."

"Oh, no, thank you."

Husband and wife both went into the kitchen. Felicia heard them wrangling. When Antony Zawacki returned, Felicia saw that he had replaced his apron with a skimpy jacket. It made him look clumsy. A tin stud was buttoned into his shirt collar.

There was an air of plebeian uncouthness in his gaze, his mustaches, his unshaven jaw, and thick neck with its swollen veins. He carried in a wooden tray with a carafe of wine, glasses, and cookies. Katarzyna had by this time also changed her clothes. She wore a yellow dress with a pleated bodice. Felicia regretted that she had allowed Marian to persuade her to visit his parents unexpectedly.

Although in no mood to drink wine, Felicia sipped it and remarked that it was good. The cookies were hard as pebbles. Katarzyna kept returning to the kitchen and her pots.

"The esteemed Countess sees us for what we are: common folk," Antony Zawacki said. "We've earned everything with our own hands—the house, the workshop. Marian had a good head for books. I wanted to make a shoemaker out of him, but he said: 'Papa, I haven't the patience for heels and soles.' 'What do you want?' I asked him. 'To become a priest and have maidservants confess to you?' In short, he wanted an education. 'Well, go ahead and study,' I said. He filled the whole house with books. I gave him everything he needed, but he got hold of a boy, some lame-brain who needed help with his lessons and whose parents could pay. Well, let him be a student, I thought. In this way he got through high school and earned a gold medal. He could have studied at the university here, but he insisted on going to Krakow. His mother began to carry on: 'So far away!—my only son.' I had another son too but no more. Well, to make a long story short, I sent him to Krakow and he studied there. Afterward, he went to France. A war started there and I read in the papers that a rabbit cost fifty francs. There the currency is francs, not guilders. A cat was fifteen francs, and one egg five francs. They have a park where they keep animals, and all the bears and peacocks and the others were eaten. My wife began to wail: 'Our Marian will starve to death!' But, somehow, he came back healthy, if emaciated. He said: 'Papa, I want to marry Countess Jampolska.' 'Where did you meet a Countess?' I asked. 'You may be a doctor, but your father is a shoemaker.' 'Well,' he said, 'times

151

have changed.' What do they call it? De-mo-cracy. He said, 'Naked, we all stem from apes.' 'Well,' I said, 'if it's all right with her parents, it's all right with me. Your wife,' I said, 'will be like a daughter to me—' "

Katarzyna returned from the kitchen. "What's the difference what you said? If our boy loves someone, we like her too."

12

Many letters arrived for Calman proposing a second marriage, and matchmakers visited the manor frequently. Although his reputation was now blemished because of Miriam Lieba's apostasy, Calman on the other hand was the father-in-law of the Marshinov rabbi's son, and related to the Jampol rabbi and to Reb Ezekiel Wiener. He was also a man of wealth and not quite fifty years old. Girls, young widows, and divorcees were offered to him. A letter came from Binneleh, the Chmielev rabbi's wife in Marshinov and Temerel's sister-in-law. Binneleh wrote that she had been lying awake in bed one night and it had suddenly occurred to her that Calman should marry her sister-in-law, Temerel, Jochanan's mother. What could be finer? Binneleh had not as yet discussed her idea with Temerel, but was certain that Temerel would consent. Temerel had been a widow for too long. As long as she had had to arrange suitable marriages for her children, she had been unable to think of herself. Now that she had married off both her daughters and Jochanan was married to Tsipele, it was a different matter. Binneleh's letter was full of insinuations that the rabbi, her father-in-law, was gravely ill. His days were numbered and her brother-in-law Reb Shimmon planned to succeed his father by force. Binneleh compared Reb Shimmon to Absalom, who had wanted to rob his father, King David, of his kingdom. Calman nodded. He read between the lines. An undeclared war was being waged by the two brothers, Reb Shimmon and the Chmielev rabbi. It was the two sisters-in-law, Menucheleh and Binneleh, who kept the feud going. Binneleh probably reasoned that a match between Calman and Temerel would be a blow against Reb Shimmon. Reb Moshe, the Chmielev rabbi, apparently had no desire to take his father's following, but he begrudged it to his brother and wanted to effect a compromise with Jochanan, the nephew.

Although Binneleh claimed that she had not yet discussed the matter with Temerel, Calman suspected that she had, in her clever way, gathered that Temerel would not be adverse to the match. But the proposal did not attract Calman. It was a great honor, of course, that the daughter of the Marshinov rabbi wanted to marry him, but Temerel would be no wife for him. She was very pious, a scholar, whereas he was almost ignorant. Moreover, she was already in her late forties, perhaps even fifty. For half a lifetime Calman had been married to a wife who had been devout and sickly; in her final years, he had almost never approached her. Lust boiled within him as in his youth. Not even hard work could subdue it. He needed more than a pious female.

Binneleh's letter arrived a week before Pentecost. It had been Calman's intention to go to Marshinov to spend the holiday with the rabbi, and also to visit Tsipele and Jochanan. But the letter confused him. Now he was ashamed to go.

Acting on Calman's indecision, Shaindel was able to dissuade him from spending Pentecost in Marshinov. Ezriel had returned from Warsaw for the holiday, and Shaindel wanted the two men to be together. As a result, Mayer Joel traveled to Marshinov alone and Calman remained at the manor. Cooped up in the house, Calman had nothing to do during the long days. He argued with Ezriel, and Ezriel spouted heresy. "Who," he asked, "saw God give Moses the Torah on Mount Sinai? The Jews have their Torah, and the Christians have something else. If their religion can be false, so can ours.

Hasn't each generation added new laws and new miracles? Is there any mention in the Scriptures of the hereafter or resurrection? No, there isn't. Ecclesiastes states categorically that everything ends with death. All the legends of another world, of a final reckoning, the talk of a Messiah, and a wild ox, and the leviathan are later developments. If there is such a thing as immortality and the soul is rewarded in paradise and punished in Gehenna, why don't the Prophets mention it?"

A great bitterness overcame Calman. He could not answer any of Ezriel's questions and so he rebuked him and then regretted it. Upset, Calman went out for a walk in the fields, occasionally touching an ear of wheat, and counting the grains. If everything went well and there was neither too much rain nor hail, the harvest would bring him thousands. Fruit hung heavy on the trees, cows calved, hens laid. Lime now brought a half groschen more per forty pounds, so that even if the duke didn't renew his lease, Calman would be left with plenty.

Suddenly he saw someone approaching. He recognized the porter from the railway depot, who as he drew nearer stopped and removed his hat. "A telegram for you, sir."

Calman did not know whether it was proper to accept the message on a holiday, but took it, promising the man a tip when the festival was over. When the porter had thanked him and left, Calman tried to decipher the scrawled handwriting of the telegram, but was unable to do so. He noticed two women approaching him, but from a distance he could not make out who they were. It was evident from their attire that they weren't peasants. On the other hand, Jewish young ladies would not venture outside the limits of the settlement on a holiday.

It occurred to Calman that it must be Clara and one of her friends. Smoothing his beard and buttoning his gaberdine, he walked toward them, Yes, the taller of the two was Clara, and with her was Tamara Shalit. Clara had on a wide-brimmed straw hat with a green band, and a light-colored dress, and she

F

carried a parasol. She was fanning herself with a handkerchief. Both women were laughing, and then Clara called out, "Think of it, Reb Calman, I won a ruble because of you!"

"Because of me?"

"Yes, I had a bet. I said it was you approaching, and Tamara said that—"

"Be quiet! I said nothing—" Tamara slapped her arm.

"Happy holiday! I was out for a walk and the porter met me with a telegram. Now you cross my path. Everything at once."

"What did the telegram say?" Clara asked curiously.

"I can't make it out."

"Let me try."

Calman handed the sheet of paper to Clara, who snatched it from his hand. Scanning it rapidly, her eyes lit up.

"You're a lucky man!"

"What is it?"

"It may be a secret. I'd better whisper it."

"No, I'll walk away," Tamara said, turning back.

Clara came closer to Calman and her hand touched his ear. A strange warmth coursed through him.

"Wallenberg is planning to build another railroad. He wants you to come to Warsaw," Clara whispered, "as quickly as possible!"

As she spoke, her hat slid back on her head and remained suspended by a pin. With her hat askew, she appeared younger and more graceful. She was so close to him that his beard rested on her shoulder. She winked and said, "Lots of luck."

11

By chance, Clara accompanied Calman to Warsaw. Though he had already purchased a third-class ticket, when she saw him standing on the platform, she asked him to join her in her second-class compartment. Clara had with her a valise, a hat box, a bouquet of flowers, and a small satchel. She wore a checked suit and a straw hat with cherries on it. The train remained standing for a long time, and some Jampol Jews saw Calman join her. Daniel Kaminer stood on the platform and spoke to his daughter in Russian through the open window of her compartment. Clara's presence did not deter Daniel Kaminer from making coarse jokes. "Watch her closely, Calman. Don't let them abduct her in the big city . . . She's worth money!"

"Papa, you should be ashamed, the way you talk," Clara said reprovingly.

"I lost whatever shame I had a long time ago."

In the car, Clara told Calman the purpose of her trip. She had broken the catch on her pearls and there was only one jeweler in Warsaw who could fix it. She also needed a new dress, and Jampol's Nissen was incompetent. And she wanted several hats, and her aunt in Warsaw, a Mrs. Frankel, was a milliner. Whenever she visited the city, Clara stayed at her aunt's house. She smiled and chattered, bent down and took refreshments for herself and Calman out of her small satchel —chocolates, marmalade, cookies, even an orange. When the train stopped at a station, she sent him out for tea. Beneath her jacket, which she removed, Clara wore a white blouse, so transparent that her bodice and part of her breasts were visible. She removed a flower from her bouquet and fixed it in Calman's lapel. Speaking confidently, she gave him all kinds of advice. First, he must not permit Wallenberg to get the best of the bargain. Wallenberg was a multimillionaire, and labor was more expensive than ever. Calman must not sign any contract in a hurry, because in furnishing railroad ties, a fortune could be lost as easily as it could be made.

Second, Clara reminded Calman that he must come to an agreement with the duke. She had heard that attempts were being made to outbid Calman for the manor. Losing the manor would be the same as losing a hand. If he wanted to maintain the lime quarries and supply the ties, he had to keep the manor, for without it, he would be unable to furnish food for his laborers. It would be impossible if he had to buy every sack of meal and every quart of milk. Calman could not stop marveling at Clara's business sense. She spoke more like an experienced merchant than a woman. He was unable, Calman confessed, to locate the duke, who was on a world tour and hadn't answered his letters. There was a way of solving this, Clara said. She knew a Warsaw lawyer, a drinking companion of the Governor-General and a frequent visitor to his castle. She also had military contacts. Her father was a bosom friend of both Colonel Smirnoff and General Rittermayer, who moved in the highest circles of the Russian aristocracy. They could be counted on to further Calman's cause.

Calman could not help comparing Clara to Zelda, who had done nothing but torment his soul and make him demean himself, live parsimoniously, and surrender everything to his enemies. Clara was young, attractive, clever, and she had a masculine mind. She was honest with him because she wanted to become his wife. She was feathering her own nest, in a way, but that's how things were. Calman moved away from her a little, as the scent of flowers and perfume made him dizzy. After a while, Clara again moved closer to him and, joking, tugged good-naturedly at his beard. Once she placed her shoe over his boot. Her knee moved close to his. Calman literally went pale with desire. He began to pray that the Lord deliver him from temptation. If Clara was destined to be his future wife, he would lead her to the wedding canopy. Lying back on the plush-covered seat, Clara tried to nap. Calman gazed out the window at the parting fields which made a path for the train. Forests danced by, flocks of birds careened overhead, frightened by the scarecrows with their torn clothes and ragged hats. Over everything there was a blue sky with little silver clouds, floating, curling to become pillows, sheep, brooms, and curtains. God's sunlight fell on every leaf, every blade of grass, every flower. Peasants could be seen between the seed beds, pulling up weeds. Peasant women worked over the potato patches. Cattle-filled pastures flitted by, cows with black and yellow patches, their udders milk-laden. A cowherd played on his fife, young men built campfires, horses grazed or simply stood, neck to neck, mutely exchanging secrets. What could be pleasanter than sitting next to Clara and looking out at God's summery day? Everything was beautiful: each windmill, each straw-laden roof, each marsh and pond where geese and ducks splashed.

"If she were my wife," Calman thought, "I could ride like this with her for days, weeks, months! She's young, and might still bear children, a son. I can still have the pleasure of watching my heir study the Torah." Calman hung his head. "Well, but does she really want me? Perhaps she's making fun of me? Enlightened people have a habit of mocking others. And how can I be sure that someone like her would observe the dietary laws, ablutions, and keep promises? What if her word means nothing?"

Clara opened one eye. "Why are you thinking so hard, Calman?"

Calman cleared his throat. "I was thinking of how good it is to enjoy the world without forsaking God. Because if, perish the thought, one forsakes God, both worlds are lost."

"Who forsakes God," Clara countered, "if everything one sees was created by Him?"

"It certainly was."

"On the other hand, one need not be a fanatic."

"Who's a fanatic? A Jew must observe the dietary laws, and a Jewish daughter the laws of purification."

"Do you mean the ritual bath?"

"Yes, the ritual bath." And Calman's face turned red.

"After all, what is the ritual bath? Since one must be clean, why not bathe in a bathtub or the river in summertime? Isn't that more hygienic than a ritual bath, where all sorts of filthy women dip themselves?"

"Cleanliness isn't the only purpose of a ritual bath."

"What then?"

"The soul!"

"What does the soul get out of a ritual bath? And besides, the match won't be canceled because of it." Clara winked, laughing.

Pausing for a moment, she said, "If I had my own manor and lived with a religious husband, I'd build a ritual bath of my own. That way, God would be satisfied and I'd stay clean."

III

Clara's aunt, the milliner, lived on Mead Street. It was her daughter's birthday and there was a party in progress at the apartment. Miss Celina was twenty, according to her mother, but the girls who worked for Mrs. Frankel figured her age as twenty-three. Normally one would have expected a woman of that age to have a husband and children, but everything happened late in Mrs. Frankel's home. One returned at two in the morning and didn't get up till noon; at Mrs. Frankel's a girl was still young at twenty-three. Mrs. Frankel, who had buried three husbands, had Celina by her second, the Commissioner. Somewhere or other there was also a son, who had apostasized and become a Russian army officer. Mrs. Frankel's Jewish neighbors avoided her; she was said to eat forbidden foods and did not cook the Sabbath meal in advance. Although nearly sixty, Mrs. Frankel did not wear a wig. She was dark as a crow, had a beaked nose and black pouchy eyes ringed with webs of wrinkles. Her left eye smiled, while the other blinked. She had a saucy way of talking; she called a hat a pancake, its feather a tail, and a female customer a bargain-hunter. But her crooked fingers were famous and throughout Warsaw her hats were the vogue.

It was known that countesses and princesses were among her customers. The demand for her work was so great that she employed half a dozen girls, who lived with her and were regarded as members of the family. At ten-thirty at night, everyone stopped work and helped prepare dinner. One girl fetched the samovar, another lit the stove, a third made potato pancakes or dumplings. Because of this, dinner at Mrs. Frankel's was a hit-and-miss affair. When the girls got lazy, they bought cold cuts and frankfurters. The bakery boy would bring a basketful of fresh rolls and hot bagels, and as the girls ate, the rolls would crackle between their teeth. There wasn't another workshop in town which had such lively girls. Mrs. Frankel went out of her way to find girls who had spirit; it was known in the trade that any apprentice of hers would become an expert. She even acted as a matchmaker for them. One often saw the coach from the wedding hall draw up before her house. The one thing she could not bear was faulty workmanship. If a girl was awkward, Mrs. Frankel would shriek, "All right, Miss Five Thumbs, hurry home and bake a pudding." More than one girl was known to work on a single hat for half a week.

Oddly enough, Celina had not followed in her mother's footsteps. Mrs. Frankel had done her best to teach her daughter millinery, but the girl couldn't even thread a needle. In fact, the only things she could do well were eat and sleep. Rainy days she didn't get out of bed at all, but just sat drinking tea and cocoa, eating buttered rolls, and rice with milk in her room. Celina had a narrow, swarthy face, a small mouth, a pair of eyes like plums. Her neck was long and her head was covered with black ringlets. She was forever grimacing and spoke capriciously in the manner of an only daughter who can ask for anything. Her monthly period kept her in bed for days. The chamber pot was carried out by her mother, who would complain, "Rots in bed and stinks. She'll rot like that until her hair turns gray."

But when Celina thought of getting up and going out, her mother would thrust her crooked nose out the window, sniff, and say, "Stay where you are, it's sweltering."

Clara called Mrs. Frankel "aunt," although the milliner was related to Clara's first husband. Whenever Clara came to Warsaw, she stayed at her aunt's and arrived with presents for everyone. This time Celina received a pair of gold earrings as a birthday gift. Celina had small ears; she owned a trunkful of trinkets; even while she lay in bed, she primped. But in honor of her birthday she had risen and put on a yellow dress and high-heeled shoes. Tall, with a long, thin waist, she could appear elegant when she wished. After dinner, the girls clasped each other by the hips and danced. The music was provided by one of the girls, who hummed through a comb. Clara danced with Celina, whose feet glided gracefully across the floor. Mrs. Frankel watched with tears in her eyes. Three husbands and six children and all she had left was this creature. Would the day ever come when Celina would bring her some happiness?

In the midst of the festivities there was a knock on the door. Mrs. Frankel answered it. A large, black-bearded man in a high-crowned hat entered.

"You must be the aunt," Calman said.

"Whose aunt—yours?"

"Isn't she here? Clara?"

"Oh, Clara. Yes, she's here. Take off your coat."

"Who's here? Musicians?"

"Don't worry. No one will bite you."

Calman took off his coat and suddenly felt sorry he had come. He followed Mrs. Frankel into the apartment, realizing how big and broad he was in comparison to her. The girl playing the comb stopped. Clara, seeing him, clapped her hands. "For heaven's sake, he's here. Welcome, welcome!"

The girls giggled, embarrassing Calman, who was forced to remind himself that he was one of the richest Jews in Poland and had just signed a contract to supply ties for the railroad Wallenberg was building for the Czar. "Good evening," he said. "I told you I would come, and you see, I have kept my word. I'm going home tomorrow."

"Tomorrow? What's the rush? He flies in like the prophet Elijah. Come here, sit down. Auntie, this is Mr. Jacoby. I've told my aunt about you. It's her daughter's birthday."

162

"Very nice having you here. Would you like something to eat? Our rule is that no visitor leaves with an empty stomach."

"I would have brought a present if I'd known."

"She doesn't need presents. I only wish God would bless her with a suitable marriage."

"Are you starting again, Mama?"

"What's wrong? A daughter may be a blessing, but a mother wants some return on her investment. There are no labor pains in having a grandson. Really, Clara, it's time I had some pleasure out of you, too. I would like to dance at both your weddings. Believe me, Mister Jacoby, there's no other woman like her in the world! Pretty and clever and educated, with a dowry too. I should make every month what she'll bring to a husband!"

Calman's face grew red. The girls exchanged glances. Clara pushed a chair toward Calman.

"Were you at Wallenberg's?"

"I signed the contract today."

"Congratulations! Auntie, Mister Jacoby signed the contract. I tell my aunt everything. We have no secrets."

"*Mazel tov*! Good luck to you! Clara's friends are mine. That's the way we are: one family. Body and soul. Girls, what are you gaping at? Set up the samovar! Don't stand around looking like lumps of clay."

"Thank you kindly. I've already eaten."

"And what if you did eat? The intestine is bottomless. This is my daughter. It's her birthday that we're celebrating."

"In the old times, celebrating birthdays was a Gentile custom."

"There's a saying, 'Where the Gentile goes, the Jew follows!' "

13

In the Marshinov House of Prayer, the students read quietly. The old rabbi was sick. The Warsaw specialist admitted that his remedies could no longer be effective. "It's a miracle the rabbi is still alive."

Although his sons wanted to transfer the rabbi to the big house, where it was quieter and the air fresher, the rabbi preferred to remain in his study, near the house of prayer. Reb Mendel, the beadle, had that morning propped up the rabbi in bed, dressed in prayer shawl and phylacteries. He had prayed along with the quorum. The rabbi's intimates tried to enter the room to shake his hand, but Reb Shimmon, his eldest son, had told the attendant to admit no one. Since the rabbi had lost his sight, he recited the Psalms from memory, and mumbled parts of the Mishnah. Most of the time, he dozed. Swollen, with a distended stomach and a face that changed each hour, he lay there, his eyes sunken behind his cheekbones. Even his beard seemed to have shrunk. The rabbi could no longer urinate; it was necessary to catheterize him. The catheter emptied into a pot partially hidden under the bed. Several times a day, his nose bled. All the ailments had merged: a blockage of the bladder, an inflammation of the lungs. The body could no longer contain the soul. At any moment the end would come.

Throughout Poland the news spread that the rabbi was

dying. The train from Warsaw kept bringing new loads of Hassidim to Marshinov. The rich arrived in britskas and coaches. From the small villages, people came in wagons, and even on foot. Barren women, in search of a blessing to make them fertile, squatted with their bundles on benches, on the stoops of houses, or simply on the logs and boards that lay in the Marshinov courtyard. The slow process of repairing the complex of rabbinical buildings had been in progress for several years.

Comparing rabbis' miracles, the women shook their bonnets, wiped their noses on their aprons, and dried the tears on their wan cheeks. There was much to discuss, for each rabbi's way was different and each woman had her own trouble. From time to time, Reb Moshe the Chmielev rabbi or Reb Shimmon walked by. Reb Moshe reputedly did not want his father's following. Reb Shimmon, on the other hand, wished to replace his father, but the women insisted that the true saint was Temerel's son, Jochanan, Calman Jacoby's son-in-law. As Reb Shimmon walked by, he overheard a woman declaring: "Is he a human being? He's an angel. There is no saint like him in the whole world!"

Reb Shimmon slowed down. "Do they mean me?" he wondered. He stopped for a moment and the woman continued: "That Tsipele is a saint, too."

Reb Shimmon grumbled. His black beard leaped as if it had a life of its own. He looked angrily at the crowd and barely kept himself from spitting. "Cows, sluts!" he growled. "Who needs them here, the scum? They come to excrete, to pick the bones clean. And Tsipele is a saint to them too now!"

Reb Shimmon stopped at the threshold of the house of prayer. Candles burned in the menorahs. He could hear Jews intoning Psalms, praying for the rabbi's recovery, a group of children praying with their teacher. Reb Shimmon was looking for the men of wealth, the important men, the rabbi's intimates, but they were all, apparently, at the inns. He tugged his beard, bit his lips. "Why do they babble so much? No one lives forever. Even Moses died." Reb Shimmon paced back and forth. For years he had prepared for this day. He had written thousands of letters, entertained every Hassid, committed every face to memory, every name, everyone's needs and requirements. His wife, Menuche, had entertained the women. Reb Shimmon was well aware that in all Poland there was no rabbi's son who had a memory to match his. Actually, he had sacrificed himself for the court. It was he, Reb Shimmon, who had rebuilt the ritual bath, had the corner walls of the house of prayer supported by piles of stones, fixed the roof. He himself had taken care of all debts, all duties, each attendant, each full-time student, each servant girl. Reb Moshe, the Chmielev rabbi, had spent his years in Chmielev. His mother was concerned only with her own ailments. His sister Temerel kept her nose in her prayer books. He, Reb Shimmon, ran the court. Why did they chatter about Jochanan? If Jochanan could be the Marshinov rabbi, then Reb Shimmon could be a priest.

11

Jochanan had been reading in his attic room instead of at the house of study ever since the rabbi had become sick. People crowded about him too much, Hassidim dropped all sorts of hints.

His mother looked at him with misty eyes. He heard others say that after the death of the old man he would be made rabbi, but Jochanan had decided not to accept the office. In the first place, who was he to become the Rabbi of Marshinov? Evil thoughts filled him. He was steeped in lust, wrath, pride, melancholy, and other evils. Second, even if he were worthy, he would not encroach upon his uncle Reb Shimmon, who had served all these years. He would not only be infringing on his uncle's rights but would be insulting Reb Shimmon. No, God forbid. Jochanan remembered the words of the Tal-

166

mud: it is better to throw oneself into a lime kiln than to shame someone before others. All these things—his grandfather's illness, Reb Shimmon's annoyance, all the whispering behind his back—upset him. A while ago, he had been a half-decent Jew. He had studied in peace and prayed with fervor. He had distinctly felt that he was becoming purified. Now he had grown base again. As he prayed, his mind filled with foolish notions. He studied, but barely understood the words of the sages. Suddenly in the midst of the Eighteen Benedictions, his thoughts grew oppressive, forcing him into a net of temptation. He caught himself by his sidelocks, pulling at them with all his strength, to make physical pain obliterate his desires. He had placed chick peas into his boots to sting his soles. He got up and stood at the lectern to study. He read a section of the Mishnah and recited a chapter of the Psalms, turning his eyes away from the sun, the window, the garden, and the chirping birds on branches. The birds did as God willed, they did not wish to rule one another. A crumb of food, a drop of water were all they needed to sing to God from dawn to sunset, but he, Jochanan, wanted to rule his brethren; to place himself above the crowd. Grandfather is happy, Jochanan thought, he will soon leave his body entirely. He is already more in the world beyond than here. Jochanan began to nod and shake: "Lord Almighty, save me! Heavenly Father, help me, because I am in an abject condition." He went over to the bookcase, removed a book, closed his eyes, and opened it at random. It was a book of his grandfather's. He looked and read: ". . . And know ye that there exists another sort of sadness, the sorrow of those who talk it into themselves that they must rise to the highest mansion, and as soon as they meet with obstacles, they fall all the way down as it is written about Elisha the son of Abujah. He gazed behind the curtain, and was hurt. Because he saw how far the road was and how insignificant man, he grew afraid, and because of this fear became a heretic. For the root of heresy is fear, not the exalted fear but the fear

167

of a slave who likes to transcend responsibility and loses faith in his Master. A rabbi has said: 'Serve the Lord, but don't try to outdo others in serving Him.' "

Jochanan's eyes grew moist. Woe! Heavens! Grandfather actually had spoken to him through the book he had just opened at random! No, he would stop worrying about rank. He would simply be a Jew. Evil thoughts? Let them come, let them assault him. He would pay no attention to them. He would only study and pray . . .

The door opened and Tsipele came in. Jochanan raised his eyes momentarily. A woman, yes, but she was his wife, the mother of his child. Besides, she was not menstruating now. In a long full dress, a head-kerchief, with a silken shawl across her shoulders, she stood at the door.

Jochanan pulled his beard. "Well—"

"Jochanan, my father may come."

"Father-in-law? So—"

"A letter arrived."

"Well, that's fine."

"I brought you a pear."

Jochanan looked directly at her. Almost a child when he'd married her, she was now (may the Evil Eye spare her!) grown up. His mother (may she live long!) said Tsipele was a beauty. She smiled at him. She had a narrow face, large black eyes, an upturned upper lip. Her face exuded the modesty and amiability of those who are not tempted. In one hand she held a pear on a plate; in the other, a knife. "How can she not be tormented?" Jochanan wondered. "It isn't possible that she can control herself so well. Apparently, the evil passions are weaker in women. Or perhaps she is the reincarnation of a sainted soul who came down to earth to correct some small errors committed in a former existence." Jochanan remembered about the pear.

"Thanks, but I'm not hungry. Why should I be? I just ate breakfast."

"You don't look well. Mother-in-law says so, too."

"No one is as one looks."

"I don't mean that. You're thin—" Tsipele half laughed.

"Thin? So what? Must one be stout? It says in the Treatise of Abbot, to increase the flesh is to increase the worms."

"You're not old yet—"

"Does one know when the Day of Death will come? Well, put it down."

"Where?"

"Here, on the table. I'll wash my hands later."

Tsipele came closer. Because her dress was long and wide, one could not see exactly how she walked. She seemed to float. Although Jochanan had lived with her for a year and a half, she continued to amaze him. For all her youth, she was intelligent. The other women quarreled among themselves, but Tsipele got along with everyone. She took care of him. She brought him delicacies. She was modest in bed. She was a light sleeper. When he came to her, he spoke about the Torah, related stories of saints, and she heard him out patiently. He had been favored with a virtuous female.

"Jochanan, I want to ask you something."

"Ask."

"I hear that when your grandfather—one must not say it—you'll become the rabbi."

Jochanan grew paler than before.

"No, Tsipele."

"Why not? Don't you want it?"

"I am not worthy."

For a while they were both silent. Then Jochanan asked: "And would you want to be a rabbi's wife?"

Tsipele smiled. "Why should that bother me?"

Jochanan laughed. "And does it bother you that you are not the rabbi's wife?"

"No."

"Well, well, it's all nonsense. These honors aren't worth a pinch of snuff."

"When will you eat the pear?"

"Later."

Tsipele turned to go. Jochanan's eyes followed her. A child in a bonnet and dress, and a mother too. It was all the same to her, and that's the way it should be. Since these things were of no importance, why think about them? Jochanan was lost in meditation. Yes, she had the soul of a saint, a pure body. Satan had no power over such creatures. It was said of them, they were conceived and born in holiness. Jochanan experienced a powerful feeling of love for Tsipele, who although she lived in the lower world reached those heights that were beyond all material laws. He had no such rights. He must struggle with evil spirits, or they would tear him apart. "I'm sorry I didn't say something nice to her," Jochanan thought to himself. "Perhaps give her a coin?" He promised himself that he would praise her after the evening services when she served him his groats with chicken broth.

III

Reb Shimmon paced back and forth in his attic room. Dusk was falling. He glanced out of the window at the ripening fields of grain and potatoes. Cows grazed in the meadows along the river. The woods and clouds had begun to turn from blue to rose. One cloud shaped like a fish opened its huge mouth and with red teeth seemed to be snapping at a curly round cloudlet resembling a hedgehog. Suddenly the fishlike jaws dissolved, the teeth crumbled, and the hedgehog cloud, inflating itself, floated off. Reb Shimmon's eyes grew bright with anger. It went on up there too—they swallowed each other. These days Reb Shimmon was in agony, and at night he could not sleep. Wrath, he knew, was a sin, but he rose in the mornings as angry as when he went to bed. Did they really believe that they could dismiss him like a schoolboy? He had served them faithfully, and now a mere boy was to be made rabbi because it was rumored that he was a saint. In his rage Reb Shimmon cursed Jochanan, calling him fool, idiot, hypocrite. "I won't remain silent," Reb Shimmon mumbled. "I'll see that he's disgraced; I'll tear him up by the roots; when I get finished, there'll be nothing left of this court." Terrible thoughts came to him. Perhaps he should reject his faith altogether? "God forbid, am I out of my mind?" he asked himself. He imagined himself banging on the lectern in the prayer house on Yom Kippur eve and shouting, "Listen to me, there is no God. All is chaos."

Where did such blasphemy come from? He shuddered and begged God to forgive him. The sun went down, and the river became fiery. Crows cawed; the first stars appeared. "Well, I must say my evening prayers," Reb Shimmon mumbled. But he didn't go down to the house of prayer. For the first time in years, he felt no affection for people. They were all false and his enemies. He decided to pray alone, washed his hands, and started the psalm, "Happy is he," Then, stationing himself at the eastern wall, he recited the Eighteen Benedictions, but the words had become meaningless to him. He walked to the middle of the room and announced in a firm voice, "I don't care. I must do it, no matter what the consequences." He walked to his bureau, opened a drawer, and took out a sheet of paper, and after glancing at it, shoved it into his pocket.

"He's secluding himself also," Reb Shimmon thought as he walked into the corridor. "I'll talk frankly to him. There's been enough of this hide-and-seek." He pushed open a door and found Jochanan seated at a table, studying the "Two Tablets of the Covenant."

"Good evening, Jochanan."

"Good evening, Uncle."

"Aren't you going to the house of prayer? Are you already imitating the saints?"

"Saints? God forbid."

"How is it then that you pray alone?"

Jochanan didn't reply.

"All right, Jochanan." Reb Shimmon's tone of voice changed. "I'm putting my cards on the table."

"Sit down, Uncle."

"Why should I sit? I shouldn't speak perhaps, but why all the secrecy? I'm told you want to be rabbi." As he spoke, Reb Shimmon was astonished at his own words.

Jochanan raised his head. "No, that's untrue, Uncle."

"You want to be asked," Reb Shimmon shouted.

"No, Uncle. It will make no difference if I am asked. May Grandfather's health be good, but should he die, God forbid, you will succeed him."

"That's what I thought. But I hear that you're following in the footsteps of Absalom."

"No, Uncle."

"If you want the rabbinate, I'll not oppose you, but I hate intrigue. Absalom at least announced his intentions."

"There isn't a word of truth in it, Uncle."

"Will you swear to that?"

"Is it necessary?"

"Sign a statement."

"What kind of a statement?"

"Here." Reb Shimmon pulled out the sheet he had thrust into his pocket, and read. "I, Jochanan, the son of Reb Zadock, give my word that I will not consent to be rabbi after my sacred grandfather's death. Moreover, I will not hold court either in Marshinov or in any other city. My uncle, Reb Shimmon, promises to arrange for the support of myself and my family."

Reb Shimmon paused. "Sign!" he ordered.

"So be it."

"Here is a pen."

Jochanan dipped the pen, then seeing that it had picked up too much ink, wiped it on his skullcap. Standing, he wrote,

172

"These are the words of the lowly Jochanan, the son of the saint Rabbi Zadock, blessed be his name."

IV

The rabbi lingered for days, bloated, altered, exhausted. Waking, he recalled that he was Reb Shmaryah Gad of Marshinov, critically ill, close to death. "Have I at least been saying my prayers?" the rabbi wondered. "Are they putting my phylacteries on me?" His hands must be washed; he must tell the beadle. The rabbi attempted to speak but found no words. He wished to write a will designating Jochanan as his successor, but the thought slipped from his mind. There had formed within him a network of thoughts full of Torah, wisdom, and ultimate knowledge such as man never attained in this life. As it is written of the Almighty, "He is both the One who knows and the object of His knowledge," so it was with the rabbi. His thoughts did not come from the rabbi's brain but arose with the spontaneity and ease of spiritual things. The rabbi saw and heard angels and seraphim. He met his father, his grandfather, the sacred Jacob Jospeh, the Baal Shem. He ascended with them to the Palace of the Bird Nest in the Mansion of the Messiah, saw the heavenly Temple, heard the Levites singing and playing musical instruments. He conceived the meaning of many things at once: Jacob's ladder upon which the ministering angels climbed, the Throne of Glory, the Celestial Court of Judgment, the Original Man. The rabbi skirted Gehenna and discovered that Rabbi Nachman was right; Gehenna was shame. Renegade souls despised themselves because they had not served God. Some transmigrated; others were thrown into the sling, to be whirled continuously around the earth. Adam returned to Eden, where he again met Eve and partook of the fruit of the Tree of Knowledge. The snake no longer crawled on its belly. Since everything came from eternity, how could the devil exist? Time was a hallucination;

173

darkness, merely the border of light; Satan, the tool of God. Pain? There was no such thing as pain. One and many were the same. So were also determination and free will. Does the stomach hurt? An old garment tears. The soul needs new clothing. Does the body suffer? Is there such a thing as a body? All bodies are one. All worlds, one world. How could Cain kill Abel if good and evil were indistinguishable?

The rabbi opened his eyes. "Is it still today?" he inquired. No one answered his question and his eyelids closed. He laughed to himself. "What kind of a question is that? Is it still today? I'm talking like a child. Am I hungry? Thirsty? Am I getting better? Am I dying?" Black draperies closed before his eyes; snakes wriggled. "What do the demons want? I am already beyond their power. Am I in the realm of Nogah, good and evil mixed? No, it's Satan's band. They are coming at me disguised as frogs, lizards, skunks, vipers, with horns and snouts, with claws and tails, with elephant trunks and boar tusks. Mother, I'm afraid! Help me! Father, they want to destroy me! What sort of eye is this? Red as fire. Shabriri and Briri, leave me alone! God, rebuke Satan! Who are you? Namah? Machlath? Marry you? We are not fated for one another. Force? I'll scream for help! I have Hassidim! They'll stand up for me! Mendel, robbers have attacked me, murderers, demons! Father, it's good you are here! I'm in terrible danger! Drive them away! Dogs? They are not just dogs. They're the hounds of Egypt. It's evil, evil! They want to dethrone the Creator. Like the generation who built the Tower of Babel. Who created them? There was darkness before light. Sammael is primeval. The First of the Firsts. How is this possible? It's right. Here is Mother? A good Sabbath, Mother. Yes, Mother, I'm studying. I'm beginning the Mishnah. A bride? You be my bride. The Messiah has come already. All souls are one.

"Mother, something hurts me. My head? No, my heart. Let me go, Mother! I want to return—return!"

Mendel the beadle had left the room for a few minutes.

When he entered again, he found the rabbi dead. Mendel had
kept a feather ready, and put it to the rabbi's nostrils. It no
longer moved.

"Blessed be the true Judge . . . !"

v

There was commotion in the court. Everyone rushed to the
rabbi's chamber: Reb Shimmon, Reb Moshe, Temerel, the
rabbi's daughters-in-law. The windows were opened and the
prayer of the Justification of God's will was said. Members of
the Burial Society lifted the body of the rabbi and lit candles
near his head. The curtain of the Holy Ark draped the body.
Little clusters of mourners formed here and there. But Reb
Shimmon paced restlessly through the court. He had already
prepared telegrams to be sent to Warsaw, Lodz, Lublin, and
Pietrkow. A number of the Hassidim demanded that the funeral be held the following day, but Reb Shimmon scheduled
it twenty-four hours later, so as to permit a number of his closest friends to get to Marshinov. There was no sleep that night;
the court remained noisy; lights burned in all the rooms.
Mourners wailed, women threw their arms about each other
and lamented. Reb Shimmon saw that someone was at the station to meet every train, for people were arriving by the train-
load: rabbis, rich men, distinguished members of the community. The terminal was crammed with admirers coming to
attend the rabbi's funeral.

The next day there was no merchandise left to buy in the
stores. Every oven in every bakery was in use, wagonloads of
flour kept coming from the mill, messenger boys could be seen
running back and forth through the streets. Rumors spread: a
light had hovered above the rabbi's head all night; watchers
had observed wings fluttering over the corpse; it was noted
that the rabbi's lips trembled as if he were still reciting the
Torah. The barren women wailed with piercing voices. Some
fainted. The Burial Society had already prepared the shroud.

Reb Shimmon and Reb Moshe were arguing: should the rabbi be buried in his old prayer shawl with the gold ornaments or should he wear the new prayer shawl with the silver ornaments? In the midst of all this confusion, Reb Shimmon had found time to rummage among the rabbi's documents. If the rabbi had left a will, he wanted to be the first to see it. It had been the rabbi's habit to store his papers in quilts. There were many of them, filled with notes that he had written to himself. No paper of his had been thrown away. Looking for a will in this mess was like searching for a needle in a haystack. If the rabbi had left a last testament, Reb Shimmon was unable to find it.

Though Reb Shimmon was unquestionably right in maintaining that the longer the funeral was postponed, the larger would be the crowd, pious Jews began to object. A corpse must not be left unburied too long, particularly in summer. To do so was sacrilege. Early on the second morning after the rabbi's death, purification began. The body was washed with an ablution ladle and rubbed with egg yolk. Once again the Hassidim argued. Who was to give the funeral oration? Who deliver the first eulogy? Each one of the rabbis was proposed by his adherents. Particularly fortunate were those who carried the bier. Thousands of Jews followed the body to the graveyard. Marshinov's streets were black with people. The air was filled with the lamentation of women. The crowd jammed into the cemetery. Some stood on tombstones, others climbed trees or sat on the branches. The schoolboys climbed the highest of all. The sacred body had been dressed in shrouds and a cowl and wrapped in a prayer shawl; a twig of myrtle had been placed between the corpse's fingers; there were shards on his eyelids. A body was nothing but a body.

The sons said Kaddish, Reb Moshe's sidelocks shook with his sobbing, and Reb Shimmon, raising his voice, choked back his tears. Temerel cried out, "Father," and leaned forward as if about to faint. Her daughters had to support her.

"Where is Jochanan? We want Jochanan," Hassidim

shouted as they drank brandy. "*Mazel tov*, Rabbi." Jochanan was as white as chalk; he shook his head from side to side. "No, no!" He pointed to Reb Shimmon. "My uncle is the rabbi."

Reb Shimmon's retinue gathered about him. One of his followers held a bottle of brandy; another, a bag with egg cookies and a tray with glasses. "To your health, Rabbi, to your health, Rabbi!" they shouted to Reb Shimmon.

"Jochanan! Jochanan!" The voices grew louder. "*Mazel tov*, Jochanan, *mazel tov*, Rabbi!"

Reb Shimmon turned pale and because of this his beard seemed blacker than ever. "It's insolence! Insolence and impudence!" he muttered. "Gentiles! Libertines! Heathens!"

"Jochanan! Jochanan!" they shouted. All were shouting, even those who had called for Reb Shimmon. Jochanan struggled. He did not wish to drink the toasts. He hid his face in his hands. They wrangled with him as if he were a schoolboy. They tore at him, pulled him. Boys and young men fell upon him: "Rabbi, Rabbi!" they cried. "The Rabbi of Marshinov!" This time Temerel actually fainted. The Chmielev rabbi, Reb Moshe, pushed his way to Jochanan. A path was cleared through the congestion. His voice broke with sobs. "Jochanan, the people want you!"

"No, no."

"Jochanan, you can't defy the whole world!"

"No, no, I don't wish it," Jochanan cried.

"Jochanan! Jochanan!"

Reb Shimmon lurched forward. He clenched his fists. "Murderers! You're drawing my blood!"

Mendel, the beadle, suddenly emitted a wild screech like the bellow of a bull. "Jews, I bear witness before God that the rabbi, may he rest in peace, wanted Jochanan as his successor. May I not live to hear the ram's horn of the Messiah if I'm lying."

"Liar! Fraud! Disgrace to your religion!" Reb Shimmon whined.

"If I lie, Reb Shimmon, may my children lie here!" said Reb Mendel, pointing to the freshly dug grave.

Everyone grew quiet. A thin wail spread among the women. Suddenly, a crow cawed. Reb Shimmon advanced to Jochanan. "Jochanan, *mazel tov!* You are the rabbi!"

And he handed him the document that he had signed.

Jochanan wanted to answer, but he could not. He bent over. He almost fell and had to be supported. His face had changed; it was red and bathed in tears. His wet sidelocks clung to his beard.

"Uncle Shimmon!" he gasped.

"Jochanan, you are the rabbi!" Reb Shimmon shouted. "Good luck to you!"

He turned and walked away. His retinue followed.

VI

In Jampol and the surrounding areas, two items of gossip were constantly being repeated. The first was that Calman would marry Clara, Daniel Kaminer's daughter; the second, that the duke had renewed the lease on the manor for a period of ten years, not to Calman alone, but to Calman in partnership with Clara. Jampol now had something to talk about, laugh at, and mock. Clara had been seen walking, arm-in-arm, with the duke. There were witnesses who claimed that they had seen them kissing under a tree.

Reb Menachem Mendel had been thinking of leaving the rabbinate of Jampol. But when he heard this story about Clara, he decided that he could not remain in Jampol another day. Calman, his in-law, was his only protector. But if Calman became Daniel Kaminer's son-in-law and married a hussy who went about with her head uncovered, he, Reb Menachem Mendel, could no longer accept his protection. Reb Menachem Mendel, usually calm, became unmanageable. Tirza Perl, his wife, and Mirale, his daughter, had never seen him like this before. Snatching up his prayer shawl and phylacteries, he started toward the door, ready to go to the railroad station on foot. Tirza Perl began to wring her hands.

"What kind of madness is this?" she asked.

"I am going to Warsaw! It's the end of the world! It must mean that the Messiah is coming."

"What will you do in Warsaw? We don't even have an apartment!"

"The Almighty will not forsake me."

Wiping a tear with her apron, Tirza Perl agreed. Jampol meant only heartbreak and shame. Besides, here Mirale was already considered a spinster at twenty-two. Tirza Perl could not show her face on the street. Warsaw, at least, was a large city. Ezriel was in Warsaw. Brother and sister might find an apartment together. Mirale went to the manor to see her sister-in-law Shaindel. Shaindel, whose eyes were red from weeping, fell upon Mirale, kissed her, and began to whimper.

"You know everything already?" Mirale asked.

"I can't understand it, I can't understand it!" Shaindel said. "Father is killing himself—without a knife!"

After Shaindel had wept and dried her tears, Mirale told her that her father was leaving Jampol and that she would go with him.

14

Calman wanted the wedding to be a quiet one, in the home of a Warsaw rabbi. He was a widower and she a widow; why make a fuss? But Clara had already decided to have the wedding at her aunt's apartment. Clara wished to show off her expensive gown and valuable jewelry. She had a wedding dress stored away that was practically new. Since she'd had no children, she decided she could wear white. She engaged musicians and a wedding jester who knew enough of the language to slip in some Polish jokes. Clara wanted many guests, but she had no relatives in Warsaw besides her aunt, and few acquaintances. Calman, certainly, had no one to invite. Grain the pharmacist and his wife, David Sorkess and his wife Sonya, Morris Shalit, and Tamara would, of course, come from Jampol. Mrs. Frankel's distant relatives, the girls who worked in her shop, the women who had once worked for her as milliners, their husbands, their friends and acquaintances would have to make up the rest of the list. People whom Calman had never heard of would eat, drink, and be merry at his wedding.

It wasn't easy for Calman to leave the manor for the trip to Warsaw. The Sabbath following the Fast of the Ninth of Ab fell at threshing time. Advance plans had to be made for planting the winter wheat. In Calman's forest, trees were being chopped down from early morning until sunset. No matter how diligent the guards were, lumber was always disappearing. Calman had not wanted to re-hire employees who had slandered him after he had discharged them, when he gave up his lumber business. He therefore imported help from other cities. The result was agitation and disputes. Half of Jampol owed its living to Calman, but all of Jampol cursed him. The tailor-journeymen had even composed a jingle about him that the seamstresses and shoemakers sang. The lyrics began:

> *Calman, the man of money,*
> *Found a girl as sweet as honey.*
> *Fool he was to marry her,*
> *For off she ran with an officer . . .*

Yes, Calman had already learned that envy was the people's worst trait. Even in the midst of wedding plans, plans for building a house of prayer, a ritual bath on the estate, and moving into the manor itself, he often longed to drop his responsibilities, his property, his enemies, his false friends, and settle somewhere in some village, some forest, or in a strange city where nobody knew him and he knew no one. Who could tell? Clara might even go with him. However much the people of Jampol slandered him, they literally pelted Clara with slime from head to toe.

Both Jews and Gentiles resented the fact that the Count was being forced to move out of his own house at Clara's insistence. Every day, every hour, there were new insults. In his store in Jampol, anonymous letters were left by individuals who allegedly had seen Clara with every officer, every sergeant major, every soldier in the barracks. Calman knew that it was unwise to show Clara such trash, but he couldn't keep the letters to himself. Her eyes grew fierce. "Their gall is spilling over, is it? It's eating them up, is it? I hope they all have epileptic fits!"

On the very day that Calman left for Warsaw to be married, he received a letter from his son-in-law, Jochanan, the

Marshinov rabbi. It was written in Yiddish, not Hebrew, and read as follows:

> To My Honorable Father-in-law, the Famous Philanthropist, Reb Calman,
>
> First, I want to inform you that we are all in good health. Praised be the name of God, I hope to hear the same from you and yours. And let us pray that we are saved in this world and the world to come. Second, I would like to inform you that your daughter, my wife, has heard some rumors that have caused me great anguish, and although I do not know if they are true, I would like to remind you that such matters should be considered carefully. The Talmud says that a man's second marriage is ordained in heaven according to his merits. I don't wish to insult you. I am interested only in your welfare. It is a great sin to give a Jewish daughter a bad name and everything should be investigated thoroughly. We have other troubles here, too. I never wanted to take my grandfather's place. I would have left Marshinov altogether if my mother had not prevailed upon me to stay. The Almighty should take pity upon us all. Best regards to everybody and greetings from your daughter, who longs to see you soon.
>
> Your son-in-law, who is young and poor, a threshold to be stepped upon by the feet of the sages,
>
> > The Lowly Jochanan, the Son of the Saintly Rabbi Zadock of Blessed Memory.

Calman read on and his eyes grew wet, but he said to himself: "It is too late!"

11

Usually, when Calman went to Warsaw, he stayed at Reb Ezekiel Wiener's, Mayer Joel's father's house, but Reb Ezekiel

Wiener was angry at Calman. Who wasn't angry at him? Even Shaindel, his favorite daughter, was furious at him. Calman stayed at a hotel. Since the groom must not come alone to the wedding, he arranged that David Sorkess and Morris Shalit accompany him to Mrs. Frankel's apartment. They were to call for him at about nine in the evening (the days had again begun to grow shorter), but Calman's watch said a quarter of ten and his attendants had not yet appeared. Calman sat in his room. Even though he disliked the taste of tobacco, he lit one of the cigars he had brought to give away as presents. He was startled by every footstep that passed, but no one came. Doors opened and closed. Men and women conversed in the corridors, murmured, giggled. Everyone in the hotel knew who he was and for whom he was waiting. Had he given them the wrong address? Or had Clara changed her mind at the last moment? Had something happened, some tragedy? The minute hand was already nearing ten, and still no one appeared. Calman could no longer remain seated. He began to pace back and forth. His boots squeaked. "Changed her mind, changed her mind!" he thought or mumbled. "Simply wanted to disgrace me! Who can tell? Perhaps it was all a joke? Everything is possible, everything is possible! They've made a fool of me. They've swindled me out of my property. They'll all have fun at my expense." Calman knew that it wasn't so, that it couldn't be so. Clara wouldn't go to such extremes. Daniel Kaminer was no longer a youngster. But new suspicions sprang up every minute. Maybe she wasn't a widow at all, and her husband still lived. Perhaps he would appear and break up the wedding. Perhaps Clara suddenly decided to become converted. If Miriam Lieba could commit such a sin, why shouldn't Clara be capable of it? "I knew all along that things wouldn't go smoothly!" Calman said to himself. A spark fell from his cigar and he imagined that a fire had broken out at Mrs. Frankel's. It had consumed the entire apartment. Everyone had been burned to a crisp. "I shouldn't have defied the

183

whole world! Jochanan is a saint, and when a saint is annoyed, it's not good. God Almighty, help me, help me!" Calman began to pray. "Not for my sake, but for the sake of—"

Calman heard footsteps. The door opened. There stood David Sorkess and Morris Shalit in top hats, canes in their hands—two little "Germans"—smelling of perfume.

"Here's the bridegroom!" David Sorkess cried out, hoarse with drink.

"Pridegroom, I mean bridegroom!" Morris Shalit shouted arrogantly.

Usually these men spoke to Calman with respect, for they both owed him their living. But now that he was about to become Clara's husband, he had fallen even in their eyes. From their frivolity, Calman guessed that they looked on the whole thing as a Purim prank.

"What took you so long?"

"The bride is adorning herself!" And both of them burst out laughing.

Calman went down with them. There was a slight opening of doors, revealing half faces of women. A droshky with two horses and an ornate harness waited outside. Children flocked around it. When Calman appeared, they began to shout: "Hurrah! Hurrah!" In the street, everyone seemed to know where he was going. Calman, his head bowed, sat between his two attendants on the upholstered seat. "Why are they so perfumed?" he asked himself. He was about to marry a modern woman, a Russian, but at the same time he felt contemptuous of worldly conduct. Why did they fuss so much? Why were they so gay? They wouldn't live forever.

At the gate of Mrs. Frankel's house, Calman saw droshkies, people in party clothes, obviously wedding guests. Climbing the steps, Calman felt like an ox about to be slaughtered. "Maybe it is not too late to escape?" he thought. He heard music, shouting, women giggling. The door to Mrs. Frankel's apartment stood ajar. Heat emanated from within, an odor of flesh. The orchestra had begun to play, the jester was performing, couples danced. They led him inside as if to a ball. All faces were laughing, all eyes shone. Perfume assailed Calman. His head began to whirl. It was crowded here, terribly warm. The naphtha lamps were dazzling. Some of the guests openly mocked Calman, others congratulated him, pressed his hand. The rabbi and the beadle from the Warsaw rabbinate were already there. The rabbi sat down to inscribe the marriage contract with a steel pen. He asked: "What's the bride's name?"

"Clara," said Daniel Kaminer.

"Clara is not a Jewish name. What was the name given her when you were called before the Holy Scroll?"

"She's named after her grandmother, Keila Rebecca."

"Then why didn't you say so?"

Despite the confusion, everything went according to the law. Calman was helped into a white robe, to remind him of the day of death. Four men raised the poles that supported the marriage canopy. The others carried twisted candles in their hands. Calman was led under the canopy and Clara was brought in, dressed in white silk with a tulle net over her hair. Her face was uncovered; she smiled at Calman. Saying the benediction over a cup of wine, the rabbi gave it to Calman and Clara. Clara extended her index finger and Calman placed the wedding ring on it, saying "Behold, thou art consecrated." The rabbi read the marriage contract in Aramaic, which Calman did not understand. Here and there he caught a word that was similar in Hebrew.

Oddly enough, when the rabbi began to recite the second benediction, the same girls and women who had been laughing impudently grew silent. Here and there, a woman wiped away a tear. It is not child's play to be born, to marry, to bring forth generations, to grow old, to die. These are matters no jester's witticisms can belittle. Calman's eyes misted over. Did Zelda, may she rest in peace, know what he was doing? Was her soul hovering nearby? Was he really committing a sin, or would something good come of this?

The canopy was removed. A tumult followed—congratulations and kissing. Clara and her aunt hugged one another, shaking back and forth. The men had already started drinking brandy and eating ginger cakes. Cherry brandy and liqueur were served to the women. The rabbi congratulated Calman. Afterward, Daniel Kaminer took the groom by the arm and, in his Lithuanian accent, half seriously, half jokingly, advised Calman as a father-in-law and as a friend. Calman too was served a drink. Clara, having embraced her aunt, kissed Celina, Tamara Shalit, Sonya Sorkess, Itka Grain, and then approached Calman.

"Well, don't you have anything to say? My husband!"

Calman could not speak. His eyes brimmed with tears and he could not quite see her. Finally he regained his voice. "Let us not forget God!" he said.

III

Business had taught Calman how easy it was to make a mistake. One figured and figured and then forgot that two and two make four. In accounting for the very smallest expenses, one sometimes forgot the largest. This was exactly what happened to Calman. He had been living at such a pace, had been involved in so many transactions, that he had forgotten the most important thing. Clara had promised to go to the ritual bath before the wedding, but Calman had not asked her whether she had kept her word. Sitting at the wedding banquet, he was reminded of other things that he could not understand, having missed them in the first place. Mrs. Frankel had told him that she bought meat at a kosher butcher's. But what about the salting and soaking of the meat? And what about her kitchen? Had she been careful not to mix the dairy dishes with the meat dishes? Did she consult an authority when in doubt? Dared he, Calman, eat here? Could one expect a woman with an uncovered head to keep a kosher home? He saw no evidence of respect for God here. If that were so, he,

Calman, might be eating forbidden food at his own wedding. And if that weren't enough, he would be lying this very night, God forbid, with a woman who had not made her ablutions. Calman's stomach felt hollow.

"Can it be that I am mad?" he thought. "Yes, I am in their power, in the company of Satan!" Calman choked on every bite. "What have I done? How is it possible? The Evil one must have been deceiving me! This means that all the accusations against me are true!"

The musicians played on; the jester in mixed Yiddish-Polish entertained the guests with Polish theater and cabaret jokes. The rooms were filled with noise and laughter. But Calman sat there, depressed. "Is there any way out? What must I do, according to the law?" Calman knew the answer: he must stand up and run as if a fire were chasing him. He must fast, repent, and torture himself for the sins he had committed. He recalled the words of the Rod of Punishment: How hot are the fires of the seven hells and how many metamorphoses must one bear until one can come even to Gehenna! For a moment he rose, as if to leave the table and escape. But he sat down again. Ezriel's words came to mind: "The Jews have their Torah, the Christians have their own laws. Did anyone see Moses receive the Torah on Mount Sinai? It is all legend."

"Well, well, I'm doing fine and becoming a heretic to boot," Calman thought to himself, astonished that the Evil Spirit had so swiftly steered him to the abyss.

"I must escape," he told himself, but he could not compel himself to move. He remained sitting, sipping his chicken soup, chewing the meat, listening to the peppery jokes of the jester, looking at the women with their bare arms, naked throats, powdered faces, hearing their wanton shrieks. Clara did not remain in her seat next to Calman. She was constantly being summoned elsewhere. New guests kept arriving with wedding presents as if this were a marriage between a bachelor and a young girl. Calman stared at them from beneath lowered brows. Who were they? How did Mrs. Frankel know so many people? Why were they so excited? And why had Clara wanted such a crowd? When Clara returned to him, Calman thought he had never seen her look so handsome. Her skin glowed. She wore as much jewelry as a queen. Pouring some wine for him, she said, "Drink, this is a wedding!"

And in worldly fashion she clinked his glass with hers.

"Is it kosher wine, at least?" Calman asked, ashamed of his own words. No longer confident, they sounded apprehensive and insincere.

"Kosher, kosher! Everything is kosher!" Clara scolded good-naturedly, winking as she did so. Calman understood what she meant: "*You* aren't such a saint."

Calman drained the glass and she poured him another. He recalled a verse from the Scriptures: "And wine that maketh glad the heart of man." His head reeled, his knees felt heavy. "Well, what of it? Gehenna was for people too, not dogs," he told himself. "According to the holy book, everyone ends up on a bed of nails, anyhow . . ." He began to feel a kind of resentment against the Creator. Zelda had been a pious woman, and how had she been rewarded? Work, sickness, a short life. And the schoolchildren that Chmielnicki had buried alive? They hadn't even known the taste of sin . . . Even according to Ecclesiastes, human beings and animals are the same. The dead know nothing.

By the time the crowd began to disperse, it was daybreak. Clara had rented rooms in a nearby hotel. A droshky waited outside to take them the short distance. People were rising to start the day, but Calman was going to a Gentile hotel with an unpious woman. Rows of keys hung on the wall behind the dozing desk clerk. Jerking awake, he gave the key to a servant. The marble stairway was carpeted. Clara's arm was on Calman's as they walked up. Skillfully, the servant carried the two valises, unlocked the door, and let the couple into the dusky suite. He lit a lamp and Clara tipped him. The room was large, the ceiling high. It was strangely cold. Clara opened the door to the other room. Calman thought she seemed very much at home. Before closing the door behind her, she said, "The toilet is in the hall, to the left."

When Calman returned, he found Clara in a lacy silk nightgown, her hair down, her feet in slippers. She had apparently put on fresh perfume. She reminded Calman of the queens and princesses that were engraved on banknotes and medallions. Suddenly she said in Polish: "Well, get undressed."

"Yes, certainly."

Calman was ashamed to undress before so grand a lady. Putting out the light, he began removing his new boots, which burned his soles, even though they cost fifteen rubles and were made of kid. He remembered not having said his nightly prayers, but he couldn't see where to wash his hands in the dark. He closed his eyes. Lust for Clara had faded away, and only fear remained.

15

The attic apartment of 19 Krochmalna Street, consisting of
two rooms and a kitchen, was inhabited by Todros Bendiner,
a sexton's son, who had returned to Poland after having spent
several years wandering around Berlin, jobless and hungry.
Bendiner's vagabond life had ended in illness; finally he had
settled down in Warsaw as a baker. He had ruptured himself
kneading the heavy dough and now only did such light work
as stoking the ovens, sweeping the bakery floor, and running
errands. Even though Todros Bendiner had six children, he
partitioned off an alcove in his small apartment and rented it
out.

Ezriel knew a Hebrew teacher who recommended the
room to him, and he decided to take it. Rytza Leah, Todros's
wife, served Ezriel his meals, and he paid ten gulden a week
for room and board. The tiny room had a window which
looked out on a courtyard. Ezriel's furniture consisted of a
bed, a table, one chair, and a bookcase.

As he sat at his table studying, his eyes would stray from his
book now and then to stare out into the courtyard. The building was inhabited by the very poor. The people disposed of
their slops out of the windows; there was no drainage in the
court, and deep puddles formed. Garbage was heaped high
around the refuse box and the stench was so strong that it rose
to Ezriel on the third floor.

The courtyard served both as workshop and marketplace. A dyer used it to carry on his trade; an upholsterer could be seen busily stuffing chairs and sofas. There was even a stall with cows, and women carried empty jugs and pans into the courtyard and took them away filled with milk still warm from the udder. Periodically the janitor appeared to feed potato peelings to his goat. Women hung out their wash to dry and aired clothing and bedding, beating out the dust with heavy sticks. Often the sound of animals and chattering girls would mingle with voices chanting the Torah, for there was also a Hassidic study house located in the building.

It was Monday, customarily the day for beggars to collect alms, and a tattered host swarmed through the courtyard gates and into the building. The beggars trudged up and down stairs, knocked on apartment doors, and exhibited crippled limbs. In a cheder located in the tenement, some of the children recited the Pentateuch. Most of the youngsters, however, were outdoors playing with sticks and strings and bits of broken dishes. A group of them were amusing themselves by tormenting a boy with rickety limbs, trying to knock his hat off.

Ezriel sat with Malinin's *Book of Problems* open before him. The problem he was considering involved a cattle dealer who had sold half of his oxen, a third of his sheep, and a quarter of his calves. "Well, if you want to get ahead, you've got to sweat," Ezriel remarked to himself, imitating the tone of his tutor Belkin. The small table at which he sat was covered with textbooks and dictionaries. Ezriel read, listening with one ear to what was going on outside. A candle burned in one of the windows, apparently at the head of a corpse. In these flats there lived the paralyzed, the blind, the mute, the insane, those for whom there was no room in institutions. Occasionally a woman in labor could be heard screaming in pain. People wandered about in the dark cellars, where mice scurried around even at midday. Work went on from early morning until late at night. Ezriel had long since learned that the harder people worked, the less they earned.

"How can it be otherwise," Ezriel mumbled to himself, "when it's all a play of blind forces? Matter and energy . . . the survival of the fittest. Justice? No, justice is impossible in such a universe. If there is no God, there is no sin. It's all a jungle."

Rytza Leah entered.

"Three letters for you."

"Three? Thank you very much."

Two were from Jampol—one from Shaindel and one from his parents. The third letter came from someone called Justina Malewska and was postmarked Warsaw. The envelope was blue and the address was written in an ornate hand. Inside the envelope was a sheet of matching paper. It read as follows, in Polish:

> Esteemed Mister E. Babad,
>
> I have just returned from Paris, where I made the acquaintance of your sister-in-law, the Countess Maria Jampolska. Knowing that my father has business dealings with your father-in-law, she asked me to convey her regards to you. I have just learned your address. I am generally at home until noon, and can also be reached evenings. I am a Wallenberg. I hope that we will meet soon. Best regards.

Ezriel read the letter over many times, but it did not occur to him at first that the Countess Maria Jampolska was Miriam Lieba. He now tore open the other envelopes and learned from Shaindel that a letter had come from Wallenberg's daughter which she was sending on to him. Shaindel also wrote that Yosele—Uri Joseph—was well and a smart boy, asked a great many questions and missed his daddy, and she, Shaindel, also wished it were time for him to come home on vacation. She had many other things to say; in fact, she covered several sheets, writing on both sides and along the margins for good measure. The third was a joint letter from his father, mother, and Mirale. In Hebrew, his father wrote that he could no longer take the insinuations of the Jampol elders and wanted to move to Warsaw. He had been told that many rabbis not officially employed by the community were able to earn a livelihood in the big city. Perhaps Ezriel could find a flat for him in a Jewish neighborhood? Was a rabbi by chance needed on Krochmalna Street?

His mother's postscript was full of anger: "I can no longer live among these ruffians. They make our lives miserable. Jampol is another Sodom . . ." Mirale had added two lines: "Ezriel, save us from this slime. Your sister, Mirale."

Ezriel shoved his books aside. Such fanatics! He could no longer remain cooped up in this narrow little room. He had to go out into the street. The Countess Maria Jampolska of Paris was his sister-in-law. Wallenberg's daughter invited him to her home. His father was coming to settle in Warsaw for good. Time did not stand still. Ezriel began to look over the sheet-draped garments hanging on the wall and decided to put on his navy-blue jacket. He would buy himself a new collar, and he would trim his beard as well. Luckily, the laundress had brought back his wash. He wondered if he should visit Madame Malewska that evening. No, tomorrow would be better. Picking up his copy of Euclid, Ezriel went outdoors and found the June day was sunny and warm. He walked down the refuse-strewn stairs and out into Krochmalna Street. It too was filled with noise and bustle. Slops were being thrown from open doors and filth ran down the gutters; a window opened and garbage flew out. There were many bakeries on the street and the chimneys belched smoke. The stables attracted flies. The street was alive with a thousand activities. Cobblers sat outside on their benches, mending shoes. Women seated on stools and doorsteps nursed their babies. A gang of urchins followed a mute, chanting: "Dumbbell!" Couples quarreled, and neighbors sought to make peace between them. Ezriel made his way to the ruins of the Mirowska barracks. The barracks, which should have been torn down completely as relics of the old Polish rule, instead formed the center of a mass of peasants' carts, dray wagons, and droshkies, for this neighborhood was one great market dealing in fruit, vegetables, and meat. Leaving Ziabia Street, Ezriel entered the Saxony Gardens. Because of the warm spring weather, the park was almost as crowded as the rest of the city. A charitable society was holding a lottery opposite the stand where mineral water was sold. Benches had been set up and tents erected. A poster announced that among the items to be raffled off was a milch cow. Children rolled hoops, played ball. Adults played a game called "extra," in which a ball was thrown from one player to the other, while a third, the "runner," tried to intercept it. The Russians had banned *palant* and other games that were specifically Polish.

Ezriel tried to read Euclid, but his desire to study suddenly left him. He began to stroll back and forth. For a while he remained standing at the pond. Boys in sailor suits and girls dressed up like little ladies threw crumbs to the swans. The nurses and governesses addressed them in Polish and French. Here there were no Jews in long capotes or women with bonnets and wigs. The men wore straw hats or an occasional top hat or derby. Unlike the unkempt beards of the Jews, theirs were trimmed into points, spades, wedges, their mustaches curled up like springs or jutted straight out stiff as wire. The young wore their soft shirt collars open over their jackets— Slowacki fashion—in the manner of the famous poet. But the older people, although it was summer, had on stiff collars and broad neckties. Everyone seemed stylish. Light trousers went with dark jackets, overcoats were worn or carried, shoes were polished to a high gloss, and canes were silver- or bone-handled. The gymnasium and university students walked about in gilt-buttoned uniforms. Ladies' hats looked like plates laden with flowers and fruits, and most of them had veils as well. Dresses were tight-waisted, beribboned, and pleated; gloves were almost elbow-length; parasols and fans blazed with colors. Lovers walked arm in arm, smiled into each other's eyes, hid in shaded paths. Everything here had a worldly glow: the fountain, the greenhouses, the flower beds. Bearded, white-aproned Russians carried ice-cream casks on their heads. There was a confectionery in the park, and a dairy, where young people drank sour milk. Ezriel again sat down on a bench and enmeshed himself in Euclidean theorems, but he could not concentrate.

How should he behave tomorrow at Justina Malewska's? Should he kiss her hand? Pay her a compliment? Should he address her as Madame or Gracious Lady, or Honorable Lady? What should he do if he were offered food? Should he accept it? Or refuse? How long should he stay? Should he extend his hand first? Or wait until she offered hers? Did he need a calling-card? What if he had to meet her husband, relatives, friends? How should he address them? Ezriel shook his head. He had changed! A few years before, he had been a real man and never had to demean himself. Now suddenly he was dependent, inferior. It would mean years of study for him to master Russian, Latin, Greek. So many languages and subjects were needed in order to finish the seven grades and earn a diploma. He must learn worldly manners, choose the right profession, and after all that he would still be nothing but a persecuted Jew . . . How odd, that the future world was easier by far than this one. In it, there was one reckoning, God. Here one was forced to consider countless directors, inspectors, laws, regulations, rules of etiquette, forms—a code far more complex than the Shulhan Aruk, the book containing the Jewish laws.

Ezriel sat there, absorbed in thought. Someone tapped him on the shoulder. He trembled, recognizing Mr. Wallenberg, whose office he had once visited.

"Pardon me, aren't you Mr. Jacoby's son-in-law?"

Ezriel stood up. "Mr. Wallenberg!"

"Yes. I was strolling through the park when I saw you, sitting deep in thought . . . I recognized you at once—"

"Oh, it is an honor for me! Only today I received a letter from your daughter—"

"I know, I know. We were speaking of you the other day.

Your sister-in-law, the Countess, met my daughter. A small town, this world, eh? How is your father-in-law?"

"All right, thank you."

"I believe you already have a child?"

"Yes, a little boy."

"Well, that's fine. It's been a while since I've seen your father-in-law, but I think I'll soon be doing business with him again. That is—if conditions permit. Negotiations are in progress to build another railroad, rather a large project, but so far no final decisions have been made. Don't say anything to him yet. An honest man, a responsible man, but old-fashioned. . . . My daughter tells me that the Countess is a beauty, though in terrible straits. You'll find out about it from her. I see that you've given up wearing a caftan."

"Yes, I'm studying."

"You're doing the right thing. The first time I saw you I knew you were a sensible young man. Where have you been hiding all this time? I told you once that I was prepared to help you."

"Oh, thank you, I know that you have no time."

"True, but one doesn't live for oneself alone. Come to see me. I've made it a habit to walk three-quarters of an hour each day. One feels confined in an office. This summer I intend to visit Carlsbad. I have a villa and some property on the Vistula. My family is moving there soon. I hear your mother-in-law died."

"Yes, quite some time ago."

"I know. I sent your father-in-law my condolences. What are your plans?"

"I hope to get my degree and study medicine."

"Why medicine?"

"I don't know myself."

"Well, doctors are needed too. Jews like doctors. A Jew will skip a meal but buy medicine. They *are* sick, as a matter of fact. Diabetes is especially prevalent among them, and consumption as well. Where are you studying?"

196

"Privately, with tutors."

"I can help you. The chief inspector of all intermediate schools in Russian Poland is a friend of mine. Generally, I don't approve of using influence—I believe in the honest way. But every rule has its exceptions. Are you on bad terms with your father-in-law?"

"No, we're not on bad terms."

"He isn't angry that you've removed your caftan?"

"He's happy I haven't shaved off my beard."

"A compromise, eh? I understand. What are you doing this evening?"

"Nothing special."

"Then why not come along with me? I'll only stay in the office about half an hour. Have supper with us. My daughter will be there too, and she'll tell you about your sister-in-law, and you can tell me all about your studies. I'd like to help someone. Why shouldn't it be you—for your father-in-law's sake, and for yours too, of course."

"I don't know how to thank you, but—"

"Why 'but'?"

"I'm not properly dressed."

"You are decently dressed. Clean—that's the main thing. What does one expect of a student? Come! You won't have to eat pork. You aren't religious, after all, are you? God doesn't care what you eat. All He asks is that you love your fellow man, isn't that so?" And Mr. Wallenberg, to show off, chanted in a Polish-accented Hebrew: "Thou shalt love thy neighbor as thyself . . ."

11

Who could have foretold that Ezriel would be riding in a carriage that very day! From the window he looked out at Warsaw. To his left were the Saxony Gardens. In the park, an obelisk like a huge finger pointed at the sky. Soon the carriage turned into Krakow Avenue. King Zygmunt's monument and the castle where a Russian governor-general ruled instead of a Polish king loomed in the distance. They passed Berg Street, named for the regent who had helped suppress Poland. Polish history permeated every cobblestone, every brick, but Russian was the language on all store and street signs. The sidewalks were crowded. In the gutter, among the carriages, wagons, and droshkies, a horse-drawn omnibus pressed forward—on its way from the Vienna depot to Praga. The carriage reached the wealthier section of the city. The farther they went, the lower the houses became and the greater the spaces between them. After Jerusalem Avenue there were villas, gardens, and even orchards with fruit trees. Many Lithuanian nobles, exiled to Poland after the Insurrection of 1863, lived in this neighborhood. Mr. Wallenberg's villa, located near Hozia Street, was surrounded by a garden. A watchman opened the gate, a stableboy in livery came out to tend to the horses. A servant opened the front door, bowed, and took Ezriel's hat. Ezriel was dazzled by the splendor. The parquet floors shone; paintings in carved and gilded frames hung on the walls; the lamps were decorated with crystal prisms which reflected the colors of the rainbow; earthen urns contained palms, fig trees, and all sorts of exotic plants. The rugs were thick. Mr. Wallenberg led Ezriel into a salon and introduced him to a gray-haired lady and several young men and women. Ezriel kissed the elderly lady's hand and bowed to the others. Mr. Wallenberg spoke in a deep, resonant voice. "This is Calman Jacoby's son-in-law. Just imagine—I recognized him at the Saxony Gardens . . . Here is my daughter, Justina, who wrote to you . . ."

Justina Malewska was small and dark, somewhat resembling the women in Japanese prints. Her upswept coiffure looked like a wig. Her eyes shone, keen and merry. Pearls glowed at her throat, diamonds sparkled in her earlobes. She extended a soft hand with pointed fingers covered with rings. She looked at Ezriel with mocking familiarity.

"Isn't that a strange coincidence? I write you a letter, and my father meets you in the park. My meeting with your sister-in-law, the Countess, was also a coincidence. I'll discuss the details with you later. One thing I can tell you now—she is very unhappy."

"Why?"

"A thousand reasons. The Count is completely mad. The Polish colony received him as a hero, but he has antagonized everyone. He associates with all sorts of charlatans and adventurers. All doors are closed to him now."

Madame Malewska hesitated, fanning herself.

"I'll be frank with you: he drinks. Perpetually."

"Oh."

"Everyone adores the Countess, but because of her husband, they've stopped inviting her to their homes. She's not well, either. She had a difficult delivery; she was close to death. I am concerned for her health."

"How is the child?"

"A little angel!"

The door opened and the maid announced dinner. Ezriel saw how the men offered their arms to the ladies. He did not know what to do. Madame Malewska smiled, and took his arm.

"The gentleman has no objection?"

"I am deeply honored," Ezriel replied.

The meal lasted a long time. Meat, vegetables, and compotes were served. Madame Malewska discreetly showed Ezriel how to conduct himself. He sat with a napkin tucked between his lapels, ate foods he had never tasted (the plates were decorated with pictures of Napoleon), and drank dry wine. Everything was guided by rules, each gesture was deliberate. Ashamed of his ignorance of etiquette, Ezriel determined to remember everything. His shyness seemed to have disappeared. The wine put him in a gay mood. He bantered with Madame Malewska and she laughed with her small mouth.

"The Countess spoke very highly of you. Could she be in love with you?" teased Madame Malewska.

"Why me, of all people?"

"Who can tell what goes on in a woman's heart? We'll discuss it later, but it would be better if she returned to Poland."

"With him?"

"How can he come? They would arrest him."

"What would she do here alone?"

"I don't know. Is there a chance of her making up with her father?"

"Out of the question."

"I was at her house. She is the most destitute countess I have ever met. I needn't tell you there is no lack of impoverished aristocrats in France—Polish and even French. Here in Poland, a Potocki works on the Vienna train. He's a cashier or a conductor. This world is no ivory tower. One cannot hide from reality, no matter how much one might want to."

Ezriel had thought that apostates would avoid all talk of Jews, but Mr. Wallenberg discussed Jews at the table and later in the salon. He was, apparently, well informed on Jewish affairs. Western European Jews, he said, had adapted themselves to the customs of the countries in which they lived, but Polish Jews had remained a tribe of Asiatics. When a Western European Jew died, he made provision in his will for community needs—the Auerbach Orphans' Home in Berlin, Frankel's Israelite Seminary in Wroclaw, Oppenheimer's and Magnus Levy's legacies—the huge sums given by Jews in England and in the United States, the institutions built for orphans, for poor children, to teach them trades, the funds put into schools, hospitals, rabbinical seminaries! What did the Warsaw Jews have? A filthy hospital and a wretched soup kitchen. As for Hassidism, there was no need to talk about them at all. They were savage Bedouins. And what about the conduct of the progressive Jew in Poland? He lived for himself. He felt no responsibility whatsoever for the community. His daughters were taught to mouth some French and dabble on the pianoforte. The Jewish woman in Poland bathed in luxury, even if her husband was on the verge of bankruptcy. In contrast, Wallenberg mentioned Adolf Kremier, and a Sephardic Jew from America who had taken the post of consul-general to Rumania in order to help the Rumanian Jews; he spoke of the Jewish financiers who had boycotted Rumania because of its persecution of Jews, the Parisian Rothschild who had loaned the French government two hundred million francs to help pay reparations to Prussia, and of the two daughters of the London Rothschild, Anna and Flora, who had collaborated on a history of the Jewish people. Was there anything comparable to these examples among the Jews of Poland?

Ezriel noticed that when Wallenberg discussed the Jewish question he grew as excited as if he were still a Jew himself. His voice became loud. Pounding his fist on the end table next to his chair, he almost shattered a vase. His sideburns were already completely gray. His face was red. His belly seemed about to escape his waistcoat, and his throat was encased in a high, stiff collar. His black eyes blazed with anger, then filled with that Jewish concern about humanity that no holy water could wash away. Silent and maternal, Madame Wallenberg gazed at her husband, nodding her gray coiffure as if in acceptance of age-old truths that defied all challenge. The Gentile sons-in-law listened and said nothing. The son and daughters held discussions of their own at the other end of the salon. Ezriel heard them speaking of shoes. After a while, Wallenberg was left alone with Ezriel. Wallenberg did not speak for a moment. Quickly he drank the coffee that he had allowed to grow cold.

"So you want to become a doctor—" he said finally.

"Yes."

"May I ask you something?"

"Of course, please do."

"Are you a believer?"

Ezriel did not know what to answer.

"Not in the usual sense."

"In what sense, then?"

"Some higher power must exist."

"Do you believe that this higher power revealed itself to

Moses on Mount Sinai and gave Jews the Torah and the Talmud and all the commentaries that the rabbis will continue explicating until the end of creation?"

"No, I am not that much of a believer."

"If that is so, then why are you still a Jew? I'm speaking to you frankly: no matter what you want to become, a doctor, an engineer, or a banker—you won't get there easily, being a Jew. I mentioned the Western European Jews. They are devoted patriots. Many Jewish young men died for Prussia and for France as well. A good number received decorations. During the war it came to the point where the Prussian Jews had to step out of the Alliance Israelite. One could not be at war and belong to the same organization. Recently there was a trial in France involving a crooked Jewish firm, and the rightist press immediately began agitating that Jews again put on yellow caps and return to the ghetto. During the war the Jews of Metz were nearly driven out of town. You probably don't read the newspapers, but I do. I read everything. For every Jew who gets a medal, hundreds get beatings. Our Polish press has been quite decent until now, but recently there was an angry article in *Gazeta Polska* protesting against the Jews in long caftans who attend concerts in Swiss Valley, screech jargon at each other, and don't bother to use handkerchiefs. The difference between Jews and Gentiles is that the Gentile who wipes his nose with his fingers doesn't attend concerts. A Jew does both. Can you foresee how this will end?"

"You can't expect all the Jews in Poland to have perfect manners."

"That's true, but a minority is always picked on, especially a minority with social aspirations. There was a time when I believed that if the Jews were to remove their caftans and learn to speak the native language, everything would be fine. Now I see that it's not so. To the rest of the world, the modern Jew is a ruthless competitor. In two thousand years, the Jews have accumulated a reservoir of skills that no other people possesses."

202

"What should the Jews do with their skills? Cast them aside?"

"No, but—"

Justina Malewska joined them.

"Father, I don't want to interrrupt you, but I must speak with Mr. Babad about his sister-in-law. You're talking, as I can hear, about all sorts of things, but this concerns a living person."

"Yes, Daughter, speak to him. He is an intelligent young man."

"Come, we'll go into another room."

Ezriel excused himself. Justina led him into a smaller salon or drawing room. Ezriel did not know what to call it. There was a clock supported by a satyr, and many mirrors hung on the walls, which were covered with yellow silk. Justina began to recount the circumstances that had brought her together with the Countess, as she called Miriam Lieba. Justina spoke of a dozen things at once: of her ties to the Polish colony, of her meetings with Polish leaders, writers, artistocrats, of how she had been received in Paris salons. Soon she spoke of the desperate need that dominated the Polish colony: their begging had reached the depths of degradation. The Poles had "borrowed" her last franc, and she had barely enough money to return home. Lucian was a drunkard, an adventurer, a beggar, all rolled into one. He ate in cheap soup kitchens. He constantly threatened to join the Foreign Legion, which most probably would not even accept him. The Countess went hungry. Justina paused for a moment. Her throat moved as if she had swallowed something.

"What I have to tell you will shock you, I know, but you are now the person closest to her."

"What is it?"

"She's become a laundress to keep from starving."

16

In Paris the Jampolskis lived in one room on a dead-end street of the Belleville quarter. It was a street of stables, bakeries, and laundries. Winding steps led up to the attic on the fourth floor. They occupied a room with a slanting ceiling and a tiny kitchen in which the big washtub was a permanent fixture. It was fortunate that they lived in the attic, for there was always room in the hall to hang laundry. Factory workers, an old cavalier, a rentier, and a streetwalker lived on the floors beneath them. On the roof, boys who kept pigeon coops guided the birds with long poles. In the more affluent streets, water could be drawn from taps, but here the concierge still brought up cans of water from the pump. At night, barrels of refuse were taken to the garbage wagon, and one had to hold one's nose because of the stench. Slatterns gossiped through windows, and the streets and courtyards swarmed with dogs, children, and beggars. During the siege of Paris, not only had all the cats in the neighborhood been eaten, but the mice as well. In the days of the Communes, the quarter had been the scene of mass meetings and demonstrations. Rebellious women carrying torches had come out of these streets to burn down Paris. The street boasted a number of war widows, and several of its residents had been sent to Devil's Island. Because there were few Poles in the neighborhood, Miriam Lieba had learned to speak French.

Her life with Lucian had been bitter from the start. Lucian had quickly squandered the two thousand rubles he had obtained in Warsaw for his mother's jewelry. He would come home raving each evening about how traitorous the leaders of the Polish colony were, how they had driven Poland into a hopeless uprising, how corrupt and scandalous was the Polish Military Academy in Genoa, the thievery that went on in the distribution of goods to emigrants, and how the wrangling between different factions was being used to foster personal ambitions. He had expressed his hostility so openly and for so long that he had cut himself off completely from the Polish colony. He got a job in a furniture factory, but soon quarreled with his employer. He tried other jobs, but never held one for more than a few weeks. Frenchmen were not drunkards, but Lucian came home intoxicated every night. More than once, Miriam Lieba went hungry during her pregnancy. After quarreling with her, Lucian would disappear for days at a time and return ragged and filthy. Her situation became so bad that Miriam Lieba ate in a cheap kosher soup kitchen that the Alliance Israelite had opened after the war for poor Jews. A neighbor, a laundress, advised Miriam Lieba to take in bachelors' laundry and gave her several addresses. The streetwalker on the second floor suggested a more lucrative profession.

After leaving home with Lucian that Purim evening, Miriam Lieba had enjoyed only a few happy weeks: the journey to Prussia, and later the trip across Germany. They stopped in Dresden, Leipzig, and Frankfurt and spent some time in Breslau. The Poles greeted Lucian as a hero, invited him and his young wife to their homes, banqueted them in cafés, sang patriotic songs. Miriam Lieba met Polish aristocrats, political leaders, officers, and even writers. In Paris, they lived for a while in a hotel. They took a trip to Deauville. In the warm forenoon, what a pleasure it had been to stand on the sand and watch the waves, foamy and wrinkled; to gaze at white sailboats out at sea; to hear the cry of the seagulls; to meet the rich Frenchmen, Englishmen, Germans, and even Turks and Indians who came there to bathe in the sea and gamble at the casino.

In those days, Lucian had been content. To Miriam Lieba it all seemed a busy holiday, one that would never end. Paris was full of music, everyone was singing. The war of 1870 had passed like a bad dream and Parisians mourned and celebrated. They showed Miriam Lieba where the barricades had been, the buildings that the Communards had burned, the remnants of the Bastille, the streets where artists, prostitutes, anarchists, and apaches lived. It seemed to Miriam Lieba as if France were constantly celebrating Purim. There were always people in costumes, singing and amusing themselves; tables were set out on the sidewalks, paupers played instruments, danced, sipped wine from bottles, and ate long loaves of bread. Magicians with parrots and monkeys wandered through the courtyards. Even the officers, with their braid-trimmed hats, the soldiers in red pantaloons, and the gendarmes wearing capes, all seemed part of the masquerade. There were outdoor cafés everywhere, theaters, bazaars, parades, exhibitions of books, paintings, sculpture, antiques. Here one saw a Negro, there someone in a turban, here a giant, there a dwarf. One could sit on the upper deck of a horse-drawn omnibus for a few centimes and see the carriages, the ladies, the famous palaces, boulevards, bridges, churches, monuments. Miriam Lieba remembered the names of certain streets from novels.

But Lucian's money and his good nature ran out simultaneously. For days at a time, he said nothing. When he left the house, Miriam Lieba never knew where he went. She cooked, but he did not come home to eat; the meals spoiled. He quarreled with her and cursed her; later he begged her forgiveness on his knees. First, he smothered her with kisses, then he struck her. In bed, boasting of past conquests, he made perverted demands. Miriam Lieba suffered a difficult pregnancy. She had to work until the day of her delivery. They were so much in need that Miriam Lieba took a neighbor's advice and bought horse meat. She had headaches, stomach cramps, dizzy spells. She was convinced she would die in childbirth. Although she went to church every Sunday and passionately read the story of the Christian martyrs, she slipped away quietly to a synagogue and gave the beadle half a franc to say prayers for her and light a candle for her soul.

II

Of all that Miriam Lieba endured in Paris, two torments were the most trying. First, she just couldn't manage to keep her apartment clean. She had been accustomed to a neat room since childhood, a properly made bed, things always in place, and life with Lucian had turned her into a slattern. Cockroaches swarmed in the kitchen. There was a hole in the roof, and the rain came through. The stove smoked. Mice nested beneath the floor. No amount of sweeping kept the place tidy. Lucian habitually dropped paper, trash on the floor, stuffed dirty socks and handkerchiefs into corners, scattered about newspapers, magazines, and notebooks, which he did not permit her to throw away. He acquired the habit of lying fully dressed on his bed, smoking one cigarette after another, and spitting at the ceiling. The privy in the courtyard was filthy, there was always a chamber pot in the flat. The neighbors' children urinated on the stairway. When Miriam Lieba gave up and decided to take in washing, tubs of dirty laundry littered the kitchen. A kettle of shirts and underwear boiled on the stove. There was a stench of soap, lye, washing soda, and bluing. At night, after Miriam Lieba extinguished the lamp, there was so much noise that she could not sleep. Later when the child, Wladzio, was born, the little apartment overflowed with diapers, swaddling clothes, bottles, nipples. They lived in a section of Paris infested with mice, bedbugs, fleas, flies, and beetles that resisted extermination. Cats, mouse traps, flypaper, and refuse exuded foul odors. Every Saturday night Miriam Lieba would heat a tub of water and bathe and wash her hair, but Lucian merely dipped his finger in the basin each morning and ran it across his face.

Miriam Lieba was disturbed as much by Lucian's lies as by his lack of cleanliness. He was either as silent as a recluse, or he lied. He could not even be truthful about where he bought a loaf of bread. Whenever he had a job, he deceived Miriam Lieba about his salary. He would tell her he had met a neighbor on the street—when the neighbor was actually sick in bed. He would boast of a bargain when he had overpaid at the market. Coming home, he would brag that he had helped to capture a thief or put out a fire, or had saved a girl from suicide. Although the Poles in Paris had long since severed all relations with him, Lucian would babble about his meetings with political figures, his connections with exiled leaders in Austria, Silesia, and Russo-Poland, or relate some conspiratorial plan to liberate Poland. There were only traitors in France's Polish colony, but Lucian had found patriots elsewhere who would readily sacrifice themselves for the liberation of their motherland. Promises of help had come from Garibaldi, the Sultan, President Hayes, and Bakunin, a Russian revolutionist whose wife was a Pole. In the ranks of the patriots were Mickiewicz's friend, the poet Odyniec; the writer Ujejski; a Madame Kuchokowska; the former Countess Skarbek, who had influence in Rome, especially in the Vatican; a Countess Walewska; an old officer, General Kolaczkowski . . . Miriam Lieba eventually realized that Lucian had collected the names of dead people. He even insinuated that Dr. Zawacki, who had married his sister Felicia, was a delegate of the secret organization and that he had sent Zawacki to Poland on a political mission.

Instead of finding a steady job and earning bread for his family, Lucian spent his time reading magazines, clipping ads from newspapers, and writing letters, to which he seldom received answers. Miriam Lieba sold her bracelet so that Lucian

208

could go to London to see his brother Josef. In the Channel, a storm broke out and the ship nearly sank. Lucian lingered in London for over a month. He returned emaciated, complaining that Josef had become a bourgeois, a flat positivist, and an admirer of the Jew Disraeli. Lucian was forever contradicting himself. He claimed both that Poland was lost and that liberation was near; that he was a republican and a royalist; he preached that Russia was Poland's worst enemy and then proposed a Slavophile plan for a union of all Slavic peoples to stand against West European decadence. Constantly sick, he had had an attack of bronchitis and an abscess in his ear. For a while he was convinced that he had contracted syphilis, although he solemnly swore that he hadn't been near another woman. The child Wladzio fussed at night and Miriam Lieba carried him about on a pillow and sang lullabies to him until he fell asleep. The moment she put him back in his cradle, he began to toss about again. "Throw the bastard out once and for all!" Lucian would say.

Miriam Lieba would burst into tears. "What else do you want me to do?"

She learned to scream and curse. When men visited the prostitute, she no longer ran from the window. She became adept at haggling with the market women over the price of tomatoes, a head of cabbage, a cauliflower. Although Lucian and Miriam Lieba tried to conceal the fact that they belonged to the aristocracy, the street soon found out. The postman read the title on their letters. The neighbors, the shopkeepers, the venders who sat behind the fruit and vegetable stands began half contemptuously to address Miriam Lieba as "Madame la Comtesse." What kind of countess was she? She spoke the French of the rabble. She took in washing. They discovered that she stemmed from Polish Jewry. Her husband, the Count, argued with street loafers, with school children. Dirty himself, he demanded cleanliness and quiet in this narrow street.

Now Lucian, for the hundredth time, had left home. When he was out of the house for a few days. Miriam Lieba slowly managed to clean up. Even Wladzio grew calmer. Wringing out some customer's blue shirt, Miriam Lieba bent over the washtub and glanced through the attic window. She could glimpse a great deal of Paris—chimneys, pigeon coops, attic windows, birds, church steeples. The sun's reflection flashed gold or silver in the windowpanes. In flight, the pigeons' wings grew red as fire. From the city there arose a roaring, a clucking, a singing, a sound of music, a whistling. A golden mist hovered over the eternal carnival. Miriam Lieba had lost everything, but she did not yearn to return to Jampol. Her mother was dead. Everything else was as far away and as insubstantial as a dream.

A mirror hung over the sofa. Miriam Lieba gazed into it. No, trouble hadn't aged her. A young face looked out at her, with tired eyes, pale lips, and blond hair that the sun had turned golden. She was toil-worn but still pretty. For a moment Miriam Lieba thought that if worse came to worse she could always follow the same course as Mademoiselle Meyar on the second floor.

III

Wallenberg knew quite well that one does not discuss an apostate daughter with a pious Jew and so he did not mention Maria Jampolska to Calman. Nevertheless, he had decided to help her return to Poland. Madame Malewska, his favorite daughter, was constantly reminding her father of the unfortunate Countess.

He finally obtained an audience with the Governor-General and somehow wangled an amnesty for Count Lucian Jampolski. The offense was an old one, and moreover it had been committed by a young man who had barely been able to distinguish between right and wrong. Besides, Poland was now calm; hundreds of nobles had returned from exile to settle on the land. Polish literature and the Polish press were dominated by positivism. After Napoleon III's downfall, the

Poles had lost all hope, and even the Polish exiles in France had been silenced. What harm could a Lucian Jampolski do the mighty Russian Empire?

The announcement of Lucian's pardon was officially dispatched to the Russian ambassador in Paris. A few days later, Lucian received notice of it from the consul. Madame Malewska wrote about it separately to Miriam Lieba, enclosing a few hundred francs for their fare home in the letter.

17

In Warsaw, winter came early that year. The very first day after the Feast of Tabernacles, a heavy snow fell. The courtyard apartment on Obozna Street in which Miriam Lieba now lived was in perpetual darkness. Wladzio was sick; the barber had come and painted the child's throat. Now Wladzio, a stocking full of hot salt around his neck, sat in bed playing with his toy soldiers, among them a lead Napoleon mounted on his horse. Wladzio was three years and four months old and prattled in a mixture of French and Polish. He was as fair as Miriam Lieba and had golden hair and Lucian's turned-up nose. At the moment his blue eyes were alive with anger. He didn't want to stay in bed and didn't want a hot stocking around his neck. Too young to remember winter, he recalled days filled with light, a blue sky, pigeons, puppies, kittens, an open door through which children came and went. That place had been called Paris. Here in this new place called Warsaw, snowflakes fell, the sky was gray, the door was always shut, the wind blew, and the panes rattled. Wladzio kept lining up the soldiers and knocking them down with his foot. He began to cry.

"What's wrong, angel? Does your throat hurt?" Miriam Lieba asked.

No, it wasn't that. Wladzio wanted to go back to Paris.

"Why Paris? You're home now. This is Poland, your own country."

Wladzio screamed in rage.

"Soon, dear, soon. We'll go. Be quiet and I'll play the harmonica for you."

But though Miriam Lieba played, the child remained restless. She took some French coins from a tea container and gave them to him. He continued to cry until, tired out, he fell asleep. Miriam Lieba couldn't get back to her work and sat watching him sadly. As he slept, his lips moved as if he were suckling. Occasionally his forehead twitched as though unhappy thoughts were passing through his mind, and he would rub his nose with his little fist. He had already suffered so much. He'd had scarlet fever, measles, and a difficult time cutting his teeth. Wasn't it enough that she was forced to struggle? Why had she brought another being into this world of torment? Apparently it had been God's will. She often read the silk-bound Bible, containing both the Old and the New Testaments, sent her by Lucian's Aunt Eugenia. Her favorite story was the one about Job and his sufferings, and how he had accused the Almighty. It was too bad, she thought, that she had not studied religious books sooner. If she had, she would have chosen Jesus rather than the abusive Lucian. But it was too late for her even to think about entering a cloister now.

It was time for her to begin cooking and she went into the kitchen to make a fire. Bending down, she picked up a few pieces of kindling and poured naphtha over them. Not until the fire was blazing did she shovel on a mixture of coke and coal; coal was too expensive to use by itself. Almost immediately the stove began to smoke because of the faulty flue. Whenever there was a wind, the smoke backed into the room. Miriam Lieba had several times reported this to the landlord and he had promised to have it repaired, but landlords never keep promises. The janitor had assured her that the chimney sweep would come and clean out the chimney, but no sweep appeared. Miriam Lieba closed the door to the living room to keep the smoke away from Wladzio. She began to cough. How could she stay healthy if she inhaled so much smoke and soot? And it was always so cold. She opened the cupboard and looked for something to cook. In it were only a few potatoes, a bag of rice, and half an ounce of dried mushrooms. Some lard, wrapped in paper, lay on the windowsill, but there was neither butter nor milk. Before she started dinner, she must clean up from yesterday. The night before, she had been too exhausted to stand over the sink scouring pots. Having fashioned a brush out of straw from the mattress, Miriam Lieba began to scrub the pans with ashes.

"No, I should never have left France," Miriam Lieba thought. "Wladzio was right. It's not so bad to be poor there."

No doubt about it, she had been foolish. She should have known that Lucian would be unable to keep a job. The Wallenbergs had treated them as if they were family, had given her books and dresses, rented the apartment for them, furnished it, and paid three months' rent in advance. Surely Lucian's job had been easy enough; he had been given decent clothing and a job in the office of the railroad at sixteen rubles a week. Without exerting himself, he could have advanced to inspector or even higher. But the moment he'd gone to work he quarreled with one of his associates, and before the first week was over, he'd got drunk and called Wallenberg a dirty Jew. Wallenberg had been very gracious and had asked for nothing more than an apology and a promise from Lucian that hereafter he would conduct himself properly and remain sober. But though Wallenberg had behaved like a true Christian, Lucian had continued to insult everyone and that was the end of the job. If Mrs. Malewska had not come and given Miriam Lieba fifty rubles, there would not have been a crust of bread in the house.

"Idiot! Madman!" Miriam Lieba mumbled.

Suddenly, for some obscure reason, she felt better and began to sing a Parisian street song. Wladzio was growing up and the worst was over when a child reached school age. She would become a governess or learn to be a hairdresser like Mirale. After all, she wasn't very old, not quite twenty-two. Miriam Lieba became tense. What day of the month was it? She hadn't had her period. No, she couldn't be pregnant!

II

On his return to Warsaw, Lucian had immediately gone to see Kasia. But Stachowa had died, and the neighbors told him that Kasia's father had claimed the girl. They were unsure whether Antek lived in Wola or Ochota. Lucian began working for Wallenberg and hadn't the time to search further. He had brooded about the girl for so many years, it seemed strange to be in Warsaw without her. Was he still in love with her? No, what he felt transcended ordinary love. Kasia, now barely fifteen, had been only a child when he had lived with her mother. The girl's slavish docility had fascinated him. She had made him think of the days when the Slavs worshipped idols, brought sacrifices to Baba Yaga, and kept slaves and concubines. Often in fantasies he had seen himself as a pasha or a maharaja, both the symbolic and the actual father of his subjects. During the insurrection, when the Polish press had praised Lincoln's struggle to free the Negroes, Lucian had secretly sympathized with the Confederates. The decree liberating the Polish peasantry had seemed a bad one to him. Meeting Polish emigrants, he had often insisted that freedom poisoned the multitude. The mob must serve. Also, women were only happy when they had masters; the suffragette movement, which came to Poland along with the positivist ideas, had been a sign of national corruption to Lucian.

Having fallen out with the Jew Wallenberg, he now had the time to renew old friendships. He went to see Lisakowa, Stachowa's former neighbor, who told him that she had heard that Kasia had gone into domestic service, although she didn't know where. Lisakowa also told Lucian the location and number of Stachowa's grave, and the address of a brewery at which Antek's brother worked. The brewery was on Iron Street and Lucian easily located him. Antek, Lucian discovered, was living with a woman on Freta Street. Lucian walked slowly over to Freta Street and found the woman at home.

At first mistaking him for a police agent, she denied any connection with Antek. However, when Lucian assured her that he was a former friend of Stachowa's and had just returned from France, she became more tractable. She wiped off a bench with a rag, invited him to sit down, and told him all that poor Kasia had been forced to endure during the time he had been away. The girl had been employed in many households and had already run away from several of them. Because of these delinquencies, their former neighbor Lisakowa had on her own initiative gone to the police and petitioned them to place Kasia in a home for wayward girls. At this moment Kasia was working for an old couple, the Wrobels, who lived on Furmanska Street. Antek's mistress was telling all this to Lucian in confidence, she explained, because Antek didn't want anyone to know where his daughter was.

Having at last obtained the information he needed, Lucian walked over to Furmanska Street. Pan Wrobel's house was pointed out to him, a crooked, tile-covered building; Pan Wrobel lived just behind the gate, on the ground floor. Lucian knocked and heard Kasia's voice.

"Who's there?" she inquired.

"Is Pan Wrobel in?"

"No, he's not."

"Your mistress?"

"No one's here."

"Open up, Kasia. It's me, Lucian."

Lucian heard her muffled outcry. Though she did not unchain the door, she pulled it open and he saw her face. It was the same Kasia, but older, prettier, pigtailed, her gray eyes filled with fear and astonishment. She drew back her upper lip, exposing broad teeth.

"Well, why don't you let me in, Kasia?"

"The old woman doesn't permit it."

"Do you think I'm going to steal something?"

"I'll be punished."

"Aren't you happy to see me?"

The door opened and Lucian crossed the threshold. Kasia stood there, grownup, in a calico dress, with scuffed house slippers on her bare feet. She had a woman's bosom.

"No, you're not happy to see me."

"I'm frightened." Kasia began to tremble.

"Of what?"

"I was told not to open the door. The old woman will kill me."

"Do you remember me?"

"I remember."

"I've been looking for you everywhere. I wrote to you, but I never got an answer. You're sure you haven't forgotten?"

"No."

"Do you still have the book I gave you?"

"Yes, the book and the groschen."

"Why are you so frightened of people?"

"I'm not. *They* are. The old man has a safe full of money. He counts it every night. The old woman's trunk is packed with gold and pearls. They keep the door chained and bolted."

"Do you ever go out?"

"I have a day off every other Sunday. I must be back by four o'clock. If I'm five minutes late, the old woman starts shouting at me. She beats me, too. She's sick, but when she hits me, my cheeks swell."

"Now I'm here, the beatings will stop."

"No."

"Now kiss me."

"I can't. It's not proper."

"You little fool, who told you that?" Lucian pulled Kasia to him and kissed her, but she did not return his kiss.

"You remember everything?" he asked.

"Everything."

III

"I wrote to you," Lucian said. "Didn't you get any of my letters?"

"Not a single one."

"They were sent to your mother's address."

"I know nothing about them. They probably tore them up."

"Can you read?"

"Only the primer."

"Yes, I understand. Well, it's not too late to educate you. Does your father help you?"

Kasia shrugged her shoulders.

"How can he help? All he does is take my money. If I need a dress or shoes, he buys them for me. The rest he pockets."

"You don't love him?"

"Sometimes a little."

"But you love me more?"

"More than anyone!"

"And I thought you'd forgotten me, Kasia. I wrote, though I knew it was useless. Look what they've made of you. As for me, I'm married and have a son, but my love for you hasn't changed. I kept longing for you the whole time I was away. I knew you were thinking of me."

"Yes, I did think of you."

"Did you believe I would come back?"

"Some day."

"Now I'm no longer wanted by the authorities. I've been pardoned. My sister Felicia lives here in Warsaw. She's married to a doctor. My wife was Jewish but she turned Christian.

I had a job but I couldn't stand the man I was working for. Anyway, I don't want a job. I want my freedom. Kasia, I had to find you. When I love, it's for good."

"I, too."

"I love my wife as well, but one love doesn't interfere with the other. Do you understand?"

"Yes."

"She's my wife and you are my daughter. No, more than a daughter! If it weren't forbidden, both of you would be my wives. I'd marry you, too."

Kasia looked troubled. "Is that possible?"

"Yes, it's possible, but forbidden. In our times there's so much that is forbidden. Don't do this, don't do that. It's our legacy from the Jews. Do you remember the night I left?"

"Yes."

"What did I tell you?"

"Many things."

"Kasia, I don't want you to stay in this house another minute. Come away with me."

"Where am I to go?"

"To my house or to my sister's. We'll see."

"I'm only paid once a quarter. I get two rubles. I've received nothing for this quarter."

"What's two rubles? Let them keep the money. Hurry up, get your things."

"But they might be robbed."

"What's that to you? They've worried a lot about you, haven't they?"

"The door will lock behind me. No one will be able to get in."

"They'll manage."

"No," Kasia said, drawing back. "I'm responsible for the house. I can't do it."

"What nonsense! They whip you and you're loyal to them. Do you have shoes?"

"Yes."

H

"Get dressed."

"But isn't this a sin?"

"Suppose it is? You belong to me and I can dispose of you as I see fit. I am both your father and your husband—your God also. I'll take you to my sister. Her husband is a doctor. She's a good woman. She's not satisfied with the maid she has. If she doesn't want you, you'll come to my house. That way we'll be near each other. You won't have to work hard and you'll be free to go out whenever you like. Here you're like an animal in a cage."

"When I go out to buy something, the old woman tells me not to talk to anyone. If she thinks I've been away too long, she beats me with the broom."

"And you want to be loyal to such bloodsuckers? Come along."

"They may return at any moment."

"If they do, I'll handle them. I'm a Polish count and they're vermin. You'll see, they won't dare open their mouths."

IV

To help start her husband in his medical practice—Dr. Marian Zawacki had opened an office on Kreditowa Street—Felicia had obtained a thousand rubles from her Aunt Eugenia, whose will included small bequests to Josef, Lucian, Helena, and herself. The understanding was that the thousand rubles were an advance against Felicia's share of the inheritance. Felicia had also sold half of her jewelry, and Zawacki's father had supplied the remainder of the necessary money. Dr. Zawacki, because he spoke French and had taken his medical degree in France, and was also married to a countess, attracted a rich clientele. Elegant ladies and gentlemen crowded his waiting room from morning to night. Felicia had brought furniture and paintings from the manor house and had hired a maid and a cook. The doctor traveled in a coach drawn by two horses and driven by a coachman. To Felicia it seemed that God was at last repaying her for all the suffering she had endured. The four hours that Marian devoted to office calls brought in between fifty and eighty rubles a week, and he was constantly being summoned to the bedside of aristocratic Poles, wealthy Jews, and high Russian officials. He found time for everything, for his office and home calls, for his study of foreign medical journals. He had even been invited to read several papers at the university and so had become acquainted with the faculty. At night he took Felicia to the theater or opera, or played cards with his colleagues. One look at a patient was sufficient for him to make a diagnosis. He criticized books and plays with the skill of a professional reviewer.

Whenever Felicia remembered how Zawacki had entered her life, she thanked Providence. Prepared for the worst, she had received the best. Marian seldom spoke harshly to her. Every groschen he earned was turned over to her. Although short, he was of a passionate nature. Every night with him in the wide French bed seemed like a dream to Felicia. To be lying with a man! At the time of her wedding she'd been so thin her ribs had protruded. Zawacki had given her drops to stimulate her appetite and had prescribed injections. She had already gained ten pounds and looked younger and prettier. The wrinkles around her eyes disappeared. Her fatigue, her constipation, her headaches, and the spinal pain she had had since girlhood vanished. Felicia was ashamed to admit it, but a little temporal good fortune had radically altered both body and soul.

Nevertheless, she worried. Years had passed and she was still not pregnant. How dreadful if she was no longer able to conceive! She wanted a child and so did her husband; on several occasions he had remarked that the basic purpose of marriage was reproduction. Another disturbing factor was her husband's lack of interest in religion; each Sunday he found another excuse to avoid going to church. Jokingly, he blasphemed against God, Jesus, the Apostles. Felicia couldn't understand how a grown man could preach such materialism. All truths, Zawacki claimed, could be discovered in the laboratory with the help of telescope and microscope. He agreed with Darwin that man was descended from the ape, and he contended that humans were the only intelligent beings in the cosmos. There were no truths beyond man's comprehension.

Her brother Lucian also annoyed Felicia. Now that he had lost his position with Wallenberg, he was forever coming around asking for small loans. He didn't behave responsibly toward his family. Lucian, Felicia was aware, could have found a more appropriate wife than the girl he had married, but since Miriam Lieba had abandoned her family and borne him a child, the least he could do was to take care of her. Every time she visited her brother's home, she was shocked by the disorder she found there. Lucian drank; Miriam Lieba spoke despairingly. There was a frivolity in her manner that ill suited Calman Jacoby's daughter. But even that was not the sum total of Felicia's worries. Clara, Calman's wife, had forced the old man out of the manor house. Count Jampolski was living in a broken-down shack which had once been occupied by a steward. Antosia had moved in with him and behaved as if she were his wife. Felicia had invited her father to live with her in Warsaw, but he had replied that he wished to die on the manor and he needed no one's help or advice.

On that cold December afternoon Felicia was alone, as Marian had already left for the hospital. There was snow on the ground outside. If she had been in her room in the manor house, she would have looked out on wide fields reaching to the horizon. Here on Kreditowa Street, all she could see was a mass of houses and a thin sliver of sky. Felicia sat in her boudoir in an upholstered chair, near the warm tiled stove, her feet propped on a footstool. She was attempting to read a novel by Balzac that Marian had told her was excellent. Felicia had never liked any of Balzac's works. Not only were they licentious, but they had that curious attitude toward man, a mixture of contempt and adoration, that Felicia found in all modern books. Man had become god to them, and they both worshipped and blasphemed Man-God. Felicia would read a line and then look up. Had the flowers been watered? Had the maid dusted the furniture? Was the cook burning the soup again? Someone had just entered the house and was speaking. The maid knocked on the door.

"Madame, your brother, Count Jampolski is here."

"Well, show him up."

"He's not alone. There's a girl with him."

"What kind of a girl?"

"A servant."

Felicia became tense. "All right, show them both up. See that they wipe the mud off their feet."

v

Felicia lectured Lucian reprovingly in French in the manner of an older sister; she gave him ten rubles but refused to take Kasia in. It was twilight. In the streets passersby stopped to stare at the odd-looking couple. What was this aristocratic young man doing with such a girl? Why was he carrying her bundle? Snow began to fall and Kasia wrapped herself in her mother's shawl. The shawl was too large for her; its fringes dragged on the ground.

Halting momentarily, Lucian puckered his lips as if about to whistle. Should he really take her home with him? No, Miriam Lieba would make a scene. He thought of Ezriel and Shaindel, who now lived in Warsaw and had an apartment on Leshno Street. Shaindel refused to visit Miriam Lieba because she was an apostate, but Ezriel came to the house often. Lucian didn't think that Shaindel had a maid. Perhaps Shaindel and Ezriel would be happy to get Kasia. Miriam Lieba, having just learned that she was pregnant, was in no mood to grant Lucian any favors. "She is more vicious than ever, the bitch. She's bursting with hatred. Felicia is right. I am mad, mad. I am destroying myself slowly but surely."

223

The snow continued to fall; it became colder. Lucian walked in the direction of Marshalkowsky Boulevard, searching for a droshky or a sleigh. A passing policeman looked the couple up and down and shrugged his shoulders. At Marshalkowsky Boulevard, Lucian found a droshky. He helped Kasia in and gave the driver Ezriel's address.

"Don't worry, Kasia dear," Lucian said reassuringly. "It may seem hard now, but we'll find a place for you. You've lost nothing. Remember, I'm responsible for you. You have a protector in me."

"I know that."

The droshky pulled up at Ezriel's house, which was across the street from a church. Lucian paid the fare and got out. Night had fallen. The street lamps had already been lit. Smoke fell like sheets from the chimneys. A man selling roasted potatoes warmed himself at his brazier. Only after he had walked through the gateway of the house followed by Kasia did it occur to Lucian that he should not have come here. Ezriel might be enlightened, but Shaindel had inherited the natural stubbornness of the Jew. How could he be sure that Ezriel was at home? What should he tell them? Whatever he said was bound to compromise him. Lucian searched through the list of tenants. The light was so dim and the writing so poor that he could not decipher the names. The janitor came out of his cubicle and told Lucian where Ezriel lived. The building was new and had three stories.

"Who's the girl?" the janitor inquired.

Lucian mounted the stairs without answering. How insolent these peasants had become! Lucian had a desire to punch the man in the nose, or kick him in the belly. If this was what democracy meant, to hell with it! It was all a result of that cursed French Revolution. It had destroyed the last vestige of human decency. When he stood in front of Ezriel's door, he gave Kasia her bundle and then knocked. Shaindel opened the door. Having seen her only once since his return, Lucian had difficulty recognizing her. She had put on weight and was obviously several months pregnant. Her dress was hitched up in front and was not particularly clean. Evidently she had been washing the dishes, for she held a straw brush in her hand.

"I'm Lucian Jampolski," Lucian said. "Very likely you don't remember me."

"The Count!" Shaindel took a step backward.

"I've brought this little girl along with me. Isn't that odd?"

"Come in, please. You also. Wipe your feet."

"Is your husband at home?"

"No, but I'm expecting him back any minute."

Seated on a bench in the kitchen was a young woman in her early twenties. She wore a cheap gray skirt and a blouse with a high collar. Her hair was twisted into a braid and wound around her head. Lucian stole a quick glance at her and thought that he had met her before. Though not homely, she had a bony nose and the sad expression of the Jew. Her gaze had a keenness often also found among the French and Italians. Her lips were thin and severe; her eyebrows grew together. Her forehead was higher than most women's and had something masculine about it. Lucian felt embarrassed before this stranger and began to speak without knowing exactly what he was saying.

"Do you know how long I've known this child? Ten years, and she's only fifteen now. Her mother hid me from the Russians. A fine woman, God rest her soul. She saved my life. That was just after the uprising. I regard Kasia as my own child. A sister, or a daughter! Can you imagine what her father's done to her? Put her into service with the vilest people, absolute exploiters! I just couldn't permit her to remain in such slavery. 'Get your things and come,' I told her. They tried to stop me, but I paid no attention to them. So, now she's here. I thought I'd take her home with me, but that would be inconvenient. Your sister's too edgy these days for a surprise such as this. I thought that since you don't have a maid, Kasia might be just what you need. That is for the time being. Later I intend to send her off to school."

225

Shaindel's dark eyes grew large and round. "First of all, we don't need a maid. That is, we do need one, but it's beyond our means. Second, there's no place for her to sleep."

"What about the kitchen?"

"My sister-in-law is staying the night with us. I forgot to introduce you. This is my husband's sister, Mirale."

"Oh, so you're Ezriel's sister. Your brother told me all about you. Your father, I believe, is the Rabbi of Jampol."

"He was the rabbi. My parents are in Warsaw now."

"Is that so? How did that happen? Well, that's very interesting. Anyway, I find myself burdened with this girl and I absolutely must find a place for her. It's already night . . ."

"Won't the Count come into the parlor? There's no need for us to stay in the kitchen. Wait, I'll make a light," Shaindel said.

"Forgive me, but I don't have the time. If she can't sleep here, I must look elsewhere. Perhaps I can get her a room in a hotel. A child her age can't be left on the streets, particularly in winter."

"God forbid! She'd freeze to death. But the Count can see for himself that we have no room here. We have a sofa in the other room, but that's where my sister-in-law will sleep. We have nothing to cover the girl with. If we had bedding, she could sleep in the kitchen. But without a blanket, it would be too cold there."

"Yes, yes, I see. Thank you anyway. Come along, Kasia."

"Perhaps she'd like something to eat. Would the Count care for a glass of tea?"

"Are you hungry, Kasia?" Lucian asked. Kasia shook her head.

"It's such an unfortunate accident," Shaindel said, "to have such an esteemed visitor and be unable to be of assistance."

Shaindel, attempting to speak elegant Polish, was constantly making mistakes. She knew she should inquire about Miriam Lieba, but she could not bring herself to mention her sister's name. To the family, Miriam Lieba was as good as dead.

226

Shaindel often quarreled with Ezriel about the visits he made to Lucian's house. Decent Jews were not friendly with apostates. Moreover, Shaindel feared that the wanton Miriam Lieba would lead Ezriel astray. Shaindel had been told that Lucian had even lived in sin with some woman despite the fact that he was married to Miriam Lieba. Now he came barging into her house like a thoughtless boor.

"Well, good night. Forgive me for dropping in so unexpectedly."

"My husband will be here soon. If the Count should care to wait."

"No, I'm sorry. I don't have the time. Every minute counts now. Remember me to your husband." Lucian turned to Mirale. "It was a pleasure to meet you. You do resemble your brother, but only slightly. Good night."

"A good night to the Count," Shaindel said, interrupting. "If the worst comes to the worst, bring the girl back here and we'll fix up some kind of a bed for her on the floor."

"No, we're not as bad off as that. But thanks just the same."

VI

The frost, more severe than ever, nipped at Lucian's ears; his nose grew as hard as wood. Pausing in front of the gate to Ezriel's house, Lucian peered from left to right. Next to him, Kasia, shivering in her mother's shawl, breathed submissively like an animal. Sleighs drove by, their bells ringing. The windowpanes of the houses across the street were white. Though it was not late, it was so still that it seemed to be midnight. An occasional snowflake fell, an icy dew, shining needlelike against the gaslights. Lucian placed his hand on Kasia's shoulder. In the milder Parisian climate, one could almost live outdoors. He had been able to drift along with little effort. He had longed for the bitter Polish winter, for intrigue, for the humility of the common people, whom he loved with his own kind of aristocratic passion. Now again, as after the uprising,

227

when he constantly had had to evade the Russians, he was in difficulty. "What do I do now?" he asked himself. "Perhaps I should just kill her." He toyed with the idea. "I'll take her down to the Vistula and throw her in. She won't resist." He was thirsty but he couldn't make up his mind whether it was water or vodka that he wanted. Actually it was a thirst for adventure. He needed to do something terrible, beat someone or find himself in some grand predicament. He was ready to fight the Russians, or even the Poles, who had submitted to Russian rule. He muttered curses, not knowing whom he was cursing. He wasn't really angry, just strangely irritated. "Well, something is going to happen tonight. She is again in my power," he thought. He shivered and bit his lower lip. A sleigh drove past. Lucian raised his hand and signaled it to stop.

"Driver, take me to a hotel."

"What hotel?"

"A cheap one. This child has nowhere to sleep. All I need is the simplest of rooms."

The driver shoved his sheepskin cap to the back of his head, and said, "I know a place on Mylna Street."

"What number?"

"We'll drive up there and I'll show you. But I don't know if they'll let her in."

"That's my worry."

Lucian and Kasia got into the sleigh. The ride was a short one. They drove down Karmelicka Street to Nowolipie Street, and then turned into Mylna Street. The hotel was old and decrepit. Lucian paid the driver and escorted Kasia into the building. In the lobby behind the desk stood a small kinky-haired man in a corduroy jacket. He had a round face, a broad nose, small shiny eyes, and skin yellow and pock-marked as swiss cheese.

"This girl's an orphan," Lucian explained. "Her mother was a servant on our manor. She needs a place to sleep for the night."

"Does she have a birth certificate?"

Lucian turned to Kasia. "Do you have a birth certificate?"

Kasia didn't answer.

"She must have some sort of papers. We'll look for them later. They're probably in her bundle. Anyway, it's only for the night. Tomorrow I'll find her a situation."

"How old is she?"

"Sixteen."

"She doesn't look it. Does the gentleman intend to stay with her?"

"What's the difference to you?"

"It's a difference in price."

"Suppose I do decide to stay?"

"Then the room will be two rubles."

Lucian noticed a peculiar glint in the clerk's eyes.

"All right, let it be two rubles."

Lucian took out the ten-ruble note that Felicia had given him, and threw it on the counter.

"Ten kopecks for key money," the clerk said, as he carefully examined the bill in the lamplight.

"What sort of fee is that? Oh, never mind."

"And two rubles ninety kopecks for security."

"What kind of security?"

"Security."

The two men looked at each other and the clerk's eye seemed to wink.

"Too bad I haven't my pistol with me," Lucian thought. "The next time he opens his mouth, I could let him have it." The clerk handed Lucian five rubles' change.

"When do I get it back?"

"When you leave, if everything's in order."

A barefooted woman, her apron half tucked up, appeared carrying a bucket of slops. She had piglike eyes and the clumsiest feet Lucian had ever seen. After some hesitation, the clerk selected a key.

"Is the bed in 23 made up?"

"Who for?"

"This little girl. She's an orphan."

"An orphan, eh? I'm an orphan myself. Is this your bundle?"

The woman put down the bucket and lit a candle. Lucian and Kasia followed her up stairs so steep and narrow they could barely be climbed. At the top of the stairs, the woman stopped to catch her breath. The corridor was narrow and the doors of the rooms looked like those of prison cells. In the hall was a basket filled with dirty laundry and a broom propped against the wall. Lucian smelled a strange odor, a blend of something musty and oily. He heard a mutter of voices; a woman laughed. She seemed to be alone in the room. It was mad laughter. The key to Room 23 didn't fit properly. The woman twisted and pushed but the lock remained shut. She handed Lucian the candlestick and grasped the key with both hands, turning sharply. The door swung open. Lucian smelled the stench of rotting straw. He looked into the room and by the light of the candle saw an iron bed, a broken-down chest of drawers, a rush mat lying on the floor. The mattress of the bed was a straw sack, and a coarse cloth covering served as a sheet. The pillow was stuffed with feathers, not down.

"Well, here it is," the woman said.

Lucian handed her ten kopecks. The woman looked at the money scornfully. "I never get less than a gulden."

Lucian would have liked to spit in her face. "Here's your gulden."

"You can't keep the candle burning. We've got to watch out for fire."

"Look, it's freezing in here."

"Well, the room was heated only this morning. The flue's no good; the heat escapes up the chimney."

After the woman left, Lucian attempted to lock the door but found that the hook for the chain was missing. He said, "All right, take off your shawl, Kasia. Are you hungry?"

"No."

"Then I guess it's time for us to turn in."
"Aren't you going home?"
"No, I'm staying here."
"Where will you sleep?"
"With you."

VII

Lucian awoke in the middle of the night. He'd dreamed he'd
been wrestling with an ape and the creature had grasped his
throat with its paws. He heard voices, men speaking Russian,
and he listened intently. The police! His ribs felt icy. If only
he'd had enough sense to bring along his pistol. He groped in
the dark and found his pants, shoes, and socks. Any minute, he
knew, the men would start climbing the stairs. But, no, there
wasn't a sound now. Should he wake Kasia? He slipped out
into the corridor and listened. From where he was, he could
see the night lamp burning downstairs. Suddenly he heard
footsteps and he started to back away. Was there another
exit? His hand touched doors and latches. At the end of the
hall, to the right, was a closet. He tiptoed in and found himself
surrounded by crates and baskets. His coat caught on a nail;
he pulled himself free. His heart seemed to stop; he stood listening with his entire body. A light glimmered in the corridor,
apparently a candle. He held his breath, silent, fearful, his
brain no longer functioning. Men were chattering in Russian:
someone replied in Polish, but what had been said eluded Lucian. That almost forgotten terror that he'd known when he'd
been on the run, hiding in woods and ditches, returned to him.
The light was coming closer, the figures also. Then, inexplic-
ably, the hall was plunged into darkness and there was silence.
"Could I have been imagining it all?" Lucian wondered. Yet
he dared not leave his hiding place. "Not so fast," he decided.
He didn't know how long he remained standing there. He
dozed, awoke, forgot what had happened and where he was.
The image of the ape he had dreamed of returned to him,

hairy, its teeth flashing. He shook himself and the hallucination disappeared. The corridor remained dark and silent. Slowly and with great deliberation, Lucian raised his hand and scratched his ear with one finger. Then he fell asleep and seemed to be in Paris.

He shuddered and something fell, a board or a box. He tiptoed out of the closet and advanced down the hall, trying each door as he passed. Had Kasia been arrested? Or was she still here? He did not remember which room was theirs. He had no matches. All the doors were chained and bolted. How could that be? The door to his room hadn't been locked. When he came to the stairs, he began to descend, one step at a time. Coming to a landing, he rested. It seemed to him that the stairway went on forever. The light below had been extinguished. Had they locked the front door? Was all of this merely a trick to lure him from his hiding place? Well, if it were, they wouldn't take him without a fight; he'd never surrender. At any rate, the girl belonged to him and that couldn't be changed.

Yes, the light was out in the lobby. He felt the edge of the desk and stumbled against a bench. Apparently there was a small step down at that spot. He had nearly fallen. Reaching the door, he opened it, and was almost driven back by a blast of wind. Now he remembered that he had not taken his tie and scarf. He paused momentarily at the threshold. He was free! They couldn't do anything to Kasia.

He walked out and turned to the left. As he lunged down a narrow crooked street, the cold cut into him. "Go back," he warned himself; the street looked like a dead end. He ran in the opposite direction and came to some public building in front of which a soldier stood guard near a sentry box. Lucian slowed his pace to a walk; the soldier eyed him suspiciously but said nothing. Lucian found himself on a broad avenue lit by gas lamps. He passed a watering trough and a well. Although he was thoroughly familiar with Warsaw, he didn't know where he was. This was not Karmelicka Street, toward which he had thought he was heading. Well, it didn't matter. He pulled up the collar of his coat and continued walking. At last he came to a street sign which read *Tlomacka* and he knew where he was.

He broke into a run and then stopped suddenly. Kasia had probably given the police his name. Did she know that he was a Jampolski? If she did, the authorities would certainly ·seek him out at his apartment. They might already be waiting at the gate on Obozna Street. Where should he go? If he wandered about on a night like this, he would freeze to death. What about Ezriel's? He was ashamed to go there. Felicia's? Her apartment would be dangerous, too. "Now there is no door left open to me," Lucian mumbled to himself, as if he were quoting a line from a poem. The evil spirit that dogged his footsteps had amused itself by pretending to release him from peril and then entangling him again. A very clever spirit, very clever indeed. An interesting and perverse idea occurred to him. Why shouldn't he return to Freta Street and spend the night at Antek's? His being hunted again exhilarated Lucian. He had accomplished what he had been planning to do for years. There was, he remembered, a Jewish hotel on Grzybow Place, not far from Bagno Street. He could spend the night there.

VIII

In the commissariat of police, the sergeant sat in a railed-in cubicle separated from the rest of the room. His jacket unbuttoned, the sergeant, a fat man, was half asleep, snoring slightly. On the table before him was a newspaper and half a glass of cold tea in which floated a wedge of lemon. The sergeant stirred and scratched his slightly exposed belly. A few minutes later, in walked Kasia, still wrapped in her oversized shawl and led by a Polish policeman. Her face was impassive and her manner docile. The policeman coughed and the sergeant opened his eyes a crack and smiled that typical smile of porcine complacency and disdain.

"And who's this one?"

"I picked her up in the Hotel Gwiazda on Mylna Street."

"Ah, a young whore."

"No, she's been seduced. It happened tonight. Some count did it."

The sergeant was now completely awake. He smiled, exposing the few massive teeth he had left in his mouth.

"How long did it take to think that one up?"

"No, it's a fact. We received the information from the coachman who drove them to the hotel. He's one of our people. The man's name, according to her, is Count Lucian Jampolski. She was in service on Furmanska Street."

The sergeant arranged himself more comfortably in his leather-cushioned chair, and then buttoned his jacket and tightened his belt. He did not believe the story he was being told but was nevertheless amused by it. Usually on a winter's night only drunks and old prostitutes, anxious to have a place to sleep, were brought in. The sergeant would have liked to question Kasia, but, having just arrived from Russia, knew no Polish. As he measured the girl up and down, his almond eyes lit up with destructive joy. To his left lay a protocol book. The sergeant picked up a pen, tested it on his thumbnail, and dipped it into a half-empty inkwell.

"What do they call you?"

"Kasia."

"Kasia, eh? Your surname?"

"He wants to know your last name," the policeman said, translating into Polish.

Kasia said nothing.

"Now see here, you're being spoken to. Answer!"

Kasia's face remained impassive.

"Is she deaf or something?"

"Tell him your name, you little trollop."

234

"Kasia."

"Your last name. Kasia what? Kasia is only your given name. Look, I'm called Stefan Krol. What do they call you?"

Kasia stirred slightly.

"I forgot."

"You've forgotten your own name? What's your father's name?"

"Antek."

"Antek what?"

Kasia did not answer.

"So you're a tough little nut," the sergeant said through clenched teeth. "Where does her father live?"

"He wants to know where your father lives," the Polish policeman said, translating.

"On Freta Street."

"What number?"

Kasia did not move an eyelash.

"He asked you what number."

"I don't know."

"What does your father do? How is he employed?"

"What's that?"

"Is he a shoemaker, a tailor, a blacksmith, a crook?"

"He goes to work."

"Where?"

Kasia did not know what to answer.

The sergeant winked at the policeman. They began to whisper to each other. The sergeant emitted a throaty laugh.

"What did you say the Count's name was?"

"Lucian Jampolski," Kasia replied.

"Where does he live?"

Kasia didn't know where Lucian lived.

"Where do your employers live?"

"On Furmanska Street. Number 3."

"What is their name?"

"Wrobel."

"Well, there, now listen to that. She does know something,"

235

the sergeant remarked to the policeman and to the world in general.

"We'll have to walk over to the Wrobels' and see what they have to say. How old are you?"

"I'm almost fifteen."

"Almost fifteen. You're beginning your career early. What did this Count do to you?"

The sergeant continued to question her intensively, the policeman acting as interpreter. Other offenders were brought in to the commissariat, but they were kept waiting. Kasia remembered everything clearly—that is, except for last names and addresses. The sergeant pinched her cheek.

"Are you hungry, little sweetheart?"

"No. Yes."

"Wait, I'll take care of you."

The sergeant wrote something on a slip of paper.

"All right, she's yours now."

"Come with me."

The policeman took Kasia gently by the arm and led her through a number of rooms and then down a staircase into a cellar. A door was thrown open and Kasia was pushed into a room. She was aware that she was in prison but wasn't afraid. The cell stank. Even before her eyes became accustomed to the darkness, she knew from the snores and sighs that she heard that she was surrounded by women. Finally, as in a dream, faces, eyes, hair emerged from the shadows. A hoarse voice called out to her, "Hey, you, what are you doing standing at the door? Won't you please step in and be friendly?" And the speaker laughed shrilly.

"Look, she's nothing but a kid," another woman remarked.

The snores accelerated as if the sleepers were trying to cram as much rest as possible into the time allotted them. There were yawns, growls, and a mixture of curses. Some of the women were lying down; others were sitting. Bodies were strewn all over the floor. A bluish-white light, dawn reflected by the snow, seeped in through the barred window.

236

"Hey, do you see, she has a shawl!"

"Give it to me."

"Girls, she's only a baby."

Someone made an obscene remark, making everyone laugh. A heavy-set woman lit a match.

"That's right; she's only a kitten. Come here, darling. Let me have the shawl."

I X

Twenty-four hours later, Kasia was released and taken by the policeman who had arrested her to her father's house on Freta Street. Antek was not at home, but the woman he lived with was there, busy at the tub, washing linen. Her face fell when she saw that Kasia was accompanied by a policeman.

"Is this the woman your father lives with?" the policeman asked Kasia.

"Yes."

"Are you two married?"

"No, officer. What would I do? The lazy bum wouldn't go to a priest."

"Do you know that living like that is a criminal offense?"

"I know, but, sir, what could I do? What happened to you, darling? Just look at her! What did she do? Steal?"

"No, worse."

The policeman related the whole story. They were looking for Lucian Jampolski. The woman wiped her hands on her apron.

"What a disgrace! It will kill her father. The Count was here the day before yesterday, wanting to know where she worked. Like a fool I told him."

"Oh, so you told him. Why? You'll be called as a witness."

"I'll testify. I'll swear on the cross and tell everything. In he walks, looking as handsome and stylish as you please, honey dripping from his tongue. He lived at her mother's once; the girl was just the same as a daughter to him. What did I know

237

about it? I come from humble people. I can't read or write. I said to him, 'She's working for the Wrobels on Furmanska Street. But you leave her alone, sir; her father doesn't want anything to happen to her.' He thanked me and left. I thought he had a present for her. Everything comes in handy these days. But he just went and seduced her, the fox. I call it a shame and a disgrace. She's not even fifteen. What will she grow up to be now? Antek's going to take this hard. It's his only daughter. And where were your eyes, miss? What did she go off with him for? You've made us a laughing stock."

"Don't worry, we'll catch this bird."

"Well, he should get what's coming to him. Such a smooth liar. He sat on this very bench. I didn't tell Antek because I was afraid he'd worry. He's got an awful temper. What did the Count tell you, the usual stuff? Don't you have any brains? Now, listen here, answer when you're spoken to."

Kasia remained silent.

"Well, the damage is done. She's ruined. A poor child, an orphan. Let's hope she doesn't get pregnant. It'll be awful when the neighbors hear of this. Antek will be wild. Is it my fault, officer? How could I know that the man was such scum? I was taught to answer politely when a person speaks to me. We don't live in a wilderness. I may be a sinner, but I go to church every Sunday, rain or shine. I never fail to light a candle. The day before Easter, when the priest comes to bless the bread, he doesn't leave here empty-handed. I wanted to be a mother to her. I didn't want her to leave home. Her dead mother, Stachowa, was like a sister to me. But Antek said, 'She'd better get used to working.'"

Suddenly Kasia interrupted, "You're lying. It was you who drove me out of the house."

There was a moment of silence and the woman retreated a step.

"It's you who are the liar."

"I'm telling the truth. You hardly let me have a crust of bread. You locked the breadbox."

238

"Officer, it's a lie. She's made up everything. She ought to be flailed. Antek wanted to beat her. He tried, but I burned the stick. He'd soaked it in slops. She may be your daughter, I said, but don't forget she's an orphan. Let God punish her. So it was me that he hit, my body. You ungrateful creature, you little bitch. Don't count on me any more. I don't care if your father breaks every bone in your body."

"Whipping is against the law," the policeman observed more to himself than to anyone else.

"Yes, I know, but sometimes a man just has to hit out. There was a fellow on this street who beat his own child to death. He's still in prison. He got five years; he's been in three and a half already. His wife brings him food packages every Friday."

"Beating is against the law."

"Well, God's will be done."

"You'll all be called as witnesses. And don't let her out of the house. She has to show up in court too."

"Absolutely, officer. We'll keep an eye on her."

A number of women had gathered at the door of Antek's house. When the policeman left, they moved aside to make a path for him. Then they entered the house.

"What's happened?"

"Can't you guess?"

They gathered in a corner and began whispering to each other. As the story was related to them, they glanced over their shoulders at Kasia. She stood in the center of the room, wearing a ragged shawl instead of the fine, broad one she had inherited from her mother. When Antek came in, the women grew silent. He stood at the threshold in a torn sheepskin jacket and a cap with a broken visor. His clothes were spotted with paint and mud, although he hadn't worked for a long time. Even his face was speckled with paint. Out of the corners of his close-set eyes he glanced at his daughter, and then fixed his gaze on a shelf full of pots and bottles at the other side of the room.

"What's this mob doing here?"

"A dreadful thing has happened to Kasia," the woman who lived with him announced. "It's a real misfortune."

"I've heard. But what do they want?" Antek pointed at the still silent women.

He took a step toward them and the women began to push in the direction of the door. The apartment emptied quickly. Antek looked at Kasia but said nothing. He knew what happened to girls who had no mother to care for them.

"All right, take off your shawl."

18

Calman never mentioned Miriam Lieba's name, and no one dared speak of her in his presence. He had mourned seven days for her after her flight, and she had ceased being one of his daughters. Mentally he compared her to a fingernail disposed of, to hair trimmed off forever. Nevertheless, he could not help hearing reports of her. He knew she had returned from France and was living somewhere in Warsaw with that vicious goy, and that she had given birth to a child. His enemies sent him "poison pen" letters through the mail; he'd start reading these letters and then rip them to pieces. Well, he had more than earned whatever was said. Although he avoided thinking about Miriam Lieba during the day, he could not control his thoughts at night. He had brought forth an apostate; through her, wicked men and Jew-baiters might descend from his loins. What could be worse? Yet was he any better than the offspring he had spawned? Like Esau, had he not sold his birthright for a mess of porridge?

Calman lived in the manor house, occupying the Count's bedroom and sleeping in his bed. Clara had not only taken over the house, but had purchased its furnishings. All that remained for the Count was what Clara had let him have: a mare, a cow, a few books, and a britska. Calman continued as always to provide the old Count with oats, flour, barley, and groats, and he was also permitted to hunt in Calman's forests and fish in his pond. However, Jampolski's needs were decreasing. Antosia now cooked for him only once a day, and never anything but rye dumplings with milk. Yes, Count Jampolski in his old age had divorced himself from all luxuries while Calman, the Jew, had taken up residence in a palace, amid gold, silver, porcelains, lackeys, and servants. He slept in a velvet-canopied bed, on a horsehair mattress. Next to him in a twin bed lay Clara, partner to his estate and his lime quarries. She called herself Madam Clara Jacobowa, and she was pregnant. She might even be carrying a male child. Yet even the hope that she would produce a son who would say Kaddish for him after his death did not keep Calman from realizing that he had committed a grave error.

From the very beginning of their marriage, they had argued bitterly and she had spoken like a wanton woman. She did as she pleased, without advice from him. She dismissed his help and hired her own, wrangled with the neighboring landowners, and invited guests Calman did not want in his house. Calman had always spoken kindly to the peasants and had overlooked their minor delinquencies, but Clara was extremely strict with them. Any peasant whose cow strayed into Calman's pasture had to pay a five-ruble fine. Everyone had to account to her. When she entered their office, the cashier and bookkeeper had to rise. She had quickly squandered her few-thousand-ruble dowry, buying her dresses in Paris. She was now talking of remodeling the manor house. Until she became pregnant, she had continued to go to the ritual bath for Calman's sake, performing this virtuous act with resentment and insisting that no other woman be present when she entered the water. A bathtub with a lid that could be locked had been ordered for her private use. In the opinion of the women of Jampol, the ritual bath was defiled by her licentious conduct. Her spidery stockings reached her hips and were attached to a corset, the attendants reported; her slips, chemises, and underpants were made of silk and were lavishly trimmed with lace. She rode to the ritual bath in a carriage!

Although Calman worked hard (the expenses had increased exorbitantly), he slept fitfully. Who would have imagined they could spend so much? Clara lived like an empress, flinging money about, ordering people around. Before the marriage, she had bought a queenly trousseau, and her closets were filled with clothes and accessories, but as soon as the wedding was over, she complained she had nothing to wear. She screamed at the maids and constantly criticized the kosher cook Calman had brought from Warsaw. When she wanted the smallest thing, she yanked the bellpull. All her whims and her passion for luxury were indulged, yet she never stopped complaining. The meat was either too tough or too tender, the soup too fat or too watery, the compote too sweet or too sour. Although the floors shone so brightly that Calman thanked God each day that he didn't slip, Clara insisted they were dirty. She lied so much and made so many accusations that Calman could hardly believe his ears. He knew wicked people existed; where else did wars come from, or the calamities that had befallen the Jews? But for a Jewish daughter to know so much about sin! Her words of endearment were mixed with derision. She mocked Calman's beard, his long capote, his prayer shawl, his praying, and his habitual "God willing." She would speak to him affectionately and then address him as a stranger. Although the peasants had no love for the Polish gentry, they resented the fact that a Jew was living like a count in a count's own manor house. The priests, now forbidden to complain about the Russians, vented their anger against the Jews. In Jampol and Skarshew, Calman's enemies spread all sorts of slander about him. It was rumored that in his household there was cooking on the Sabbath, that the utensils were not kept kosher, that Calman had relations with his wife on her impure days. Mayer Joel hardly spoke to his father-in-law. Jochebed avoided him. An occasional postcard came from Tsipele, but Jochanan did not add his greetings in his

243

own handwriting. Shaindel had an apartment in Warsaw. Calman wanted her to stay at the manor with Ezriel and the child Yosele, but Shaindel kept making excuses. Calman knew the truth; she hated her stepmother Clara.

Hate, hate, hate! He found it everywhere. Plots of one kind or another were constantly brewing among his lumbermen and clerks. The peasants were always quarreling. The Rabbi of Gur's Hassidim wrangled with those from Alexandrow. Tamara Shalit denounced Sonya Sorkess. Sonya Sorkess made fun of Mrs. Grain, the apothecary's wife. Everyone, Clara said, was a thief. When Calman suggested that if Clara bought fewer ornaments there would be less chance of her being robbed, she replied scornfully, "Don't think you're talking to your Zelda! I am Clara, and I love pretty things, not Jampol rags!"

I I

Twice each month Clara gave a party or *wetcherinka*, as she liked to refer to it in Russian. The same people were always invited: Colonel Smirnoff, Lieutenant Papricki, the druggist Grain and his wife, David Sorkess and Sonya, Morris Shalit and Tamara, and sometimes Dr. Lipinski from Skarshew, and such officials and minor clerks as are only to be found in a small town. A military band was hired to play. For Calman the *wetcherinkas* meant only trouble: they cost too much; Clara, preparing for them as if for a wedding, required new clothes; the floors were waxed and the house was cleaned and dusted, even though it already shone. For the few days preceding the *wetcherinka* Clara cried, scolded the servants, and threatened to run away or kill herself. Calman appreciated the words of the sages who claimed that all sinners were either partly or totally insane.

Calman found himself eating with Gentiles. The food was kosher, but what about the wine? It was strictly forbidden to drink wine with Gentiles. Although Calman himself did not taste the wine, he suffered agonies sitting beside these modern Jews and Gentiles, listening to their blasphemy, flattery, and mockery. Each time Clara wore a new dress, they praised it extravagantly. Every delicacy tasted like something out of paradise. But their praise was edged with ridicule. There was venom in their politeness. While eating their host's bread, they made fun of him. Their conversation, usually in Russian, was spiked with double meanings; their eyes winked and their tongues hissed. When the men told jokes, the women laughed wildly. Cruelty and lechery were the substance of their humor. They knew all the best spas, all the most chic hotels. They knew everybody. Calman ate in silence. He was afraid to think of the many sins resulting from such a banquet.

The *wetcherinka* did not reach its height until the musicians began to play and the dancing started. Clara passed from hand to hand. Her gowns were extremely low cut, back and front. As she danced, her skirt flew up, exposing her legs. She danced with all the men. With Colonel Smirnoff, she put her hand on his epaulette and he clasped her waist; as they danced, the spurs on his polished boots jangled. In the hallway hung the swords of the officers. Calman, more astonished at his lack of foresight than shocked at the behavior of the others, could only blame himself. What had he thought she would devote herself to—studying the Bible? Didn't he have eyes in his head? Or had Satan pulled the wool over them? How could a Jew, the son of pious parents, witness such goings on? Did the mezuzahs on the doorposts approve? And God? "I am mad, mad!" Calman said to himself. "I deserve to be torn to pieces and drenched in acid!" Licentiousness was everywhere, in every glance and smile. The ladies were bareheaded; the pianoforte tinkled, the trumpet blared, the drum pounded. A company of adulterers and harlots had gathered in his house. Could these women be anything but whores when they let strangers touch their hands, their shoulders, their hips?

Calman stood against the wall, his hand on a chair. Opposite him, in a mirror, he saw himself, in a knee-length frock coat

245

and a silken skullcap. His beard seemed shorter, even though he hadn't touched it. Had Clara trimmed it while he slept? Despite the heat of the stove, Calman felt an icy chill in his ribs. Colonel Smirnoff's face was flushed from drinking; his short blond hair bristled like a hog's, his eyes watered, his coarse laugh seemed to imply: what's mine is mine, and what's yours in mine, too. Winking at the lieutenant, he clicked his heels, calling out to the music: "Da-da! Hop! Hop!" The lieutenant's wife, on the other hand, danced with David Sorkess. That's what happened at a *wetcherinka:* they exchanged wives.

"Is it real? How did it happen? Have I forgotten God?" Calman asked himself.

The music stopped. Colonel Smirnoff bowed to Clara, Lieutenant Papricki to Tamara, David Sorkess to Nadia Ivanovna. Clara approached Calman. Half naked, adorned with rings, earrings, and brooches, she faced him, her diamonds quivering. Her cheeks were rouged; her eyes flashed as she smiled.

"Why are you standing around staring like that? Do you expect us to cry?"

"No."

"If you don't enjoy these evenings, I won't have them any more."

Calman said nothing. It was not her fault, but his. "May my name be blotted out." For the first time in his life, he cursed himself.

19

Reb Menachem Mendel Babad sat in his study on Krochmalna Street with a Talmudic commentary open before him. The book was *The Face of Joshua*. On the table, amid a confusion of manuscripts, lay a steel pen; next to it stood an inkwell. Reb Menachem Mendel had already brewed tea for himself in the samovar. As the morning progressed, he smoked his pipe, made notes, and studied. He had little time for himself here in Warsaw. Women were constantly coming to consult him on religious matters; occasionally a lawsuit had to be decided; everyone wanted the rabbi's advice, and this included thieves and fallen women, who were forever asking him to work out the proper dates on which to celebrate the anniversaries of their relatives' deaths. Observing such anniversaries was their only pious act. Near the reading stand in Reb Menachem Mendel's study was a six-branched candelabra where long candles burned in commemoration of the departed. Though Krochmalna Street required the services of a rabbi, it was not easy for the rabbi to make a living. Donations were collected weekly, but Tirza Perl suspected that the beadle who made the rounds pocketed more than the twenty-five percent due him. The rabbi's income decreased every week, and expenses were high in the city. Rent had to be paid each month, not yearly. Butter was sold by the ounce, milk by the quart, wood by the bundle, potatoes by the pound. It was embarrassing for Tirza Perl to shop at the market or deal with the butcher. Her neighbors did not buy in the small quantities she was used to. They cooked in big pots, for Russian trade had brought prosperity to Poland. Apartment houses were being built everywhere and new stores were being opened. Facing the same courtyard as the building in which Reb Menachem Mendel lived was a stocking factory and a shop for manufacturing silk thread; there were also cobblers, tailors, and joiners in the buildings. Yes, the Jews, God be praised, were doing a prosperous business. But an unofficial rabbi received no salary.

Reb Menachem Mendel pulled at his red beard. Some latter-day commentator had attempted to analyze difficult passages in the text of *Maimonides*, but his explanations were casuistic and ambiguous. His interpretation contradicted Rabbi Samuel Edels's commentary. Was it conceivable that Rabbi Samuel Edels could have been in error? The new era was almost unable to understand the ancient way of thinking. Yet one had to try, and now and again heaven assisted the scholar. Reb Menachem Mendel drew on his pipe, picked up a glass and took a sip of watery tea, put the glass down and rubbed his high forehead. Trying to solve these problems was like banging one's head against a stone wall.

He began to chant as he read. Who would have thought that things would turn out as they had? He was in Warsaw. His son Ezriel had separated himself from everything Jewish. Despite his responsibilities as a father, he had discarded the capote and was studying to be a doctor. Mirale had moved out of the house, was not interested in marriage, and was training to be a hairdresser. She spent her time combing the hair of rich ladies. Suddenly Reb Manachem Mendel had found himself childless. What had he done, he wondered, to deserve this? Somehow the guilt had to be his. Ezriel might have married the daughter of the Skarshew rabbi, but Reb Menachem Mendel had preferred a match with one of Calman's daughters. And how that had turned out! One of the other Jacoby girls had become an apostate; Calman himself had married a wanton. How did the saying go? One sick sheep was sufficient to infect an entire flock. Now it was hard to know whether anyone would recite Kaddish for him after his death. If he didn't keep on studying the Torah and storing up good deeds, he would arrive in the next world empty-handed.

"Well, let's see what *The Face of Joshua* has to say for itself."

There was a knock on the door. Tirza Perl was still asleep in the bedroom, and Reb Menachem Mendel opened the outer door himself. A woman stood at the threshold, and so he averted his face.

"Papa, it's me, Mirale."

"Oh you. Well, come in."

His face flushed. Since his daughter had left home, she seemed like a stranger to him; he was embarrassed in her presence. He looked at her. She had a hat on her head, not a shawl. The upper part of her body was covered by some fashionable-looking garment. Did she bathe herself with scented soap? Reb Menachem Mendel sucked on his pipe.

"Well, Daughter, what do you have to say for yourself?"

"I've come for some linen that I forgot to take."

"So!"

"Mother is asleep?"

"It seems so."

"Father, there's no need for you to be angry with me," Mirale said.

"No need, eh? Your brother has become completely irreligious. I'm told that he even visits that apostate, Miriam Lieba. You've left home. You've both brought us nothing but shame and disgrace."

"What have I done wrong? All I'm doing is learning a trade."

"The first thing a Jewish girl must do is marry."

"Marry whom? That good-for-nothing Jonah? You yourself said he was a fool."

"I? God forbid."

"I'd rather die an old maid than marry such a simpleton."

"Well, how old are you now? You're twenty-four, may you avoid the Evil Eye. Other women your age have children."

"What have I missed? Someone from Skarshew told me that Jonah has become an assistant teacher in a cheder. He has a sick wife and a houseful of children. I've lost a lot, haven't I? Look at me, Papa. You may look; I'm not a stranger. Do you see how I'm dressed? I work and I earn money. I don't have to depend on anyone. Is that such a sin?"

"A Jewish girl marries."

"I'll marry. I'm not seventy years old. I'll have a husband I like and not some schlemiel that Yankle the Matchmaker has chosen. How can that hurt God?"

"No one can hurt the Almighty. 'Is it any pleasure to the Almighty that thou art righteous?' The commandments were only given to assist men. When you marry, you settle down. If you associate with loose women, it's easy for you to go astray. The Talmud says that if we go into a spice shop, pleasant odors cling to us, but if we go into a tannery, we come out stinking. One is easily trapped by the words of heretics. Who are these contemporary philosophers? A pack of murderers and lechers!"

"Many of them are decent people."

"The body is everything to them. If, as they say, there is no God, then it doesn't matter what one does. At first we are tempted by some minor sin, but as soon as that is committed, the will lures us into more serious evil. Without law and a judge to administer the law, there is no reason why one should restrain oneself. Why not give in to evil completely?"

"Because one is a human being."

"A human being! If one does not serve the Almighty, one is even less than an animal. Animals kill only for food; murderers enjoy killing."

"Papa, exactly who are all these murderers? The peasants? Don't they work hard enough to feed the world?"

Reb Menachem Mendel looked at his daughter in astonishment.

"Why bring in the peasants all of a sudden? Some are decent and some are wicked."

"Where does the bread you eat come from? Someone has to plow and sow so that you'll have your Sabbath loaf. The peasant works for everyone and goes hungry himself. Do you call that justice?"

"It was destined that the peasant remain poor."

"No, Papa, it isn't destiny; it's robbery. Everyone fleeces the peasant: businessmen, aristocrats, even your pious Jews."

"Only swindlers rob people."

The bedroom door opened and Tirza Perl entered the room. Her shoes were unlaced. There was a red kerchief on her head. Her dress was baggy and she looked sallow and drawn. Warsaw had made her old.

"Well, look who's here. The debates are beginning again!"

"I ask him a simple question but I don't get an answer."

II

How unfathomable are the ways of Providence! Temerel, instead of marrying Calman, Jochanan's father-in-law, became the wife of the Komarover rabbi, a recent widower, who in addition was her daughter Yentel's father-in-law. The match was arranged by Hassidim of both courts. Although Jochanan did not approve of the match, he made no attempt to influence his mother. The Komarover rabbi did not stem from an illustrious line. His grandfather had been a dairyman. His father, Reb Abraham Komarover, had established himself by performing a number of exorcisms. Claims had been made that his touch had cured a paralytic, that a cripple had thrown away his crutches at the sound of the rabbi's voice, and that a barren woman blessed by the holy man had become fertile. His had been a lifelong war against the powers of evil; he had beaten them with his cane and driven them off to remote places. His earnings had been kept in earthen jars and had consisted of gold, silver, and copper; he had refused to accept paper money. He had left everything to his son, Shraga Mayer. Shraga Mayer had named his youngest son after Reb Abraham, and it was this youngest son who was now married to Yentel.

Although Shraga Mayer had inherited his father's mannerisms and his following, not even the most ardent Komarover Hassid was under the illusion that Shraga Mayer was the old man's equal. Reb Shraga Mayer shouted and stamped his feet, but the demons paid no attention to him. Neither barren women nor the spiritually ill, neither those afflicted with hiccups nor those possessed by demons came to him for help. His beard was a fiery red, his eyebrows disheveled. More than once Temerel burst out laughing, watching him. He made such strange gestures, prayed so noisily, and the religious commentaries he attempted to write were illiterate. But Temerel wanted to get married. Who likes to live alone?

Her mother agreed to the match. Reb Shimmon was opposed, but the negative attitude of her brother only convinced Temerel that she was acting wisely. So the marriage took place and Temerel settled in Komarov. A few weeks after the wedding, she took a trip to Marshinov to visit her son.

"How are you, Mama?" Jochanan asked.

"Praised be the name of God," Temerel answered.

"How are things with the Komarov rabbi?" Jochanan knew that he should have called his stepfather "uncle," but could not bear to say the word.

"What do you expect? He manages. When benedictions have to be said, he says them. He ushers in the Sabbath and he sees it out." As she spoke, a mischievous glint came into Temerel's eyes. Suddenly she pulled out a handkerchief and blew her nose loudly. "Jochanan, I've signed my own death warrant." Tears flowed down Temerel's withered cheeks.

Jochanan trembled. He pitied his mother but dreaded hearing about the many grievances she had against her husband, since the Law prohibits listening to gossip. Yet, how could he prevent her from complaining?

"Don't worry, Jochanan, I'm not going to talk about forbidden matters," she said teasingly.

"Maybe things will get better."

"How? You can't make a silk purse from a sow's ear."

What had she expected, Jochanan wondered. A man from such a family! He changed the subject. "Is Yentel all right?"

"I guess so. But what use is she? That husband of hers is another barbarian. In all my life I've never met such vulgar people."

"Well, well . . ."

"What am I going to do, Jochanan? They're unendurable. They constantly grate on my nerves."

"You can't expect all people to be the same."

"Your poor father was a true saint. May the qualities that he had not die out! You take after him, Jochanan, may you live to a ripe old age. Your uncle Reb Shimmon is a hard man, but nevertheless wise. The rest of them! Do you know what they do after they eat? They—forgive the expression—belch. Come one o'clock in the afternoon, they're all snoring like bears. At three, they're famished again. They can only think of one thing: food."

"Mama, the rabbi's a scholar."

"Jochanan, you speak like a child. Even I, a mere woman, catch him in errors. If his scribe Reb Israel didn't correct everything, people would laugh themselves sick. Whatever has to be written is written by Reb Israel. And what does he get out of it? He's starving to death. My husband pays him in promises. The man's not a rabbi; he's nothing but a crooked peddler."

253

"Mama!"

"Why are you shocked? Because a man is called a rabbi, does that make him one! A water carrier can have the soul of a rabbi and a rabbi be nothing but a swindler."

"You're right, Mama."

III

Usually great throngs of Hassidim descended upon Marshinov during Pentecost, but not many people came in the weeks immediately preceding the holiday. Though Jochanan was devoted to his followers, he welcomed this lax period. Nothing suited him better than seclusion. He opened the book known as *The Two Tablets of the Covenant* and began to study the treatise dealing with the rituals and customs of Pentecost. He had been in a melancholy mood that morning, but his spirits improved after prayers. Why was he worrying? He did not have to be a saint. Supposing he did burn in Gehenna? Since there was a Creator, what did man have to fear? Jochanan listened to the birds twittering. A rooster crowed, perhaps one of the fowl which would be slaughtered for the holiday. Well, what difference did it make? Slaughterer, knife, rooster were identical. There was no death. Life existed in every tree and every blade of grass. Jochanan listened more intently, heard crickets chirping, frogs croaking. In the study house, men were chanting the Torah. Somewhere close by, children were reciting a passage from the Pentateuch—or was it the Mishnah? Suddenly a butterfly flew into the room and alighted on the page of the book Jochanan was reading. Love for this creature which had no knowledge of evil and served the Creator in its own way welled up in him. He wondered if it were capable of thought. Did it somehow sense the sanctity of the holy book on which it was resting? Its speckled wings were as delicate as silk. Was it trying to read something? Was it thirsty or hungry? On the table before him was a glass of tea he had been sipping as he studied. He poured out a few drops

254

of the liquid and dissolved some sugar in it. "Drink," he said, addressing the insect.

The butterfly did not move. But the sugar did attract a fly. It stood on the table bending its tiny head, somehow getting itself entangled in its hind legs. Another fly dropped down, landed on top of the first. Jochanan saw what the creatures were doing. All living things united, the small as well as the large. Everything was either male or female. Suddenly the meaning of the passage, "And rejoice with trembling," became clear to him. He himself was trembling in a kind of ecstasy. Who could help but exult when God's greatness was to be seen everywhere? When winter came, this poor fly would die of the cold. He himself would probably live somewhat longer, but no one was immortal. Only the soul mattered. Then what was the sense of worrying? One must serve as one could. One must be joyous. Jochanan rose and began to pace up and down. God was present, watching him and listening to his thoughts. Sinners were to be pitied; they were God's children also, but having forgotten their father, they suffered torment even while indulging in their sensual pleasures. Yet the suffering that they inflicted upon themselves served some purpose. God had created Satan so that man should have free choice, although the path chosen by sinners was the more painful one. Transgression! Ruin! Jochanan rubbed his forehead. His thoughts were too dangerous. He must dismiss them from his mind.

The Hassidim had told him of a Russian organization whose members were committed to overthrowing the Czar. They wanted to help the peasants, taught them to read newspapers. Some of these people had assassinated a governor or a prince, and had been exiled to Siberia. Jochanan grasped his beard. How could the Czar be overthrown? And what if he were? Another Czar would come along. Meanwhile, the revolutionaries suffered. In Siberia, the winters were very cold. But was a soldier who killed on orders guilty? He only did as he was told. As for the Czar, he had been born Czar. Jochanan had learned that some of the revolutionaries were Jews. He groaned. Small wonder! Those who abandon the Torah and associate with the wicked and speak their language become ensnared.

The door opened and Mendel the beadle entered.

"Rabbi, there's a stranger outside, a Hassid, who would like to see you. He wants to get your opinion on something."

Jochanan raised his hand. He constantly prayed that his following would decrease, but nevertheless the Hassidim continued to come. His opinion? What advice did he have to give? Yet how could he refuse to see the man?

"Well, tell him to come in."

As Jochanan spoke, a small, yellow-haired man entered. His beard was also yellow. Everything about the man was yellow: his freckled face, his hat, his patched coat, even his eyes. An odor of axle grease and far-off places came into the room with him.

"Peace be with you, Rabbi."

"Peace be with you. Good day. Be seated."

The man remained standing.

"Where do you come from?"

"I'm from Wysoky. Actually I'm a Turisk Hassid. Where I come from, you go to the court either at Turisk or at Beltz. In our town there are a few Hassidim of other courts as well, but they don't have houses of worship. One of them is an old Kotsker Hassid. He likes to tease the community by smearing cheese on his mustache on the ninth day of Ab to make people think he's eating on a fast day. May it never happen to you, Rabbi, but my daughter began to suffer from terrible stomach pains. The doctor in Zamosc told her to go to Lublin and have an operation. By the time she arrived in Lublin, the pains were gone, but the doctor said that didn't matter, that she must have it anyway—how do you say it?—surgery. We went back to Wysoky and the rabbi said, 'Well, if it's better, it's better. Anyway, I don't believe in the knife.' But when she got home the pains started all over again. She almost climbed up the walls. I was told to take her to Warsaw. In Warsaw one specialist says cut it out—I forget what he called it. Another specialist says, wait. The rabbi, may his life be long, has a reputation as a saintly Jew, and although I'm a Turisk Hassid, I've run up expenses coming here. Whatever the rabbi thinks best, I'll do. Forgive me, Rabbi, I forgot to give you . . ." And the Turisk Hassid pulled a piece of paper and a silver coin out of his pocket.

"Thank you, I don't accept money," Jochanan said. "How can I advise you? God is the adviser."

"You don't take money?"

"No. But thank you just the same."

"In Turisk, even paupers give. It's said that nobody is helped by a rabbi who refuses money."

"Obviously the Turisk rabbi needs it. My father-in-law is a wealthy man."

"Rabbi, what should I do about my daughter?"

"How can I tell you that? I'm not a doctor. You pray and I'll pray. One never knows whose prayers will be answered."

"But I need your advice, Rabbi. I'm an uneducated man. How can I come to a decision when the specialists don't agree? The Turisk rabbi doesn't believe in the knife, but there are times when it's needed. The daughter-in-law of the rabbi had an operation herself. She went to Vienna for it."

"So? It was probably necessary."

"The rabbi was against it, but she didn't listen to him. The doctors say the operation saved her life. Her father is a rabbi, too, and he insisted that she have it."

"Honoring your father is most important of all."

"Rabbi, what should I do?"

"Ask another doctor."

"I don't have a gulden left. I spent my last one to come here. You must tell me something, Rabbi."

Jochanan looked down and saw something that startled him. There was a gold watch in his satin waistcoat, a wedding present from Calman. Jochanan was overcome with shame.

He had been searching in his drawer in an attempt to find a few groschen to give to a poor man and here in his vest pocket was a scrap of that gold from which the ancient calf had been carved. Woe unto him. How easily one forgot and was ensnared by Satan. He lifted the watch as if it were unclean.

"Reb Shloime—that's your name, isn't it?—take this watch and sell it. Don't tell anyone I gave it to you. It's gold, pure gold."

"The rabbi's watch? No, I couldn't."

"Please, Reb Shloime. I am forbidden to have anything like this in the house. The longer I keep it here, the graver my sin. Believe me, you will be helping me. Perhaps because of you I will be forgiven. I should not have worn it even for one day. See a specialist, and if you have any money left over, use it for traveling expenses."

"I just can't take the rabbi's watch. One must give to a rabbi, not take from him."

"Reb Shloime, please. The Almighty will assist you because you have helped me."

"I refuse to take it."

"I command you to."

Jochanan knew that he should not have used the word "command." A word such as that was only uttered by a saint. But there was no other way to overcome Reb Shloime's obstinacy. Silently Jochanan prayed for the Hassid's agreement. The Wysoky Jew's yellow hands began to tremble.

"Rabbi, you're a saint, a great saint."

"Please, you mustn't say such things. I am only doing what the Law commands. You wouldn't have found a groschen on the persons of the ancient rabbis, but in my house there's gold. This trinket can save a life. What good is it to me? Take it. God will certainly help you."

"The rabbi swears to that?"

"With the Almighty's help."

"I won't leave until the rabbi promises me my daughter will get better."

Jochanan was disturbed. What did the man expect of him? How could he give such assurances? He himself was a transgressor. For all he knew, he had committed a host of such sins as he had discovered today. How many other things had he forgotten? Now the Evil Spirit was forcing him into the ways of pride. The only solution was to flee, go into exile. Yet should he promise? If he did not, the man might consider his unwillingness a bad omen.

"Yes, I promise you."

"She'll get well?"

"With God's help, she'll bring you joy."

"Rabbi, my business is bad."

"He who giveth life also giveth food."

"Rabbi, my wife's knee hurts. They say it's hermetic."

Jochanan found it difficult to keep from smiling; Reb Shloime meant rheumatic. He bit his lip and reminded himself of the Diaspora, of the destruction of the temple and of the sufferings of the Jews. Removing his hands from his face, he said, "Your wife will recover completely."

20

I

When a son, Alexander Jacob—or Sasha, as Clara called him
—was born, Calman was ecstatic. God had granted him an
heir. Clara had had a difficult pregnancy, had grown unusually
large. In the middle of winter, she had a craving for cherries
and Calman had managed to obtain them from a rich landowner who had his own hothouse. Sasha entered the world
large and husky. The Warsaw accoucheur said it was a miracle that the child was delivered without tearing his mother's
womb. He bellowed like a six-months-old baby and had a
head of black hair. The circumcision was like a wedding and
included a banquet for the poor. Both the Skarshew rabbi and
the new Rabbi of Jampol came to the ceremony. The child's
grandfather, Daniel Kaminer, recited the benediction. Although Clara's breasts were heavy with milk, she engaged a
wet nurse. The nursery was decorated sumptuously. Clara
bought a scale in which to weigh the infant, imported a baby
carriage from Berlin, read books and articles on child care.
The child grew and began to walk and talk in his tenth month.
Calman bought the boy an amulet to ward off the Evil Eye.

Before Sasha was even three, he started to climb trees.
Wildly mischievous, he mistreated the pets the peasant
woman brought him as gifts, stepped on the puppies, at-

tempted to strangle the kittens. He threw a baby chick into the water. He dismembered his toys. Finding a knife somewhere, he cut off a doll's head. At first Calman consoled himself saying that it was all because the boy was, may the Evil Eye spare him, so amazingly strong. But as time went on and the child remained incorrigible, Calman's fears increased. He complained to Clara that the boy ate too much. He forbade the child toy whips, swords, and guns. But Clara warned Calman not to interfere.

Jampol found the boy a subject for gossip. They laughed at him and cursed him. Clara bought him a pony and a small britska with a fancy harness. She forbade him to speak Yiddish and hired a French governess. He was taught not to answer when he was addressed as Senderel, to respond only to Sergei and Sasha, his Russian names. Eventually Clara herself began to have trouble with him. He grew fat from overeating, hit his governess and the maid. He laughed wildly. The townspeople nicknamed him Ishmael. Calman was furious, but the name was appropriate—Sasha was a savage.

Finally, after much discussion, Calman convinced Clara that a tutor should be engaged to teach the boy religion. Sasha pulled at his teacher's beard and laughed at the man's fringed garment. It was said by Calman's enemies that his son's black eyes concealed a devil. The boy made fun of everyone, stuck out his tongue, spat, ridiculed Yiddish. Suddenly he acquired a passion for lighting fires. It was impossible to hide matches from him. Whatever fell into his hands burst into flame. The servants predicted he'd burn down the manor house. Clara finally slapped him herself. He broke into laughter and hit back. He began to howl and retch. One afternoon he set fire to a haystack. That day Calman spanked him. The boy shrieked, "You dirty Jew," and kicked his father.

Calman lost control of himself and hit Sasha with all his might, then locked himself in his office and wept. It was the first time since Zelda's funeral that Calman had cried out loud.

Sasha's nose was bloody; he had a swollen cheek. Clara pounded on the office door and, when Calman opened it slightly, shouted, "If you ever touch my son again, I'll kill you."

Calman threw the door wide open.

"Go ahead and kill me, you slut. Your filthy blood flows in his veins."

"Be careful, Calman; I'm not going to warn you again."

Calman fasted the next day and recited the whole Book of Psalms. He swore that this was the end, that he would never make peace with his wife, but she came to him that night, kissed him, tickled him, playfully counted the hairs of his beard, and promised to stop her private war against the Hebrew teacher. But several days later she decided that the manor absolutely had to be renovated. She had waited long enough. The building was impossibly old-fashioned, the roof an incredible patchwork.

"It was good enough for the Count. Why not for you?" Calman protested.

"The Count! You know he's an old idiot."

The reconciliation scarcely over, another quarrel began. It would take many thousands, Calman said, to rebuild the manor. His money was tied up in the business and he was short of capital. Besides, God's needs preceded everything and he had promised to build a prayer house on the estate. Clara laughed, wept, threatened, called him names and warned him that she would run away with the child, or commit suicide. She even announced that she would take a lover and make Calman a cuckold. He sat on the bed in his long nightshirt, skullcap on his head, his beard in disarray, dangling his feet. Clara disliked arguing in the dark and had lit a candle. Calman saw his reflection in a mirror; there were gray hairs in his beard. The world beyond was already calling to him and he was spending his time wrangling with this bitch who had borne him a monstrous child. She paced up and down the room in her bare feet, her hair hanging down over her shoulders, her naked breasts visible through her nightgown. As always when they argued, she addressed him by the formal "you."

"You're wasting your breath arguing, Calmanke. The house will be renovated. All this talk will do as much good as bleeding a corpse."

"I'll build a prayer house and a ritual bath first."

"A ritual bath? Who are you going to soak in it, the Queen of Sheba?"

"You foul-mouthed woman!"

"You feeble old lecher."

Calman could no longer listen to such wickedness. During her pregnancy, when she had feared for her life, she had prayed to God. Now that she was well again, she blasphemed. He picked up his pillow and a blanket, and went into another room to sleep.

11

Clara wrangled with her father as well as with Calman. In his old age Daniel Kaminer had grown foolish and wanted to marry Celina, Mrs. Frankel's daughter. Clara was anxious to prevent the marriage. She was his only heir, and if he married he might spawn a half-dozen more children. Father and daughter spoke to each other sarcastically, argued and bickered. Clara informed him that his contract with the government might easily be cancelled. General Rittermayer would prefer to do business with her. Since she controlled the manor, she could underbid Kaminer. Moreover—as she pointed out in a guarded manner—she was in a position to expose him. The old man became so furious that he burst out laughing. They didn't come any smarter than his daughter. He suggested a compromise; he'd give her half his fortune now. Why should she wish him dead? But maybe she'd poison him anyway. Clara laughed. "If you weren't my father, I'd marry you myself."

"Yes. And if your grandmother had wheels, she'd roll."

"Honestly, what do you want with Celina?" Clara asked, crossing her legs. "You're much better off living as you always have. You know what I mean."

"Ah, it's different when you get old."

"Does she really appeal to you? She's such a mess. Some day she and her room will float off together. Till now she's spent her life sleeping at her mother's house; she'll finish it sleeping at yours."

"I'll wake her when I need her."

"What a man!" Clara said, laughing. She adored her father. The two of them understood each other perfectly.

"How do you know she'll have you?" Clara asked.

"We'll have to talk it over with Auntie."

"Who'll do the talking?"

"You," Daniel Kaminer said.

The conversation continued, each trying to be wittier and more salacious than the other. Daniel Kaminer denied that his fortune was as large as his daughter claimed it to be. But she knew where every ruble was invested. Pencil in hand, she worked out an exact division. The two of them haggled like tradesmen. Then they started teasing each other all over again. Suddenly Daniel Kaminer grew sad. "If only your mother were alive." His eyes moistened. Clara wanted to cry, too. She went to the credenza and took out a bottle of brandy and a carafe of liqueur, poured a drink of brandy for him, liqueur for herself. It annoyed her that in his old age her father wanted a woman to replace her mother. But having been appointed matchmaker somewhat mollified her. Nevertheless, she anticipated having difficulties with Celina; the silly girl would be unable to make up her mind. It would have to be made up for her. On the other hand, it was pleasant to have an excuse to visit Warsaw. And then, of course, best of all was the money she was to receive from her father. Why wait for an inheritance? She hoped that he would live to be a hundred, or even longer. Who was there in the world closer to her than he?

She had been wanting to go to Warsaw for some time, and for a number of reasons. Her plans to renovate the manor required the services of an architect. She was also anxious to consult her lawyer. Moreover, there were a number of people she wanted to see, among them Miriam Lieba and her mulish husband Lucian; Ezriel, too. Until her pregnancy, Clara had been busy courting the Wallenbergs, but the difficult time she had had bearing her child had interrupted her social activities. After the delivery, there had been a procession of wet nurses, maids, and governesses to add to the confusion. Since Sasha's birth she had visited Warsaw only a few times and then always to see doctors. It was now more than three years since the baby's birth and Clara looked younger and prettier than ever. However, the trip was not as easy as it might seem to arrange. Sasha was so wild that Clara did not like to trust him to the servants. Leaving her possessions behind worried her, too; she dreaded the possibility of thieves breaking into the manor house. On the other hand, she couldn't stand guard over her property forever, like a dog chained to its kennel. What sort of a life would that be for a rich, intelligent woman? She must hire servants she could trust. She'd have to find the right tutor for Sasha. Boys respected men more than women.

So as not to leave an angry husband behind her, she made up with Calman. Let him build both his ritual bath and his synagogue! In Warsaw she would get estimates on how much the construction of the buildings would cost. Clara went even further. She told Calman about her agreement with her father, and offered to lend Calman money to assist him in his plans. After all, she was his wife, the mother of his son. "Calmanke," she said, stroking his beard and peering into his eyes, "you don't realize it, but I'm the best friend you have."

"If you could only be like this all the time," Calman replied gruffly. "All I want is that we live like human beings and remember God."

"And what do you think I want? If only half of what I wish for you would come true . . . Your good fortune, Calmanke, is mine."

Calman, after having satisfied his lust, was soon snoring, but Clara lay awake for a long time. The clock seemed to her to be ticking at a feverish pace. Her pulse was beating just as quickly. She couldn't stop planning, wanting, and hoping. It was as if her blood were boiling within her. "What's happening to me? Why am I so driven? And what am I so afraid of?" she asked herself. She knew the answer; obstacles always littered the path to her happiness.

III

In Warsaw, before going to Mead Street, Clara drove to Marshalkovsky Boulevard to buy gifts for her aunt and Celina. What madness, Celina was to be her stepmother! Men were so stupid . . . Clara bought a pair of large gold earrings for Mrs. Frankel and a fur stole for Celina. She saw her own attractiveness mirrored in the knowing glance the sales clerk gave her. "I'm a pretty woman," she thought. "It's worth having a guilty conscience because of me." She imagined herself a man in love with such a woman. When she got into the droshky, she put the packages on her lap. There was no one, experience had taught her, who could not be bribed. You could even buy off God with a ritual bath or a prayer house. The summer day was warm, not hot, and a breeze blew from the Vistula. The odors of fresh fruit and new potatoes permeated the air. Street cleaners splashed the gutters with a white fluid resembling diluted builders' lime. Despite the din created by droshkies, omnibuses, coaches, and pedestrians, the chirping of birds could be heard. It was already noon. Clara had had nothing to eat since an early breakfast but she did not want to arrive at her aunt's with a full stomach. No insult was greater to Mrs. Frankel than a guest who had just eaten. Mrs. Frankel loved to serve and be served food, to give and be given presents. A variety of aromas floated down the stairway; the odors of borscht, cutlets, tomatoes, parsley. Clara inhaled deeply; the smells titillated her appetite. When she knocked, two girls ran to open the door and began to clap and shriek as soon as they saw who it was; Clara never arrived empty-handed. Shears in hand, Mrs. Frankel hurried toward them. In her haste, she had neglected to remove the scissors from her fingers. She kissed Clara first on the lips, and then on both cheeks, and topped it all by screaming with joy. Clara kissed the girls, too.

"Where's Celina?" she asked.

Although it was afternoon, Celina was still in her bathrobe and slippers. "Well, if she appeals to him, it's all right with me," Clara thought, kissing the girl.

"She has an ache in her shoulder," Mrs. Frankel explained apologetically. "Last night we rubbed her down with turpentine, but it hasn't helped. So I told her to sleep as long as she wanted to. Anyway, there's no reason for her to get up."

"You never can tell; she might hatch a few eggs . . . Auntie, I've brought you both a little something."

"A little something! What a spendthrift you are, Clara."

"What do you want me to do, take my money to the grave with me? These earrings are for you. Pure gold!"

"Oh, it's too much, Clara. I can imagine what they must have cost."

"And this little neckpiece is for you, Celina. Feel the nice furry animals."

"Look, Mother. Isn't it gorgeous? Oh, Clara, it's just exquisite."

"Shush, don't make such a fuss. You're a good-looking girl and you should wear nice things. All right, the rest of you, don't stare. I haven't forgotten a single one of you. You'll all get something. Honestly, Auntie, I'm as hungry as a bear."

"Hungry, are you?" And Mrs. Frankel skipped girlishly into the kitchen. There was a pot roast simmering on the stove; peas were boiling. Whatever the peddlers had hawked that day in the courtyard, Mrs. Frankel had bought: raspberries, gooseberries, cherries, and currants. There was bread left over from breakfast, but Mrs. Frankel sent a girl to the bakery to buy a fresh loaf and some warm Kaiser buns. Clara removed the jacket of her suit and her ostrich-plumed hat, one of her aunt's creations. With only a blouse and skirt on, the thickness of her waist and the fullness of her bosom became apparent. Childbirth had filled out her figure. Now she no longer needed to pad her hips and her buttocks. "Oh, Clara, you have such wonderful taste. Isn't that brooch new?" The girls looked at her with admiration. Everyone had to examine and touch her. One girl, an expert on fabrics, lifted Clara's skirt to inspect the material on the left side. Clara began to answer questions. Having read the Parisian magazines, she could describe the very latest fashions. In the midst of the commotion, Mrs. Frankel entered, bringing hors d'oeuvres. As if addressing a yard full of hens, she called out: "Scat . . . Shoo." Laughing, the girls hurried back to their wires and feathers. They were busy preparing for the winter season.

Clara refused to eat alone, insisted that Mrs. Frankel and Celina have something with her. Mrs. Frankel pointed to her throat and swore that she was full up to there, but as soon as she took a bite of food her appetite returned miraculously. Celina scarcely touched anything. Her mother grimaced scornfully. "Just look at the girl, Clara. This is her breakfast."

"I've already had a pretzel with milk."

"That's food? What's going to become of her?" Mrs. Frankel's tone changed. "Clara, darling, she'll kill me. I don't sleep at night. There's scarcely a trollop in the world who doesn't find a husband. But Celina's still an old maid. It hurts me here," she said, placing her hand on her chest. "A girl who refuses to leave the house."

"I suppose you'd let me?"

"Be quiet, or I'll slap that saucy face of yours. A young man used to come to see her, handsome as a picture, a ladies' tailor; he had a tiny little mustache. When the girls saw him, they almost fainted. He worked at Silvermintz's, earned twenty rubles a week, and he was exempt from the draft. No wonder the girls buzzed around him. Who gets such a prince these days? Originally he'd come because of a customer, but when he saw Celina I thought he'd been striken with an epileptic fit. It made me feel good. Who knows? Perhaps they were destined for each other. My fine friends were envious already. But did that girl make an effort? About as much as a wall. He talked and she yawned. Pretty soon he lost interest. Did you ever hear of anything so awful?"

"What's so awful about it? I didn't like him."

"Whom do you like, you idiot?"

Clara smiled. "What's he like, Celina?"

"Oh, he's just a fop. Tries to give you the impression that he's Mr. Somebody."

"And just who are you? It happens that you're my daughter and I've got to love you. But if you weren't—"

Mrs. Frankel didn't finish the sentence. Tears fell from her eyes. She took out a handkerchief and blew her crooked nose.

When Clara announced that afternoon that her father was not getting any younger and was looking for a wife, someone he could trust, Mrs. Frankel's left eye snapped open. It had occurred to her that if Daniel Kaminer were not so avaricious and lewd, he would be a perfect husband for her. A man who lived by himself was worse off than a dog. And how long could she struggle with her shop? Her strength was ebbing.

"You understand, Clara, I'd have to talk it over with Celina."

"With whom else?" Clara asked. "It's Celina we have in mind."

Mrs. Frankel puffed herself up like a brood hen hatching an egg. Her eyes looked bloodshot. A piercing note entered her voice.

"I thought you were a smart woman, Clara," she exclaimed shrilly. "But you're talking like a fool."

"Auntie, let's not kid ourselves, Celina's no child. Before you

269

know it, she'll be thirty. It's time she got married. And my father's no octogenarian; he's not even seventy."

"I don't want to talk about it any more, Clara. I'd rather see her in the Gęsia Street cemetery."

"Well, no is no, but you don't get such an opportunity every day."

"Clara, you've hurt me. All right, he's your father I know, but what else can be said for him? He's nasty, a Litvak, and he talks like a lecher. Can't you find something better for Celina? You should be ashamed of yourself."

"All right, I'm ashamed. But I'm not speaking for myself; my father sent me. Don't think I'm going to get a matchmaker's fee. Let's forget that Celina's your spoiled darling and look at the facts. She's not young, can't do anything, certainly not keep house! Of what use is she? My father knows all that. Suppose she did get a young man! As soon as she started to act the way she does with you, he'd serve her with divorce papers."

"What are you talking about? She's a charming, sweet girl, and good-looking, too. I'll admit she's a trifle spoiled, but she'll make someone ,a good wife. She doesn't run around like the sluts of today."

"Who's she going to get? The ladies' tailor? Well, he hasn't asked her yet. From flirting to behold-you-are-consecrated is quite a jump. And even if he does stand under the canopy with her, what's twenty rubles a week? You'll have to give her a dowry. A young man doesn't want to work for somebody else forever. He's probably younger than she and she'll have to mother him. The first time he swears at her, she'll come running home. Auntie, I only want the best for Celina. I love her like my own sister. But we must be practical."

"Oh, so you want to be practical? Your father's an old man and a drunkard to boot."

"How old is he? Let me tell you, he's a lot stronger than

most of the young ones. Have you ever felt his grip? He's thin, but powerful. He does take a drink now and then, but never too much. And I've never met a smarter man. You should have the money he makes. He's educated too, a Hebrew scholar. I know that I sound like a matchmaker, but after all we're family. He'll sign over one of his houses to her, or something comparable. What's more, there'll be a money settlement written into the marriage contract. She can be sure of one thing: she won't be in want. Look at me! Didn't I marry a man twenty years older than myself? I was not much older than Celina when I went to live with Calman."

Mrs. Frankel shook her head from side to side. "Clara, you're such a schemer. You have a man's head on your shoulders. Calman's not like your father; he's a respectable man. He lost his wife and he remarried. Your father's been a widower for thirty years. You can't do anything with a man who's a profligate."

"Well, no is no. But you can't turn me against my father. If I weren't related to him, and didn't have a husband, I'd take him myself. He knows the world. You can talk to him. Every word he says is worth listening to."

"He should have a wife his own age."

"Why, when he can get whomever he wants? Don't be offended, Auntie: there's an old saying that one has the right to proposition even the rabbi's wife."

"I'm not offended."

Both women lapsed into silence. Mrs. Frankel sat, her nose wrinkled, her lower lip protruding, trying to contain her anger. Her legs felt heavy. She knew full well that Celina couldn't be dragged to the wedding canopy, but the fact that someone had had the audacity to suggest an old widower for Celina was insulting. It was now clear to her why Clara had been so generous with her gifts. "The sly witch," Mrs. Frankel thought. "Insinuates herself into my confidence and then spatters me with mud. It would be better for Celina to die a spin-

271

ster." Clara's eyes glistened as she thought to herself, "A lot of difference it makes to me. That's some bargain he's losing. Anyway, she hasn't given her final answer."

Clara rose to her feet. "Auntie, let's not be enemies."

"Why should we be? Have I lost anything? Sit down and I'll bring you your applesauce."

"No, Auntie, I've got to run along."

Clara took a quick look at herself in the mirror, and then left. Mrs. Frankel's knees were trembling. Even her own workshop seemed unfamiliar to her. She stood at the threshold of the workroom and watched the hustle and bustle. One of the girls was ironing, another was pulling felt, a third was sprinkling water on some material. The room was infernally hot and clouded with steam. There was the odor of something burning. "Devils in Gehenna. What are they doing? What do I need all this for? I don't have the strength to go on any longer." She rushed off in search of Celina, found her in the bedroom, taking off her nightgown.

"Mama?"

"Just look at you!"

Mrs. Frankel slammed the door shut. She had a bitter taste in her mouth. All of her life she had worked hard, and what had she got for it? Other mothers could take satisfaction in their children. She had given birth to something rotten. A girl who spent her life in bed, who wouldn't even dip her hands in water! Did she deserve anything better than an old man? What would happen to her when she didn't have a mother to depend on? There wasn't any money for her to inherit. Mrs. Frankel imagined herself dead. Who would dress her in her shroud? Suddenly she remembered God. "Why am I living?" she asked herself. "What will become of my soul?" One thing she could do while she was still alive: buy a plot in the Gęsia Street cemetery and order a tombstone. Otherwise, when she was buried, she would be completely obliterated.

When Miriam Lieba and Lucian had returned from France, Clara had tried without Calman's knowledge to find a job for Lucian. She was impressed by the fact that her stepdaughter was a countess. There was also the fact that Clara had taken over the Jampolski estate and wanted to make some amends. Lucian, however, had ignored her halfhearted attempts, and Miriam Lieba had not been interested in her favors. Every now and again Clara would hear something about Lucian. He had come to terms with Antek and had taken Kasia in as his maid. For a while he'd worked for the Warsaw Benevolent Society, but then something dreadful had happened. A number of the charitable ladies who supported the Society had formed a group which staged dramatizations of stories and poems by various Polish writers. Only a very select audience attended these performances, which were held in the drawing room of a member of the group. Occasionally some highly placed Russian official would be invited, sometimes even the Governor-General himself. The ladies and their daughters made the costumes. The dialogue was written by an amateur writer. Lucian didn't care much for his work at the office, and managed to get himself sent out on loan to the ladies. After he'd taken part in several of the plays, the women agreed that he was a born actor. His name was even mentioned in the *Kurjer Warszawski*. But the older ladies, having heard rumors about him, began to insist that he no longer be invited to participate in the plays. They didn't think it safe for their unmarried daughters to meet him. The younger generation argued that a hero of the uprising should be treated with charity.

Then suddenly scandal broke. Clara, who at that time was still tied down to the baby and was not coming to Warsaw, had never been able to learn the details. She did know that there had been an antique music box involved. Apparently the box had disappeared from a house after a visit by Lucian. He had come through the front door to see the lady of the house and later the same night had returned through the back door to visit the maid. The lady of the house had found him in bed with the maid and had chased him into the street, clad only in his underwear. He had been arrested and sent to jail for two weeks. Later it was discovered that he had embezzled money from the Society and had been planning to elope with a young woman student. Oddly enough, the Wallenbergs had stood bail for him. They had also made good the sum he had stolen from the Society. The music box had turned up later in an antique shop on Holy Cross Street.

For a time, Clara lost track of Lucian. Then she was told that he had become the protégé of the widow of an actor, a certain Elzbieta Bobrowska, a seamstress, and was doing walk-ons at the Rozmaitosci Theater. Kasia had given birth to a child, who had immediately been deposited in a home for foundlings. She was now acting as housekeeper for a widower on Chmielna Street. It was said Lucian had sold her to the man. These stories fascinated Clara. She remembered how little interested Lucian had been in her when they had first known each other. He had promised to write to her but hadn't kept his word. Clara forgave him. All right, he had acted foolishly. The one thing she couldn't forget was that he had never once tried to kiss her. Nor had he been the only man with whom she had failed. Her good looks and her aggressive manner did not assure success with everyone. Grisha, her first husband, had left her before he'd got consumption. Men would start off hot in pursuit of her and then suddenly lose interest. Colonel Smirnoff's ardor, for example, had cooled off considerably. Finally he'd been transferred to another garrison. The same thing had happened with General Rittermayer. Curiously enough, the only man who couldn't stop wanting her was Calman.

Often on sleepless nights Clara would meditate on this. When she'd attended the gymnasium she'd had crushes on her teachers and on a number of boys, but had always been rejected. It was these failures that accounted for her marriage to so crude a man as Calman. Not being able to get love, she had settled for money. She remembered the evenings she'd spent at Grain's, playing cards with the Sorkesses and the Shallits. Good cards had always flown her way. They'd all joked about her good fortune at cards which meant failure in love. Every so often David Sorkess would kiss her, and Morris Shallit liked to pinch her bottom. But they never took her seriously. Even the inscriptions that officers and students had written in her school album had been more ironic than romantic. Whenever Grisha got angry, may he rest in peace, he would curse her for being so vulgar. But in just what way was she vulgar? She certainly dressed with chic. She knew how to play the piano, could speak Polish well and Russian perfectly. Her French wasn't too bad either. What did other women have that she did not?

That afternoon, having left Mrs. Frankel's, Clara paused in the courtyard at the gate and looked about her. She'd been so anxious to get to Warsaw, but now that she was there she didn't know what to do with herself. Should she go to see the unfortunate Miriam Lieba, or pay a visit to Shaindel? Perhaps she might look in at her tailor's. She had been given the address of an architect but wanted to find out more about him before seeking him out. There was her lawyer, of course, but he was always so busy. From the newspaper Clara had learned that a famous Italian composer was that day conducting one of his own works at the Dolina Szwajacarska. But she couldn't attend a concert by herself. Alas, a woman could not go anywhere unescorted. Men were lucky. Theaters, cabarets, clubs, and even the hangouts of thieves were open to them. A man could buy a woman for a few rubles if he wanted to. He could indulge all of his desires, no matter how perverse, and his reputation didn't suffer. If only she had been born a man, she would have shown the world a thing or two. Clara finally decided to visit Miriam Lieba on Obozna Street.

The droshky that she hailed took her down Hozia Street

and out into Krakow Boulevard. Clara had the coachman draw up at various shops, where she bought toys for the children and some flowers for the Countess. She made clear to the shopkeepers that the gifts were to be wrapped attractively because they were intended for members of the aristocracy. The sales people smirked and bowed politely. Now that it was summer, Obozna Street didn't look as desolate as it had when Clara had last been there. The acacia and fruit trees were in bloom. Birds were singing; dogs were chasing each other. Small girls sang as they rolled hoops in the middle of the street. Their song was about a haughty lady who refused to become an empress and later disdained saving her life by marrying the executioner. Clara listened. Young though the children were, they were already singing of love. She was overcome with desire. Her father was planning to take a girl as his wife, and she, his daughter, had shut herself up with an old man, a religious fanatic. "A ritual bath, of all things," she mumbled. "It's high time I found myself somebody else." She paid the driver and entered the courtyard of the house where Miriam Lieba lived. She knocked at the janitor's door and gave the man a gulden to go upstairs and announce her. Clara stood watching the janitress pump water. A crippled old woman hobbled across the narrow yard, tapping with her cane and grumbling to herself.

The janitor returned, cap in hand. "Forgive me, madam," he said, "but they refuse to open the door. They've locked themselves in."

"Maybe they've gone out."

"No, the Countess is there. I heard her. She shouted at me."

"Where are the children?"

"The children? A lady took them away. Dr. Zawacki's wife . . . to the country . . . to Wilanow."

"Well, thank you," Clara said, and she tipped the man again.

He bowed deeply. "God bless you, madam. Perhaps I can be of further assistance to you?"

"No, never mind. I'll go up there myself."

"Something may be going on there. The Countess is in a bad mood."

"It doesn't matter."

Clara mounted the stairs, holding the packages in one hand and her pocketbook in the other. When she reached the door of Miriam Lieba's apartment, she gave it a kick. She didn't know quite why, but she was determined to beat on the door until she received an answer. There was the sound of footsteps within.

The door was flung open. Clara saw a woman dressed in a cotton skirt that was too short, and wearing scuffed slippers on her bare feet. The woman's half-faded golden-blond hair had been hastily combed and was held in place at the top of her head with a single hairpin. Yes, it was Miriam Lieba. But she was so changed that Clara had difficulty recognizing her. In a few years she had become old and emaciated. Her cheeks were pale and hollow; her eyes, sunk deep in their sockets, were underlined with heavy shadows. Lusterless, they were the eyes of a person who has grown tired of life.

"Well, what do you want?" Miriam Lieba spoke angrily. On her breath was the odor of vodka.

"Forgive me, Countess. I am your father's wife—Clara. We met several years ago."

The two women studied each other. Miriam Lieba's lip curled as if she were about to say something cutting.

"Clara?"

"Yes, your father's wife."

"What are the flowers for? We haven't had a death here yet."

"God forbid. They're for you, Countess."

"Well, come in."

Clara was surprised to see what sort of a place the Jampolskis lived in. The plaster on the kitchen walls was crumbling; the stove was littered with dirty pots and pans. Onionskins, potato peels, the remainder of a bag of chicory were scattered

277

on the floor. The window was shut. There was a cloying, sweetish odor that suggested the apartment had been neither aired nor swept in weeks. Miriam Lieba took Clara into the living room, which was in the same disorder as the kitchen. The drawers of the dresser were open and clothes and laundry were scattered everywhere. On the table was an empty liquor bottle. Here, too, the windows were closed. Miriam Lieba shuffled to the center of the room and remained standing there.

"It's a mess, isn't it?"

"It doesn't matter."

"Some very generous people have consented to keep my children. I'm here by myself. There's no sense in doing any housework. What shall I do with the flowers? There's no water in the barrel. I stopped tipping the janitor and so I don't get any water. Just put the flowers on the table. Let them wither. Everything around here withers anyway."

"I'll have the janitor bring you a bucket of water."

"No, don't bother."

Clara laid the bouquet on the table and put the packages on the windowsill. She looked for a chair to sit on, but all of them were piled with clothing and other objects. Miriam Lieba took hold of a chair, tilting it to clear it of clothing.

"Won't you sit down? No one comes to see me, that's why . . . Did you send the janitor up? He knocked on the door."

"Yes, I asked him to announce me."

"Why did you do that? I never let him in. We're at war with each other. He's a spy, too. Gives information about me to the comissariat. They've already registered my furniture. The marshal came in with a policeman to attach my possessions. I owed eighteen rubles and fifty kopecks. What brings you here? Now no one comes to see me."

"But you are my stepdaughter."

"What? I'm still someone's daughter? I'd forgotten. Sometimes I feel I've never had anyone. I just exist, like a stone on the riverbank. Well, how is he, my father? I call him Father

278

although he's disowned me. When I left, he told everyone I was dead. He observed shivah."

"Countess, you can be sure that he thinks of you."

"He thinks of me? What does he think? I can't even remember what he looks like. Is his beard gray?"

"A little, not entirely."

"You have a child now, don't you?"

"Yes, a son. Sasha. He always asks about his sister the Countess. When he was **born,** I wrote you a letter, but I never received an answer."

"You wrote? When? The letter probably came when Lucian was at home. He steals my letters. He steals everything. He must have taken that, too. Well, now that I'm a grown woman, I'm blessed with a brother! That's really funny. When I was a child, I always wanted a brother. I envied girls who had little brothers to play with. But now it's a trifle too late for something like that." The tone of Miriam Lieba's voice changed. "This seems to be the final act of my little tragedy, or perhaps it's a comedy after all. What difference does it make? Unfortunately I don't have a thing to offer you, not even a glass of water." Miriam Lieba rose, ready to show her guest out.

2 1

At last Ezriel had enrolled at the Szkola Glowna, which the Russians had transformed into a royal university, and was studying medicine. Wallenberg had kept his word and had helped. He knew most of the faculty and was friendly enough with the dean to have him to dinner. Ezriel found studying for a degree difficult. The Russian language still confused him, although he did well in mathematics, physics, chemistry, and botany. He had heard that students in foreign universities led a gay life, drank endless tankards of beer, and played all kinds of pranks on the rector and the university administrators. Nothing of the sort went on in Warsaw. One had to work hard to get into the university. Political activity on the part of the students was discouraged by the Russians. The Polish press was constantly preaching the same sermon: industrialization and culture was its theme. Polish youth was becoming increasingly preoccupied with education. It was almost considered a patriotic duty to become a doctor or an engineer.

Ezriel was now the father of two children; the older one, Uri Joseph, or Joziek in Polish, already attended school. The younger child, Zelda or Zina, went to kindergarten. But Ezriel still walked about in a student's uniform. Evenings, while Joziek did his homework, Ezriel looked over his own lecture notes. He was taking courses in the history of medicine, analytical chemistry, surgery, and ophthalmology. Anticipating the curriculum, he was always ahead of the assignments and frequently read additional books on the subject, not required in the course of study. He rummaged about, frowned, hummed to himself. The habits of the study house stayed with him. The Polish and Russian students were not as serious as he. They joked in the morgue. For him, medicine was no laughing matter. First of all, it was a science and an art. Second, it bordered on mysterious realms. How little was known about the functions of the brain! No one had as yet discovered how traits were inherited. Wherever one looked, one was presented with riddles. The study of medicine was a great responsibility. Ezriel's throat constricted and his mouth became dry each time he entered the morgue. The corpses lay on the metal tables, covered by sacks. The smell of formaldehyde made Ezriel's head reel. He couldn't grow accustomed to the rigid cheeks, glazed eyes, deformed noses, and sagging chins of the dead. These bodies had only recently been living creatures, hoping and planning. Ezriel could almost hear them whispering to him, "Too late, too late." It seemed to him that in death they had discovered a truth that would have altered their lives radically if they had learned it in time.

Once Ezriel saw a student put a cigarette into the mouth of a girl who had died of poisoning. The other students winked at each other and laughed. They found life and death equally funny.

That year Calman had again invited Ezriel and Shaindel to visit the manor with their children. Clara thought well of university students. Besides, Zina, Ezriel's daughter, was about the same age as Sasha. In any case, whom else could Calman invite? The apostate Miriam Lieba? Tsipele, the wife of a rabbi? Jochebed and Mayer Joel, who remained aloof? Ezriel and his children were the only ones who could possibly stay at the manor. However, Ezriel and Shaindel were in no hurry to accept the invitation. Shaindel still found it difficult to pass even a day with Clara. One look at her father's new wife,

Shaindel said, gave her a spasm. Ezriel liked the manor's fields, forests, and meadows, its rural calm, but if Shaindel wasn't happy there, what sort of vacation would it be?

In the summer evening Ezriel sat at the table reading a biology text by the light of a lamp suspended from a chain. As he read about centrosomes, chromosomes, protoplasm, and cytoplasm, he listened with one ear to the activities going on in the apartment. Ezriel liked quiet, but Shaindel was noisy. Or maybe it just seemed that way to Ezriel. He still loved Shaindel, but her increasing corpulence disturbed him. After the birth of each child, her waist broadened several inches. Her bosom had grown pronounced, her hips too round. Only her face and legs remained maidenly. Constantly warning her to eat less chocolate, jam, and halvah, he had shown her published proof in a medical journal that sweets ruined the teeth, accumulated fat around the heart, and even led to diabetes. Shaindel ought to be especially careful, he told her, since her mother had been diabetic. Shaindel insisted that it was Ezriel's fault she overate. She longed for him constantly and it made her yearn for food.

Actually, Shaindel had remained provincial. She could not give up her small-town habits, and bore a grudge against Ezriel for studying so much and reading so many books. She still spoke the Polish of a peasant and could not even write an address properly. Her own son, Joziek, caught her in errors. Shaindel no longer wore a wig—but she had remained a pious Jewess. She attended the ritual bath, asked advice of rabbis, threw coins into the alms box for the holy rabbi Mayer, the Miracle Worker. For two and a half weeks out of the month, Ezriel was not permitted to go near her. When a child sneezed, she tugged at its ear. On the eve of a new moon she gave the children a potion to prevent worms. Behind Ezriel's back, she consulted wonder rabbis and even gypsies. At times it seemed to Ezriel that Shaindel played a perverse game with him, regressing as he advanced. How had he harmed her, that she should wish to oppose him?

Her jealousy of Miriam Lieba had developed into a mania. He had to promise solemnly not to visit her sister, or even speak to her. Shaindel swore on her mother's memory that if she found he had visited Miriam Lieba or had even spoken to her on the street, she would take the children and run away, or commit suicide.

"I'll leave and you won't know where I am!" Shaindel would scream. "My blood will run down the gutter!"

And although time and time again he swore to avoid Miriam Lieba and not answer her letters, Shaindel continued to harangue him: "You fiend!" she wailed. "You filthy liar. Hurry up, rush off to her. When you come back, I'll be lying with my feet toward the door . . ."

In her rage she would pound her head against the wall.

I I

Ezriel did not have to look far to see the workings of heredity. Joziek took after his mother. The boy was small and darkskinned, had black eyes and hair, red cheeks, and a small nose. He was as good-natured as Shaindel had been when Ezriel first met her. In his cap and brass-buttoned black jacket with its military collar, he looked like a toy lieutenant. Joziek got the very highest marks, nothing but four pluses and fives. He spoke Russian like a native, and had acquired fluent Polish from his playmates. Ezriel had engaged a French mademoiselle to teach the boy, and he had learned French quickly. No subject proved too difficult for him. He was a favorite of both children and teachers. Shaindel often said that she had grown stout merely from looking at her Joziek.

Zina, nearly three years old, was blond and blue-eyed and tall for her age. Shaindel had to discipline her constantly. When Zina was denied anything, she had a tantrum. She had started to talk early, but in a language of her own. She put everything that she found into her mouth, and had once swallowed a button. At times expressions appeared on her face that

K

reminded Ezriel of his grandfather Reb Abraham Hamburg. Whenever Zina threw her toys about, stamped her feet, or cried, Shaindel remarked, "Look at that temper. There's no doubt about who her father is."

Yes, the drop of semen, barely visible through a microscope, had somehow carried from one generation to another thousands of physical and spiritual characteristics. How were the mannerisms of Zina's Turbin grandfather hidden in the chromosomes? Was it the work of a few molecules? Or did some kind of tiny soul dwell in the semen? Anything was possible. Was not matter itself a secret? No one had seen an atom or a molecule. Nor was the true character of gravity, magnetism, electricity, or sunlight understood as yet. What then *was* known? Indeed, was knowledge possible for man when all his experience had to be filtered through the prism of space and time and the purely subjective categories of quality, quantity, and causality? Ezriel knew that he should devote all his time to his medical studies, but he found himself drawn to the works of Spinoza, Kant, Fichte, and Schopenhauer. How could one go on living in the midst of such mystery?

"Ezriel, come to bed."

"Yes, dear. In a moment."

"You'll ruin your eyes, Ezriel. You don't let me sleep either."

"I'm coming. I'm coming."

Ezriel was still not making his own living, and Shaindel's dowry had already been consumed. Nevertheless, they had hired a maid. Her name was Tekla. Ezriel heard her rearranging the straw in her mattress. Evidently she was about to retire for the night. She had her own little world. She ate and slept in the kitchen. It was there that her friends and suitors visited her. Sundays she went to church. Once a month she received a letter from her native village, written by the county clerk. Ezriel would read it to her: "First of all, we are happy to report that we are all in good health. God grant that you are healthy also. Second, we would like you to know that our cow

284

Kwiatula has calved . . ." Under her pillow, Tekla kept an Egyptian dream book. She dreamed nightly of gold pieces, broken eggs, black tomcats, and dreadful men who chased her with sticks and swords. Ezriel turned off his lamp and went into the bedroom.

"Shaindel, are you asleep?"

"How can I sleep when you have the light on and keep on rustling pages? And Zina will have me up at six."

"I must study. I can't accept your father's generosity forever."

"If you'd listened to me, you wouldn't need my father's help. Look at Mayer Joel. He's a rich man."

Ezriel undressed and got into bed. He wanted to take Shaindel in his arms, but she was still in an "impure" condition.

Ezriel said good night, tried to fall asleep, but sleep wouldn't come. In the dark he visualized the morgue, the tables, the sacks, the dead faces. Why had the tall young man hanged himself? Why had the redheaded girl jumped into the Vistula? How much did a person have to endure before he was driven to do such a thing? Were they now at peace? Was their sleep actually eternal?

Ezriel tossed, doubt-ridden, in bed after the work-filled day. Was it worthwhile to struggle so to become a doctor? Did he really have an aptitude for the profession he had chosen? He was permitted to practice a little now under the supervision of a doctor, but it seemed to him that his diagnoses were rarely correct. And why bother to cure people when hundreds of thousands perished to advance the political ambitions of Queen Victoria or to indulge the caprices of Abdul-Hamid? Here in Warsaw, people lived in dark cellars, three families to a hole. They were devoured by lice, hunger, consumption. What good was medicine if people were driven to death?

Ezriel had had great hopes that progress could be achieved through education. Yet knowledge itself turned out to be extremely precarious. The entities which were said to constitute matter seemed to have almost magical properties. Moreover, the various materialistic theories, and Darwinism in particular, had put almost all values in jeopardy: the soul, ethics, the family. Might was right everywhere. Man's ancient beliefs had been bartered for the telegraph. But what could Ezriel do about it? For him the old traditions were already destroyed. He was left with nothing but examinations and dread. He had forsaken God but he was dependent upon all kinds of bureaucrats. He had made a mistake, Ezriel felt. But what exactly had been his error? How could it be rectified? As he lay in the darkness, it occurred to him that the young man who had been found hanging in an attic room in the Old City and whose dissection Ezriel had witnessed must have had much the same thoughts as he was having now.

III

Mirale had rented a room on Dzielno Street. She had been lucky. She was gifted at the trade she had decided to learn. Six weeks after beginning her apprenticeship, she knew how to set a coiffure. She was sent to the houses of wealthy ladies and given a percentage of the fee by her employer. The women on Marshalowsky Boulevard and Senator Street were delighted with the way Mirale curled locks or braided chignons. When spoken to, she listened respectfully. None of her clients were scratched by combs or hairpins. She pulled gray hair out by the roots so that it would not grow back. She was skillful with scissors, tweezers, and curlers. Would anyone have thought that this quiet girl had so many ideas of her own? When Mirale returned to her room in the evening, she became another person. She put a pot of water for tea or potatoes on the stove and took some bread and herring from the table drawer where she stored food. While preparing supper, she did the lessons that Ezriel's friend, Aaron Lipman, had mapped out for her. She was studying Russian, Polish, and geography. Aaron read

286

to her from Buckle's *History of Civilization in England* and Mill's *Principles of Political Economy*. He analyzed for her Czernishewski's novel, *What Must Be Done?* Mirale, however, learned even more from Aaron's conversations with her than from the books he read to her. Things were happening in the world. The Parisian communards had been hanged, but their ideas could not be destroyed. Aaron told her about the nihilists, the Narodniki, the European socialists. The serfs, though they had been freed by Czar Alexander, remained uneducated and in peonage. Europe was moving forward, but Russia refused to budge. In England, Parliament had more power than the Queen. France was a republic. Lincoln had freed the American slaves. But Russia was still governed by an autocrat. The Jews of Western Europe spoke civilized languages and sent their children to modern schools. Here the Jews spoke a barbaric jargon, dressed like Asiatics, and believed in dibbuks.

How long could they exist in such ignorance? There was only one remedy, Aaron said—education. When people were conversant with the laws of nature and informed about what had happened in the past, they could no longer remain docile. Aaron's program for the future was not always consistent. One day he insisted that the Jews learn Polish, and the next that they study Russian. He had periods when he believed that Poland's salvation lay in forgetting her national aspirations and getting down to the real business of industrializing herself and educating her citizens. At other times he regarded the ousting of her oppressors as her most important task. Whatever his program, he was certain of one thing: the Jews must assimilate. Whenever Ezriel dropped in, he backed up his friend. After all this time, it wasn't very likely that the Messiah was going to come. The Jews would remain in Poland. Since that was so, they'd better reform their synagogues and schools and start dressing like everyone else. This was the second half of the nineteenth century, not the Middle Ages. Ezriel and Aaron did not agree about everything. Aaron was a partisan of the Narodniki. Ezriel did not think that the Jews should get involved in Russian politics. Their first job was to stop being religious fanatics. Anyway, their allegiance was to Poland; let Russia worry about itself. The men would argue and bicker angrily, using terms that Mirale did not understand, referring to people of whom she had never heard. Aaron made fun of the leaders of the world: priests, generals, aristocrats. He considered the Russian peasantry superior to everyone. Ezriel was always so negative in his attitude that Aaron nicknamed him "the pessimist." Finally they would stop debating and sit down to a game of chess. Ezriel would start out boldly and seem the better player, but he soon became bored with the game. Aaron would tug at his remnant of a beard and meditate about each move interminably.

"Where do you think I should put my bishop?"

"That's no bishop. That's your queen."

"Oh, it's my queen, is it? Well, yours isn't worth a pinch of snuff." Suddenly Aaron would begin to chant from the Book of Esther: "Will he force the queen also before me in the house?"

Mirale would break into laughter. Although they spoke constantly of assimilating, they couldn't stop quoting the Scriptures. Aaron was small and dark, and had a high forehead. He was a student of law at the university and supported himself by teaching at an orphan asylum. He was also the founder of a group dedicated to self-education. The group met three times a week in Mirale's room. Ezriel, too, sometimes came to the meetings. The group studied economics, sociology, biology. They were constantly arguing about the important issues of the day: the plight of the peasants, women's rights, the new books. Aaron had a way of attracting people to himself. Among those who came were Alexander Zipkin, a student whose father had once managed the Lithuanian estate of a Polish landowner; Sonya Rabinowitch, a midwife; and Esther Eisner, who had come to Warsaw from Bialystok after having been divorced from her husband, a manufacturer.

Esther was now a seamstress and conducted her own business. Vera Charlap, another member of the group, was the daughter of a rabbi. Vera had run away from home to study at the conservatory. She had developed consumption and had been forced to spend three years in the resort town of Otwock. Now she supported herself by giving piano lessons to the children of wealthy Hassidim. The language spoken at the meetings was a mixture of Russian and Polish. Vera also knew Hebrew. The oldest member of the group was Sonya, who was an inveterate cigarette smoker. Esther Eisner amused everyone by mimicking the gossipy shrews who patronized her shop. Mirale loved to listen to the lectures and the debates that followed them. What was the difference between absolutism and democracy? Did a woman have the right to do as she pleased with her body? What road should today's youth take? The names of well-known writers, critics, and revolutionaries were mentioned. There was talk of the French Revolution, and the young Russian intelligentsia, men and women who "went out among the people." Karl Marx had founded the Internationale; Bakunin had created the Alliance; a student by the name of Karakozoff had attempted to assassinate the Czar. In foreign countries, Russian socialists were publishing revolutionary books and magazines that were being smuggled into Russia. Yes, both in Russia and in Free Europe history was on the move. The arguments went on so long that the floor became littered with cigarette butts. Although what they were doing was not forbidden, Mirale kept the curtains drawn. The Warsaw police became suspicious any time young people gathered in a group. Any stranger seen entering an apartment was reported to the comissariat by the janitor of the building.

IV

After leaving Miriam Lieba's, Clara went to Ezriel's apartment, but he was not at home. She chatted with Shaindel and for the hundredth time invited her to visit the manor. Shaindel explained that Ezriel was at his sister's and suggested that if Clara wanted to see him she would find him there. By the time Clara arrived at Mirale's, Ezriel had gone. Alexander Zipkin offered to escort her down the stairway, which, he warned her, was so dark one could easily slip. Zipkin was a tall, bushy-haired man. Under his jacket he was dressed Russian style in a satin blouse, striped trousers, and a tasseled belt. A cigarette dangled from the corner of his mouth. He had dark eyes and heavy eyebrows, a lean face with side whiskers, and a thin, straggly mustache. As Clara descended the stairs, he took her arm casually and spoke to her in the confident tone of a sophisticate. When they reached the street, he made no motion to return to Mirale's. Clara asked where he was from and what he was studying. Zipkin explained that his father had originally been Prince Radziwill's bailiff. Berish Zipkin had been so highly thought of by the Radziwills that he, Alexander, had been taught by the same tutors as the Prince's children. Consequently he had become a good horseman and an excellent swimmer. But after the uprising a large portion of the Radziwills' land had been divided among the peasants. Although the Prince had escaped complete ruin, he had no longer required the services of a bailiff. So Berish Zipkin had moved into town. Alexander had begun studying medicine in Kiev but had transferred to the University of Warsaw, where he had met Ezriel, who had introduced him to Aaron Lipman and the other members of the self-education group.

"The truth is, it's a complete waste of time," Alexander told Clara.

"How can you say that? Education is very important."

"For the people perhaps, but not for a bunch of old maids."

Clara suggested that he visit the manor during his vacation, mentioning Sasha's need for a tutor. She hailed a droshky and they drove to a confectionary on Theater Place. They sat talking over a cup of coffee about love, literature, money, and the situation in Russia. Zipkin, it turned out, had spent some time in Lomza and had patronized the same apothecary as Clara. Alexander had had some experience in teaching and as a tutor had gained entry into the homes of a number of wealthy families. As a matter of fact, he was living for the summer in the house of a rich merchant who was vacationing in Carlsbad with his family. A maid had been left in charge of the house, but Zipkin had let her go off on a visit to her parents in the country. "If you doubt my word, madam," he said casually, "you're welcome to come and see for yourself."

"You know very well that a respectable woman doesn't visit a bachelor's apartment."

Zipkin laughed. "I haven't raped anyone yet."

"There's always a first time."

"My victims would have to absolutely implore me."

"Well, believe me, I'm not the imploring type."

The apartment was only a few blocks away, on Leshno Street. Despite the lateness of the hour, they decided to walk and sauntered down Tlomacka Street past the newly erected synagogue. No lights were on in the building. Piles of lumber and bricks still littered the yard. Zipkin stopped and looked at the Star of David on top of the cupola.

"Now what's the sense of all that?"

"Jews still believe in God."

"Not the ones who built this synagogue."

The conversation turned to religion. Zipkin said straight out that he was an atheist. People spoke of God, but where was He? Had anyone seen Him? Each race worshiped a different idol. Man, as Darwin had proved, was descended from the apes. He was just another animal: *homo sapiens*. Zipkin began discussing the doctrines of Marx, Lassalle, and Lavrov. The Polish Jew, he said, had once had a real place in society. Before the liberation of the serfs, he had acted as an intermediary between the landowners and the peasantry. He had outlived his role and become little more than a parasite. He wasn't productive, didn't speak the language of the country in which he

291

lived, and sent his children to cheders. How long was the Jew going to wash himself in ritual baths and walk around in tzizis?

Clara burst out laughing.

"What's so funny about that?"

"You don't know why I'm in Warsaw. I'm looking for someone who can build a ritual bath."

"You're joking."

"No, I'm not."

And Clara, with a smile on her lips, told Zipkin about Calman's plans. When Zipkin asked her why she had married such a man, she replied, "I can't explain it even to myself."

Clara knew that it was unseemly for her to go upstairs with Zipkin, but she had no desire to go back to her aunt's and listen to her complaints. And Zipkin was interesting. She liked the way he spoke Polish. He quoted the modern writers, had seen the fashionable plays, visited the latest exhibitions of both the Polish and foreign painters, and knew many of them personally.

When they approached the house and Zipkin rang the bell, Clara glanced quickly over her shoulder as if she suspected that she was being followed. Someone was waiting for her, she mumbled; she must go home. Zipkin paid no attention to what she was saying. The gate opened and the janitor appeared. Zipkin tipped the man and taking Clara firmly by the arm guided her through the doorway. She climbed the stairs with him, her face burning as if from a slap. Her heels were too high; the stairs were too long.

"Just where are you taking me?" she asked. Her mouth had become dry.

"I've already told you."

When they reached the third floor, Zipkin opened a door which led into a hallway. As soon as they were in the hallway, he pulled her to him. His presumption repelled Clara.

"Please," she said, pushing him away. "I want you to light a lamp."

He did as she asked, and led her into a drawing room. The place was dusty. Two brass candlesticks stood on the sheet-draped piano as if at the head of a corpse. As she moved around the unfamiliar room, inspecting the pictures and knickknacks, Clara felt both fear and desire. Zipkin had wandered off somewhere. The air was heavy with the odor of camphor. The dry furniture squeaked, and she felt warm and sticky. A moth began to flutter about the candle Zipkin had lit. Clara looked into a mirror and studied her reflection. She tried to smile at her image, but it gazed back at her with grave aloofness. How many more years of youth did she have? She'd had husbands, but no lovers. If she waited much longer, she might be denied that experience. The candle was smoking. A bit of dust dropped from a stove with a gilded cornice. For a moment Clara thought she heard a key in the door that led to the hallway. Were the owners of the house returning? Her heart began to pound. "I mustn't die here," she thought.

Zipkin returned. He had taken off his jacket and looked taller in his belted blouse. He was carrying two glasses of wine. He handed Clara one and touched his glass to hers.

"To your health."

"My, it's strong."

"Unfortunately there's not a thing to eat in the house."

Clara was aware of the passion in his look. His face was pale. His dark eyes seemed insolent, yet humble too. He spoke in incomplete sentences and breathed heavily. As a rule, Clara was overcome with laughter when men tried to approach her, but this time she remained serious. An unfamiliar sadness took hold of her. "Let's not do anything silly," she protested.

"It's even sillier to do nothing and wait for the grave."

He went into the corridor and bolted the front door, remaining there for a time as if listening for footsteps. He was tense when he returned.

"The neighbors are all at the spas. The whole building is like a cemetery," he said.

"Sometimes I think the whole world is a cemetery," Clara

answered, astonished at her own words. Zipkin moved a bit closer to her.

"True, but one can have fun even in a cemetery."

v

Late that night Zipkin escorted Clara to her aunt's house. No droshkies were available after midnight and so they had to walk. They stood at the gate to the courtyard exchanging the weary kisses of those who are only half awake. When the janitor opened the door, Clara tipped him twenty groschen. Zipkin gave her a final quick pat on the shoulders. She climbed the dark stairway, then paused for a moment to lean on the banister. "Am I happy?" she asked herself, and listened as if waiting for an answer. No, she was not. But why shouldn't she be? She had wanted a lover. Was it weariness or was she ashamed of appearing at her aunt's at such a late hour? No, those were not the reasons. What did men really think of women such as she? How did they talk about them? Zipkin had sworn not to say a word to Ezriel, but he would surely boast to someone. They were to meet the following evening at Semodeny's Confectionery and would discuss Zipkin's visiting Jampol during his vacation. "Well, what's done is done," Clara said, yawning. It was bound to happen sooner or later. She knocked on the door of her aunt's apartment and waited. Her high heels made her feet ache. Her corset cut into her flesh. Her temple was throbbing. Mrs. Frankel appeared, wearing a long nightgown and holding a candle in a brass candlestick. She seemed extraordinarily old and wrinkled; her hair was disheveled and witchlike.

"Oh, it's you. What a scare you've given me. How can a person just run off and not return until dawn? If I'd been sure you were out having a good time, I wouldn't have cared. Let your husband worry about you. But who knows what can happen. The droshkies fly by so fast, you've got to have wings to escape them."

294

"No, I wasn't run over, Auntie. I was just out somewhere and I lost track of the time."

"Oh, you lost track of it, did you? Well, come on in. I lay down but I couldn't shut my eyes. That's how foolish I am. If everyone isn't in the house, I toss and turn like a worm. Well, now that you're here, tell me, are you hungry?"

"Hungry? No, I'm just so tired I can't stand."

"Well, your bed's made. How about a glass of milk?"

"No, Auntie, thanks just the same."

"You remember our little talk. Well, I've had one with Celina, too. One tries to keep things to oneself, but out they come. I told her everything, the whole painful truth."

"Why did you do that?"

"I don't know why she should be so choosy. Well, we'll talk about it in the morning. A mother can fool herself, but never completely."

"So, she's reconsidered already," Clara thought, but without any feeling of triumph.

She walked into the bedroom and began to undress. Though the room was warm and stuffy, Clara felt cold. She was accustomed to having things happen as she willed them. That night a man had done with her as he had willed, a strange madman who seemed to have dropped from the sky. Clara took off one shoe and then sat still on the edge of the bed, her head bowed. What was his name? Oh yes, Zipkin. What did he look like? She couldn't remember clearly. She was content that her longing to have a lover had at last come to fruition. Yet behind her satisfaction there was a threat of failure. Too easily, too easily, she murmured to herself. He will never take me seriously. Well, and Calman? Certainly he did not deserve it . . . Clara had told her aunt she was not hungry, but her stomach felt hollow and she was thirsty too. It was an effort to stretch herself out on the bed, as if during the night she had become twice as heavy. She heard a dog barking and a neighbor's child crying. My God, I may be pregnant. She was amazed the thought had not occurred to her sooner.

She closed her eyes but couldn't fall asleep. Again she entered the confectionery, and heard the orchestra playing. Once more she strolled down the street with Zipkin. She heard him say, "Where is God? Has anyone seen Him? Man is just another animal." Dozing at last, she dreamed that she was mortally ill and lay in a wide bed, propped up by pillows. On her bedside table were medicine bottles and glasses, as well as half an orange, not yellowish gold as oranges usually are, but red. "Probably to give me blood," Clara said to herself in her dream. "But why do I need blood if I'm going to die?" Calman was there also, wearing a white beard and long sidelocks like a rabbi's. A young man who looked like Zipkin came in, but it was her son Sasha. Clara said to him in Polish, "Now you'll have to get along without me."

"No, Mother."

"It's not my decision."

Clara awoke shivering. Her foot seemed to jerk of its own accord. He heart beat rapidly just as it had in that unfamiliar drawing room when she had thought that she was about to be discovered by strangers. She sighed. It was already morning but the light seeping through the draperies was dusky and reddish. She knew she had had a bad dream but could not remember it. Someone had been sick. A rabbi with long sidelocks had come in. Only the image of the half orange returned to her clearly. Suddenly she recalled what had happened the previous night and sat up in bed. She wanted to look at herself in the mirror. "I'm to meet him at Semodeny's," she said to herself. "God in heaven, who would have thought that it would have happened so quickly! As if it had been fated." There was the sound of birds chirping. Turning her face to the wall, Clara went back to sleep. Again she saw the half orange, the medicine bottles, and the old man who was supposed to be Calman. And she was ill, about to die.

22

The crops were not abundant in Poland that year. On Calman's estate, the wheat was sparse, and the grain fell out before it was threshed. Calman's losses were heavy. The wages he paid out to the farmhands were greater than his income. There were duties to be paid, and the duke always demanded his rent on time. The potatoes were small and coarse. There had been no rain for weeks and the grass was scorched. Since there was insufficient hay to last the winter, the peasants sold their cattle cheaply. Normally in August wagons lined up in great numbers before Mayer Joel's water mill, and the peasants waited for days to have their grain ground into flour. But this year there was little to grind. The peasants stopped buying not only luxury items like dry-goods, shoe leather, female trinkets, and herring, but even staples like naphtha and salt. At night they sat in the dark or burned kindling wood, discussing all manner of things. Old peasants said that a flaming witch had been seen in the sky; she rode a broom and was followed by three fiery rams. In the forest, near the village of Maciejow, an old crone was said to have met the Antichrist complete with tail and horns. Frogs and worms had rained down on the village of Lipsk.

The peasants blamed the drought on the Jews. How could there be plenty, when the Jews dried up the earth's juices, drew turpentine from the trees, chopped down the forests, and fouled the air with smoke from lime kilns? Calman had imported threshing machines from Germany. He lived in the Count's manor house with his haughty young wife and their rebellious child. The boy now had a tutor called Zipkin, a man with black eyes and curly hair. Calman himself they could tolerate, but his wife was hostile to the peasants. In the harvest heat Clara went riding each day with the tutor from Warsaw. An amazon in riding clothes, she waved her crop and went off with the stranger into the thick forest among the bogs and caves. What was there to prevent such a trollop from sinning with that spoiled young dandy? Some peasants had even surprised the couple bathing in a forest stream, he in his underpants, and she in her chemise. The peasants chewed turnips, spat up saliva out of starved bellies, and their women remarked: "Oh, well, a young stallion is better than an old nag."

The talk of the peasants and the gossip of the Jews reached Calman's ears. Calman himself was suspicious. He warned Clara that no good would come of her loose behavior. Clara laughed at him. What was he thinking of? One man was enough for her. She didn't give a hoot for Zipkin. Horseback riding— why not? It improved her health. Bathing—what should she do in a heat wave, sit huddled by the stove? She was no frump; she was a sophisticated woman. Let God have His due and man his. She had lent Calman money to build a house of prayer and a ritual bath. What more did he want? Zipkin had done wonders with Sasha, had practically made the boy over. In a few weeks Sasha had learned more from him than from all the previous teachers put together. Hadn't Calman noticed how much calmer the child was? He kissed his parents' hands, no longer set fires, stopped hitting his governess. Zipkin was a born teacher—if only he could be prevailed upon to remain. Unfortunately, when the holiday recess was over, he would have to return to the university. Why, then, was Calman so annoyed? People always had big eyes and long tongues. They even slandered the rabbi.

To prove to Calman how much she loved him, Clara came to his bed at night and kissed and fondled him. She said amusing things and behaved so comically that Calman was forced to laugh and forgive her. Suspicion had stimulated his lust. He could not get enough of her. Laughingly Clara complained that he was breaking every bone in her body. He fell asleep exhausted, satisfied that she had told him the truth. But like Noah before the flood, he both believed and did not believe. He knew that it was a sin to hate—"Thou shalt not hate thy brother in thy heart"—but he could no longer look Zipkin in the eye. He refused to eat at the same table with him. Even Zipkin's effect on Sasha's manners did not please Calman. The boy was not being trained according to the *Ethics of the Fathers*, but was learning stunts like a dancing bear. Now he bowed and scraped and said thank you like the officers and dandies. He walked with a mincing step and had a false smile on his lips. Calman actually preferred the earlier period when Sasha behaved like a savage.

At night Calman sighed in his sleep. When he awoke in the morning, he was ashamed to put on his prayer shawl and phylacteries. As he recited the Eighteen Benedictions, tears ran down his beard. At night Clara's words confused him, but his judgment returned with dawn. "What could the son do except sin?" Was Zipkin a Joseph the Saint? And where would Clara have learned the fear of God—at the Russian school she had attended, or from mixing with officers? Certainly not from the cheap novels she bought or the plays she saw in Warsaw that taught women how to be adulteresses? Clara herself had told him what took place in those farces. The husband always turned out to be a simpleton and the lover a brilliant fellow. Calman recited a saying from the Proverbs: "She eateth and wipeth her mouth and saith: 'I have done no wickedness.'" Yes, Clara had sinned and was still sinning. He had signed over his property to her, and now she was making a fool of him. People stared, pointed, and laughed at him. A man with horns! But what should he do—drive her away? The law

299

was on her side. The judges, lawyers, courts of law had been created to protect the wicked. They would take everything away from him and give it to the adulteress who had never once soiled her hands in dishwater. This was what the Gentiles termed justice.

"Father in heaven, what kind of filth am I walking in?" Calman cried out, clutching his head. "How can this have happened? I am after all the son of God-fearing people." Did he dare recite his prayers, or put on his phylacteries? He was unclean. His home was a bawdy house. No, he was not worthy to utter holy words. Calman put his phylacteries away.

11

Calman did not sleep that night, he lay in his bed still and tense. He could hear Clara snoring and talking in her sleep. She cried out, "Alexander." A man nearing sixty, Calman lay curled up in bed, combatting Satan. From the netherworld of passions a voice rose bidding him grab an ax and first hack Clara to death and then her lover. God forbid that he should yield to such an impulse. Yet it showed to what depths a man had sunk when the Evil Spirit made such suggestions to him, and in the month of Elul, just before the High Holidays. God knew what he, Calman, son of Sender Jacob, was thinking. How could so many catastrophes have befallen him? His daughter was an apostate. He, himself, was only one step away from the abyss. Was it his wealth that had led to such disasters? He had always had a bad temper. Once Zelda (may she rest in peace) had so provoked him that he slapped her. He had forced himself to forget this wickedness, but the Almighty remembered.

Though he found it painful to remain lying on his side, he did not change his position. He should be tortured. But what should he do about Clara? Good and evil warred within him. The Evil Spirit assured Calman that he was already lost. "Rise up and avenge yourself," Satan screamed. "What sort of a man are you? Show the lechers that Calman is no fool. Beat them! Kill them. The peasants will testify in your behalf. It is the mighty who rule; let them know who is most powerful. Remember that even the Talmud says: 'Whoever is the strongest is the victor.' Did not Phineas, the son of Eleazar, with a spear kill Zimri, the son of Salu, and Cozbi, the daughter of Zur? She is a married woman; she deserves death. But you don't have to kill her. Cripple her so that no man will ever want to look at her again. Don't wait, Calman. She'll have respect for you then, and when she grovels at your feet, you'll spit on her."

Calman clenched his fists. He felt if he rose now he would be so strong that he would not need an ax and could smash her skull with his bare fist. He was a giant. He would not allow himself to be shorn of his locks like Samson.

Though Calman's anger increased, the voice of reason continued to whisper. "How much longer do you have to live, Calman?" it asked. "Your beard is already gray. Run away from them, Calman. They have sinned, not you. You're still a decent Jew. Remember your father and mother and your saintly ancestors."

Calman could lie still no longer. He sat up in bed, waking Clara.

"What is it, Calman?" Clara asked.

Calman didn't answer.

"Calman, what's wrong?"

"Shut up, you whore!"

His spirit no longer thirsted for revenge. He bent over and made his ablutions with water from the pitcher that stood on the floor. Then, having put on his slippers and his dressing gown, he groped his way toward the door, bumping against a candelabrum. In this vast building, Calman never knew where he was. He walked out of the house and down the stone steps into the cool night. The sky above him was dense with stars. Staring into the darkness, Calman realized that only a single step separated life from death, piety from evil, truth from falsehood. How careful one had to be! He breathed deeply. The sweat dried on his body. His wrath subsided. He sat down on a stone. The sky seemed close enough to be touched. No, he was not a man of violence. There was a God. Calman knew that his first concern must be for his soul.

The front door of the house opened and Clara came out into the night, dressed in a long white nightgown.

"Calman, what's troubling you?"

"I don't have to tell you, Clara."

"It's all false, Calman. I swear on my mother's grave."

"You did not lie with him?"

"He's never even touched me. I swear to you before God."

Calman sat there, trembling with fear. "Do you know what an oath is?"

"I know, Calman. Believe me, I do."

III

In the morning Calman entered the dining room. Clara was breakfasting with Zipkin. Calman was not dressed in his capote and vest but had on a quilted jacket and skullcap. He walked over to Zipkin. "We have no need for a tutor here," he announced. "Please be good enough to leave my house." Zipkin stopped eating. For a moment Clara was speechless, but then she said: "Calman, have you gone mad?"

"Clara, I'm still master here. I don't want him around."

Zipkin half rose from the table. Clara leaped to her feet. "Don't listen to him, Alexander. He's out of his mind. He can't give orders around here. Everything in this house is mine."

"Pack your bag. Your train leaves at eleven."

"Calmanke, you'll pay for this." Clara picked up a knife from the table as Zipkin walked out. Calman took hold of her wrist and twisted it until the knife fell from her hand. She began to scream.

"Help me, someone! He's broken my arm."

The servants paid no attention to her. They were on Calman's side. The night before, Calman had planned exactly what he would do. Now he moved calmly about, putting his plan into action. He ordered Antoni, the coachman, to drive Zipkin to the train in the britska. He himself led the horses from the stable and harnessed them to the coach. Then he packed his books and clothing and loaded them into the vehicle. Apparently in anticipation of spending the winter on the road, he took along his fur coat.

Clara at once sent a messenger on horseback to her father. She stood at one of the attic windows, pale and frightened. Her husband had set upon her like a brigand, had driven Sasha's tutor away, and injured her hand. Calman was leaving the manor at a time of economic crisis. Zipkin had fled like a coward, hadn't even said goodbye. Clara considered going downstairs and throwing herself at Calman's feet, but she was ashamed to humble herself before the servants. Nor was it likely that the gesture would help her. Calman's eyes were ablaze with anger as he greased the carriage wheels and skillfully arranged the harness. Clara began to calculate just where she stood at the moment. She was co-holder of the lease on the manor, but the lime quarries would not be hers until Calman's death. The demand for railway ties was only half what it had been. The mill belonged to Mayer Joel. Clara was familiar with court procedure but she had had no experience with a divorce action. Perhaps Calman would bring witnesses into court to testify against her. Clara went into the nursery, where Sasha's governess was giving him his French lesson.

Taking the boy by the hand, she led him downstairs.

"Go and say goodbye to your father," she told him, and then returned to the attic window.

Sasha approached his father hesitantly. "Papa, are you going somewhere?"

"Yes, I'm going away."

"Where to, Papa?"

"Back to the Jews."

Sasha felt an impulse to laugh. His father was so comical. He looked more like an old beggar than anything else. He had a long beard, wore strange clothes, and was always walking around with a prayer book in his hand. All he talked about was God and the Jews and what you could and couldn't do. Clara once more descended the stairs and walked out into the courtyard.

"At any rate, kiss the child goodbye," Clara said.

Calman remained silent.

"The coach doesn't belong to you. You have no right to take it."

"Everything here is mine," Calman said.

"That remains to be seen."

"Stay away from me or you'll be sorry."

"Do you want a divorce?" Clara asked.

"I want to be rid of you."

Clara was silent for a moment and then said, "There's one thing I think you ought to know. I'm pregnant."

Calman had a desire to seize her by the hair and drag her along the ground as had been done to adulteresses in the old days. He spat.

"There is a God."

"Come, Sasha darling. If you want war, Calman, you'll get more than you've bargained for."

Why did I keep quiet so long? Calman wondered, after Clara and the child had gone back into the house. Now that he had discarded his worldly pride, his courage had returned. She had committed adultery, not he. Let the wicked feel shame, not the righteous. He had visited Marshinov just once since he had been married to Clara. During his marriage he had been unable to face Jochanan and Tsipele. Now Calman had decided to spend the Days of Awe in that holy place. Let everything at the manor fall apart; he had been working for the devil anyway. Antoni returned, having taken Zipkin to the station, but Calman planned to do his own driving.

Calman, to the amazement of the town's inhabitants, drove into Jampol without a coachman. He went first to his office, located next to a granary. At the back of the building there was a tool shed in which were stored the implements needed for lumbering as well as various odds and ends he had accumulated from the tavern he had once owned.

"Well, you're busy, eh?" Calman said as he walked into the office.

The surprised bookkeeper and clerks had their account books and ledgers open before them. No one said anything. Calman was sure they had been gossiping about him a moment before.

"I'm leaving to visit my son-in-law the rabbi," Calman announced. "I'll be in Marshinov for the holidays, perhaps longer."

Morris Shalit reached for the pencil he carried behind his ear.

"You're going to become a Hassid."

"No, only a Jew. Mayer Joel will take care of things in my absence. He'll sign whatever papers are necessary."

"Mayer Joel? He'll need a power of attorney."

"Yes, we'll have to go to the mill. Take along pen and ink and the sealing wax."

"Do as the boss tells you," David Sorkess said, quoting the proverb.

Calman did not usually issue orders without first hearing the opinion of his employees. Now he stood in the office, silent and determined, whip in hand. The clerks quickly finished the tea they had been drinking. When they tried to pile into the coach, they found that it was so loaded with Calman's possessions that no more than two of them could get in. Ignace Herman climbed up on the box beside Calman. The Jampol merchants came out of their shops to stare. The women, too, left their duties to observe this strange phenomenon. The disheveled heads of girls appeared at the windows. It was obvious to everyone what had happened: Clara had driven Calman from the manor. It was known that a mounted messenger had brought a letter for Daniel Kaminer and, not finding him at home, had trotted off to the barracks in search of him. The Jampol Jews shrugged their shoulders: Calman had made his bed, let him sleep in it.

The carriage trundled along the dirt road that led to the mill. The few wagons waiting their turn there made way for Calman. The peasants doffed their caps and bowed. Mayer Joel came out. He was covered with flour—even his black beard was powdered gray by it. Calman dismounted, and took Mayer Joel aside to speak to him. Mayer Joel was to superintend operations at the lime quarries for a couple of weeks and also take care of Calman's interests at the manor. Calman could no longer endure living with a depraved woman. Mayer Joel listened and stroked his beard. This was the beginning. He had always known that eventually he would take over the property for good. Who else? Ezriel was no business man, and Jochanan was a rabbi. Mayer Joel stood with his father-in-law near the dam. As they spoke, they watched the foaming water spill over the wheel. It was a mild, sunny September day. "*Babie Lato*"—woman's summer—was the way the peasants described this time of year, when the air is full of gossamer. The odor of hay, manure, the scent of pine were everywhere. Chickens and roosters clucked and crowed. Some peasants were transporting logs and boards for a barn which they were building. A ladybug landed on the lapel of Calman's coat.

"Do come into the house, Father-in-law," Mayer Joel said. "You know that you're always welcome here."

"You must ask the clerks in too."

"Never mind them. Let them stay outside."

Jochebed had been busy baking bread and had not seen the coach drive up. She stood with a spatula in her hands, a kerchief on her head, and a broad apron tied around her waist. There were flat cakes in the oven, and on the stove chicken soup was boiling in a pot held by a tripod. Teibela, Jochebed's oldest daughter, was peeling onions. The boys were off at the cheder in Jampol. Jochebed's youngest child was in its standing stool, busily banging with a ladle. Calman stopped in amazement. Jochebed was almost the image of Zelda. He shuddered. She had the same narrow chin as her mother and a similar wart with three hairs growing from it. Seeing her father, Jochebed put down the spatula and clapped her hands in exactly the same way as Zelda would have done. In her eyes was that look of melancholy that no amount of prosperity could banish. A smile brightened her face for a moment and then disappeared.

"Father."

"Jochebed."

She spoke to him just as Zelda would have, love and reproof mingling in her tone. Why did he visit them so seldom? The children were constantly asking for their grandfather. He had become almost a stranger to them. Then, reaching into the pocket of her apron, she pulled out a soiled handkerchief and blew her nose. Calman noticed a prayer book lying open on the table.

"You bake and pray?"

"I was reciting a few chapters from the Psalms."

"How's your stomach? Do you still get that burning feeling?"

"When I eat sharp food."

"Why don't you see the doctor?"

Jochebed's lips puckered in disgust. "What do doctors know? As long as you keep breathing, you're all right."

"A woman your age should be in good health."

"I'm not so young any more. Teibela has already had a proposal."

Teibela's lips tightened. "Oh, Mama, are you starting that again?"

"Have I said anything false? It's true, isn't it? I just want to live long enough to dance at your wedding."

Calman listened awe-struck. Those were the very words Zelda had once uttered. It was as if his dead wife had miraculously risen from the grave.

Mayer Joel interrupted, "Wouldn't you like something to eat, Father-in-law? Let's go into the living room."

They sat talking for a long time. Finally they called in the clerks. Mayer Joel knew all about Calman's lime quarries and the lumber business. The questions he asked showed that he was a clever businessman, even shrewder than Calman. "How does he know so much?" Calman wondered. "Has he been spying on me all these years? Has someone been revealing my business to him?" Mayer Joel could take over the running of Calman's various enterprises at once; he revealed that he even had a lawyer who could handle any litigation that might come up.

"I can die," Calman thought. "I am no longer needed." It was not death that he wanted, however, but the life of a Jew.

THREE

23

After giving orders that she did not wish to be disturbed, Clara locked herself in her room, sat down at the desk, and wept. Her good fortune had lasted not seven years but seven weeks. It was hard for her to believe that it was all over. Both her lover and her husband had deserted her.

Now she had just had an unpleasant visit from her father. Daniel Kaminer had spoken sharply. One either behaved properly or stayed unmarried; at least one did not go around in broad daylight with a university student. Kaminer already knew that Calman had for the time being signed over his business to Mayer Joel, and he suspected that the son-in-law would be a tough nut to crack. For one thing, Mayer Joel visited the gentry, and for another, he was on good terms with most of the officials. Rittermayer was now in St. Petersburg; Smirnoff had been transferred. It was said that the new colonel was vicious, but Daniel Kaminer had not as yet even met him. As things were, Kaminer could do little to rectify his daughter's mistakes. Moreover, he was about to be married and was going to Warsaw to visit Mrs. Frankel and Celina.

As her father spoke, the tears ran down Clara's cheeks. "If I should die," she said, "please take care of Sasha."

"You're not dying yet, Daughter. You'll outlive me."

And Daniel left, slamming the door behind him.

When Mayer Joel came to the manor to talk things over with Clara, she refused to see him. Her message to him was, Do as you please. Two days later she departed for Warsaw, leaving Sasha behind with the governess.

On this visit to the capital, Clara did not stay with Mrs. Frankel, but went to the Hotel Krakowski. As soon as she entered the hotel room, she threw herself on the bed and wept. Later, having made herself presentable, she took a droshky to a small restaurant which was located near the university and was frequented by students. She looked around for Zipkin, but the first person she noticed as she entered was Ezriel. If he had not caught sight of her as well, she would have left immediately. He was drinking tea with another student.

"Good heavens, this is a strange coincidence," he said, rising and hurrying toward her.

Clara had difficulty in restraining her tears.

"Why didn't you visit us during the summer? What do you have against me?"

"I told you we couldn't, Clara."

"Why does Shaindel dislike me?"

Ezriel had no doubt as to whom Clara was looking for. Zipkin himself had not only told Ezriel what a jealous old fool Calman was, but he had not spared Clara. He had called her a parvenue, citing as proof a ridiculous error she had made in quoting a Latin epigram. Having made his excuses to his friend, Ezriel escorted Clara to another table. He was nervous and sat on the edge of his chair, which was turned at an angle away from the table. Clara ordered a cup of black coffee. For a moment there was a strained silence, neither knowing quite what to say. Finally Ezriel remarked that Zipkin had not attended classes that day.

"Why not?" Clara asked. "Is he ill?"

"I don't know."

"Let me tell you, your father-in-law is a fool. A big fool!"

312

And Clara began to relate in short, abrupt sentences how Calman had chased Zipkin from the house for no reason at all. God was her witness that she had done nothing to be ashamed of. "If there had been the slightest truth in his suspicions, it wouldn't hurt so much. I don't care what people think of me." Clara began to sniffle and sob. Everything about her was overdone: the hat she was wearing had too many plumes; her cheeks were too heavily rouged; she had on too much perfume. The students looked at each other and smiled. A woman dressed so extravagantly was a rarity there. Ezriel lowered his head and blushed.

"Don't take it so hard," he said hesitantly.

"But it's all been so humiliating and painful."

Clara seemed on the point of crying again. Finally she managed to get control of herself. "I must tell him how sorry I am. It was a misunderstanding. Do you know where he lives?"

"No, I don't. It's somewhere on Leshno Street in some businessman's apartment. The owner is away taking the baths at some spa."

"Doesn't he have his own rooms?"

"I really don't know."

"I'm not staying at my aunt's this time. I'm at the Hotel Krakowski," Clara said, as if to herself. Ezriel understood that he was to pass this information along to Zipkin. Both of them were silent for a long time. Clara did not even wait for her coffee. Aware of Ezriel's embarrassment, she got up. Ezriel rose with her.

"I must go. I have a great deal of shopping to do. The coffee? Well, don't inconvenience yourself . . ."

"It doesn't matter. I'll drink it."

"Come to my hotel, I'll take you to the theater. Bring Shaindel along."

"Will you be in Warsaw long?"

"I don't know. My father has decided to marry in his old age. My aunt's daughter, as a matter of fact." And Clara dabbed her eyes again.

Ezriel said goodbye to her. They were now being looked at with open mockery. The students grimaced and whispered. As soon as Clara left, they surrounded Ezriel. "Who was that bit of fluff? Why was she sobbing? Have you gone and got her with child?" Half guiltily, Ezriel swore that it was his stepmother-in-law, but the students shook their heads: "Tell that to your grandmother!"

Clara strolled along New World Boulevard. What a stupid coincidence—of all people, she had to run into Ezriel and cry right in front of him. That was how a pregnant chambermaid conducted herself. Clara shuddered; *she* was pregnant. For the second month she had missed her period. "Well, I'll do as the chambermaids do: throw myself into the Vistula." Pausing in front of a shop window, she glanced at the manikins dressed in autumn coats with fur collars and muffs. "What's wrong with being a doll like that?" Clara mused. "They don't even know they exist. Death is the only consolation. It cancels all errors, all sins, all failures."

Clara walked on. Whenever she had fallen in love, bad luck had always followed, bringing vexations, complications, and misunderstandings. What should she do now? She did not know Zipkin's address. She could not compromise herself further. The students' leering had been apparent to her.

11

Dinner was being served in the home of Jacob Danzinger on Leshno Street. Danzinger, who sat at the head of the table in an armchair, was a small, ruddy-cheeked, bright-eyed man. He wore a gray goatee and was dressed in a black suit, a high stiff collar, and a ribbed vest. Jacob had a huge napkin tucked under his collar. As he ate, he joked with his two daughters and his son, Zdzislaw. The family had only recently returned from Carlsbad, where they had gone to drink the waters. Because of the tariff war between Russia and Germany, the price of woolens had climbed, and Jacob looked forward to making a large profit on the goods stored in his warehouse. Although not a worldly Jew, he owned a pew in the reformed German synagogue. He spoke Polish fluently, but with an accent, read the Hebrew daily *Morning Star*, was a follower of Reb Abraham Stern, may he rest in peace, and knew Reb Chaim Selig Slonimski, both leaders of the Enlightenment in Poland. His wife, Rosa, the daughter of a wealthy merchant from Kalish, had a large red birthmark covering one side of her face. This birthmark had brought Jacob Danzinger a dowry of eight thousand rubles. Mrs. Danzinger spoke French and played the piano. When she argued with her husband, she called him "Zydek"—old-fashioned Jew.

Sabina, the oldest of the girls, was in her twenties. She was short and stout and had a head too large for her body. But, on the other hand, she had been fortunate enough to inherit her mother's blond hair, and had blue eyes and a snub nose. Sabina had attended a fashionable boarding school to which only a very few Jewish girls were admitted. She had studied French, English, and Italian literature and wrote poems in Polish which she never showed to anyone. For years she had been working on a translation of some sort. Her father had put aside a considerable amount of money for her dowry, and each year the accrued interest made the sum larger. Sabina had refused to have a marriage arranged for her. She was so fastidious that if a dish were not cooked to her satisfaction she would not touch it. Garlic, radishes, onions, and herring she considered taboo. Most of her classmates were already married and had children, but Sabina was not even officially engaged. She spent her days and evenings in her "Blue Room," reading difficult books, and was perpetually warring with her family. Her sister Anna was still in high school; her brother Zdzislaw worked for his father and was about to be made a partner in the firm.

In the middle of dinner, the family heard the doorbell ring. A few minutes later the maid entered to announce that a messenger was outside with a letter for Mr. Zipkin.

L

"What do you want me to do about it?" Jacob asked.
"Take the letter."

"He won't give it to anyone but Mr. Zipkin himself."

"You know that Mr. Zipkin has moved."

"He wants his new address."

"We're not an address bureau," Mrs. Danzinger announced, raising her eyebrows.

"Let me speak to him," Zdzislaw said, and went to the door. A moment later he returned carrying a blue sheet of paper in one hand and an envelope in the other. Zdzislaw, the family clown, was short and stout; his neck was thick and bullish and his hair was curly as a sheep's. He had dropped out of the gymnasium without graduating, but had been taken into his father's firm. Zdzislaw had assured the messenger that he was Zipkin. Now he planted himself ceremoniously in the center of the room and, having raised one of his hands dramatically, began to declaim:

> My dearest Alexander,
> I arrived in Warsaw yesterday, and went immediately to the restaurant near the university, but couldn't find you. I am staying at the Hotel Krakowski, Room 8. I have been enduring the tortures of hell; I cry constantly. Come quickly or I will die. Please give this messenger your answer.
>
> Forever,
> Clara

When Anna burst out laughing, Mrs. Danzinger banged on the table with her hand. "Anna, be quiet. Let me see that letter, Zdzislaw."

"Mother, don't make so much noise," Sabina said crossly. She glared at her sister Anna, a tall, slim girl who already went to balls and won prizes for dancing. Numerous young men pursued her. Sabina pushed her plate away. She had just received a blow from which she would never recover. Nevertheless, decorum must be maintained. Sabina had always known in her heart that Zipkin was a liar and a charlatan. She had never believed any of his sweet words. The man was an egotist who acted as if what happened to the world concerned him deeply. He had written her passionate love letters while carrying on an affair with this woman who awaited him breathlessly in a hotel room. Sabina could no longer remain seated. The tears that she was seeking to restrain threatened to spill forth at any moment. Her cheeks became flushed; her forehead perspired. She folded her napkin and walked from the room, her head bowed. Her feet could be heard in the hall, and then the sound of her door being locked. Mrs. Danzinger put on her gold-rimmed glasses and having picked up the sheet of paper held it at arm's length.

"How disgraceful," she said, and then she turned to her son. "You shouldn't have done that."

"We had to find out the truth sometime, Mother. I told you he was a fake."

"All men are beasts."

Jacob Danzinger continued chewing a chicken leg. "He's coming here this evening. I'll have a talk with him."

"And what will you talk about?" Mrs. Danzinger asked, taking off her glasses.

"I'll tell him to fish or cut bait. Either marry or go to hell."

"Jacob, what language. Remember this is Warsaw and not Lodz. How do you know she still wants him?"

"As soon as you marry, you forget such nonsense."

"Students are forbidden to marry."

"He'll quit the university. He'll never become a doctor anyway. He doesn't have the patience. I'll take him into the business."

"Into the business? After such behavior? A fine father you are." Mrs. Danzinger rose from the table. "I've lost my appetite." And she walked out of the room.

The others finished dinner in silence. Now that his wife had left the table, Jacob no longer used his fork. As he sucked loudly on a chicken bone, he plucked a crumb from his beard and tossed it into his mouth. He kept shaking his head and sighing.

Zdzislaw seemed pensive. He already regretted his prank. He pitied his sister. Anna's face had become serious, too. She realized that she should not have laughed. Sabina would never forgive her. What had happened was not funny. There were no limits to the treachery of the male species. Anna thought of all the men who had sworn their eternal love for her; they were probably just as false.

III

At precisely eight that evening Zipkin arrived at the Danzingers' carrying a small bouquet and rang the bell. The new room he had moved into on Dluga Avenue had turned out to be far from satisfactory. As Zipkin saw it, his entire summer had been wasted; he had become so involved with a woman older than himself that her husband had ordered him out of the house. He was behind in his studies, and for that matter in everything else. On his way to the Danzingers', Zipkin had reviewed the situation for the hundredth time. He had behaved foolishly at Kiev University and had almost lost his life in a useless demonstration. It was a miracle that he was once again at school and not in exile in Siberia. But had he abandoned his ideals? Perhaps he lacked the necessary strength for revolutionary action, although he still believed that the masses must be educated and given their freedom. Zipkin considered himself an atheist. He had no intention of being married by a rabbi. Marriage was a barbaric rite, and absolutely out of tune with the times. But that had not prevented him from telling Sabina that he looked forward to the day when they would stand together under the wedding canopy. He had made promises he could not keep, had borrowed money he could not repay. He forgot to write to his parents and to his sister Sonya, who had made herself sick worrying about him.

"What's happened to me?" Zipkin asked himself. "I used to

be such an earnest fellow. I told everyone the truth, even Radziwill himself. Everything's gone wrong because I have been too cowardly to leave this country. I am too egotistical, too much in love with comfort." A revolutionary had once said to him: "Anyone who likes white shirts becomes a reactionary sooner or later."

"Yes, I do have too much dislike for dirty shirts and I despise vermin."

The maid opened the door. "Ah, flowers," she said, looking at him mockingly. "I'd better put them in water." And she gave him a spare smile. When Zipkin entered the dining room, he found only Jacob Danzinger at supper, not the entire family as he had expected. There was one other setting on the table, apparently for him. "What's going on here?" he wondered, and asked out loud, "Where's everyone?"

There was the hint of a smile on Jacob's lips. "My wife has a headache. Anna's off somewhere. Sabina's locked herself in her room. Zdzislaw's seeing to his own business. I'm here all by myself."

"Is it all right for me to see Sabina?"

"If she'll let you in."

"Something's happened," Zipkin thought. On his way over, he'd had an odd premonition that he was heading for trouble.

Jacob Danzinger stroked his beard. "Sit down. I'd like to have a little talk with you."

"Certainly. Thank you."

"Just a minute."

The maid brought in two plates of rice with milk and cinnamon, a dish that was only served at the Danzingers' when no one special was expected. Zipkin took a spoonful of the concoction but found himself unable to swallow it. Jacob Danzinger picked a grain of rice out of his mustache.

"Alexander, it's difficult for me to talk about this. You understand I'm only speaking for myself. I have no idea what is going on in Sabina's mind. After all, I'm not God."

"What's happened?"

319

"We've reached a point," Jacob Danzinger said, with an amused twinkle in his eyes, "where we have to know where we stand. Either your intentions are honorable or they are not. If they are, you must cut out the nonsense and get married." The last word was spoken with great speed.

"Get married? The Ministry of Education doesn't permit it. There was supposed to be a new decree, but . . ."

"Tell me, who is Clara?"

Zipkin turned pale.

"Are you spying on me?"

"Not at all. But you can't keep such things hidden. A letter came for you today. It was opened accidentally."

"When? What kind of a letter?"

"I have no idea. Zdzislaw read it. I know boys will be boys, but there is a limit. Tell me, who is she? Does she live at the place where you were working—on that estate?"

"This is sheer madness."

"If you're in love with her, then you can't have my daughter. On the other hand, if you have some feeling for Sabina, you and she must settle the matter between you."

"I would have to leave school."

"I am speaking as a father. A man of my age can forgive a lot. What Sabina will say is something else again. Well, go ahead and eat your rice; it's not poison."

Zipkin lowered his head. How could she have done such a thing? He had specifically told her not to write him at the Danzingers'. She had done it purposely to compromise him. He pushed his spoon into the rice but forgot to remove it. His face had become flushed. His ears burned as if they had been slapped. Lifting his eyes from the table, he stared at the lamp above him with its bronze chains and its porcelain lampshade. Zipkin became conscious of the wall clock ticking. He noticed how the silver shone on the credenza. Outside, it was cool and still and dark, already September. Should he give up the university, he asked himself, should he become an employee of a capitalist? Jacob Danzinger seemed to have read his mind, for he said, "If you don't want to go into the business, you and Sabina can go abroad. In France, even a grandfather can be a student."

"Yes, that is true."

The maid brought coffee. Jacob Danzinger began to talk shop. Because of the tariff war between Russia and Germany, trade was prospering. Lodz was growing with the speed of yeast and was already known as the Russian Manchester. Why did Russia have to import so much? There was nothing that could not be produced in her factories. If only the Jews would be given a free hand, as in the rest of the world. Jacob Danzinger subscribed to the Polish newspapers and to the one Jewish magazine published in Polish. He remarked to Zipkin that old Montefiore was again planning to go to the Land of Israel. In Kesheniev, money was being collected to resettle Jews on farms. A Hungarian Jew had become an Egyptian pasha. Who would have believed such things possible a few years ago? And was it true that the fires in the villages around the Volga had been set by people called nihilists?

"Anything is possible."

"What's the value of such fires? It's the poor who are left homeless, not the rich."

Zipkin did not answer.

"Such people will destroy the world," Jacob Danzinger said, dipping his hand into a finger bowl.

IV

In Sabina's room, blue was the predominant color. There was a blue rug on the floor, the wallpaper was blue, there was a chair of blue; even the lamp had a blue shade. The gilt cornice of the tile stove and the gilt-framed pictures on the walls were all the more conspicuous in contrast to the prevailing color. Sabina sat reading a book bound in velvet at a round table that was covered with a blue tablecloth. A white blouse and a dark skirt clothed her plump body. The light of the

321

lamp fell on her blond hair. When Zipkin entered, Sabina continued reading, to show that she was much more interested in poetry than she was in him. Finally, she raised her large head and stared at him with her blue eyes.

"Ah, it's the Don Juan of Nalewki Street."

Zipkin bit his lip. "Sabina, I didn't come here to listen to your humor."

"No, of course not. You expected me to give you a medal. Come closer. Sit down. Here on the chaise."

"Thank you."

"Don't think your behavior surprised me," Sabina said in the tone of one who has considered a matter carefully and now understands it thoroughly. "I never trusted you. That's the plain unvarnished truth."

"I hope that this does not affect our friendship."

"Why should I be friends with a fraud?"

Zipkin paled. "I guess I'd better go."

"Wait. You'll leave when I permit it, not before. Your kind doesn't have the right to leave when he pleases." Sabina laughed, exposing wide yellowish teeth. Despite her outward gloominess, Sabina's sense of humor was famous in the family.

Zipkin crossed his legs. "What are you reading?"

"What difference is that to you? Just who is this Clara? The wife of that landowner you wrote me about in Carlsbad?"

"Possibly."

"Why don't you go to her? Poor thing, she can't stop crying. She's at the point of death."

"Is that what the letter said?"

"More or less. Perhaps she'll divorce her rich husband and marry you. According to your letter, her son must be a dear little boy."

"Stop being sarcastic."

"You described him yourself. I never took you seriously. That consoles me now. Just how many women do you have on the string?"

322

"Sabina, I didn't come to confess to you, but to say good-bye. I want to thank you for the happy hours we spent together."

"You needn't thank me. They weren't so happy. You had better times with Clara. Have you had supper?"

"Yes, thank you."

"Who else was in the dining room?"

"Only your father."

"Oh. What did he say to you?"

"He's angry, too. Nevertheless, he would like us to get married." Zipkin blushed when he said the word "married," which seemed to have slipped from his mouth against his will.

Sabina seemed on the verge of laughter, but her face became stern. "Get married, to a charlatan?"

"Darling, no one's going to force you."

"I should think not. If my dear father could, believe me he would. How did you meet her? You've never wanted to take a job before."

"We met here in Warsaw."

"And you fell madly in love?"

"If that's what you want to call it."

"What else? She never stops crying. I have one question I'd like to ask you. Please give me an honest answer for once."

"What's your question?"

"No, I want you to swear first. Give me your hand."

Zipkin rose hesitantly and took Sabina's hand, which was warm and moist.

"On your word of honor."

"On my word of honor."

"Go back and sit where you were. I don't like a big hulk like you hovering over me."

Zipkin seated himself again.

"Did you bring her here? I mean, to this house?"

Zipkin swallowed hard.

"I did."

"And she sat on this bed?"

"I don't want you to faint if I tell you."

"Do you think I'm the swooning type?"

"Yes, she did. Is there anything else that you want to know?"

Sabina's face had grown white. But, as with her father, a trace of laughter remained in her eyes. "Tell me, do you think there's anyone lower than you are?"

"I have no idea."

"Well, I have. Get out of here and never come back. I don't want to hear from you ever again. Is that clear?"

"Clear enough."

And Zipkin rose to leave.

"Not so fast. I told you I'd throw you out when I've finished. When did all of this happen?"

"I didn't write the date down. One evening."

"Did the janitor see you?"

"No, I don't think so. The gate was still open when we got here," Zipkin lied.

"And when did she leave? The next morning?"

"No, the same night."

"I'm getting rid of this mattress. And the bed, too. Incredible as it may seem, it felt strange to me. Why did you do it?"

"Because you wanted to stay a virgin."

"Did you expect me to become a streetwalker like her?"

"She's not a streetwalker."

"What did my father say?"

"That we should get married at once."

"Oh, at once. Don't worry, I'll let you go in a minute. Remember, it was you who swore eternal love for me. I didn't even like you at first. I thought you were a poseur. You told me how heroically you behaved in Kiev and how deeply concerned you were with humanity. I never lied to you. You knew that I didn't believe in free love. I thought that somewhere, underneath everything, there was a spark of decency in you. Well, tell me what are you going to do now?"

"Leave the country."

"With her?"

"Don't be foolish. As far as I'm concerned, she doesn't exist."

"Who does exist for you? What will you do when you go abroad?"

"I don't know. Throw myself into my work."

"What sort of work? Making bombs? Agitating?"

"Not agitating, enlightening."

"*You* enlighten *others?* That is funny. Well, all right, get out. Now I mean it."

"Good night, Sabina. Forgive me."

"Good night. Don't ever come to see me again. Don't try to write to me. Whatever I felt for you is gone. When you cross that threshold, you cease to exist for me."

"Well, stay in good health."

Sabina did not answer. She had already picked up her book and had resumed reading. Zipkin closed the door quietly. For a moment he stood in the hallway as if he expected to be called back.

"Well, that's done with," he said to himself. This was the second time he had been thrown out of a house.

v

It was early as yet, not even ten o'clock. Zipkin walked out of the unbolted gate and lit a cigarette. He was not angry with Sabina; she had acted as a correct young woman should. But Clara he did not understand at all. What did she want? She knew quite well that the Danzingers had returned. She was a shrew and must be avoided like the plague. Zipkin did not want to return to his room. He needed company. Having crossed Karmelicka Street, he turned into Dzielna Street, looked up and saw that there was a light in Mirale's window. Shadows moved across the curtain, signifying that Mirale was entertaining guests. Zipkin entered the building. "Well, it seems that I'm destined to sacrifice my life for humanity," he muttered as he mounted the stairs, and immediately wondered what a materialist such as he could mean by destiny. Who had destined it? Such mad thoughts passed through one's head. "Well, now I'm finished with lies. I'm free at last. That's the end of just living for myself." He experienced the kind of momentary relief one feels when one has lost everything. He even felt physically light and buoyant. It didn't matter that he lacked even the price of a meal. From now on, he would have to support himself by tutoring. He rapped three times on the wall, a sign that it was not the police, and the door opened.

"Look who's here," Mirale said, extending her hand.

"What's all the noise about?" Zipkin inquired.

"Oh, there's a big discussion going on. Come in. Ezriel and Aaron are battling to the death."

She entwined her arm in his and led him into the apartment. The room was warm and smoky. There was a babble of voices, everyone talking in Polish. It was the usual crowd— Ezriel, Aaron, Esther Eisner, Vera Charlap, and Sonya Rabinowitch. Some were drinking their tea from glasses, and others from their saucers, Russian style. Zipkin heard Ezriel say, "If you take that position, anything is justifiable. You say that Nechayev had the right to kill Ivanov. In effect, you are deifying the murderer. He becomes the defender of the people. That's what your *Catechism of a Revolutionary* says. Its idol is Bakunin, a common murderer."

"Oh, so Bakunin's a murderer. Those who go about hanging working-class women are as innocent as lambs, I suppose. You know what would have happened if the Jacobins hadn't used the guillotine: the revolution would have failed and the Bourbons would have kept their stranglehold on France and Europe as well."

"Was Napoleon an improvement over Louis? Besides, the guillotine did a lot more than cut off the heads of the Bourbons. What about Danton and Robespierre?"

"There are always some errors. You know the saying, 'When you chop wood, you must expect shavings.' The French Revolution had to happen. Europe had to enter the new era. Russia hasn't had a revolution, and where are we? Lost in darkness. Whatever we have now, we owe to the French: the Internationale, the strikes in England, the fact that we're talking together the way we are now. Would the serfs have been freed if there had been no French Revolution? And let me tell you, we wouldn't be students at the university, either. You and I would still be packed away in the ghetto."

"Bravo, Aaron," Sonya Rabinowitch exclaimed, clapping her hands. Then suddenly seeing Zipkin, she called out, "Well, here's a latecomer." Everyone became silent.

"Just what is the point at issue?" Zipkin asked.

"Oh, it's just the usual babble," Ezriel replied. "Although England has had no revolution, she does have a parliament. Your friends take a contradictory position: they are both for and against the use of violence. In fact, they want to be constitutional nihilists . . . They're forever trying to reach the masses, who don't want to have anything to do with them. What do the muzhiks do to the young women sent out to teach them? They rape them. The men are handed over to the police. The whole theory of *Obshchyna*, going out to the people, is ridiculous. Who are the avengers of the people? Nothing but bandits. It was the peasant Komisarov who captured Karkov, wasn't it? Isn't that typical of the entire movement?"

"All right, let's hear your program."

"Do nothing unless you know what should be done. I say that we should follow the injunction of the Hippocratic oath: never harm, only heal. Of what value were the last two Polish uprisings? Did the Paris Commune help anyone? Or the Dolgoshunzes? Whom did the Fifty benefit? What good will come from the execution of those political prisoners who have been condemned? I understand that out of 193 prisoners, twelve have already committed suicide and thirty have gone mad. These terrorists simply don't have what it takes to be revolutionaries. It's as if when a surgeon is needed a butcher is sent for. The government is definitely sick, but terror can't make it well."

Zipkin drew himself up to his full height. "Just what butchers are you referring to? Czernishewski? Herzen? Lavrov? Exactly what do you suggest, Ezriel? Whom would you choose to sponsor the revolution, a group of old ladies? And what of those who are in power? Have they taken the Hippocratic oath? Do they think twice about destroying hundreds of thouhands of people? Have you read the recent revelations about the Turkish War and the machinations of the Great Powers? Why don't you write to the aristocracy and suggest that they all take the Hippocratic oath?"

"Because I'm not entirely mad."

"No, that's not the reason. You want to be safe and stay out of prison. You have your career as a doctor to think of, but there are others who are willing to lay down their lives for the people."

"Don't you want to be a doctor? Anyway, sacrificing your life doesn't feed the hungry. No one eats because cities are razed. Moreover, what people are you referring to? You consider yourself a Russian, Zipkin, but this is Poland. And, as a matter of fact, the people in this room aren't even Poles. They're Jews."

"Jews? Why bring up the Jewish question?"

"Well, what will happen to the Jews? Are we to be destroyed because we don't have a peasantry?"

"Who's talking about destroying? In the new society, Jews won't be storekeepers and usurers. Today the Jew is still on the side of the exploiters. He's owned by the gentry."

"Does this include your own father?"

"You should be ashamed of yourself, Ezriel. Yes, my father, along with the rest. True, I am his son, but I can see the role that he plays in society. He's been nothing but Radziwill's tool. In the morning he prayed; the rest of the day he stole from the peasants. Why should the peasants love him?"

"And why should you be on the side of the peasants? If the peasants could, they'd kill both you and your father."

Mirale began to shout, "Ezriel, you're getting too personal. Leave our parents and the Jews out of it. Sit down, Zipkin. I agree with you. A parasite is a parasite, even if he's your father. You'll have some tea, won't you?"

VI

They continued to drink tea, eat bread and cheese, and argue. Zipkin, Ezriel saw, had suddenly become the most violent of extremists. He spoke with enthusiasm of Vera Zasulich's assassination of Trepov. There were times, he said, when it was necessary to burn one's bridges behind one. He had a higher ideal than just getting a diploma. He even ridiculed those revolutionaries who put all their hopes in the establishment of a parliament. "What's come over him?" Ezriel wondered. Ever since he'd come to Warsaw, he'd been one of the moderates. Moreover, he'd been squiring a wealthy young lady, and had begun to talk like a Polish positivist. Did this sudden change have something to do with Clara? But how? The question under discussion was whether, in the process of liquidating the aristocracy, one had the right to risk the lives of innocent bystanders. Ezriel argued that this was a crime, but all the others were against him. "One can't consider individuals when the world's future is at stake," Aaron declared. Sonya Rabinowitch commented that this was not a war to be waged with powder puffs.

"Just tell me this," Mirale said to her brother, "when they fight, do the aristocrats consider the people?"

"Do we have to follow their example?"

"Your brother would like to have freedom brought in on a silver tray with a lace doilie on it." Zipkin was joking, but there was an angry smile on his lips. He poured some tea into a saucer and sucked on a lump of sugar. All of the women agreed with him. "Why are they all so bloodthirsty?" Ezriel wondered. They were Jewish women, members of the race which had sworn to uphold the Ten Commandments. Mirale was only one generation removed from their father and mother. Only a short time before, she had been reading their mother's prayer book. How old was she? Ezriel began to calculate. He recalled the winter day in Jampol when Mirale had entered the study house to tell him that Calman Jacoby had come to meet him. Now he spent his time cutting the dead apart, and Mirale plotted to kill the living.

"When one talks about sacrifice," he said, "one must think of oneself as the offering. Let us assume, Zipkin, that Utopia has been achieved, but to win it you have had to forfeit your life. There is singing and laughing in the streets, but you lie in your grave. There is no life after death. After all, we don't believe in the immortality of the soul. When you die, you're dead forever."

"Stop scaring the chickens. Do you think life is such a bargain? What about the soldiers who are dying in this war? Who's going to lead them to paradise?"

"I didn't kill them."

"You killed them with your so-called positivist ideas and your acceptance of tyranny. You shiver over the suffering of one poor innocent, but what of the millions who die of consumption, rot in prison, and swing on the gallows? Do you know what the death rate is among the muzhiks? Every year, tens of thousands of peasants starve to death."

"He knows that, but he'd like to forget it," Mirale cried out.

"How does that give me the right to sacrifice another?"

"Who's speaking of anyone else? Those who are fighting sacrifice themselves."

"You speak of all this fighting as if it were something new. People have been fighting for thousands of years. What have all those battles produced?"

330

"Civilization. Our modern world, with all its virtues and faults. Mankind has moved forward, not backward."

Sonya Rabinowitch clapped her hands. "Bravo, Zipkin, bravo."

Finally, Ezriel and Aaron began a game of chess. Zipkin talked with Sonya Rabinowitch. Esther Eisner paced back and forth on high-heeled high-buttoned shoes, chewing on a piece of bread. Esther, the divorcee, was small and dark-complexioned and looked much younger than she was. She wore her hair in a bun with a comb in it, not upswept in the current fashion. Esther was considered illiterate, even though she associated with intellectuals and spoke their jargon. She spoke Polish fluently but swallowed the last syllables, so that one couldn't make out the case endings. Sonya Rabinowitch, who had completed gymnasium and was a serious reader, didn't care for Esther and enjoyed catching her in errors.

Vera Charlap sat down and watched Ezriel and Aaron play. The doctors had assured Vera that her lungs had healed, but she still occasionally coughed blood and became feverish. She predicted that she would die some rainy day and that none of her friends would attend her funeral. A rabbi's daughter, she knew Hebrew well and liked to draw Ezriel into religious discussions so that she could exhibit her knowledge of Jewish lore. Whenever Vera felt sick, she sent her maid to fetch Ezriel. She had thick red hair and a porcelain white face. There was always a string of artificial pearls around her long neck, and heavy earrings dangled from her ears. Vera suffered from homesickness, especially on the Sabbath and during the holidays. She would sit at Mirale's enveloped in a beaded silk shawl and wail, "Now Father is praying. Now they are singing the Sabbath hymns in my house."

Mirale, who despised religion, would say angrily, "If that kind of fanaticism appeals to you, why did you leave home? Go back and marry a Talmudic scholar."

"That's easy enough for you to say, Mirale."

331

VII

Zipkin stood at the bookcase, browsing among Mirale's books. He opened a volume without looking down at the page. What a fiasco. He had lost everything—both Sabina and Clara. Why had Clara written that letter? Just to embarrass him. There could be no other reason. Zipkin suddenly remembered that he owed Jacob Danzinger hundreds of rubles—he had no idea what the exact amount was. Sabina was right when she had called him a fraud. He had once read that a man only blushed in public. But as he stood there in the shadows, with his back to his friends, he felt the blood mount to his face. He had to return the money. Now! At once! But how? He had nothing. It was true—he was both a seducer and a thief. "I should never have taken money from them." It occurred to him that in a similar situation Radziwill's son Ludwig would have killed himself. Had he not tried to commit suicide when he had lost five thousand rubles in a card game? Zipkin shook his head from side to side as if to rid himself of such nasty thoughts. "Yes, I have fallen low." Zipkin tried to read so as to forget his disgrace momentarily, but the words danced before his eyes. "Well, I will kill myself. At least I'll prove that I'm no embezzler." He took a step in the direction of Ezriel and Aaron.

"Whose move is it?"

"No kibitzers, no kibitzers," Aaron mumbled, his body swaying.

Ezriel lifted his head and looked at Zipkin out of the corner of his eyes. He had never liked the man but was unwilling to indulge in petty spite. Clara wanted Zipkin to know where she was, and Ezriel would deliver the message. But Zipkin wasn't leaving yet . . . Ezriel moved his rook and bit his lip. He knew the move was wrong, but he had already lost the ambition to win.

"So that's your move," Zipkin interjected.

"Yes, that's it. Why haven't you been to school?"

"To hell with the university."

"So soon? Are you through studying?"

"I'm through with everything."

"What's happened? Did you win the lottery?"

"I've either won it all or lost it all," Zipkin said, his words spilling out at random. It occurred to him that Ezriel was to blame for his misfortunes. If Ezriel hadn't taken him to Mirale's and introduced him to that ridiculous self-education circle, he would never have met Clara. No, it had not been Ezriel but Aaron who had first brought him to the group. "Well, what's the difference? They're all a bunch of Polish idlers."

"Well, I think it's time for me to go."

"Just a moment, Zipkin. I have a message for you."

"What is it, Ezriel?" Zipkin felt a knot in his throat.

"It's confidential."

Zipkin was sure that Ezriel was the bearer of more bad news. He was about to receive another slap in the face. Hatred for Ezriel, Clara's step son-in-law, welled up in him. His hands grew moist. They'd probably been talking about him all evening, and he, idiot that he was, had stumbled in like a blind horse into a ditch. Out loud he said, "Well, let's hear the big secret."

"Come outside."

"What secret do you two have?" Aaron asked in astonishment.

"Whenever there's a secret, look for a thief," Vera Charlap announced, translating a Yiddish saying into Polish.

Zipkin said goodbye to everyone. Usually he shook hands when he left, but this time he merely said, "Well, ladies, don't slander me too much."

Mirale smiled. "My, he is in an odd mood today."

"Why are you so flushed?" Sonya Rabinowitch asked.

Zipkin left, followed by Ezriel. The conversation in the room ceased. As soon as Ezriel had closed the door, Zipkin said, "All right, Ezriel, let's have it. I have bared my breast. Plunge the dagger in."

"It's nothing like that. Clara's been looking for you. She's in Warsaw."

"She is. Where?"

"At the Hotel Krakowski."

"Where did you meet her?"

"At the restaurant—near the university."

"Well, that's strange. Thank you, Ezriel. I want to apologize. I thought that . . ."

But Zipkin did not finish. "Good night. See you soon."

Ezriel returned to the chess game.

Zipkin remained standing in the dark. So that's how it was. She was in Warsaw. She had come to look for him. His heart felt lighter. Tears came to his eyes. It wasn't because he loved Clara. But someone still wanted him, and Ezriel, whom he had regarded as an enemy, had been decent enough to give him the message. Not everyone in the world, it would seem, was corrupt. "I am a deplorable egoist," Zipkin confessed to himself. "I don't think enough about other people. That's why things have turned out as they have." He considered not going to see Clara, and thus ending the affair. All the same, he knew that he would go. He hoped that she had not yet checked out of the hotel. The janitor opened the gate for him; Zipkin tipped him ten groschen. He walked quickly, every now and again looking around for a droshky. "Well, what shall I do? She's young and her husband is old. She's never loved him . . . The whole institution of marriage is nothing but a mire." He began to walk faster. "What was that nonsense about burning my bridges behind me? What should I do, really? Partition land that does not belong to me? Become a lumberjack in the summer and sleep with my boots beneath my head? Everyone is so mixed up."

Suddenly Zipkin looked up and saw that he was standing in front of the Hotel Krakowski.

334

VIII

The lobby was empty. The clerk who usually stood behind the desk was not there. Zipkin looked around. "If I only knew which room she was in." He caught sight of the guest register and started to scan the pages. Yes, there was her signature— Clara Jacobowa. But what was her room number? The clerk appeared, a small, chunky, flaxen-haired man with the pink eyes of an albino. He was in his shirt sleeves.

"Who are you looking for?"

"Mrs. Clara Jacobowa."

"She's probably asleep. Who are you?"

"Her brother," Zipkin said quickly, astounded at his own lie.

"What do you want with her? I can't allow you to go upstairs at this hour."

"It's very important. Her child's ill. I've just come from Jampol."

Zipkin took out a coin and gave it to the clerk, who eyed it suspiciously, hefting it in his hand.

"She's in room 8. That's on the first floor. But she can't be disturbed."

Zipkin ran up the stairs. Arriving at room 8, he knocked on the door. When there was no answer, he began to beat on it.

At last he heard a voice, "Who's there?"

"It's Alexander."

He stood holding his breath, his eyes lowered, listening. He could hear her striking a match and then moving about in her slippers. When she opened the door and he saw her, she seemed like a stranger to him, older, as if in the last few days she had suddenly become middle-aged. Her hair was tucked beneath a net and she was wearing a dressing gown.

"I thought you'd get here much earlier," she said, looking at him sadly.

335

"How could I? I didn't know you were here."

"Didn't the messenger tell you?"

"What messenger?"

"I sent you a note. Didn't you receive it? Well, you'd better come in."

In the room, a candle was burning in a bronze candleholder. The bed was rumpled. A magazine, a bagel, and a garter lay on the table. For a moment there was a strained silence and then Zipkin said, "I told you I wasn't living there any longer."

"But you didn't say where you were living."

"I didn't get your note."

"Who got it, then?"

"The Danzingers."

"They opened it?"

"Yes."

"The man who delivered it said he handed it to you personally."

"It wasn't me. It was Zdzislaw. That's the son."

"He sent the reply?"

"He must have."

"Well, then, how did you know I was here?"

"Ezriel told me."

"When? Where? Well, it doesn't matter. That I survived the last few days proves to me I must be immortal."

When Zipkin took her in his arms, she leaned her head on his chest and sobbed softly. There were deep circles under her eyes.

"I thought you were finished with me," she said, once more addressing him with the familiar "thou." "I kept waiting and waiting. I almost went out of my mind. Calman's left. He's run off to his son-in-law, the rabbi. He deserted me."

"Is that what he said?"

"He took his winter coat with him. Mayer Joel is taking care of his business interests."

"Well, I understand."

"What right do they have to open your letters?" Clara asked. "Are you engaged to that girl?"

"That's finished."

"I asked you whether you were and you denied it. Why is it over? Because they opened my letter?"

"I don't love her."

"But you were engaged?"

"Not really."

"What then? Well, it's clear enough to me. A woman becomes fond of a man, and immediately she's in trouble. What do I do now?"

"That's simple enough. Give me a kiss."

"Alexander, I'm pregnant."

Zipkin's hands fell from his hips. He took a step backward.

"Whose child is it?" he asked, the tone of his voice suddenly altered.

"You know whose child it is."

"How can you be sure? You told me that you slept with him, too."

A bewildered look came into Clara's eyes. She didn't know what to answer.

"I'll get rid of it if I can. It's a very dangerous business for me."

"No more than for anybody else."

"If you want me to die, I will die."

Where is the other garter? Zipkin asked himself, staring at the table. All this talk of pregnancy and abortion had cooled his ardor. He had a desire to flee. Zipkin looked toward the door.

"Don't run away," Clara said. "Sit down."

As Zipkin seated himself, he noticed the other garter lying on the rug, and touched it with the tip of his shoe. How complicated everything had become. The affair reminded him of one of those illnesses which start with the sniffles, a cough, or a headache, and before you know it, the patient lies dying.

337

IX

Zipkin stayed with Clara that night. He left early the next morning, before the servants awoke. As they kissed and fondled each other, he made all sorts of promises to her that he had no intention of keeping. This coarse woman who slept with two men would never become his wife, nor would her child receive his name. It was one thing to have an affair with Clara and quite another to marry her. It seemed to him that this distinction should be obvious to her, as well.

Zipkin was to meet Clara at Semodeny's at one o'clock. He hadn't had much sleep and was on his way back to his room on Dluga Avenue. He stopped off at a coffee shop on Bielanska Street to have breakfast. He was more sleepy than hungry. The waitress brought him a newspaper along with his eggs and rolls. Zipkin ate, alternately scanned the paper and dozed. Clara had promised to pay him two hundred rubles for tutoring Sasha, and he was determined to send this money to Jacob Danzinger as partial settlement of his debt. On the other hand, was it proper for him to take so large a sum for a few weeks of tutoring? Wasn't it really nothing but a bribe?

In the newspaper Zipkin read an article about the summer horse show. It criticized the Poles for considering horseback riding vulgar. In London, the paper pointed out, ladies rode in the public parks and even hunted on horseback. Almost every article and news item in the paper contained allusions to Western Europe and the United States. In other countries, the houses had plumbing, the cities wide streets, sidewalks, and clean gutters. Here in Warsaw, a woman was criticized for being a pediatrician. Abroad, that sort of thing was no longer even news. In foreign cities policemen helped school children across the street; circuses and exhibitions were lit by electricity; the universities lent students books; one did not have to inform the authorities when one moved to a new apartment, or constantly show one's papers. Zipkin turned the pages of the paper and yawned. Yes, it was a large world, a free and enlightened one, and he was buried in Poland. "I must get out of here before it's too late," Zipkin thought. "I've had enough of the provinces."

Zipkin had forgotten his key and was forced to knock on the apartment door.

"Oh, it's the master," the Gentile maid said, throwing the door open. "You've been away all night."

"I stayed with a friend."

"Shall I bring you breakfast?"

"I've already eaten."

"There's a letter for you."

Zipkin entered his room and found the letter lying on a chair. It was from his father. Berish Zipkin wrote that business was bad and that his wife had had an attack of gallstones. Sonya was tutoring. There was a postscript in her handwriting, written in Russian: "Is life as tedious in Warsaw as it is here? There's just nothing in this town. The young men have only one ambition—to make their boots squeak." Zipkin lay down on his bed in his clothes. "Yes, Sonya dear, it's boring here, too," he mumbled. "More boring than you can imagine."

He fell asleep and dreamed that he was wandering through a series of rooms all constructed of petrified wood. Petrified mushrooms grew from the walls and ceilings. In front of him was a pit and to the rear a body of water. There was a bridge over the water and a passageway that led into the pit. He didn't know which way to go. He was hiding from someone —an informer, or an *agent provocateur*. "No, they won't take me alive," Zipkin said in his sleep. "I'd rather drown myself." Thirty years of life were enough.

He awoke with a start. It was raining outside. Streams of water ran down the windowpanes. From far off came the rumble of thunder; to Zipkin it sounded as if furniture were being moved in a room upstairs. A moment later there was a knock on the door and the maid entered, carrying a pink envelope. "This came by messenger," she said, and she stood

there in her shabby slippers, staring at the sleepy-eyed Zipkin.
"Thank you," he said, taking the letter.
"The man's waiting for your answer." There was a look of wonder in the woman's eyes, the rustic's astonishment at the complexity and deviousness of city life.

Zipkin recognized the stationery. The letter came from Sabina. He opened it and saw her ornate, curlicued handwriting:

> Dear Pan Zipkin:
>
> Circumstances beyond my control force me to write to you. I have no particular passion for ownership, but you did borrow my volume of Musset's poetry. The book was a present from a friend who is no longer alive. Please return it to me at once. There are also several small matters that I would like to discuss with you. Would it be possible for you to meet me at Spivak's Confectionery at four o'clock? I have purposely chosen a confectionery on Nalewki Street, so that you will be in the kind of surroundings that suit you best. Don't forget the book.
>
> > Your devoted
> > Sabina

24

It was predicted in Marshinov that this year the town would be half empty at Rosh Hashana. Reb Shimmon had left Marshinov and had moved to Stiktin, taking with him the richest supporters of the court. Most people thought that the remaining Hassidim would also defect. The proprietors of the town's inns and rooming houses held a meeting to discuss the situation. Jochanan was called a procrastinator, a schlemiel. Also present were Marshinov's butchers and fishmongers; in fact, all whose living was dependent on the court. Everyone agreed that Jochanan had wrecked the town's economy. Reb Shimmon would not have abandoned Marshinov if Jochanan had paid more attention to the business of the court instead of soaking himself in the ritual bath day and night. Many suggestions were offered, among them that the rabbi be warned that unless he made peace with Reb Shimmon, the town would take action against him. A butcher demanded that Jochanan be driven out of Marshinov with sticks. Some recalled the story of a rabbi who one hundred years before had been expelled from the town in a wagon drawn by oxen, and on a Friday, so that he had been forced to spend the Sabbath on the road. As was usual at such assemblies, after a great deal of angry debate and shouting, the only decision that was reached was to hold another meeting. What was there to be done with a rabbi who was determined to destroy himself? Marshinov had enjoyed many years of prosperity. Those years were over; from now on, Stiktin would have all the luck. Yet, while all the talk was going on, Marshinov was filling up with people. Several hundred Jews had already arrived by the time of the first penitential prayers. Many of them were Hassidim who had come to the court for the first time. Those who had predicted that the prayer house would be empty were embarrassed. Every train brought hosts of worshippers. The teamsters did not have enough space at the station to pull up their wagons. Many visitors walked from the train, carrying their bundles. The innkeepers brought down straw mattresses from the garrets, and cooked in huge pots and kettles. High rates were demanded in advance for a night's lodging. The butchers went out into the villages to buy up cattle. The fishmongers sent Gentiles to set up nets in the Vistula. Suddenly Marshinov seemed too small to hold all of Jochanan's following. Not since Marshinov had become Marshinov had anything like this happened. People wracked their brains for an explanation.

Jochanan himself was apprehensive. He had been indifferent to the attack of his mother and advisers when they upbraided him for permitting Reb Shimmon to leave. He had never wanted to be rabbi and still could not understand why he had been appointed a leader of Jews. Now that a following of thousands had assembled, with more expected, Jochanan was terrified. What did heaven want? He remembered what the Scriptures said about vanity: "Pride goeth before destruction and a haughty spirit before a fall."

Was this another form of temptation? Or was he one of those who never earn Paradise but get their just due in this world? As he prayed and studied, his tears wet the pages of *The Two Tablets of the Covenant*. Oh, how simple it would have been for him if his grandfather had been there to guide him. But his grandfather had gone to heaven and dwelt among the celestial sages, leaving the burden to be borne by him.

Thousands of Jews longed for him to pray for them. But with what good deeds could he approach the Lord of the Universe, he who possessed only evil thoughts and worldly ambitions? Shouldn't he leave Marshinov? Jochanan asked himself. Shouldn't he go into exile and fast and castigate himself—in summer prick himself with thorns, in winter roll in the snow? If he were a mere wanderer, no one would pay him homage. Tsipele, long may she live, would not serve him soup or milk or preserves and indulge him in luxuries.

But dare he run away? Did he have the right to abandon his congregation because he longed for martyrdom? No, he did not, particularly not now on the eve of the Holy Days. Jochanan probed himself daily. He was a mass of faults, but he did have one virtue: he loved the Jews. The sight of beards and sidelocks filled him with joy. Only embarrassment kept him from kissing every Jew he met. His love for his people was apparently a gift from heaven. Jochanan clutched his beard. "God Almighty, help me. Father in heaven, we are only weak humans. What thou dost not bestow upon us, we do not possess."

11

Calman Jacoby was among those who came to Marshinov for the holidays. He drove his carriage himself, one of the first of the faithful to arrive. Tsipele ran out to meet him, followed by two of her children, Zadok and Zeldele. Gadele, the baby, was in its cradle. Tsipele, now grown tall, wore a bonnet on her shaven head. Although she was only twenty-four, she had a son old enough to be studying the Talmud. Zadok was fair, light-eyed, yellow-haired, and wore breeches, a velvet hat, a long gaberdine, and knee-length stockings. As he walked, he played with the fringes of his sash, winding them around his finger. Zeldele, a graceful child, resembled her grandmother Temerel. Tsipele could barely keep herself from hugging her father unrestrainedly. She had disapproved of his marrying

343

Clara, but she had heard how much his wife had made him suffer. Relief and sadness mingled in her gaze as she noticed the baggage he had brought with him: the prayer books, the clothing, his fur coat. He had changed so much since she had last seen him. Now his beard was almost entirely gray and his body was shrunken and bent.

"Oh, Papa, Papa," she cried out and could say no more.

"This is Zadok, eh? Almost ready to get married!"

"Grandpa."

Zadok kissed Calman's hand. Zeldele hung back shyly. A moment later Mendel the beadle and Kaila the maid came out of the house followed by a host of yeshiva students and hangers-on. And then finally Jochanan appeared.

"Sholem aleichem, Father-in-law."

"Aleichem sholem, Rabbi."

"Welcome to Marshinov. You've been away from us too long. We all missed you. I trust that you are in good health."

"Praised be God, yes."

Jochanan checked his natural inclination to ask after the rest of Calman's family, so as not to have to mention the names of women. He did not even glance at Tsipele. When others were present, the rabbi and his wife did not address each other.

"How was your trip?" Jochanan inquired.

"Thank God, good."

"The children are thrilled. They missed their grandfather."

"I have some gifts for them in the carriage."

"Gifts? It is written that he who hateth gifts shall live," Jochanan said.

"Oh, but they are children."

"They must be taught correctly from the beginning. 'Train a child in the way he must go.' "

Finally Jochanan returned to his study, having invited Calman to join him there later in the day. Tsipele herself helped carry in her father's baggage. His room in the attic had a brass latch on the door and a mezuzah enclosed in an engraved sheath on the doorpost. Calman unpacked the presents which

344

he had purchased in Warsaw, where he had stopped on his way to Marshinov. For Tsipele he had brought a pair of diamond earrings; for Zadok, a prayer book bound in cedarwood and decorated with pictures of the Wailing Wall and Rachel's tomb; for Zeldele, candies and an assortment of small presents. Calman had even brought presents for the rabbi and Temerel, who had come to spend the holidays with her son. To show her respect for her father, Tsipele herself brought him a pitcher of water, a towel, and a basin. Though he assured her that he was not hungry, she insisted that he wash his hands and sit down to eat. At dinner, Calman found that his appetite had returned. A circle of people formed around his table. Tsipele and the children were there, as well as a number of students. Calman was embarrassed. Why were they honoring him? There was nothing extraordinary about him. At the manor, he had been treated with contempt. He dipped his bread in the gravy, and his eyes became moist.

"Why did I wait so long?" he asked himself. "This is heaven and that was hell."

"Grandpa, is there really a salamander at your place?" Zadok suddenly asked.

"A salamander? No, I've never seen one."

"Why not? The fire in the lime kilns has been burning for seven years."

"Not continuously. Besides, the heretics deny the existence of salamanders. No animal can live in fire."

Tsipele bristled.

"Why must you repeat what the heretics say?"

"They say, God forbid, that this year there'll be a shortage of citrus fruit for the Feast of Tabernacles," one of the onlookers said, removing his pipe from his mouth.

"Why?"

"Because of the Turks."

"But citrus fruits come from Greece, not from Turkey."

"Aren't the Greeks Turks?"

"No. The Turks are the sons of Ishmael, and the Greeks the

345

sons of Javan," Calman replied. The students listened in silence. Here in Marshinov, Calman was a man of the world. After grace, he retired to another room with his daughter and seated himself in an easy chair. Tsipele sat opposite him. The beaded bonnet that she wore gave her youthful face a sedate appearance. Her dress was so long that the tips of her shoes were barely visible. This was no longer the playful Tsipele who had once ridden on Calman's shoulders, but the wife of the Marshinov rabbi, the mother of three children.

"Oh, Papa," she said, "you can't imagine how much it means to me to see you again."

"I missed you, Daughter."

"I used to wake up at night, worrying about you."

Tsipele asked after Jochebed, Mayer Joel, Shaindel, Ezriel, and all of the children, including Senderel. She did not mention Clara. Suddenly Calman thought of Miriam Lieba. This daughter of his, the wife of a scoundrel and the mother of Gentile children, was still alive somewhere. She was a branch that had been torn from the tree. Calman would go for months on end without recollecting her once and suddenly, as now, the memory of her would come without warning. Calman's eyes became moist. Tsipele lowered her head, sensing of whom her father was thinking.

III

Although the countries where Jews lived in exile continued to war against each other, killing and plundering, for the Jews, thank God, this holiday season was the beginning of a period of devotion and prayer. Rich men and paupers prayed in the same words; all attended the Rosh Hashana banquet, and ate the traditional dishes, challah with honey, carrot stew, carp, the head of a sheep. A benediction was made over a fruit tasted for the first time that season. It was usually pineapples or grapes. None of the Jews in Marshinov went hungry, God forbid. True, Mendel, ignoring the rabbi's instructions, made certain that all the rich men whom Reb Shimmon had not taken with him were seated at the table, while the poor were left standing. But what was so bad about standing? When one came to a rabbi's, one expected to be jostled and pushed; sweating there dissolved one's sins. As long as one was in Marshinov, there was no need to worry. A prayer shawl was a prayer shawl, whether brocaded or not. Though Rosh Hashana was a judgment day, Marshinov was delirious with joy. The rabbi prayed. He wept. His tears made the congregation exult, for it was known that the angels collect the tears of a saint in a wineskin to intercede for the children of Israel when Satan the accuser brings indictments against them. The praying continued both days until four o'clock. Because the study house was overcrowded, the younger men strolled in the orchard wearing their prayer shawls and their skullcaps.

Yellow leaves drifted down; occasionally an apple, a pear, or a chestnut dropped from a tree. The sun shone. Cool breezes blew in from the fields. The rabbi missed no part of the liturgy, but the Hassidim managed to find time to discuss the intricate matters that they were studying, and Reb Shimmon's defection from Marshinov. Women were to be seen everywhere, strolling down paths and across the grass. The older women wore old-fashioned dresses with trains, bonnets ornamented with bows and satin ribbons, and fur-trimmed velvet capes. Long earrings dangled from their ears; tarnished necklaces, long out of style, hung about their necks, their finest jewelry having already been given to their daughters and daughters-in-law. They walked haltingly, their bodies stooped, holy books and large handkerchiefs in their hands, their lips moving in prayer. All of them requested the same things from heaven: a year more of life, enough to live on, the company of their children and grandchildren, the coming of the Messiah. For when the Messiah came and the dead arose, there would be no more death. The old people noted that

M

three men and one woman had died that very day in Marshinov, so that their deaths must have been decreed in heaven the previous Rosh Hashana.

The young matrons wore silk capes and fashionable bonnets and walked proudly with a light step. Small earrings sparkled in their ears and thin chains glistened at their throats. Their prayer books had copper or silver clasps and gold-trimmed covers. Their shoes had high heels and pointed toes. It was hard to believe that these frivolous-looking creatures bathed in the ritual bath and had husbands with beards and sidelocks. Temerel, who had come to Marshinov to observe the holidays, and her sister-in-law, Binneleh, the Chmielev rabbi's wife, set the style for the women. Temerel wore a white satin dress embroidered with flat beads and edged with lace at the sleeves. She had on a kerchief embroidered with diamonds. Binneleh, daughter of a rich man, a woman whose face was still unlined and rosy-cheeked, promenaded in a silver bonnet and a dress styled according to the latest Paris fashion. When she moved, her silver slippers showed from the hem of her dress. Concealed in her handkerchief was a tiny vial of perfume which she sniffed constantly when she sat in the women's synagogue with its odors of wax, dust, and perspiration.

The day after Rosh Hashana, most of the faithful left to go about their business. Jochanan's prestige had now been fully restored. His words were repeated everywhere and he was compared not only to the Pzhyscher rabbi but even to the famous Kozhenitzer preacher. There was also a good deal of talk about Calman. Everyone had seen him praying at the Eastern wall in his shawl and white linen robe. It was noticed that he remained standing during the reading of the scroll. He had paid for the lodging of ten poor Jews and had been called to the lectern the second day of the holiday. He had, however, not left when Rosh Hashana was over. From this it was deduced that relations between him and Clara were strained.

A few days later, a new horde descended on Marshinov for

Yom Kippur. There was a run on roosters, sacrificed before the holiday for the redemption of sins. Temerel reserved a white rooster for Jochanan. The prayer house was again filled to capacity for the night prayers. Early on the morning before Yom Kippur, the rabbi and his family gathered to offer the sacrifice. Gadele was also there. Tsipele held the baby in her arms. The men held the roosters by the feet and swung them overhead; the women did the same with hens. This sacrifice, which ended with the eating of the chickens, always caused Jochanan anguish, even though the Torah stated explicitly that animals had been placed on earth to feed men. Did one have a right to be more pious than the Pentateuch? It was known that when an animal was slaughtered according to the laws of kashruth and the benediction was devoutly said, the spirit of the creature was purified. Migrant souls, the souls of saints, were imprisoned in animals. Nevertheless, it disturbed Jochanan to take a fowl by its claws and feel its body trembling. Although birds committed no acts of piety, neither did they sin. Who could say that he, Jochanan, was more worthy to live than the creature sacrificed for him? The ritual slaughterer, who had arrived at the court at dawn, slaughtered the birds with a short-bladed knife. Jochanan stood nearby, his head lowered, his face pale, remembering the story of Cain and Abel as well as the words, "And the preeminence of man over the beast is naught." He began to rub his forehead. Thousands of Jews had assembled to draw new faith from him, but he doubted.

In fact, Jochanan had been disgusted with bodily existence for a long time. He never stopped envying his father and grandfather, who had already cast off the burdens of material life and now existed in supernal regions.

349

25

During the holiday season, Calman had no desire to leave
Marshinov. What awaited him at home? An adulteress and an
ungovernable child. He was no longer young. He had had his
fill of business. At the feast of Succoth, Calman prayed in the
Tabernacle and spent the night there with Jochanan and his
inner circle. It was good to lie under a feather comforter and
look up at the stars through the branches which made up the
roof. On the seventh day of the feast, he stayed up all night
praying with the Hassidim. On the eighth day, he recited the
prayer for rain. On Simhath Torah, he participated in the first
procession celebrating the Torah. It was a long time since he
had been so happy. He danced with the other worshippers and
treated them to wine and mead. Although no one got drunk,
everybody was slightly tipsy. Calman contrasted his pleasure
now with the misery he had known at Clara's parties. He
calculated that he had enough money with him to enable him
to remain in Marshinov for five years. After that, it would be
up to God.

But as soon as the holidays were over, the Hassidim departed and snow fell on Marshinov. The House of Prayer was
empty. The courtyard grew so still one could hear the last
leaves tearing away from the branches. Only a few yeshiva
students and hangers-on remained. The old men, having been

in each other's company for so long, grew irritable. They dozed by the stove, or sat over their books sucking their pipes. Calman busied himself studying a volume of the Mishnah. But how much study could he stand?

He paced nervously back and forth through the rooms of his daughter's house. Gadele, the youngest child, had the measles and Tsipele would not leave his bedside. The window of the room was draped with a red curtain. When Calman entered the room, Tsipele would put a finger to her lips to indicate that the child was sleeping. Calman went to his own room and lay down on the bed, but how could he sleep when he had been doing nothing for weeks? That evening rain drenched the windowpanes. A dry warmth rose from the stove, and there was a rustling sound as if a friendly house demon was burrowing among the rags and feather dusters. Calman knew that with the coming of Hanukkah Marshinov would again be as pleasant as it had been. But this was only the beginning of the month of Heshvan, and there were almost sixty days to Hanukkah. After the evening services, the maid' brought him a plate of soup and some beef stew, but he had no appetite. He put on his overcoat and walked out into the night. Tsipele called after him that it was foolish to go strolling about in such weather. Calman walked, not knowing where he was going. His fur coat became wet. The darkness was almost impenetrable, and he tapped with his cane like a blind man. Finally he reached the station. There was a tiny lamp burning, but the ticket agent's cage was closed. No train was due in for hours. Calman sat on a bench, staring off into the darkness. Was there no place in the world for him?

He rose and started back to Tsipele's. The rain had turned to snow. It fell at an angle, dry as hail. As he trudged along, he felt his face swelling and his eyelids congealing. He'd been through many blizzards, had spent nights by himself in the forest, but never before had he experienced such darkness. It seemed to him that he had been walking for hours. At the rabbi's house, the only light visible was in Jochanan's room.

Everyone else had retired. Calman was about to knock on his son-in-law's door, but changed his mind. There would be nothing to say. He must not take Jochanan, who was a godly man, away from the Torah.

He returned to his room and lit a candle. Its reflection flickered beyond the windowpanes, where a second Calman fidgeted, imitating his movements. Calman seated himself on his bed. The chimney whistled. The shingles on the roof rattled. A cold wind blew through the room from corner to corner. Calman recited the prayer spoken before retiring. He was afraid that he would not be able to sleep, but as soon as he closed his eyes he dozed off. Clara came to him; she was naked and she coiled her hair around his body, laughing like Lilith. Calman awoke, burning with lust. Not even in his youth had he known such desire. He threw off his blanket. Sitting up, he listened. A mouse was gnawing at the floorboards like a creature with a saw in its jaws. Calman reached down, picked up one of his boots, and with it pounded on the foot of his bed.

"Be still, devil."

11

The snow fell. The flakes whirled in the wind. Every gust was laden with white. Snowdrifts formed. The wind scurried over the earth, tearing up straw roofs in the hamlets, knotting braids in horses' manes, exposing furrowed fields and sweeping paths and highways. Occasionally Calman was struck in the eyes as if by a handful of salt. At times it seemed as if cold fingers pressed on his lids. He kept shaking off the snow. Had he been in a sleigh, the trip would have been difficult enough. But the coach skidded constantly, and when it did, the horses stopped dead. Calman was reminded of the story of Balaam's ass. Nevertheless, if one says alpha, beta must follow. If one sets out, one must continue on one's way. Calman, dressed in his fur coat, a bashlyk on his head and straw overshoes covering his boots, sat on the box, arguing with himself. He should

352

have remained in Marshinov. Why was he going to Jampol? Whom did he want to see? His wife, who had slept with another man? It was true that Reb Alter, the assistant rabbi of Marshinov, had ruled that the Law permitted Calman to live with his wife. As long as there was no witness to prove her adultery, she was presumed innocent. On the other hand, Reb Alter had warned that in a case where there was the slightest suspicion it would be best for a man of faith not to go near her, especially if she could not be trusted to practice the prescribed ablutions.

"Gee-up! To the right! Brrr! . . ."

The snowfall grew even denser. Jampol was not far away, not more than fifteen verst, but Calman was afraid, God forbid, of losing his way. He drove into a tempest. Swirls of snow fell across the plain like whirling sprites. From time to time, an entire pillar rose like a white column of locusts ready to drag him and his coach and team off to the Treasure of Snow, to the Congealed Ocean. The chestnut-colored horses turned white as if they had suddenly aged. Their hindquarters seemed to be moving on the same spot. The snow piling up on Calman's shoulders and fur cap transformed his head into a sugar cone. Who could tell? Perhaps he was destined to perish in the storm. He had thoroughly earned his punishment. A man of his age who could not control his lust deserved death. Calman pulled a flask of brandy from his breast pocket and took a swallow. It wouldn't do to get drunk, but it would be worse to catch cold. The frost penetrated his fur coat, his jacket. His feet were numb. Where should he go? To the manor or to the mill? Calman stopped directing the horses, no longer signaled them with his whip. He concentrated on searching for signs of the road. Here and there he made out traces of the highway. As long as it remained light, he realized that he was in no real danger. Behind the clouds, the sun shone. Shadows raced across the plain. Occasionally a flash of red glowed on the snow like a glimpse of a sunset.

Thanks be to God, the coach rolled onto a forest road

353

on which one could no longer lose one's way. Firs lined the road on either side, the snow lying like white cats on their branches. It was already twilight. God forbid lest a highwayman emerge from behind the thickets. Calman was too weary to defend himself. He prayed to God, although he was ashamed to do so. The good who travel with an innocent purpose suffer no harm; but the goal of his journey was evil. What help could he expect?

The snow continued to fall but not as heavily as before. Occasionally Calman heard the cawing of a crow. How could these creatures stand the cold, Calman wondered. It seemed to him that he had been riding through snow and winter for weeks, months, years. Night came and the darkness descended in an instant, as if suddenly the lights in the sky had been turned off. One moment the snow was still blue and gleaming with diamonds, and the next, everything had turned black. The coach had lanterns, but the panes were frosted over and Calman's fingers were so stiff he couldn't strike a match. He would have to rely upon the horses. Animal's eyes were keener than man's. The horses were moving so slowly that Calman had to call out to them, "Gee-up. Gee-up." He felt like laughing. Here he was, a sixty-year-old man, imperiling himself for a woman who had betrayed him. He thought of Zelda, God rest her soul. If she wanted him to be punished because he had married a loose woman, the sight of him in such a predicament was all the revenge she needed.

As Calman drove into the manor, the dogs tore at their chains and barked at him. Apparently they had forgotten their master. At last, Antoni the coachman appeared and took the horses. The half-frozen animals were led into the stable and covered with blankets. Calman could barely climb from the box. He restrained himself from inquiring about Clara, and walked into the kitchen, where a fire was burning. When he removed his coat, which was stiff and round as a barrel, it remained standing on the floor. He pulled the icicles from his beard, stepped out of his overshoes and boots, and began to warm his feet. Suddenly Clara appeared. She had on slippers, and a sleeveless coat over her nightgown. A net was thrown over her hair. "You certainly picked a fine time to come," she said.

"Well, I'm here," Calman replied, "and I'm alive. I have God to thank for that."

Calman was hungry, but it seemed that in his absence Clara had discharged the Jewish cook. He was afraid to drink even a glass of tea. He sat near the open stove, chewing on a dry crust of bread like a beggar. He added a few pieces of kindling to the fire. His face was flushed. Clara kept pacing back and forth in front of him.

"How's Sasha?" Calman asked.

"He's in Warsaw."

"In Warsaw? By himself?"

"No, he's at school there."

"I don't understand what you're saying, Clara."

"Well, it's not very difficult."

"But who's taking care of him?"

"His governess, of course. I rented an apartment for him, and hired a maid."

"What kind of a school is it?"

"A private school."

A Gentile school, of course. I deserve what I get, Calman thought. Who else would return to such a shrew? For no reason at all he threw a piece of bread into the fire. A childish thought occurred to him. It was like a sacrificial offering. He moved away from the stove to avoid singeing his beard.

"Don't you miss him?" he asked. "I have other children. He's your only child."

"He won't be for long."

Calman became pensive again. "When did you see him last?"

"I go to Warsaw constantly."

Now it was all clear to Calman. She was carrying a bastard. She had rented an apartment for herself and her lover and had so managed that she had an excuse to go to him whenever she wished. Though Calman was in anguish, he marveled at her cunning. His running away had fitted conveniently into her plans. He knew that he should not share her room, but all the other rooms were unheated. He walked into the room, lay down on the bed, and covered himself with a feather comforter. Tired though he was, he could not sleep. Clara, who was also wakeful, coughed continuously. It was the cough of an enemy. Still, he did not regret his difficult journey back to her. In Marshinov he had nourished the illusion that a reconciliation between them was possible. But now her adultery was revealed. She had sent his child away, his only son, his heir. The boy was almost certainly eating non-kosher food. There was no longer the possibility of arranging a truce. He could not even eat a spoonful of food in his own house. Everything was unclean. She might even try to poison him. Once started down the road of evil, there was no end to what a person could do.

"Well, why are you so quiet?" Clara suddenly asked. "Usually when a husband returns from a trip, he tells his wife about it."

"What is there to tell you?"

"You didn't even bring me a gift."

"What kind of a gift? There's nothing to buy in Marshinov."

"You might have sent me a postcard."

Calman was disgusted with her falseness.

"I didn't have anything to write. There was nothing to say."

"What did I do to you? Drown your ducks in the lake?"

"My worst enemy couldn't have hurt me more."

"Is it my fault that you're crazy, and obsessed with Zipkin?"

"I'm not crazy."

"Calmanke, you are. You should go to a doctor. You've nothing to be angry about. The child must be educated. We can't let him grow up to be a peasant. If you want him to have a Hebrew tutor, they're not hard to find in Warsaw. As far as I'm concerned, he can study the Torah with the greatest rabbi."

"He's eating non-kosher food."

"Why non-kosher? The maid is Jewish."

"Why did you discharge the cook?"

"Because of you, Calman. What point was there in keeping her when you weren't here? If you stay home and behave like a normal person, we'll start obeying the laws again. Your Mayer Joel treated me as if I were a thief. What a boor he is."

Calman knew that everything she said was untrue. Nothing but lies. Yet his anger began to disappear. Her voice soothed and caressed him. He wanted both to beat and to hug her. If he made up with her now, he told himself, he was lost. She would demean him. It would be as if he himself were delivering his soul to Asmodeus.

"Calmanke, come to me."

"I swear before God that I'll never touch you again. If I do, may all the punishments recorded in the Book of Curses fall upon me."

The next morning, Calman moved out of the manor house and into the house where he had once lived with Zelda, may she rest in peace. He hired a woman from Jampol to be his housekeeper and began to live alone.

26

Just as the Simhath Torah dances and the prayers for rain ended, winter began in Warsaw. On the Sabbath on which the first section of Genesis is read, snow and hail fell. It was unnecessary to tear down the Tabernacles after the holiday. The wind had already scattered the branches in all directions. The wealthy freeholders lit their ovens and went about wearing felt boots, plush hats, and fur coats. They ordered their wives and servants to prepare hot soup with barley, dried mushrooms, and beans cooked in fat. The early frost took the poor by surprise. According to the newspapers, sickness and starvation were rampant in Poland. There was a shortage of coal in Warsaw because the locomotives were unable to haul enough freight cars, and flooding rivers disrupted transportation. The news from Galicia and Upper Silesia was also bad. In Warsaw, because of a shortage of glaziers, a broken windowpane often could not be replaced and many windows were boarded up. Without shoes, underwear, and warm clothes, the children sickened. The Children's Hospital on Alexander Street was filled to capacity. Convalescent patients could not be discharged because they had nothing to wear, and they moved about in the wards among the sick. At night, long lines of homeless people gathered before the police commissariats. These indigents were permitted to sleep on the commissariat floors, but in the morning they were driven out into the cold.

The Polish press appealed to the public. The Warsaw Chamber of Commerce began preparations for a ball, the proceeds of which were to be used to assist the poor. A number of philanthropic organizations proposed holding a bazaar. Famous actresses, singers, and society ladies promised their services as salesclerks in the booths. Wallenberg pledged a large donation. But the number of those who were to receive help far exceeded the number who could give it. It was difficult to know whose need was the most urgent. The peasants had eaten their seed and were now starving. Even some of the wealthy Warsaw freeholders were unable to obtain fuel with which to heat their homes. Most of the coal that reached the city went to the factories.

The situation was even worse among the Jews. Mobs of paupers convened outside the community house, but the beadles refused to let them in. The angry crowd wept, scolded, cursed the Hassidim, whom they accused of allying themselves with the assimilationists, thus delivering Warsaw into the hands of semi-converts. A feud had raged between the Hassidim and the non-Hassidim, ever since the Russians had issued a modern dress decree. The non-Hassidim had wanted all Jews to adopt European-style clothes: hats, long trousers, shoes with laces or buttons. It was said that the Rabbi of Kotsk had been in favor of European dress, but the Rabbi of Gur and his followers had insisted on the Russian capote, trousers tucked into the boots, a kerchief around the neck, and the Russian cap adapted to the native style. In addition, Hassidim had for some time been agitating against Reb Yukele the Chief Rabbi of Warsaw. But on his death, no new chief rabbi had been appointed. Instead, a rabbinate was placed in charge of religious matters. Among those who came for assistance to the community houses were mourners with corpses at home. They had been unable to secure burial plots, shrouds, hearses.

Lucian and Miriam Lieba were also homeless. Lucian could

359

spend the nights at the house of Bobrowska, the seamstress and actor's widow, who was his mistress. An old friend of hers, Cybulski, a director of a small theater, from time to time gave Lucian parts as a walk-on. Miriam Lieba's sister-in-law, Felicia, had practically adopted Lucian's children, Wladzio and Marisia. But she would not take in the children's mother because Miriam Lieba drank. Miriam Lieba herself did not want to become a burden. Ezriel helped her out. He rented an attic room for her on Leshno Street, opposite Kercelak Place, which contained an iron stove with a tall smokestack. Ezriel bought her a bed (Lucian's furniture had been sold at public auction), a kitchen cabinet, and two chairs. It was a narrow room with a slanting ceiling and a window perched high on the wall like a small head on a hunchback. In order to look outside, one had to stand on a bench. The place did have one advantage: a private entrance.

Since there was no coal available, the room was nearly as cold as the street. The window was caked with ice. The water that Miriam Lieba brought up from the pump froze in the pail. The crumbling, unpainted walls became brown with mold. Although Miriam Lieba wrapped her jacket around her feet, she couldn't get warm. Ezriel brought her bread, cheese, herring, sausage, knowing that she would spend whatever money he gave her on whisky. She ate hardly anything and complained that Ezriel's gifts only served to attract mice. When he didn't visit her, she missed him; when he did, she spoke harshly to him.

"What do you want of me? Let me die in peace."

"Miriam Lieba, you must get a grip on yourself."

"Why should I?"

Ezriel went about dressed in his student uniform, his collar turned up, and his hands drawn into the sleeves of his jacket. He himself was susceptible to colds. His children had been ill the entire winter. Shaindel had been forced to have the doctor in to prescribe for them. Evenings, Ezriel sat beside Miriam

Lieba's bed, listening to her complaints. "Who can understand the ways of nature?" Ezriel would ask.

There was a soup kitchen on Iron Street where a meal cost only six groschen. The menu never varied: it was always barley soup with a dumpling or a tiny piece of meat in it. Lard was used for cooking. The kettles boiled from early morning until late evening, and the place was patronized by poor laborers and the unemployed. As soon as one batch of patrons was finished eating, they were hurried out to make room for another. The intellectuals sat by themselves at the "Gentlemen's Table." Lucian had lunch there every day. One of the habitués was Zbigniew Chwalski, a former landowner who blamed his ruin on the liberation of the serfs, but who actually had gambled away his fortune. Chwalski, who was tall and heavy, always brought along his small, thin wife, Katarzyna. Katarzyna's face was as dry as a fig, and her snub nose was perpetually red. As she ate, she berated the Russian tyrants, the perfidious French, the Polish *nouveaux riches*. She was forever talking about that convert Wallenberg who helped the Jews, was an intimate of the Russians, and lived in a palace while Polish aristocrats were forced to eat in soup kitchens. The Chwalskis were not the only anti-Semites at the "Gentlemen's Table." Zhulkowski, who wore a beard and still dressed in a caftan, was even more vehement on the subject than Chwalski. He always brought along a tin pan for his ration. He would place it on the table reserved for the gentry, add enormous amounts of salt and pepper, and begin his diatribe. According to him, the Freemasons and the Jews were responsible for every conceivable evil. They had plotted the partition of Poland, to undermine the Catholic faith. In fact, it was impossible to differentiate between Masons, Protestants, and Jews. They were all the same. Disraeli, Bismark, the Rothschilds, and Wallenberg all took orders from the same masonic high priest. Alexander II was a secret member of the conspiracy and had abolished serfdom for that reason. He had made a Russian Jew by the name of Ginsburg a baron. Sarah Bernhardt was not only an actress but one of the secret couriers of this organization composed of nihilists, liberals, and communards. To what depths Poland had sunk was exemplified by the fact that two Jews, Leventhal and Orgelbrand, headed the country's principal publishing concern. Another Jew, Ungar, was the custodian of Polish art.

Whenever Zhulkowski began to speak, a group gathered about him. Sooner or later, his conversation would get around to the Old Testament. Had not Abraham saved his life by deluding Abimelech into thinking that Sarah was Abraham's sister? Hadn't Isaac followed his father's example? Hadn't Jacob cheated Esau out of his birthright? Hadn't his brothers sold Joseph into slavery? By nature the Jew was a coward and a usurer, a worshipper of the golden calf, physically dirty, haughty, obstinate, and dishonorable. His aim was to monopolize the wealth of the world. Zhulkowski quoted a German writer to the effect that Cain was the prototype of all Jews. At first Lucian had argued with Zhulkowski. Were all Catholics as innocent as lambs? Didn't Christians consider the Old Testament sacred? But Zhulkowski had a dozen answers for each question, and gradually the two men became friends. Lucian told Zhulkowski about Miriam Lieba. Over a glass of beer, he outlined a plan to rob Wallenberg. Zhulkowski shook his head in criticism. Robbery? Theft? That was the way the Jews behaved, not Polish aristocrats. Zhulkowski had a much better plan. They must found an anti-Semitic party and publish books and periodicals to inform the people of how they were being betrayed. Zhulkowski referred to similar movements in Prussia, Hungary, Rumania, and Russia. Had Lucian read the articles of Lutoslawski? Did he know about the "Black Hundreds"? Was he familiar with Renan's essays on religious history? Had he read about the proposal Victor de Istochy had

362

made in the Hungarian parliament, the gist of which was to deport all Jews to Palestine? Did he know that in Prussia everyone was saying: "The Jew is our misfortune"? Even the *Gazeta Polska* had recently run an article attacking Yiddish, a jargon closely associated with the nefarious Talmud that taught Jews how to cheat Christians and defile the Host. Was Lucian aware that the modern Jew, the so-called "assimilationist," was even more dangerous than his old-fashioned brother with his long capote and sidelocks? For the latter at least stayed in the ghetto, while the former had pushed his way into every strata of Polish society and was carrying on his destructive work.

Oddly enough, Zhulkowski toured the Jewish-owned book and antique shops on Swiętokrzyska Street every day after lunch and continued his discussions with fellow customers in the stores' back rooms. He was forever mounting the ladders placed against the bookshelves, and fetching down musty volumes to browse through. Although he never bought anything, the Jewish proprietors always addressed him respectfully. He carried on high-flown discussions with the Jewish salesgirls. He even borrowed books from the shops. For years, Adam Zhulkowski had been gathering material for some vast work. His hatred of the Jews had begun when a manuscript of his had been rejected by the publisher Leventhal. Catholic publishers had also rejected his essays, but it was Zhulkowski's theory that they had been influenced by the opinions of the Jews.

III

It had reached the point where Lucian could not stop talking about murder. When he visited Miriam Lieba on Saturday nights, he always spoke of his plans to do away with Bobrowska. Lucian never failed to bring with him a bottle of vodka, some food, a small pail of coals, and a bundle of wood. He would light the iron stove, lie down under the blanket with

Miriam Lieba, put out the lamp, and babble for hours. He would rob Wallenberg, kill Bobrowska, and then run off to Sicily or Corsica with Miriam Lieba and Kasia. Though his words were only the ravings of a drunk, Miriam Lieba noticed how much they excited him. He could no longer make love without such talk. As he spoke, he would flourish his pistol, place the muzzle against Miriam Lieba's forehead and say: "Darling, shall I shoot?"

"Go ahead, shoot."

"You'd be killed immediately."

"The sooner the better."

When he was with Bobrowska, Lucian spoke about killing Miriam Lieba. Miriam Lieba paid no attention to his antics, but Bobrowska begrudged him the murder of his wife. She wanted to do it herself with a knife, not a gun. Bobrowska would then suck the blood from Miriam Lieba's throat like a vampire. Later, while Miriam Lieba was in her death agonies, Bobrowska would lie with Lucian. Although only a seamstress, she was descended from the nobility. She boasted of how her grandfather had lashed a score of peasants to death. She related how during the uprising of 1863 Cossack officers had used flagellation to arouse aristocratic women sexually. In the morning, Lucian and Bobrowska would tell each other their dreams.

Lucian was not able to see Kasia as much as he wished. He could only visit her when her employer, Pan Chodzinski, was at the steam bath. He began to think about murdering Chodzinski too, and asked Kasia where the old man kept his money. "Why talk about it?" Kasia replied. "You won't kill him."

"How can you be so sure of that?"

"You're just not a killer."

"Yes, I am. I'll put an end to that old dog."

"Why? He's going to die anyway."

"I want his money."

"You'd be killing him for nothing. You wouldn't find it. No one knows where he's hidden it."

Though Kasia was too much of a peasant to appreciate Lucian's perversities, he kept asking her if she were not jealous of his wife and Bobrowska. Wouldn't she like to revenge herself on Bobrowska? How would she do it? He kept putting words into her mouth and forced her to comply to his perversions. He wheedled and begged until she gave him money. Lucian had arrived at a new low and he was aware of it. He was without a job. His children had been taken from him by his sister. He ate in a cheap soup kitchen, lived off Bobrowska, and hung around waiting for a walk-on at the theater. The only thing that kept him from being a complete derelict was his appearance. But even keeping himself looking presentable became more and more difficult. Bobrowska's apartment was infested with vermin. Though hot water was poured into the cracks of the woodwork and poison scattered about everywhere, the bugs always returned. Miriam Lieba managed to keep herself moderately clean but slept on a torn pillow, the feathers of which blew all over the apartment. Bobrowska washed Lucian's clothes and occasionally pressed his suit, but all his clothing was worn out and needed to be replaced.

Lucian's rage had grown so intense that he could not repress it. Whether awake or asleep, he dreamed perpetually. In the morning, he always awoke tired and with the urge to lie down again. He was constantly yawning and stretching. Formerly, he had enjoyed cold weather, but now he could not bear it. His fantasies were always of South Sea Islands or South American plantations where natives toiled while he sat drinking wine on shady porches. Thoughts of love and murder never left him. He became incapable of dealing with everyday matters. It was almost as if he had been swallowed up by his grandiose dreams.

IV

Pan Chodzinski, the man for whom Kasia worked, left for Grodzisk to spend Christmas with his sister. He was to be away for several days and possibly over New Year's. Kasia remained to take care of the house, but Chodzinski had arranged for her to eat her holiday meals with a neighbor, a shoemaker, because it was not right for a girl to be entirely alone during this happy season. Although Chodzinski had bought a Christmas tree, he would not have it decorated with candles, for fear that his apartment would catch fire. Nor would he allow Kasia to go to church, because there were so many thieves around during the holidays. He particularly did not want her to attend Midnight Mass. Kasia was glad that her master had left. Despite his impotence, he continued to harass her. Kasia's young son, Bolek, was being brought up by a woman who lived almost at the very end of Dzika Avenue, near the Catholic cemetery. Kasia paid a ruble a week for the child's board, thirteen rubles a quarter. All that she earned in that period was five rubles. The rest she managed to scrape together by selling bones, potato peels, the presents that Chodzinski gave her, and the occasional coins she got from Lucian. Kasia, though barely twenty-one, already had a handsome five-year-old boy who resembled Lucian. If it had not been for her father's assistance, Kasia would never have been able to raise the child. Chodzinski must never learn that she was the mother of a bastard. It was only on rare occasions that she could visit the boy. Even on Sunday, her day off, Chodzinski insisted that she go to church with him. Now that Chodzinski was not around, Kasia could behave like a mother for a few days, and Lucian could again visit her freely. Recently it had become more difficult to see him because Chodzinski had given up going to the steam bath on the same day each week. Sometimes he skipped a week, and there was no predicting on what day he would go. The young men on Chmielna Street did not know that Kasia had a lover and a child and pursued her as dogs do a bitch. But Kasia was only interested in Lucian. Though Lucian came to her drunk from the arms of another woman, a visit from him was still a holiday for her. She served him cookies and jam from Chodzinski's larder. Lucian hid nothing from her, told her all his sins, and revealed to her his most private thoughts. Although she did not understand much of what he said, it was good to listen to him. She often caught him in lies, but that didn't matter. Men liked to boast. Although he was so much older than she, Kasia thought of him as a child. He chattered like Bolek, laughed and grimaced exactly as the boy did. At times he would threaten to murder Chodzinski, strangle Bobrowska, do away with his wife, the Jewess, or merely commit suicide himself after killing Kasia first. What did all such babbling mean? Thus far, the only one he had harmed was himself. Kasia dreaded only one thing—becoming pregnant again. But Lucian had learned a trick that prevented conception. Thank God, her period came regularly. Despite her poverty, she dropped a groschen in the church box each month and had a candle lit at the altar of her patron saint.

While Pan Chodzinski was away, Kasia would be able to spend some of her nights with Lucian. Lucian had promised to buy the boy some presents and take Kasia in a droshky to Pawązek to visit him. Lucian hadn't seen Antek in years, but had even agreed that they meet and visit Bolek together. How strange it was that his former enemy should now be his father-in-law, Bolek's grandfather. Antek now had his own woman, and plenty of work to do. A great many homes were being constructed in Warsaw, and he had become a mason. He earned seven rubles a week, sometimes as much as ten.

Lucian had meant every word when he made these promises to Kasia. Unfortunately, that Christian soul Felicia had prevailed upon her husband to invite Lucian and his wife to Christmas dinner. At first Zawacki had been stubbornly opposed to the idea. He was determined not to have his charlatan brother-in-law or his psychopathic wife around. But Felicia's eyes had grown red from weeping. After all, Lucian was her brother. Besides, the children were asking to see their mother and father. Felicia could not rob her angels of their parents. After much discussion, Zawacki gave in. Felicia sent clothing and fifteen rubles in cash to her sister-in-law so that Miriam Lieba could make herself presentable. Felicia also wrote Lucian a letter begging him to accompany his wife and to conduct himself like a gentleman, at least during Christmas.

Miriam Lieba gave Lucian the letter that Felicia had sent to him, and also three of the fifteen rubles. He must have some money in his pocket. Then Miriam Lieba made Lucian swear on the crucifix that he would accompany her to his sister's, no matter how low his opinion was of Felicia. As if this were not enough, Bobrowska announced that she was planning to give a dinner to celebrate God's birthday, and that if Lucian disappointed her on this occasion she would have nothing more to do with him. She knew that Chodzinski was going away and suggested that Lucian bring Kasia along. Why should the girl be left alone on such a holy day? Bobrowska was too old and clever to be jealous. Actually, she had wanted for a long time to have that fresh young thing around, to talk to and drink whisky with. Later all three of them could carry on in the manner Lucian had suggested to her.

How was Lucian going to convince Kasia to visit Bobrowska when Pan Chodzinski had forbidden her even to attend Midnight Mass and had arranged for her to eat her holiday meal at the shoemaker's? And how was he to celebrate Christmas Eve with his sweetheart when he had to accompany his wife to his sister Felicia's? How, too, would it be possible to make Kasia feel friendly toward Bobrowska when Kasia hated her, called her crazy, bitch, and the like? Lucian had still another plan in mind, but the obstacles to its fulfillment were many. Yes, he had ensnared himself in a web that even the devil could not escape. Usually, Lucian's lies got him out of his predicaments, but this time it looked as if the stew he had cooked would choke him. However, Lucian had often observed that if one kept one's head, one always found a way out, or else chance offered a solution. And that is exactly what happened. Despite his helplessness, Lucian felt lucky. The

368

angel that watched over him would extricate him from all entanglements.

As it turned out, the shoemaker's wife at whose house Kasia was to eat came to tell the girl that she could not have her to dinner after all. On Christmas Eve, if there were an odd number of guests, there was a superstition that one of those present would die before the year was out. The shoemaker's family consisted of eight people and she could only include Kasia, who was a paying guest, if Pan Chodzinski were willing to pay for two instead of one. But Chodzinski was known in the courtyard as a miser and the shoemaker's wife doubted that the old man would even pay for Kasia. The janitor proposed that she eat at his house, but Kasia hated the janitor and his household. A large family was cramped into one tiny room, where the laundry was washed as well. With a Christmas tree in it, not even another pin could fit into the room. Besides, the janitor owned a dog, blind in one eye, who barked and bit. Eating at the janitor's was out of the question. Pan Chodzinski had left on the stagecoach at three o'clock on the day of Christmas Eve. Lucian arrived at Kasia's around three-thirty, carrying a bottle of sweet brandy and a bag full of cakes. Kasia told him what had happened and Lucian consoled her. It seemed to him that Providence itself was working for him. Sitting with the girl in the kitchen, he poured a drink for her and for himself. Kasia made a face. The liquor was too strong, and Lucian ridiculed her. "You call this liquor? It's water!" After the third glassful, Kasia stopped grimacing. Her gray eyes twinkled. Her upturned nose became red. She began to mutter that she would get drunk and forget her troubles. Lucian embraced her, kissed and flattered her. He was not drunk, but seemed to be. He played their old game, calling himself her husband, lord, and master. Whatever he told her, she must do, even if he ordered her to jump into the Vistula. Suddenly he said: "Get dressed quickly. Come with me!"

"Where? I must not leave the apartment."

369

"Let the apartment go to hell!"

"Where are you taking me? The old man will kill me!"

"If the old rascal lays a hand on you, I'll chop it off!"

Kasia mumbled something about her duty, thieves, the janitor, but Lucian assured her that he would take full responsibility for her going. Kasia put on her high-buttoned shoes, her Sunday dress, and threw a shawl over her shoulders. Lucian seldom went out with Kasia. The few occasions on which he had taken her for a walk or to visit their child, he had waited for her at the end of Iron Street. This time he made no attempt to hide. All the neighbors in the courtyard were already drunk. For the girl, his walking out with her was a sign of his devotion. He was no longer ashamed of her. Kasia fumbled with the lock, and Lucian helped her hang it on the door. He dropped the key into his own pocket. To avert her suspicions he told her that he had bought Bolek a toy sword. They strolled along arm in arm like lady and gentleman. He led her to Iron Street. Kasia asked: "Where are you taking me?"

"To Baba Yaga, into her caldron."

"Oh, do be serious!"

"I'm taking you to a brothel and turning you over to a pimp."

When Kasia realized that he was taking her to Bobrowska's, she objected violently. She even tried to run away. But Lucian held her fast. "Don't be an idiot. She is a goodhearted woman, a motherly soul. If you're not happy there, you can always leave. She doesn't eat people alive . . ."

He reminded her that she had promised to obey him blindly. He muttered something about her sainted mother, Stachowa. He even poked Kasia lightly in the shoulder, a sign that he was displeased and that it would be dangerous to thwart him. Before entering Bobrowska's house, he took the bottle of liquor from his pocket and gave Kasia a drink.

"Take a deep one . . ."

Bobrowska's room was half swept when Lucian brought Kasia inside. Sawdust was sprinkled on the floor. In the window stood three candles of different colors, in memory of the Trinity. The Christmas tree was already decorated with ornaments and tinsel. Odors of carp, cake, vegetables, and ginger permeated the apartment. Bobrowska was still in her petticoat. She was doing many things at once—cooking, baking, hemming a dress. On the table stood a pressing iron filled with glowing coals. The apartment was warm and steamy. The parrot shrieked like a human being. Bobrowska's red and perspiring face lit up with a smile. Although Lucian had promised to bring Kasia, Bobrowska had learned by now that his word could not be depended on. Suddenly there he was with the girl. Bobrowska had already had a few drinks. She ran to Kasia, embraced her, kissed both her cheeks, and sang out: "Don't say a thing. I know all there is to know. Take off your shawl!"

Lucian hesitated for a moment and then said: "I must go out again."

"Go out where?" Bobrowska asked suspiciously. "It will be dark soon."

"I'm afraid I'll be somewhat late for dinner."

"Where are you going? What's wrong with you? I was planning to call in my neighbor so that we wouldn't be an odd number."

"You needn't do that. I won't be here for dinner."

Bobrowska's green eyes lit up. "You were fooling me, eh? Why did I prepare everything? Why did you bring this girl here if you're running off to your wife?"

"Elzbieta, I'll come later. I can't tear myself to bits. Meanwhile, you two get acquainted."

Lucian whistled in relief and slammed the door. She heard him running down the stairs. For a moment Bobrowska was transfixed. Then she screamed in a voice unlike her own: "Madman! Maniac! Parasite! Dog!" She opened the door as if to run after him, but instead she turned to Kasia and commanded: "Take off your shawl. You're staying here . . ."

371

V

From Iron Street, Lucian ran back to Leshno Street, in the direction of Kercelak Place. It wasn't snowing, but some invisible, prickly substance was falling from the sky. Even at this late hour, Christmas trees were still being peddled. Pine needles covered the sidewalks and the air was permeated with the odor of pine and wintry forests. The stores were selling starch cakes shaped like stars, crosses, pictures of holy figures with wings and halos above their heads. Colored candles, glass balls, and tinsel for decorating trees were displayed in the shop windows. Hay for placing under the tablecloth and stalks of wheat for standing in the corners of rooms were also on sale. Drunken revelers staggered down the street, hoarsely bellowing their songs. Choirboys passed by in their surplices and cowls. Lucian sprinted along. Having eaten little in the last few days, he had grown light, as though he were hollow. He would go to bed irritated and arise with the same feeling. Within him something fluttered constantly, as if his heart hung on a thread. He had had his hair cut for Christmas. Bobrowska had removed the stains from his clothes. His dress shoes had been half-soled. With his derby hat perched sideways on his head, in his fresh collar, wool shawl, and polished shoes, he still looked the dandy. He had not wished to disgrace Felicia by his shabby appearance. When he reached his wife's attic room, he opened the door and saw a transformed Miriam Lieba. Combed and dressed almost to perfection, in a skirt a trifle too short—Felicia was an inch shorter then she—Miriam Lieba stood there, a hat on her head and a fur neckpiece over her shoulders. She wore earrings given to her as a wedding present by Lucian's Aunt Eugenia, may her soul rest in paradise. Miriam Lieba had apparently powdered and rouged her face, because she was not as wan as usual. Lucian stared at her, astonished. All winter, he had never seen her out of her nightclothes. She had always been huddled in a thick shawl. She was still pretty. God, what had he made of this woman!

He said: "Truly, you look marvelous!"

"Go on, laugh at me—"

"No, dear, it's the truth."

"Oh, my cough is choking me," said Miriam Lieba, and she began to cough into a handkerchief. She put on a worn plush jacket. On the bed was an old muff and numerous little boxes and bags.

"What are those?"

"Stars for the children. I bought something for the adults, too. You forget, Lucian, that you are a father."

"No, I don't forget. Come, it's getting late."

"I can't walk in these shoes. We'll have to hire a sleigh."

"Do you have any money?"

They added up their small change. Miriam Lieba hung a lock on the door, and they walked down the stairs, which were covered with mud. The odor of cooking carp came from all the doors. Miriam Lieba suddenly remembered Passover evenings in Jampol. How different it had all been, and how long ago! . . . Someone, carrying up a Christmas tree, blocked the passageway. They had to wait a long time for a sleigh. Miriam Lieba seated herself, and Lucian, playing the cavalier, covered her with the sheepskin lap robe. The sleigh skidded right and left, almost spilling Miriam Lieba out, and she clutched at Lucian's arm. How long was it since she had seen her children! Not since the end of the summer. Actually, she had not gone outdoors all winter. She had sat at home, just as cold as those Polish patriots who still languished freezing somewhere in the Siberian tundras. If not for Ezriel, she would have been completely isolated from the world. Choking as she coughed, she sucked on some rock candy. Yes, Felicia was a Christian soul, but it wasn't easy for Miriam Lieba to visit her own children as if she were an outcast. The driver drove to Kreditowa Street through Iron Street. They passed by the gate that led to Bobrowska's apartment. Afterward they turned into Grzybowska Street, and from there to Krolewska. Miriam Lieba could not believe that the world was still full of people who dressed up, primped. The short section of Marshalkowsky Boulevard that they crossed was filled with sleighs, crowds, and pre-holiday excitement. Luxury goods jammed the shop windows. The newspapers spoke of shortage and starvation. Yet, in spite of all the poverty, new fashions still appeared. On this street there were women dressed in fox furs, sables, and magnificent hats, and elegant gentlemen with racing dogs.

When Lucian and Miriam Lieba walked into the Zawackis' apartment, the household was already prepared for the holiday ceremonies. Presents for the servants were piled on a table in the drawing room. Balls, bells, pine cones, and silver tinsel hung on the Christmas tree, which had a star on top. At the foot of the tree stood a miniature manger inherited from Felicia's parents and grandparents. In it were displayed figurines of sheep, cattle, shepherds, angels, the Child Jesus, the Blessed Mother, the three Wise Men from the East, their slaves, donkeys, and camels—everything painted gold or silver and covered with artificial snow. Felicia embraced Miriam Lieba, kissing her on both cheeks. She also kissed Lucian. A governess brought in the children. Miriam Lieba's eyes filled with tears. She glimpsed Wladzio and Marisia as if through a mist. Both had grown in the few months they'd been away from her. Wladzio had on a velvet suit with knee-length trousers, and his blond hair was parted in the middle. It was the same Wladzio, but a patrician affluence emanated from his face. Marisia's dress was trimmed with lace, her braids tied in red ribbons. Wladzio blushed, bowed, hesitated a moment before leaping into his mother's arms. The little one began to move backward, her face wrinkling to cry . . .

Kissing the children, Lucian was filled with resentment. "I'll take them away from here! I'm still alive. After today, everything will change. They will forget this period of their lives

374

. . ." He decided he would settle in Sicily or Corsica and take along Kasia and Bolek. All he needed was the fare and a sum of money to purchase a house or a bit of land. He would begin anew and wed his Slavic strength to the southern sunshine . . . The democratic refuse that the French Revolution had spread throughout Europe would sooner or later in turn be swept away with a fiery broom . . .

Dr. Zawacki spent the entire time in his office, reading a medical journal. He despised sentiment, tears, impassioned conversation, and waited for the family, in his own words, "to soak itself out." What the devil was the sense of all these holidays? he wondered. How much longer would people cling to these empty myths? Would mankind remain ignorant forever? The following day he would have to visit his father, the shoemaker, in the Old City; listen to his and to his mother's reverent observations, eat all the cooking and baking that lay so heavily on the stomach. What came of all these festivities? The priests, those wastrels, went around sprinkling holy water, robbing the poor of their last few groschen. The rabble glutted itself, and appendicitis attacks, stomach poisonings, heart failures, and apoplexies followed. Coffinmakers and undertakers would have a busy season.

Hearing Felicia's step, he put the journal aside. She had come to summon him to their guests. To please her, he even planned to attend Midnight Mass. "Well, what is love?" he reflected. "Another irrational thing . . ."

V I

Even before the meal had ended, Lucian rose and announced that he had to leave, promising to return later. Although Miriam Lieba had become reconciled to his insulting treatment of her, she had never imagined that he would run off and leave her and the children on Christmas Eve. She gazed at Lucian in bewilderment. Felicia pleaded with her brother to remain and attend Midnight Mass with the family. "A little prayer won't

375

hurt you," she argued. Marian Zawacki was in the midst of presenting historical evidence that Christmas had never been a Christian holiday and that, even from the theological viewpoint, there was no indication that Jesus had been born on the twenty-fifth of December. The fasting and celebration on that date were relics of pagan times when the populace feared the angry spirits of the winter solstice. Wiping her tears away, Felicia begged her husband to stop blaspheming.

In the midst of it all, Lucian said goodbye.

Zawacki called after him: "Come back, little brother-in-law. There is a present here for you, too."

"Yes, thank you. I'll be back."

Lucian hurried out. His watch indicated a quarter to nine. The frost that night had become drier and more piercing. Lucian walked down Marshalkowsky Boulevard and turned into Chmielna Street. Sleighs glided by, their bells ringing. Through half-frosted widowpanes there gleamed the light of candles and Christmas trees. Drunks staggered by, croaking songs, rushing forward to kiss people. The streetwalkers loitered as usual at the end of Chmielna Street. Lucian's plan was simple. He would get into Chodzinski's apartment, locate the money that the miser had hidden somewhere, and before the gate was closed, steal out into the street and go on to Bobrowska's. Kasia had often told him that her employer kept money in the house. The only problem was where. The old idiot wasn't due back until the day after next, or perhaps not even until after the New Year. There would be plenty of time to cover up the traces. Racing over the icy sidewalks, breath coming from his nostrils, Lucian considered the situation. He had hoped for a long time that Chodzinski would go on a trip. He had frequently urged Kasia to get to know Bobrowska better. Bobrowska had even promised to teach Kasia how to sew. But Kasia had obstinately refused to hear of it. All at once, both his wishes had been granted. Now he could manage everything without interference. Weren't these omens that the beginning year would be a lucky one for him? Despite his having just finished a large meal, he felt light. In the street, the flames of the gas lamps cast trembling shadows. The sky was filled with stars. Lucian glided rather than walked. The wind, blowing from somewhere on the North Sea, thrust him forward. "Oh, it's a good frost. It's good to be alive," Lucian exulted. "A sin? The old man's money would be squandered anyway, or he would leave it to some church . . ." Lucian daydreamed about Corsica, where there was hardly any winter. One walked among palm trees by the shores of the Mediterranean. Laws were not taken too seriously. As in Napoleonic times, bandits still operated there.

A streetwalker accosted Lucian. "Not now, girlie," he said. "Maybe on my way back . . ."

Everything seemed to be working in his favor. He met no one going through the gate. Unobserved, he walked up the stairs. A lock hung on the door, but Lucian had taken both the big and the little keys. Although no light illuminated the stairway, he quickly found both keyholes. Removing the lock, he replaced it so that it only appeared to be locked. If the janitor decided to check, he would find everything in order. Entering, Lucian closed the door, bolting it from the inside. In the breast pocket of his overcoat lay a loaded pistol, but Lucian knew that he would not have to use it. The janitor had more alcohol in his head than in his glass. Only one thing would be dangerous—lighting a candle. Lucian decided to work in the dark. At the threshold of the living room, he let his eyes grow accustomed to the dimness. A street lamp and the lights from the neighboring apartments broke the darkness. The reflection of the snow on the roof across the street cast a luminous light of its own. It was now about a quarter after nine. A good hour and a half remained before the gate was locked. Lucian decided to begin with the bedroom. Misers habitually secreted money in mattresses. Lucian pulled apart the bed linen, searched beneath the pillow, felt the mattress. Should he slash it open with his knife? The mattress was old, its stuffing almost gone. There was nothing to be found in it. A commode

377

stood at the left of the bed. Lucian tried to open it, but all the drawers were locked. Should he force it—but how? He needed some sort of tool, a file or crowbar. How could he have forgotten to bring such a thing along? He walked into the kitchen. The darkness seemed to grow less from one minute to the next. He could see everything, the pantry, the pots on the stove, as if it were midday. A cleaver hung on the wall. He removed it and hefted its weight in his hand. This was not the proper tool, but if he lingered until the gate was closed, he would be left in a trap.

Cleaver in hand, Lucian turned back to the bedroom. He was calm, but warm. He wanted to remove his coat, but finally decided against it. In this kind of situation, one could easily forget something. There were letters and papers in his coat. Just as Lucian had felt confident he would have no trouble in entering the apartment, he now sensed that there was no money in the commode. He would force the drawers and lose time for nothing. Nevertheless, he broke open a drawer and began to tap around inside. There were collars, magazines, cuffs, all sorts of knickknacks. He tore open the second drawer, which creaked and squealed. The brittle old wood smelled of starch. He dumped out shirts, handkerchiefs, neckties, scarves, and socks, to reach the drawer bottom more quickly. It was unnecessary to force the third drawer, which he struck from the inside with his fist, loosening it immediately. Again he found all manner of foppish accessories. "How he indulges himself, the devil!" Lucian snarled. He began to grow angry, his armpits perspired. His throat grew dry and he had to cough—two deep coughs and one light one that brought up the phlegm. He wiped his mouth with a handkerchief.

"Have I missed anything?" he asked himself, resting for a moment. Apparently he had grown unaccustomed to physical exertion. His arms ached, his heart pounded. He was not jittery but tense. He had just eaten, but something like hunger began to gnaw at him. Perhaps the old codger kept some

378

whisky or liqueur on the premises? As he stood there, sparks drifted before Lucian's eyes. A dreamlike design formed—spots, stripes, flowers—of green, blue, and violet. They changed shape, assuming all kinds of geometric patterns, both tangible and ethereal. What was this? As a child, when his nurse had tucked him into bed, he had had similar visions. Oddly enough, he even recalled the colors, the combinations, the whole dreamlike design.

Lucian shuddered. There was no time for fantasies. He had to search through everything and leave before the gate was closed. Every second was precious. Everything hung on a scale between life and death . . .

Going into the living room, he went to the window, tucked up the curtain, and consulted his watch. It was later than he had imagined. The small hand pointed to ten and the large to five. Only half an hour remained.

VII

The church bells rang. Everywhere, from all the streets, all the houses, from palaces and cellars, from luxurious apartments and attics, people were on their way to Midnight Mass. The churches filled rapidly. At every altar stood a stable with a crib representing the birth of Jesus in Bethlehem.

The Russian New Year fell thirteen days later, but Poland always was, and remained, a Catholic country. Even the Czar could not uproot the faith of the people. The Russians continued to build new Greek Orthodox churches. In Praga, they had constructed a *sobor*, its crooked Greek Orthodox cross of solid gold gleaming on high. It was said that similar *sobors* were to be built in Warsaw and in other large Polish cities. But what was the use of spacious structures, copper cupolas, the rich holy decorations, when inside, the churches remained empty and the priests preached to the walls?

Bobrowska ate Christmas dinner with Kasia. By candlelight, surrounded by the scent of the Christmas tree, Bobrowska

N

spoke frankly to the girl. "What a savage that Lucian is! What a deceiver, numbskull, hothead! How little one can depend on him! He has a talent for ruining himself and everyone who has anything to do with him!" Drinking and talking, Bobrowska refilled Kasia's glass. Kasia made a face with each mouthful, but Bobrowska urged her on: "Drink, darling, drink down your sorrow! Life would be unbearable without lots of brandy."

Bobrowska stuffed Kasia with delicacies until the girl's stomach ached. Kasia drank until her eyes became glassy. She began to mumble words in the peasant jargon she had picked up from her parents in her infancy. She used such comical expressions that Bobrowska was forced to laugh: "Hey, girl, you're a peasant, all right! You drank it in with your mother's milk . . ." Bobrowska asked how often Lucian visited her, where he slept with her, when, how—but Kasia only smiled drunkenly, revealing her widely spaced teeth. Suddenly, as if severed, her head fell on the table. Bobrowska laughed: "You're drunk, girl, completely soused . . ." Bobrowska's knees were shaky too, but she managed to stand up, and led, almost carried Kasia to a windowless alcove which contained her spare bed. There she lay the girl on the bed where Lucian usually slept. Kasia gasped once and lay as if in a faint. Bobrowska smiled to herself: "What a scoundrel! What a fool, swine, rogue! Left two sweethearts and went off to his own wife, that Jew bitch. Or who knows? Maybe not to his wife, either. He must have found himself another whore. Did it mean anything to such a rake, such a pimp? Did he have anything to worry about?" He gorged himself at her house, snored in her bed, loafed the days away in soup kitchens among the derelicts. Even the few gulden he got in the theater he earned because she, Bobrowska, had recommended him. And how did he repay her? Of all times, on a holiday, he runs off and makes a fool of her.

Bobrowska was angry, but inwardly she laughed. "Just let him come here! Don't worry, he'll come."

She'd greet him with a broom and a slap. She'd land one on his jaw, one on his lousy undershirt. Let him just step across the threshold . . . Bobrowska wobbled back to the table. There could no longer be any question of going to church. She was too tired, too drunk. As they rang, the bells lulled her. Each chime stirred her deeply. She had once been young, handsome, had had desires, dreams. She had had a father, a mother, brothers, sisters. Where had they all gone? All had become dust and ashes . . . She had loved Bobrowski and Cybulski, who was now an important theater director and had no time for her, the son-of-a-dog . . . He was busy, terribly busy . . . But he had plenty of time for the whores. "Well, let them have their way. I earn my bread! What's already happened, even the devil can't take away from me . . ." Bobrowska tried to pour herself some vodka, but only a single drop remained. She placed the glass to her nose, inhaling. Suddenly the door opened and Lucian walked in. Bobrowska laughed joyfully. She wanted to make a cutting remark, but could not get the words out. He looked pale, disheveled. "Here comes the squire!" she crooned.

And she pointed at him with an index finger.

Lucian bristled.

"Where's Kasia?"

"I ate her. Hee, hee . . ."

"Where is she?"

"In the alcove. Dead drunk."

Lucian waited a moment, then moved a step closer to her.

"Elzbieta, I've killed a man!"

Bobrowska's smile froze on her lips. "Killed?"

"Yes, killed."

"And may I ask whom?"

"The janitor in Chodzinski's courtyard. He didn't want to open the gate for me, so I shot him in the stomach."

"The janitor? What were you doing in Chodzinski's yard, with her here?"

"I was . . ."

"So you're a murderer, too—" And Bobrowska, half sobered but feeling unusually heavy, remained seated. Her legs seemed paralyzed. She hiccuped and belched at once.

"Are you joking?"

"No, it's the truth."

"Well, that's just fine. Fine and dandy!"

Bobrowska, still smiling, stared at him, startled not so much at what he had done as at her own indifference and sluggishness. Fatigue had overpowered her. She seemed to have become rooted to the bench. Her tongue was stiff and she knew that whatever she said would sound foolish.

"Well, did it pay, at least?" she asked.

Lucian looked at her with the bewildered expression of someone who didn't quite understand what was being said to him.

"I found nothing. He had papers there, but they were junk as far as I'm concerned."

"Yes, I understand."

"He must have taken everything with him."

"Uh-huh."

"I must go away at once. The *glinas* may come here looking for me any minute." Lucian used the underworld nickname for the police. He stood there lopsided, pale, his clothes unbuttoned, his hat shoved back on his head, his hands in his pockets. Taking out a cigarette, he thrust it into his mouth and then spat it out. Bobrowska remained seated. Her stomach was as inflated as a drum, but she was completely sober now.

"Why did you do it? We could have had such a happy holiday."

"—I did it. I needed money."

"What will happen now?"

"I don't know, I don't know."

"How will they know that you did it?" Bobrowska asked after a while.

Lucian was silent, lost in thought. Then he said: "Kasia will run home tomorrow and they'll learn everything from her. She's a fool and a peasant—"

"You're just finding that out? We won't let her go home."

"What do you mean?"

Bobrowska did not reply. Lucian removed his overcoat and laid it over the cover of the sewing machine. He doubled up like someone with cramps.

"Are you hungry?" Bobrowska asked. "I left everything for you."

Lucian raised his brows questioningly, as if he did not understand what she was saying.

"Hungry? No. But do you have something to drink?"

"No."

"Slopped up everything, did you? Well, I'm dead tired."

Noting a chair in the middle of the room, Lucian sat down. He did not remove his hat. His eyes remained shut for a while as if he were about to doze off. Then he opened them again. They expressed no regret, no fear, only a weariness and the perplexity of someone awakened out of a dead sleep. Bobrowska slowly turned in her chair to face him.

"I put her down in your bed."

"Well, let her rest."

"You shouldn't have done it, Lucian. If at least you'd killed the old man. How was it the janitor's fault?"

"A clod, I wanted to get out and he wouldn't let me. He tried to hit me with the key."

"Did he recognize you?"

"I doubt it."

"Oh, it's a sin, a sin. He was surely a father of children. And on this holy night besides."

"Shut up!"

"You shouldn't have done it, dear, you shouldn't have done it. What will you do now? Unless throw yourself in the Vistula."

"The Vistula is frozen over—"

383

"What will you do?"

"I'll go away and that will be that."

"Away where? And what will become of me? I'm not even thinking about your children—"

"What happens will happen."

"Now I understand why you brought the girl here."

"You understand nothing. It was a coincidence. It was because the shoemaker didn't want to have an odd number of guests."

"What shoemaker? What are you talking about?"

"I know what I'm saying. Tomorrow, keep her here as long as you can. I'll leave first thing in the morning. I'm too tired now. Or should I kill her too, to keep her from going home?"

Bobrowska shivered.

"What are you saying? Not in my house. They'll question me as it is."

"No one will question you."

"Yes, they will. They'll ask the girl where she spent the night and she'll lead them to me. You'll make off and they'll drag me to the police station."

"So what do you want me to do? Give myself up?"

"You shouldn't have done it, Lucian. What good did it do you? You got nothing anyhow."

"He hid it, the scurvy dog. Under the floor, or somewhere. I should have stayed until morning. I simply didn't have the time to search."

"Certainly. You should have stayed until daybreak. In the morning, you could have come out and no one would have been the wiser. You would have spared yourself committing this sin—"

"I wanted to come to you. I knew you were waiting."

"I would have waited a while longer."

"It's all your nagging. Well, now it's too late. You all brought me to this. You gnawed at me like a worm. And Miriam Lieba, that Jew bitch, kept berating me. I wanted to take

384

another look in the daytime, but Kasia would have raised a fuss. Everyone hindered me, that's the truth."

"I didn't hinder you. I prepared a meal for you. For you and your sweetheart. You went away and left us like two fools."

"I went away because my sister, that lunatic, wanted to do a good deed . . . A gang of women have climbed on my back, each one pulling in her own direction . . . Well, I'm tired."

"I'll make the bed right away."

Bobrowska wanted to rise but was unable to do so. Lucian stood up and went to the alcove. Kasia snored. It was ink-black there, hot and stuffy, smelling of food. For a while Lucian stood over Kasia's bed, listening to her breathing. Perhaps he should strangle her? He felt no animosity toward her, but human life no longer had any value for him. He knew that in the courtyard there were cellars for storing limestone. He could carry her down, throw her into some cellar, and it would be weeks before she was found. By that time he would long since have escaped to America, or to Africa . . . Everyone was in church. There would be no witnesses . . . Lucian had even begun to extend his hands toward Kasia's throat when he suddenly changed his mind. No, not now . . . It would be better at daybreak . . . Let Elzbieta get to sleep first . . . He stretched out on the wide bed, placing his hat on the floor beneath it. He lay there still, hollow. "I don't even have pangs of conscience," he mused. He was somewhat concerned about wrinkling his suit, but he didn't have the strength to undress. On that evening years ago when the police had searched the hotel on Mylna Street, he had nearly died of fright. Now, all fear had left him. He had even buried his pistol in a snowpile, leaving himself unarmed. Lucian closed his eyes. He neither slept nor remained awake. A black stillness enveloped him. He had a strange sensation as if for the first time in his life he was really resting. Death must be like this. After a while, he began to dream. Wool was being

385

wound around a huge ball by dwarfs. "Who needs so much yarn?" he wondered. "And could it all have come from one spinning? No, I'm dreaming . . ." He heard footsteps. Elzbieta came in. She was barefoot and in a bathrobe. She bent over him, kissed his forehead. "Well, don't be so despondent!"

"I'm not despondent."

"Pray to God, poor man, pray to God!"

"I'll pray to no one."

"Wait, I'll undress you."

Elzbieta knelt, unbuttoned his shoes, drew off his socks. Afterward, she began to take off his trousers, jacket, shirt. She fussed over him as if he were sick. She had difficulty in taking off his collar and he helped her remove the collar pin. Finally she lay down beside him.

27

Events moved swiftly. Catastrophes, coming one on top of the other, recalled the passage from the Book of Job about the messengers with evil tidings. It started with the bomb thrown at Alexander II, followed by the pogroms in Warsaw! The beatings, the lootings, the smashing of windowpanes and furniture, the tearing of bed linen, lasted three days. Twenty-two Jews lay wounded in the hospital. Oddly enough, many Warsaw Jews had fought back, and twenty-four Poles were wounded. The Jewish community protested. The Polish press published a condemnation of the incident and declared that Ignatiev's agents had suffered a defeat. The Polish nation would not permit itself to be incited against the Jews by the Russian conquerors. Warsaw was not Elisavetgrad or Kiev or Odessa, where large numbers of peasants had taken part in the pogroms. But the shame, the disappointment, and the sobering effect the massacres in Russia had on the modern Jews in that country were felt just as strongly by the enlightened Jews in Poland. A proclamation issued to the Ukranian peasants by the "Ispolnitelny Committee" was reprinted in the sixth issue of the clandestine newspaper, *Narodnaya Wola*, and had found its way to Poland. The proclamation called for further pogroms. The pogroms were also welcomed by the followers of the *Czorny Peredel*. It was known that a Jewish revolutionary was one of the authors of the proclamation. Jochanan, the Marshinov rabbi, was not surprised. Why shouldn't evildoers make pogroms? And what was the difference between Gentile evildoers and Jewish ones? As long as Jews were associated with the wicked, how could they rise above them? Jochanan felt that the last throes preceding the arrival of the Messiah had begun. In the Zohar he had found an allusion to the war between Gog and Magog and the beginning of the End of Days, which indicated they were about due. Reb Menachem Mendel, Ezriel's father, the Rabbi of Krochmalna Street, was attacked by a hooligan. While Tirza Perl, his wife, put a cold compress on Reb Menachem Mendel's hand, he sat down to study a page of the Talmud. Was it something new for Jews to be beaten?

It was the shaven ones, who emulated the Gentiles and spoke their language, who cried out in protest. In Kiev, as the Jews in the synagogue were mourning the victims of the pogrom, a group of Jewish university students entered. One of them, Alenikov, ran up to the reading desk and called out: "We are your brothers! We are Jews like you! We regret we tried to be Russians. The events of the past weeks—the pogroms in Elisavetgrad, in Balta, and here in Kiev—have opened our eyes. We've made a tragic mistake. We are still Jews!"

The Jewish-Russian newspapers, *Russki Yevrey*, *Razsviet*, and *Voschod*, published a series of articles discussing the events. It was obvious that many Jews would have to leave Russia. But where would they go? Factions formed: one in favor of emigration to America; the other, to Palestine. Both sides planned to organize socialist colonies. Both preached that the Jew must stop being a middleman, must settle on the land and be productive. Aaron Lipman and Mirale had a falling out. Aaron had become an adherent of the Palestinian faction. "What could be crazier," he argued, "than sacrificing oneself for the muzhiks who kill Jews? How can Jews be connected with a party that incited massacres in the name of social jus-

388

tice?" In his room, Aaron had a secret library, several scores of volumes of brochures, as well as bound editions of clandestine newspapers. He tore them up and burned them in the stove, spitting into the fire. Stomping his feet, he shouted: "May their names be blotted out! Thou shalt utterly detest it and thou shalt utterly abhor it, for it is a cursed thing."

When he came to Mirale and told her what he had done, she said: "You're no better than a rioter yourself!"

And she pointed the way out of her house.

Aaron's eyes seemed to turn inward.

"What do you want to do? Lubricate the revolutionary machine with Jewish blood?"

He went out, and Mirale slammed the door behind him, bolting and chaining it as if fearing he might change his mind and return. But this had not come as a surprise. For weeks they had been wrangling over the same question. Many other young Jews in Russia had reacted like Aaron, had become frightened by reality, infected by a contagious nationalism. Did they think a revolution could be made with silk gloves? Did they imagine that in the struggle against exploiters Jewish shopkeepers would be spared? Didn't they understand, the cowards, that the pogroms against the Jews were simply the beginning of the general rebellion that was sweeping the peasantry and even the working classes? How did they think absolutism would be smashed? With ringing phrases? How strange! It had been Aaron who had taught her to understand all this. He had brought her books, brochures, had read to her Lassalle's *The Essence of the Constitution*, had explained Jan Mlot's brochure, *From What Does One Live?*, and had familiarized her with the works of Belinski, Pisarev, Herzen, Lavrov. Aaron had guided her as if she had been a child. But now that she had grown spiritually and could stand alone, he had become a renegade. Palestine had become the only salvation of the world for him, a desolate country where some baron or other, an exploiter, was trying to establish colonies for a few confused students. What madness!

"Jews! Jews! Jews! Everything was measured against the Jewish yardstick! But didn't chauvinistic Russians, Poles, and Germans do the same? Didn't all misfortunes stem from the efforts of ethnic groups to pull only for themselves, prepared to sacrifice mankind to their own insignificant interests?" Ezriel had told Mirale that their father had been beaten. She was upset. But how could one acquire a world view from such incidents? And who was he, this father of hers? A zealot, a parasite who produced nothing, ate the peasants' bread, lived off the workers' labor, while he disseminated false ideas and superstitions. "Certainly, it wasn't his fault. He had been raised that way. But how long would the people continue to sleep?"

It was not easy for Mirale to break off with Aaron. How long was it since they had planned to live together? Now it was all over . . . Mirale began to pace back and forth. She glanced out the window at the Pawiak Prison. The windows were not only barred, but wire netting had been placed over them so that neither air nor sunlight could enter. The prisoners confined within were fated to perish from hunger, in damp and darkness. Mirale had not yet actually done anything to help redeem mankind. Aaron had prevented her from becoming involved. He had postponed the final step with words, theories, yeshiva-student philosophies. Now that he was gone, she would act.

11

All the windows in Wallenberg's villa had been smashed by hoodlums. There had been no mention of the incident in the newspapers, the censor having specifically forbidden it. The shutters remained closed for a long time because it had become difficult to obtain glass. Surely it was a disgrace that so distinguished a family (it was connected by marriage with the best families of Poland) should suffer the same indignities as the poor Jews. Wallenberg wasn't very distressed about it. On the contrary, this action against him by a handful of rowdies had finally convinced him to do something about a project that he had had in mind for a long time. For years he had been dreaming of giving Poland a truly liberal newspaper. He had also thought of founding a publishing house, and a magazine dealing with popular science. Wallenberg feared that positivism was beginning to lose its attraction for the Polish people. Instead, many of the radical intellectuals were accepting the Russian theory of social revolution. Polish nationalists, on the other hand, still indulged in hopes of a new patriotic uprising against the Czar. Ideas such as these could only result in further unrest and repression. The Polish press, ostensibly loyal to Russia, was badly edited and ran pedantic articles that were utterly incomprehensible to the ordinary person. Now that there had been a pogrom in Warsaw itself, Wallenberg felt it was high time for the masses to be educated. He purchased *Czas*, a newspaper that had recently gone bankrupt.

Wallenberg decided to call his newspaper *The Courier*. There were enough enlightened persons in the cities of Poland to provide a readership for a paper whose mission it was to combat that new monster known as anti-Semitism. Conservative Poles, too, might in time be numbered among its readers and would learn how their religious fanaticism and isolation endangered them. The paper would also try to stem the growing interest of Jewish intellectuals in anarchism and nihilism. Such a paper would have to be staffed not only by experienced journalists and writers but by those who in addition were thoroughly familiar with the Jewish way of life. Suddenly Wallenberg thought of Calman Jacoby's son-in-law, Dr. Ezriel Babad. Wallenberg had helped liberate that young man from the study house. He had seen Ezriel grow from little more than a dreamer into a practicing physician whose specialty was nervous diseases and mental ailments. Wallenberg knew that Ezriel's office was on Nowolipie Street and that he was on the staff of the Bonifraten Mental Hospital. Ezriel had already published several articles dealing with medicine in the Jewish-Polish magazine *Jutrzenko*. Wallenberg was one of those people who read everything, even articles in medical journals. Ezriel Babad's style was light and his articles had evinced a healthy skepticism rare among Jews. The Jewish writer in Poland, it seemed to Wallenberg, was either a committed atheist or fanatically religious. Neither type was right for *The Courier*.

Wallenberg was celebrating his sixtieth birthday at a party in May, and he sent an invitation to Dr. Ezriel Babad. The Polish Benevolent Society, the Society for the Development of Art, and a number of orphanages and homes for the aged, jointly announced plans for a testimonial dinner in his honor. The Polish newspapers published his photograph, and he received a handsome medal from St. Petersburg. The Governor-General and the Police Commissioner sent him their congratulations. Wallenberg, however, accepted only those honors he dared not refuse. These people praised him to his face, but conspired against him behind his back. The Ministry of Communications often received anonymous letters containing accusations against him. The very same newspapers that now praised him so highly had in the past carried articles in which he had been called a Shylock and a bloodsucker. His life consisted of one crisis after another, all of them the fabrications of envious people. He sometimes thought of himself as a circus performer constantly forced to walk a tightrope over a mass of hissing adders. And now a testimonial dinner. For what reason? No, he did not need the congratulations of his enemies and competitors. His birthday party would be for his family and close friends only.

Wallenberg's invitation to Ezriel included Shaindel, and caused quite a stir in the Babad household. Shaindel said she had no intention of visiting a convert. For many years now, Ezriel had been begging her for his sake to improve her Polish. It wasn't right for a doctor's wife to speak Yiddish or the illiterate Polish of the peasants. Ezriel himself had begun giving her lessons. Somehow or other, she couldn't learn. He realized that it was not inability but obstinacy that made her such a poor student. Other women learned from their children, but Shaindel spoke to hers in Yiddish. As if this were not bad enough, she had begun to neglect her appearance, although she did keep the house clean, if not tidy. It finally got to the point that Ezriel considered her too dowdy to take visiting. At first, she had not been interested in going, but now she accused him of being ashamed of her. It was true. Other doctors' wives had graduated from the gymnasium. Shaindel, when she was in the company of such women, was afraid to open her mouth. Taking her to the Wallenbergs' was out of the question. Actually, Ezriel was somewhat apprehensive about attending the affair himself. He had not learned to dance and, though a physician, was as ignorant of the great world as a yeshiva student. Each time he attended a party, he envied those young men who since childhood had spoken the Gentile tongue, worn modern clothes, and mixed freely with girls. How confidently they strutted about in their stiff shirts and tailcoats. How gracefully they kissed the women's hands. Ezriel could not get used to this way of life. The cheder and the Talmud had made him unworldly.

Whether he wanted to or not, he felt he had to put in an appearance at Wallenberg's party. Dressed in his doctor's smock, Ezriel wandered around his office. He was no longer surprised by anything his patients, both men and women suffering from nervous maladies, told him. He even felt an affinity with the inmates of the asylum where he was a staff doctor. His brain was a little insane asylum of its own. There weren't many patients that morning. His clientele usually came in the afternoon. Ezriel paced the freshly waxed floor with nothing to do for the moment. He had not chosen to be a "giver of enemas" but had entered a branch of medicine that was still almost totally unexplored. What went on there in that piece of white matter whose parts were designated the cerebrum, the cerebellum, and the medulla oblongata? Was free will also one of its constituents? If not, how was it possible to talk about responsibility and duty? When he listened to

393

the voice of his own spirit, it seemed to him that he heard the cry of all the generations. He recognized the voices of his parents and grandparents within himself. At times it seemed to him that he heard even more ancient voices, the idolatrous ones of pagan ancestors. Existence had always meant the same chaos; the ego had always wanted everything for itself—money, fame, sex, knowledge, power, immortality. But this savage was constantly coming up against the resistance of the world with its restrictions and taboos. Was it any wonder that people went mad? How much strain could the mental mechanism stand? Ezriel heard the doorbell and buttoned his smock.

The patient, ushered in by the maid, was a young man who had been married for three months. As he spoke, his eyeglasses became foggy with tears. His wife wanted to leave him, he told Ezriel. The neighbors knew all about it. His mother-in-law and father-in-law kept tormenting him. What was he going to do? He needed a woman, but as soon as he drew close to one he became impotent. Ezriel suggested hydropathy. Oddly enough, the young man's words made Ezriel nervous. Words, he knew, had a strange magnetic power. Once a woman had told him that whenever she sat down to eat, her plate would suddenly fill up with lice. A short time afterward Ezriel was seated at dinner and had the illusion that the same thing was happening to him. Was it any wonder that mental doctors were more susceptible to insanity than other physicians? The fact was that there was a touch of madness in everyone.

The young man paid his forty kopecks and departed. His office hours over, Ezriel sought out Shaindel, whom he found in the kitchen ironing a shirt for him to wear to the party. Shaindel was again pregnant, already in her fifth month. Ezriel's suggestion that she have an abortion had infuriated her. Seeing him enter, Shaindel turned over the ironing to the maid. In her view it was improper for a doctor to enter the kitchen. She and Ezriel went into the living room.

"What was the matter with that young man?"

394

"The same old story. Nerves."

"My nerves are killing me, too. I'm forever wanting to cry."

"I still think that you ought to go to the Wallenbergs' with me."

"Let's not talk about that again. I don't intend to eat pork in the house of some convert."

"The Wallenbergs don't serve pork."

"I wouldn't go there even if my life depended on it."

For a while, husband and wife remained silent. There was a sadness in her eyes that Ezriel had never noticed before. She seemed terribly afraid of something and at the same time ashamed of her fear and anxious to conceal it. Ezriel shook his head.

"Remember that Simhath Torah when you balanced a melon on your head and said that you were the Empress of Jampol?"

Tears came to Shaindel's eyes. "It's hard for me to believe that it ever happened. It seems like a hundred years ago."

III

Wallenberg had written that the party would be for an intimate group, but that evening, as Ezriel's droshky pulled up before Wallenberg's mansion on New World Boulevard, not far from Hozia Street, a long row of coaches lined the driveway. They were occupied by distinguished couples. A number of the men were in uniform. The horses, their necks drawn up, could barely stand still. The liveried coachmen helped the gentry from the carriages. Over everyone the purple luster of a large sun shone, as it rolled over the orchards, gardens, and streets that trailed off toward Wola. For a moment Ezriel felt that he had seen and experienced all this before. He seemed to recognize the pale blue sky, the formations of the clouds, the odor of horse dung. There was even a dusky familiarity about the strange faces. Ezriel himself did not know why, but the city of Turbin came to his mind, his grandfather, the eve before a holiday. In a specially made dress coat, a top hat, and white gloves, Ezriel now felt shy, as he had in his childhood when on the first night of Passover he went to prayer wearing his new boots, new velvet hat, and new capote, with a fistful of nuts in its pocket. Wasn't he overdressed? Was his tie crooked? Did his clothes seem too new? Everyone spoke French. Although Ezriel had studied French, he had never learned to speak it. There was a hymn sung during Pentecost the words of which stated that if all people were writers, all skies parchment, and all forests pens, it would still be impossible to write out all the secrets contained in the Torah. In a way, this was also true of worldliness. Ezriel was sure that he was committing some blunder, even though he tried his best to conform to all the rules of etiquette that the secular Shulhan Aruk prescribed, and which could never be fathomed by those who were not brought up on it.

In the foyer, Ezriel gave his top hat and cane to the Swiss servant, and the gravity with which the man accepted these articles assured Ezriel that he did not appear inferior to the other guests. At least not yet. He walked into the drawing room with the humility of one who has done everything possible and, because of this, must feel confident . . . Wallenberg and his wife stood at the entrance. Wallenberg looked inquiringly at him as if not recognizing him at first, then suddenly pumped his hand and remarked that he had planned an affair for a handful of people but that it had turned into a ball. Ezriel had not seen him for years. He had grown stout and his sideburns were completely white. Madame Wallenberg looked like an old woman. Her white coiffure shook in sympathy as she told Ezriel how sorry she was that Shaindel had not been able to come. After a while, Madame Malewska approached. She too had grown round and heavy.

Everything happened too quickly and smoothly, as when one is in a state of semi-intoxication. Ezriel was introduced to bemedaled men and to women with deep décolletages. He heard the announcements of high titles, famous names—he

396

discussed the weather with total strangers. In the huge dining hall, tables were set for about one hundred and fifty guests. Silver, porcelain, crystal, flowers, and candles glittered. Ezriel did not know where to look first: at the amazingly beautiful ladies smiling down from gold-framed portraits or at the living women who swarmed about—somewhat less comely than their counterparts on canvas, but each with her upswept hair, her jewelry, her special expression. This was not a house party, but a première at the opera, an exhibition at the Zachęta. Here, at a converted Jew's mansion, the elite of Warsaw society had assembled. The Governor-General had suddenly come down with the grippe, but the Chief of Police was there, the dean of the Warsaw University, and numerous other dignitaries, each with his epaulets, stripes, and decorations. Russian was heard, as well as Polish, French, and even English, which had lately become the fashion. Lackeys sped about noiselessly, showing the guests to their seats. Ezriel sat at the foot of a long table, where apparently the younger guests had been placed. He was joined by a boyish-looking young man whose pointed mustache seemed pasted on, and by two girls who appeared to be twins. Madame Malewska came over and introduced Ezriel to his neighbors, announcing names that he forgot as soon as he heard them. He realized that he was the only Jew at his table. A young woman with a sharp nose said to him: "Isn't the dining room divine?"

"Yes, magnificent."

"Everything has been rebuilt, enlarged. Have you noticed the new painting by Matejko?"

"Matejko? Where?"

"There."

And she pointed her finger toward the other end of the room.

"I prefer Brandt to Matejko—" a young man remarked.

"I'd give them both up for Zmurka . . ."

A discussion on painting began. For a while Ezriel thought he would be left sitting there, excluded from the conversation.

From his limited experience, he knew how painful this could be and how long such a meal could seem. He began to search for a subject that could, at least for a while, link him to these people. Should he ask the young man a question? Should he attempt to discuss art? Should he wait until someone spoke to him? He had arrived in a more or less confident mood, but now he was one step from despair. The others apparently noticed what he was enduring, and their eyes seemed to avoid him. There ensued the kind of mysterious anathema, cast by those who are speaking, upon someone who had not joined in at the beginning. Well, I'd better be quiet. I won't burden anyone, Ezriel decided. As if his decision had been secretly revealed to the others, two of them addressed him simultaneously. One of the twin sisters asked him to pass the salt shaker. At the same time, a young man remarked casually: "We were introduced, but I did not get your name. My name is Gewalewicz. Julian Gewalewicz."

"I'm honored, my name is Babad."

Ezriel quickly realized that it wasn't polite to give only his surname, but he could not, in this place, utter two such Jewish names as Ezriel Babad. Numerous times he had spoken, half in jest, of changing his first name to make it sound more Polish, but the name Ezriel did not readily lend itself to alteration. It was a stubborn name that would not allow itself to be assimilated. The young man inquired whether Ezriel was a visitor to Warsaw.

Ezriel realized that he could not conceal the truth.

"I was born in Turbin, in the province of Lublin. My father was the rabbi there. I am in medical practice here on Nowolipie Street."

For a moment there was silence. Ezriel's simple words had ended all tension. Ease replaced it, and the kind of intimacy that only truth can produce.

"Where is Turbin? Near what city?"

A conversation began about the Lublin region, about its peasantry, gentry, Jewry. It seemed that the twins had an aunt

398

near Tomashow and that the mustached young man also had relatives in that section. A squire sitting nearby, who had been listening, also joined the conversation. He had some knowledge of Jewish affairs and asked Ezriel if he had studied in a yeshiva.

"Not actually in a yeshiva, but I did study the Talmud."

"The Talmud?"

Everyone grew curious. In what language is the Talmud written? Hebrew? Chaldean? What is Chaldean? Does anyone speak it? Is it written from the right to the left? And what, for example, is written in the Talmud? Ezriel answered everyone. He became so deeply involved in conversation that he was not quite aware of having finished his meal. The toasts began. Prelates, generals, editors, the Russian chief of police, the president of a scientific society—all joined in toasting the great intelligence and benevolence of their host. The company shouted "Hurrah!" and "Vivat!" and drank his health. Here and there at the table someone made a sarcastic remark. It was clear to everyone that all the praise and devotion proffered this converted Jew had one basis—money.

IV

When the dancing started in the drawing room, Ezriel's shyness returned. But the rich feast, the wine, and the entertaining experience at the table had left him cheerful and somewhat made up for the fact that he wasn't dancing. He wasn't the only one. There were other guests who stood near the wall watching the couples. Some gathered in side rooms. Men conversed and smoked cigars. In a corner, an elderly woman fixed a young girl's gown that had apparently come loose at the waist. As the older woman fussed, the young one tapped her foot in pique. Her face was remarkably red. Ezriel understood the cause of her annoyance. She was missing a dance she had anticipated. Just as he was, everyone was taking this affair much more seriously than was reasonable. Despite the music, the drumming, the polkas and mazurkas, the fashionable clothes, the costly jewelry—there was still the tedium that is always present when strangers without common purpose assemble, each with his own pride, ambition, and humility. There really wasn't anyone to appreciate all the elaborate coiffures, all the toil that the tailors, hairdressers, and corsetières had put into these toilettes. People kept introducing one another, and the men never stopped touching feminine hands with their beards and mustaches. Ezriel remained standing for a while before a painting: hunters, pointers, snow-covered fields, a distant forest. A deer had been shot and a trickle of blood stained the snow. All had been painted with expert knowledge of the subject, yet the picture did not hold Ezriel's attention.

"Why am I so impatient?" Ezriel wondered. "I used to stare for hours on end at the awkward illustrations in my mother's *Haggada* . . ." Suddenly someone poked him in the side with a familiarity that startled him for a second. He turned and saw Wallenberg, and a lady of about thirty, a brunette, whose hair was combed simply into a chignon. She was dressed differently from the others. Her gown, barely ornamented, seemed to have been made by an ordinary seamstress. She was smiling the smile of a Jewess who encounters a compatriot among Gentiles. She had heavy eyebrows and black eyes, and the kind of attractive down often seen on the upper lip of a dark-complexioned woman.

Wallenberg said: "I thought you were dancing, and I find you admiring my pictures. Madame Bielikov, this is the young man I've been telling you about, Dr. Babad, a neurologist. Madame Bielikov comes from your home town. You're from Vilna, aren't you?"

"I from Vilna? God forbid! I come from the Lublin province."

"Oh, yes, what am I taking about? You are, of course, Calman Jacoby's son-in-law. Madame Bielikov comes from Lithuania. Her husband was a neighbor of mine. That is, we were neighbors for a while in Druskenik, near the Nieman River. I owned a villa there. Ah, how time flies! There is something I'd like to talk to you about, but I don't know when. Could you come to my office perhaps? What do you do on Saturdays?"

"The same as the rest of the week."

"And you are a rabbi's son! How about this Saturday at two?"

"Certainly."

"Well, that's settled. I'll be expecting you on Saturday. I must go now. Talk to each other. Madame Bielikov understands Yiddish."

After Wallenberg left, they both stood there for a while, not knowing what to say. Finally Ezriel remarked: "His hair has turned completely white."

"Yes, one grows older, not younger," Madame Bielikov observed in Polish, but with a Russian accent. "When we lived in Druskenik, he still had black hair. Do you practice in Warsaw?"

"Yes."

"My husband was a doctor, an army doctor." And the woman grew silent.

"I'd never want that kind of career," Ezriel said, after an overlong pause.

"Why not?"

"I'm not fond of barracks."

"Oh, my husband had nothing to do with the barracks. He was connected with a military hospital. Sometimes that is more convenient than a private practice."

"Do you live here in Warsaw?"

"Yes, on Zielna Street, not far from Prozna Street."

"Is that near Kreditowa Street?"

"Kreditowa Street is on the other side of Marshalkowsky Boulevard."

"Yes, of course. I know a Dr. Zawacki who lives there."

"I know Dr. Zawacki."

"I come from the village of Jampol. Dr. Zawacki is married to the daughter of the local squire."

"Yes, I know. Madame Malewska told me about you and about the Countess—how is she related to you, is she a cousin?"

"My sister-in-law. She and Madame Zawacki are sisters-in-law."

"Madame Malewska told me all about it. Now I understand. So you're the one! Madame Malewska is a friend of mine. We used to see each other more often. Lately she's been busy, and I've been occupied with my children. My husband is dead."

"I see."

"Well, Warsaw is a small town. What's become of your sister-in-law?"

"She is sick and miserable."

"Unhappily, one hears of such things. People lose themselves and go to pieces. Where is she?"

"Some place in Otwock. For a while she was in a sanatorium. Now she's found a place of her own."

"Consumption?"

"Yes."

"And her husband—what's his name? Is he still in prison?"

"Lucian? Yes, but he'll soon be out."

"I've heard of all sorts of crazy things that seemed to be sheer madness. Apparently the Wallenbergs did everything they could for him."

"Yes, they did."

"There are people who must hurt themselves. It's hard to understand why they do it. Would you care to sit down?"

v

They sat on a chaise longue and talked. Her parents were Jewish. Her father had taught school and as a sideline had written petitions to the Russian authorities. She, Leah, or Olga, had

402

been orphaned early and had gone to live with a wealthy aunt in Vilna. There she met her late husband, Andrey, who had been studying in St. Petersburg. His father had been a ladies' tailor, a pious Jew, but he had adopted the Greek Orthodox faith. When Olga married him, she had also "converted a little." Madame Bielikov had been speaking Polish, but the last words were said in Lithuanian Yiddish. She smiled sadly as she said them. Well, what was the difference? There was no God anyhow. If there were a God, so many tragedies would not occur. She and Andrey had been happy. One day he had gone to bathe in a tiny stream where one could scarcely wet one's knees, and had been found drowned. How had it happened? Perhaps he'd suffered a heart attack. But he had never complained about his heart. Suicide? Why should he have committed suicide? He had led a happy life. Only one thing was peculiar. He had been discussing death the day before. What had he said? That if he were to die, he was not to be wept over, for a dead person was like one who had never been born. He had said this half jokingly.

When had it happened? Almost two years ago. How was she getting along? They had saved up a little money and she received a small pension from the government. It was, to be truthful, difficult. Wallenberg had offered help, but she had refused. Andrey would not have wanted it. He had been a proud person. The Petersburg University had published his dissertations. He had left an extensive library in four languages. Andrey had not only been interested in medicine. He had been an amateur astronomer. She still had a small telescope somewhere about. In Druskenik he would sit up nights at a time, observing the stars.

At first, Ezriel asked the questions. Then her turn came. She had still not quite figured out his connection with Dr. Zawacki. His sister-in-law was also Felicia's sister-in-law. Lucian was his brother-in-law. "How in the world does a person make such a mess of himself?" Madame Bielikov asked.

"The human brain is the greatest enigma of the cosmos—"

Madame Bielikov looked at him with surprise.

"Odd, those were Andrey's very words."

They rose and walked into the salon. She said: "Of course you do not know how to dance."

"No."

"There could be no doubt about that with a yeshiva student."

"Do you dance, madame?"

"Not any more."

Madame Bielikov had to leave early. She had a maid, but the girl was inexperienced, having just come from the village. Madame Bielikov's boy, Kolia, was only four years old. He woke up at night and cried and only his mother could calm him. Ezriel offered to escort her home.

"You needn't ruin your evening because of me."

"I have no reason to stay."

They left without saying goodbye, according to the English custom. It was difficult to find a droshky in this neighborhood. They strolled diagonally across New World Boulevard. The night was warm, somewhat humid, and filled with vernal odors. There were gardens and orchards nearby. Crickets chirped as if in the country. Birds awoke, twittering. The flickering gas lights made the darkness seem denser. Every now and again, a coach or wagon passed by. Lightning, flashing at the edge of the sky, foretold hot weather. Between the trees and bushes, villas could be glimpsed, mansions with pillars, garrets, carvings, fountains. Shadows moved behind the draperies. Occasionally, a dog barked. The sidewalk was uneven, and Madame Bielikov nearly fell. Ezriel took her arm.

"A strange night," Madame Bielikov remarked.

"All nights are strange."

"Yes, you are right. And all life is incomprehensible."

After a while, they got a droshky. It was not yet midnight, but Warsaw was already asleep. The streets were empty except for a few late pedestrians and streetwalkers. The droshky turned into Berg Street and passed Kreditowa Street. At the

404

intersection of Marshalkowsky Boulevard and Prozna Street the driver went into Zielna Street. Madame Bielikov pointed out a two-storied building with balconies, and reached for her pocketbook.

"No, madame, God forbid!"

"Why should you pay for me?"

"Just because."

"How can I thank you? Well, it was really very pleasant. In my situation it's burdensome to attend a ball. How nice that we met!"

"I wouldn't have known what to do with myself either."

"Someone would have taken pity on you . . ."

Ezriel helped Madame Bielikov out of the droshky. He stood with her at the gate, waiting for the janitor to open it. She smiled at him, inquisitively, as if to say: "Is this all?" She exuded a secretive familiarity. The janitor's footsteps could be heard. Madame Bielikov extended her hand to Ezriel. Her glove was warm. She squeezed his hand slightly.

"Good night. My thanks again."

"Good night."

The gate closed. He did not hear her steps immediately, as if she too were lingering on the other side. Only then did it occur to him that he might have asked to see her husband's medical library . . .

VI

The doctors who worked at the Free Clinic for the Poor generally dropped in at their lounge before leaving for home. Most of the young ones were involved in social-service activities and had founded an association of their own called "Health," which issued pamphlets in both Polish and Yiddish. The subject they talked about was always the same—the filthiness in which the poor Polish Jews were forced to live. A doctor who was on the staff of the Jewish Hospital on Pokorna Street described the terrible conditions there. Mice ran through the corridors; there were no decent toilet facilities for the patients; the Jewish Society for the Sick brought preposterous foods for the invalids, heavy Sabbath puddings, onions fried in chicken fat. Another doctor spoke of the new Jewish hospital that was to be built and of the great need for Jewish nurses. Ezriel thought of the women who had brought their lice-infested undergarments to his father, the rabbi, in cases of irregular menstruation, to avoid the sin of cohabiting while unclean. An elderly doctor who specialized in diseases of the lungs said, "We're still knee deep in the Asian mire."

"But look what advances have been made by the Jews of Western Europe."

"They don't have the Hassidim to contend with."

Ezriel was about to leave. Suddenly the porter who made tea and swept up handed him a letter in a blue envelope. Ezriel's heart skipped a beat. The letter was from Madame Bielikov.

> Honorable Dr. Babad:
> Perhaps you remember me? We met at the ball at Pan Wallenberg's. I told you then that my boy, Kolia, awakes at night in fear. I have been told that he suffers from Pavor nocturnus. Since neurology is your speciality, I would consider it a privilege if you would consent to examine the child. Kolia and I are almost always home and we will be happy to see you at your convenience. You must certainly not go to any special trouble. Although we only met briefly, I feel as if I have known you for a long time. I hope you have not forgotten me entirely. If I am too bold, do not take offense.
> With my esteem and my best wishes,
> Olga Bielikov

Ezriel read the letter again and again. It emanated warmth —in the address on the envelope (E.P., E.P.—Esteemed *Pan*, repeated twice, the most formal salutation), in the penmanship, the uneven margins, even in the blot on the paper. It

406

seemed to Ezriel that between the lines he could detect the woman's proud hesitation before she had sent it. Only the day before, he had been reading about telepathy. Wasn't this an example of telepathy? He had thought about her and his thoughts had forced her to write to him. He was not the only neurologist in Warsaw. Ezriel still had a little time and he decided to read up in the medical encyclopedia on the subject of Pavor nocturnus. "Should I bring flowers?" he asked himself. He read, without really knowing what he was reading. "Is it possible that I have fallen in love with this woman? It would kill Shaindel . . ." His heart pounded and the letters danced before his eyes. "Should I go there today? Should I wait? What suit should I wear?" Suddenly his weariness left him and he was filled with anticipation. Everything had changed—the desk, the bookshelf, the courtyard, the formations of the clouds. What innumerable combinations of vapor and light there were! How inadequately words described it! What, for example, was now going on in his brain? If only one could see all the physical and chemical changes! Nerves trembled, cells moved, substances blended. The few words that Madame Bielikov had written had started a turmoil in his marrow, blood, stomach, sex organs. Not only the brain, but every part of the human body reacted to symbols.

He started toward his house. He had already missed lunch and had more patients to see in the afternoon. Ezriel had often envied the doctors with more tangible specialties than his—the internists, venereologists, dermatologists, gynecologists. They more or less knew what they were about. He had entered a domain where almost nothing was known.

VII

Ezriel had brought flowers for the mother and a box of chocolates for the children. Natasha, the older girl, curtsied gracefully. Kolia aped her in childish fashion. Jadzia, the maid, hurried off to place the bouquet in a vase. The country girl with her flaxen hair and plump cheeks flushed with delight at the sight of a male visitor. It was a warm evening outside, but indoors there was a springlike coolness. A mild breeze blew in through windows that opened on densely leaved trees. Ezriel compared this apartment with his own. Here the parquet floor gleamed. Everything was in its place. Each article had been polished, scrubbed. He could not get Shaindel to keep their rooms tidy. There was always some disorder.

Ezriel examined Kolia. Seating him on a bench, he tapped him below the knee, looked into the boy's eyes, listened to his heart, his lungs. Organically, the boy was sound. The eight-year-old Natasha was already studying the piano, and her mother asked her to play for the doctor. Then Jadzia led the two children off to bed. The brother and sister bowed, said good night, and thanked him for the chocolates. Ezriel sat on a chair, Madame Bielikov on a sofa. The floor lamp with its green shade cast a diffused light. How erect she held herself! How cleverly and tactfully she spoke! How discreet was her smile! In this room, European culture was not a phrase but an actuality. Ezriel explained to Madame Bielikov that Pavor nocturnus was a form of nervousness, one of those functional disturbances the origin of which is not known. Nevertheless, he asked whether there was any insanity, epilepsy, or other nervous disorders in the family.

"Andrey was a nervous person," Madame Bielikov said thoughtfully.

"Oh."

"I myself have my moods."

"Who doesn't?"

"There are some people for whom everything goes smoothly—both internally and externally."

The maid brought tea, cookies, fruit. Afterward, she asked her mistress for permission to take a walk. "For as long as you like," Madame Bielikov replied.

"Good night, Doctor sir."

They drank tea and conversed with the ease of old acquaintances. She inquired about his practice. He told her about the insane at the Bonifraten Hospital: the quiet ones who dreamed while awake, and the maniacs who had to be confined to strait jackets; the melancholics steeped in perpetual gloom; the paranoics who convinced themselves that they had inherited great wealth, had buried treasure hoards, and were connected with the royal court. There were a fantastic number of Messiahs among the Jewish patients. Women were more susceptible to erotic insanity than men. Insanity was really a disease of the brain, but more than any other affliction it was linked to social factors, culture, and religion. Ezriel remarked that, in the broad sense, knowledge of the brain included all the sciences, all the arts, all thoughts and feelings. We study the psyche even when we are studying Latin or tailoring.

Madame Bielikov smiled. "Would you call a tailor a psychologist?"

"There is a philosopher who believes that all things are ideas. As pure logic, this premise is more consistent than all the other philosophic theories."

"Andrey used to toy with such thoughts. For a while he attended courses of the philosophy faculty, in Russia and in Germany."

"Have you been abroad?"

"No. When we met, he had already completed his studies. We always planned a trip to Switzerland, to France, to England, but we never went. The children—"

"I, too, would like to see what's going on on the other side of the border."

"You are still young. You'll see it. Andrey always used to speak of the Alps."

"I've never seen a mountain of any sort. Neither a mountain nor the sea."

"Nor I . . ."

There was a balcony in the apartment. Madame Bielikov suggested that they go out on it. There were two chairs. Ez-

409

riel and Olga Bielikov sat in the darkness, conversing. The sky was filled with stars. Stillness reigned in the street. Ezriel could not quite make out Olga's face. He only heard her voice. She discussed her home, her parents, the gymnasium. She had always been a serious person. Other girls liked sunny days, but she had enjoyed the rain. She had preferred to bury herself in books and above all to daydream. Especially after her parents had died. She used to argue with her mother as if she were still alive. She had literally seen her a few times. How was this possible? She spoke of her relatives. Somewhere in Bialystok she still had an uncle, her father's brother. There were some cousins, too. She remarked: "When I became converted, I naturally estranged myself from everyone. They must have cursed me."

"Do the children know about their Jewish ancestry?"

"Yes, they know. You can't keep anything from them."

"Do you have friends here in Warsaw?"

"Friends? Not really. I still don't know what I'm doing in this city. I came here by chance after Andrey's death, and somehow I remained. Actually, Warsaw is alien to me. Yes, the Wallenbergs—they're really my only connection."

"They're very important here."

"I know. But I wouldn't exploit a friendship. Actually, I hesitated to write to you concerning Kolia—"

And Madame Bielikov suddenly stopped speaking. Ezriel summoned up courage. "If you hadn't written, madame, *I* might have written—"

"Why do you say that?"

"Oh, I don't know. I've been thinking about you. Sometimes a casual acquaintance makes an impression—"

"Yes, of course. I am not naturally bold, but I think that you still retain a touch of the yeshiva student."

"I'm afraid so."

"Actually it's appealing. Andrey was a worldly man. But a modest one as well. An odd mixture of boldness and shyness. He could tell a general the truth without blinking. He said things that could get one banished to Siberia. But at the same time he was as timid as a schoolboy. Natasha is exactly like him. Kolia is more like me—"

"Both are unusually handsome children."

"Thank you."

"And the stars in the heavens perform their own function. They sparkle and blink."

"Yes, the stars. I believe I've told you that Andrey was an amateur astronomer."

"Yes."

"He would spend entire nights at it. I sometimes looked through the telescope, too, at the Milky Way and other things up there. What is the meaning of it all?"

"We know nothing."

"If you come again, I'll take out the telescope. It's packed away somewhere. It's a small one, but one can see a great deal through it. The moon is particularly interesting . . . What's your wife like?"

"A good woman. A devoted mother."

"Well, how much more can you ask? Most men are satisfied with that. Besides being husband and wife, Andrey and I were like two comrades. We always had something to talk about. But so much happiness is not allowed by the powers on high."

VIII

Was it on his third or fourth visit? He took her in his arms and kissed her. She started but did not pull away. They were standing on the balcony. He had been thinking about it constantly, but it seemed to happen of itself. In the dusk, she clasped his wrists.

"No, don't!" she whispered.

"Why not?" he asked.

"It's too soon. I take these things seriously . . . The time hasn't come yet."

And her voice seemed to break.

o

Had he offended her? Other young men had had love affairs, but he was a novice in such matters. Looking at the sky he wondered: "What place do all these petty complications occupy in the universe?" He listened to the beating of his own heart. It was as quiet here, on Zielna Street, as in a country meadow. There was an incessant rustling which might have come from crickets, the wind, or a ringing in the depths of the ears. It seemed to Ezriel that the summer night, so full of things, was waiting too, absorbed in its own kind of cosmic tension. He was about to apologize to Olga, but within the shadows of her face he saw her black eyes gleaming with a mixture of timidity and joy. She came closer to him.

"Funny—before my husband's tragedy," she said, "I thought I would be the one to die first. I don't know why. I was young and healthy. I just had a premonition. Ever since I was a child I've always been uneasy when things went smoothly. I would be overcome by an expectation of disaster. But that anything should happen to him never occurred to me. You surely don't believe in superstitions."

"I no longer know what to believe in."

"Andrey was a rational man. Perfectly so. Still, sometimes he'd say things that astonished me. I myself am somewhat superstitious. I have always been a fatalist. 'Simple luck,' as they say in Yiddish, guides a man. A mysterious hand. But why should God devote himself to each person individually?"

"If there is a God, He is capable of that, too."

"What do you think of spiritualism? There's a big stir about it in Warsaw right now."

"I don't believe in it."

"Neither do I, but—a woman talked me into it. She said she could put me in contact with him. The very thought of it struck me as a desecration. If he were able to reach me, he would have found a way to give me some sign. How many nights I have lain awake and prayed. Ah, I can't explain it to you. At first he was always absent from my dreams. Lately I've begun to dream about him."

412

"What do you dream?"

"I don't know. I can't remember. I don't feel that he is dead —still, somehow I do. It seems rather that he is gravely ill. Like a person who has suffered a stroke. He is in great peril, and because of that, he's especially dear to me. What are dreams?"

"No one knows."

"What is known? What is the purpose of all this? I lost my father very early and I used to dream of him every night. Afterward, when Mother died, Father was thrust into the background and Mother replaced him, as if there were not room for both of them in my dreams. Isn't that odd? Now Andrey comes every night. He is so pale, listless, sad. It is indescribable. As if he's ashamed of what happened to him."

"What does he say?"

"I can't remember. Nothing important. When I wake up, I wonder why he has such trivial things on his mind. Later, I forget it all. Why are dreams so quickly forgotten?"

Suddenly there was a childish screaming and weeping from the bedroom. Madame Bielikov caught hold of Ezriel's hand. Kolia had awakened and was crying loudly. He was having an attack of Pavor nocturnus. Olga began to pull Ezriel after her and he followed her to the children's room. Standing beside the bed, he listened as she calmed Kolia. "What is it? Darling, sweetheart, my little angel! Oh, he is completely drenched in sweat!" She pressed her lips to Kolia's face, hugging him and comforting him in the words of a mother. Natasha's breathing could be heard from the other bed. Finally, Kolia fell asleep again. After his mother had straightened his pillow and blanket, she tiptoed out of the room, followed by Ezriel, who took her arm. They stood on the threshold between the bedroom and the dimly lit living room. Ezriel felt the warmth of her trembling body.

"Is it really Pavor nocturnus?"

"Yes, a mild form."

"There can't be anything between us—" she said in a

muffled voice. "You have a wife . . . It just doesn't make sense . . . What would become of us?"

"Logically, you're right."

"How can one not be logical?"

They walked into the living room. The clock pointed to half past eleven.

"Well, I'd better be going."

She led him into the hall. She closed the door to the living room and once more they were in darkness. They stood silently, tense, with a sense of anticipation, an inner tautness. They seemed to be listening to forces that were about to decide their fate. He started to reach for his hat but did not take it. As if with a light of their own, Olga's eyes glittered in the dark.

"Can't we just be friends?" she asked.

"Yes, of course."

"I scarcely dare say this, but you're so much like him—the same sort of temperament . . . his kind of pride . . . It seems unbelievable . . ."

He embraced her and they kissed—long, silently, with the desperation of those who can no longer resist their passion.

IX

Ezriel sat in a droshky on his way home. He was not so much happy as astounded at what had happened. For years he had read about love. Now he was having an affair of his own, a real affair, full of secrecy, and danger. After all, his marriage to Shaindel had been a prearranged match. She had grown prematurely stout and frigid. Warsaw was asleep. Ezriel leaned against the side of the droshky, inhaling the cool air. His childlike pleasure in being pulled along by a horse was mixed with the adult satisfaction of having succeeded with the opposite sex. Fortune had been good to him. He had finally involved himself in a risk-laden game with secret encounters, hidden pleasures. Mundane boredom suddenly gave way to a

414

life full of expectation, as in a novel, a play . . . But what should he tell Shaindel? Where had he been? How long would he be able to deceive her? She was pregnant, in her late months. Divorce her? He could never do that. He had Shaindel to thank for everything. Even his having been invited to Wallenberg's was due to his being Calman Jacoby's son-in-law. Foolish ideas ran through his mind. "I am a doctor, I am carrying on an affair. What could be more European than that? I've gone pretty far since Jampol." He fell into a blissful little reverie. Startled, he awoke from his daydream. He had imagined that Shaindel had died in childbirth and that he had married Olga. They had left the country and settled in St. Petersburg on Nevski Prospect . . . He shook himself, mumbling, "God forbid! May she live to be one hundred and twenty!" Involuntarily, he began to pray to God: "Lord of the Universe, protect her, make sure that she be delivered safely! I vow to contribute eighteen rubles . . ." Again he caught himself, realizing that he was praying. "What's wrong with me? I have all the symptoms of a neurasthenic!" The horse stopped. "How wonderful animals are, compared to humans! They have everything—humility, serenity, faith, inner detachment . . ."

For a long time he tugged at the gate bell. The night was warm, but he felt cool. He was a non-sleeper in a city sunk in slumber—a debaucher returning after a night's revelry . . . "What shall I tell her?" He could not think of an explanation. If the world were truly nothing but atoms and combinations of atoms, how could there be anything like sin? The same molecules of water into which a ship once sank might today rescue a child dying of thirst. How could the endless transmigrations of matter be kept track of unless there existed a universal ledger of accounts . . . A dog began to bark. The janitor came to open the gate. He was in his underwear. Ezriel gave him twenty groschen and he took the tip without saying thanks.

Ezriel climbed the stairs. How dark it was! His childish fear of the dark had never quite been uprooted. "What would I do if a demon grasped me?" He visualized a dark being, tall as if on stilts, soft as cobwebs, with elf locks, goose legs. Ezriel smiled to himself. "How difficult it is to rid oneself of superstition. It possessed an atavistic power; though, according to Weismann, acquired characteristics could not be inherited. Well, that hadn't been definitely established. And why couldn't they both be correct, Lamarck and Darwin?" Ezriel ran up the last few steps, as when a boy in Lublin he had returned from some night errand. He knocked hastily and soon heard Shaindel's footsteps. Evidently she had not yet been asleep. She had on a nightgown and her abdomen protruded. Her hair was disheveled, her face sallow.

"Where were you? Woe is me! What I feared should not even befall my enemies!"

"I was with a patient."

"What sort of patient?"

Ezriel entered the apartment.

"A child. He's suffering from Pavor nocturnus. He wakes up in the middle of the night in fear. It's a disease."

"Did you sit there waiting for him to wake up?"

"That's the only way one can make a diagnosis."

"And what would you have done if he had awakened two hours later?"

"I am a doctor, not a shoemaker," Ezriel said, amazed at how easy it was for him to lie. Nor was it actually a lie. Shaindel stood looking at him in astonishment.

"Why didn't you tell me that you would be so late? You know how I worry."

"I decided to go there at the last minute. This is the first time I've had such a case."

"Who is it? Where does the family live?"

"On Zielna Street."

"Don't they have other doctors there?"

"Wallenberg referred them to me."

"Are they young people?"

"They have two children, a girl of eight and a boy of four. Converts."

"Converts? A person goes off and disappears—" Shaindel began to speak forgivingly. She realized that Ezriel was telling the truth and she was overcome with remorse. She had doubted him and without reason, poor man. She was much too jealous, always filled with the worst suspicions. He worked hard, days and even nights. "Oh, I couldn't live without him. If, God forbid, he ever deceives me, I'd kill myself!"

She said: "You must be hungry."

"Hungry? No."

"Did they at least give you a glass of tea?"

"They are fine people."

"What does the husband do?"

"He is an army doctor."

"A doctor himself? If that's so, you don't even get paid."

"It's an extremely interesting case. When you need an accoucheur, it'll be free too."

"Well, it's your business. Most doctors rake in money, and you only deal with madness and nonsense. Waking up like that is sometimes caused by the child holding its hand over its heart . . . Is the woman good-looking?"

"A devoted mother."

"Is there another kind? I thought you'd become disgusted with me and run off with someone else," Shaindel said, despite herself.

"You silly woman!"

"I get such crazy ideas! On the other hand, what am I? A frump. I cause you nothing but trouble. Often you seem like a saint to me. You are a doctor and I am a drudge. You can't even show me off to your friends."

"Don't talk such nonsense. You are my wife and I love you. You're the mother of my children. If not for you, I wouldn't be a doctor."

"Well, that's enough flattery for tonight."

417

28

During vacation, Clara's children, Sasha and Felusia, went to Jampol to visit their grandfather Daniel Kaminer, who now had three children by Celina. Clara was still annoyed with her father for not having kept his promise to turn over half of his property to her before marrying Celina. But Daniel Kaminer was anxious to see his grandchildren, who in any case could not stay in the city during the summer. Then, too, Calman had insisted before divorcing Clara that their son be permitted to spend a few weeks each year with him. Calman paid fifty rubles a month for Sasha's support. It had also been agreed that Clara would engage a Hebrew teacher for Sasha, keep the boy out of school on Saturday, and maintain a kosher kitchen. Although Clara neglected to fulfill the other terms of this agreement, she feared that if Sasha did not visit his father, Calman would stop sending her money. Clara gave Sasha a prayer book that he had received for his bar mitzvah to take along on the trip, as well as a fringed garment, which he was to put on before meeting his father. Since the divorce, Calman and Daniel Kaminer no longer spoke to each other. It was now Mayer Joel who managed Calman's property and discussed whatever business was necessary with Kaminer.

Clara was distressed to see the children leave. On his summer visits, Sasha was showered with presents by his father.

Calman attempted to study the Pentateuch and Mishnah with him, let the boy ride horseback, and indulged all his whims. There was a constant struggle between Calman and Daniel Kaminer for Sasha's favor. Calman would not even look at Felusia, although allegedly she was his daughter. The girl sensed that there was something wrong and was jealous of her brother. She often announced that she had two fathers, Papa Jocoby and Papa Zipkin. At times she insisted that she was not her mother's child but had been left in a sack by a gypsy. Clara was unable to calm the child's fears. To quiet her own feelings, Clara bought her daughter expensive dolls, and dresses, and pampered her with sweets. Sending Sasha and Felusia to Jampol was no simple matter for Clara.

Nevertheless, the children needed fresh air, and Clara time for herself. Their governess Louisa accompanied her charges. Clara was determined that this summer she would at last do something she had been planning to do for a long time. Zipkin's in-laws were summering in Carlsbad. Sabina was suffering from a stomach ailment that had been diagnosed by some doctors as gallstones, and her parents wanted her to go along with them. Sabina had refused to go without Alexander. She pointed out that while she was taking the cure in Carlsbad, Alexander would be spending his time with Clara. Rosa, who was forever urging her daughter to get a divorce, argued that here was the opportunity to get rid of that charlatan. Rosa assured her daughter that in Carlsbad she would meet really interesting men. Sabina was still young. She would fall in love with someone worthy of her. Her dowry had remained in her name and was still on deposit at the bank. A divorce would free her from her suffering.

Sabina, however, did not want a divorce, and her father too was opposed to ending the marriage. The couple had a child, a darling boy, Kubuś, and Zipkin was in charge of the firm's bookkeeping and accounting. Though he wasn't much of a businessman, at least he was honest. Zdzislaw, now married to a girl from Lodz, wanted everything for himself, and Alexander sided with his father-in-law. Jacob Danzinger didn't dare go off to Carlsbad and leave everything in Zdzislaw's hands. Zdzislaw was unstable, a speculator; his wife, avaricious; and his father-in-law, a bankrupt ne'er-do-well. Alexander, although he did have faults, was dependable.

Finally, Jacob Danzinger had his way. What was there to worry about? To begin with, Jacob didn't believe that there was anything between Alexander and Clara. Anyway, if a man occasionally made a fool of himself, it was no tragedy. What did all the salesmen and business agents do to amuse themselves on the long trips they took into the heart of Russia? One couldn't keep too close a watch on a man these days. Alexander was Sabina's husband. They had been married according to the laws of Israel as laid down by Moses. Alexander was the father of Sabina's child. Why suffer because of a lot of nonsense?

This family dispute had been going on since Pentecost, with Sabina constantly changing her mind as to what she should do. One moment she was ready to accompany her family to Carlsbad, the next moment she was not. She agreed to a divorce and then accused her mother of trying to break up her marriage. Alexander pretended that he didn't know what was going on but privately hoped that he would be free of Sabina for a few months. She had grown progressively surlier and more disagreeable, was cold, and imagined she had all kinds of outlandish diseases. Of late, for example, she had become worried about her breathing and was constantly visiting doctors to have her lungs examined. Whenever Zipkin was with Clara, he assured her that Sabina would be away for the summer, and Clara and he would be free to enjoy themselves.

At the last moment (she already had her passport) Sabina changed her mind. Instead of going to Carlsbad with her parents, she leased a villa in Polanka, one station away from Warsaw. Her reason was obvious to Clara. The village was so close to Warsaw that Zipkin need not stay overnight when he went to the city. There were frequent trains to the suburb all year, and in summertime their number was even increased. Clara felt that Sabina had played a trick on her and decided to pay back in kind.

She sent a messenger to Zipkin's office with a letter in which she wrote that after a sleepless night she had decided that the time had come for Alexander to make up his mind. It was either Clara or his wife, but not both. She was tired of deceit. She'd suffered enough insults. Actually, she didn't even have the status of a mistress. If Zipkin decided to remain with his wife, Clara's heart and her door would be closed to him for good. She had signed her name in blood, an act which even she recognized as vulgar.

II

Clara had instructed the messenger to deliver the letter and not wait for a reply. Zipkin opened it immediately, although when he received it there were some customers in his office. He paled, recovering quickly. "It was bound to happen sooner or later," he thought. "Perhaps it's better this way." As long as he was occupied with business matters, it was easy for Zipkin to accept his dismissal. "Affairs are not meant to go on forever. Such a bargain isn't hard to replace." That day the books were being closed for the month. Zipkin sat in a rear office with the assistant bookkeeper, Rubinstein, a young man with a large shock of curly hair. The abacus clattered continuously. Both men were smoking cigars. One moment they would be discussing debits and cash accounts, and the next, actresses and opera singers. Zdzislaw kept coming into the room, playing the boss. The firm's letterhead actually read *Jacob Danzinger & Son*, but in fact, Zdzislaw had little power.

Jacob Danzinger had made sure that he would not become another King Lear, to use his own expression. He had, however, let Zipkin know that Sabina was being left the larger portion of his estate. "Well, one can't have everything," Zipkin said to himself. Clara was an excellent mistress, but not suitable as a wife. Sabina, Zipkin assured himself, would become a different person as soon as Clara was out of the picture. The whole business with Clara had been nothing more than a bubble that had to burst.

Nevertheless, as the day wore on, Zipkin became lonesome. He read Clara's note over and over again. By twilight her signature in blood had begun to look ominous. He had intended to stay in town that night, to have dinner at Clara's and then take her to a concert, or a play. They would have been as free as birds. Suddenly to present him with such an ultimatum! Zipkin picked up the letter once again and read each word carefully. There wasn't a sentence, not even a phrase, that didn't exude passion. "You know how much I long for you. Each time we met was an adventure for me." What would he do with himself now? Sit in Semodeny's Confectionery with no one to keep him company? The thought of his sister Sonya came to him. She had recently come to live in Warsaw. She had a dark room on Dzika Avenue and did some tutoring. Although Zipkin loved her, he had avoided her because Sonya had friends who were active in the political underground. Sonya was one of those women who become beautiful and arouse admiration at a very young age. By the time they reach their early twenties, their charm has already begun to fade, and they become a disappointment to their parents, friends, and to themselves. At sixteen Sonya had received marriage proposals from the wealthiest and best-educated young men in the town where she lived. Now at twenty-six she was considered an old maid who had missed her opportunities. She had dark hair, dark eyes, a fair skin. Her figure was good, but her eyes had become sad and her personality reflected her state of resentment. Her rare meetings with her brother in Warsaw always ended in a quarrel. She quoted mediocre writers, and used phrases which, to Zipkin, seemed utterly banal and silly. She kept a diary and would announce that she had gone to sleep at two o'clock the night before because she had written ten pages in it. When Zipkin asked her what she wrote about,

422

she would answer: "Oh, about many things," and she would smile secretively. Zipkin could not help insulting her whenever she was with him. She would cry softly, and then smile and say: "It won't help you, Alexander. I love you anyway."

It was odd that after living in Warsaw for years Zipkin now found himself isolated. He no longer maintained any ties with his classmates at the university. The group of self-educators had disappeared. Some of its members had been arrested; others had fled. Still others, provincial boys and girls, had committed suicide, although no one knew exactly why. A handful had emigrated to Palestine, where, in settlements founded by some baron, Hebrew was being spoken. Although the *Israelite* was critical of this newly created Jewish nationalism, its opposition did not prevent the movement from spreading. Meetings were held and were well attended, particularly by the Lithuanian rabbis and the opponents of Hassidism. The revolutionaries, too, were again agitating silently. Zipkin was no longer interested in such activities. Only at Clara's did he meet liberals and radicals with whom he could converse about what was going on. As for business friends, there were Zdzislaw and his crowd, who thought of nothing but money.

After leaving the office, Zipkin proceeded to a restaurant where he read the newspaper while he ate. Without Clara, life seemed gray and uninteresting. The scandals in Bulgaria, the economic rivalries between German and British companies in East Africa, the fuss about gold in the Transvaal, all seemed trivial to him. Here in Warsaw everyone was excited about the horse races and the lottery being held in the Saxony Gardens. These activities were of little interest to a man who had been thrown out by the woman he wanted to make love to. Zipkin started for home. As he walked down New Senator Street, he asked himself, "Are all these strolling couples really happy?" If they were, perhaps it was because they'd never known real love. "Take that old fellow barely able to drag his feet along. What is the purpose of his life? What does he hope for? Why is he pulling at his beard? No doubt he has a small hoard hidden away somewhere." Zipkin climbed the stairs to his apartment, unlocked the door, and lit the kerosene lamps. All the furniture, the ottoman, the armchairs, the piano, were covered by sheets to protect them from the dust. The place smelled of naphthaline. He opened a window. Should he go to a cabaret? Or drop in at the chess club? The last train to Polanka might not have left yet. But the thought of traveling to the station, buying a ticket, getting on the train, and then getting off and walking in sand through the dark repelled Zipkin. Yes, the air was fine in Polanka, and Kubuś was a splendid boy, but Sabina would begin lamenting and complaining about her ailments as soon as Zipkin arrived. For all he knew, she might even treat him worse than before when she discovered that Clara had broken with him.

"I'll read a book," Zipkin announced to himself. He glanced at the volumes in the bookcase and immediately lost interest in them. He reminded himself that he owed his parents a letter, but lost the desire to write as soon as he looked at the inkwell. He began to rummage about, pulling out drawers in the writing table and chest in search of he scarcely knew what. How could one endure the sort of life he was leading? "If only I had a bottle of whisky." He sat there staring at the wallpaper. Suddenly he was overcome by the urge to abuse himself like an adolescent. He started to tremble. "I'd better go out and look for a whore." He closed his eyes. "No, I wouldn't enjoy it. I might even not be able to do anything. I'll go see Clara. She won't throw me out. There's no reason why we can't discuss this matter."

He arose quickly. For all he knew, she might not be home. Probably she'd already started going out with other men. He had a bitter taste in his mouth and felt nauseous. He closed the window, thinking it might rain. Sabina dreaded the smallest drop of water, the tiniest ray of sunlight. He must not get to Clara's too late. When he put out the light, he stumbled in the darkness, unable to locate the door, like someone just awakened from a deep sleep.

424

Finally, after banging his knees against a chair, he found himself outside the apartment, racing down the stairs. He didn't hail a droshky because Berg Street was so close it was faster to walk. At last he caught sight of Clara's house. Yes, there was a light on in the parlor. Was she alone? "She's not above bringing a man to her place," he thought, and stopped to catch his breath. He was ashamed to be so dependent on a woman. But what else was there to be addicted to? To heaven? He had not yet decided what he planned to do, but he knew that it would be something extreme that would alter his entire life. It occurred to him that this must be the way a man felt when he entered the casino at Monte Carlo determined to wager all that he possessed.

III

He rang the bell and, as he waited, listened. Apparently there were no guests inside. Finally he heard footsteps and then Clara's voice.

"Who is it?"

"It's me, Alexander," he said hoarsely.

There was silence. She was probably deliberating. Zipkin held his breath. He knew that everything hung in the balance. If she ordered him away, he would never see her again. Perhaps Clara realized this also. She drew the bolt, unfastened the chain, and swung open the door. She wore a dressing gown and slippers. She had changed her hair style and seemed thinner than when he had seen her last. There were dark rings under her eyes, yet somehow to Zipkin she seemed more alluring than before. They stood gazing at each other.

"Apparently you don't recognize me," she said in Polish.

"Oh, I recognize you."

"Well, come in."

Zipkin walked into the hallway and then into the living room. He took off his straw hat but kept it in his hand. Although his cigarette had gone out, he did not remove it from

425

his lips. He noticed a change in the living room, but couldn't figure out what it was. The curtains? Were they different? No, she had removed the chair in which he usually sat. Clara glanced at him, and he paled. An expression of girlish obstinacy came into her eyes.

"I hope you've come to a decision," Clara said. "If not, you're just wasting your time."

"I can't understand what's got into you."

"You know well enough. You're not a simpleton. I don't care for the position that you've assigned to me."

"What exactly do you want?"

"I told you in my letter. You must choose between us."

"I just can't divorce her like that."

"It's either her or me. This two-woman arrangement has to end."

"If I leave her, I'll lose my job," Zipkin said, and regretted his words immediately. He began to blush.

"Are you telling me that you get paid for your love? All right. But I've had my fill. I'm not the fool you take me for. Why I put up with it for so long is beyond me. I don't intend to haggle with you. I've told you already: it's either here or there."

Clara smiled. It was the same smile that appeared on her lips before she jumped all his pieces when they played checkers. In that smile were mingled victory and feminine compassion. Zipkin said nothing. He removed the cigarette butt from his mouth. The tone of her voice annoyed him. He didn't like the way she stood with her hands on her hips. He moved over to the stove and reached out his hand as if to warm himself. If he deserted Sabina, he would be left without a kopeck. Her dowry had been kept in her name. Anyway, he wouldn't think of taking money from a woman whom he was abandoning. What should he do? Should he marry Clara? Was he to give his name to a woman who had already had two husbands and had gone to his room the very first night they met? Could

426

he become the stepfather of that barbarian Sasha? And for how long would Clara interest him? She was certainly already forty, if not more. "Well," he said, "you can't expect me to come to such a decision immediately."

Clara hesitated for a moment. "Forgive me for saying so, Alexander, but the place for you to think such a matter over is in your own home."

"You're telling me to go?"

"No. But I'm ready to free you from all your responsibilities, even from your obligations to your own daughter. I can't stand this sort of life any longer."

"It's hard for me, too."

"Exactly how hard? We just can't go on talking forever. Words, my dear, are no longer of any use. Don't think this decision has been easy for me. You'll never know how much I've suffered."

Zipkin began to pace up and down the room. What should he do? He glanced at the window and then walked over and pulled back the curtain. Then he turned slowly back toward Clara.

"All right," he said. "I've made up my mind."

"Yes?"

"I don't want her. I want you. But we can't remain in Warsaw. We must leave."

"Where will we go?"

"Out of the country."

"So . . ."

"If not, there'd be too much for us to contend with."

"Yes, that's true."

"Are you willing to go with me?"

"Yes, I'm willing."

They looked at each other in amazement, surprised at the turn their conversation had taken.

"Where do you think we should go?" he asked.

"I have no idea."

427

"Perhaps America? At least one can earn a living there."

"What will you do—sew pants?"

"Possibly."

"All right. I wanted Sasha to graduate from the gymnasium, but if he can't, it's just too bad."

"One can go to school there, too."

"He'll have to start all over again. But I don't care. If my father wants to keep him for a few years, I won't oppose it. The boy is still young. He's just starting life. I'd like to make the most of the few years that I have left."

"Why do you say the few years?"

"I don't know. Just because. One can't be sure. If I can't be your wife, I don't want anything."

"Come, let's go to bed."

"I'll go anywhere you want to go, but you must swear that it will be as we've agreed. I want it in writing."

I V

In the middle of the night, Clara awoke, terrified. Someone was ringing the doorbell and pounding on the front door. Through the cracks of the shutters came the first blue light of dawn. Zipkin and Clara had not been asleep for long. Clara shook Zipkin awake.

"Alexander, someone's knocking on the door. Don't you hear?"

"Do you have any idea who it can be?" he asked.

"None whatsoever."

Clara put on a dressing gown, and Zipkin a robe and slippers. Finally, after some discussion, it was decided that Clara should go to the door while Zipkin waited in the parlor. The foyer was dark.

"Who's there?" Clara asked. She had the feeling that the person on the other side of the door was coming to destroy her happiness.

"It's me. Sonya."

"It's your sister," Clara shouted to Zipkin. She opened the door and Sonya slipped in, seeming almost more shadow than girl.

"Forgive me, madame. The circumstances that have brought me here are quite unusual. I've been wandering the streets since eleven o'clock. The police were going to arrest me."

"What for? Alexander, come out here." Zipkin hurried into the foyer.

"What's happened, Sonya?"

"Oh, so you're here. They've searched my house."

"When?"

"At about eleven. I had been to the theater with Mirale, Ezriel's sister. On Przejazd Street. She was with a young man. He's not Jewish. When I got to Dzika Street, Notke, the landlord's son, said to me, 'Go somewhere else. Your place has just been searched.' I went to your house, but the janitor wouldn't let me in."

"What were they looking for? Have you done anything?"

"Here in Warsaw? Nothing. You know—I've moved to the place Mirale used to have. I told you—they have a printing press now. They're living together. Oh, I shouldn't have said that. It's a secret. They ran away too, even before I did. As soon as they heard the word 'search,' they just rushed off."

"Well, come on in," Clara said, at last recovering herself. "What are we standing out here for? Mirale was supposed to do my hair, but she never showed up. I thought she was sick. Who is the young man?"

"Oh, he's nice. One of them. Their leader. They met me yesterday and took me along."

"How did you know that I was here?" Zipkin asked embarrassedly.

"I had no idea that you were. I thought you were at home or out of town. I don't even have my birth certificate with me. I came here because I thought Madame Clara would be sympathetic. It's all so strange to me somehow. I really don't know what to say in apology. There was someone following me. I don't know who it was."

"A police agent, perhaps?" Clara asked, half in anger. "He followed you here."

"No, not an agent. He left when I arrived at your house, Alexander. As soon as I rang the gate bell, he walked on."

"Let's get out of the hall," Clara said sharply. "What a night it's been. It's dawn already. Forgive the way the place looks. We have our own problems. Alexander, may I tell her?"

They walked into the parlor. The curtains were still drawn, and the room lay in a twilight that made their faces appear pale, blurred, like images on a dimly lit stage.

"Tell her what, Clara?"

"We're to be married, Sonya. Alexander's leaving his wife."

"Alexander, is it true?"

"It is, Sonya. I never loved Sabina. My marrying her was a mistake."

"But what will become of Kubuś?" When no one answered the girl's question, she continued in a different tone of voice. "I never cared for Sabina either, and she doesn't like me. Well, congratulations. Your happiness is mine. Now Felusia will have a father."

Clara, choked with emotion, coughed to clear her throat. "Well, both Alexander and I have made our mistakes, Sonya, but that's over with now. We're leaving the country."

Zipkin interrupted, "We'll take you with us, Sonya. It's best that you leave at once, perhaps even before we do. Don't you think so, Clara?"

"Unquestionably. What does she have here that's worth staying for? Sonya, our plan is to go to Paris, and later, if possible, to America."

"To America? Oh, my God."

"Alexander, you go back to sleep. I'll make a bed for her on the sofa. If you're hungry, Sonya, I can give you a glass of milk and a roll. A stale one, I'm afraid. I was in such a state yesterday that I ate nothing. Suddenly your brother appeared and everything was all right again. What sort of printing press do they have? Does she live with the Gentile?"

"Not like man and wife, if that's what you mean. They wanted me to join the organization, but I gave them no definite answer."

"Don't get mixed up in all these conspiracies, Sonya," Zipkin said. "The time isn't ripe for that sort of action. Here and in Russia the reactionaries have taken over. There are *agents provacateurs* everywhere. It'll end with you being packed off to jail. Who'll get you out then? You see my situation. I can't stay in Poland any longer."

"Yes, Alexander, I understand perfectly."

v

The clock in the living room struck ten. Zipkin opened his eyes. Clara was still asleep beside him, snoring as if it were midnight. Zipkin ran his hand across his brow. Had he been dreaming? No, Sonya had in fact arrived in the middle of the night. There had been a police search. He had given Clara his word that he would divorce Sabina, had even signed a paper to that effect. So, that was how things were! He lay there and looked at Clara, amazed at where his passions had led him. Yes, she dyed her hair. He could see some gray growing in at the roots. As she slept, Clara's face looked fat and middle-aged. There were wrinkles on her cheeks and her skin was pitted. Had she had smallpox? Last night, consumed by desire, nothing but lying next to her had mattered. Now, seeing her in the morning light, he wondered, "Where will I go with her? How will we live?" He got out of bed and put on a robe and slippers. When he opened the door, he saw Sonya seated on the sofa which she had used as a bed, reading a book.

"So you're up already," he said.

"I didn't sleep a wink."

"Why not? You said you were so tired."

"All this has unnerved me, Alexander."

"To what are you referring?"

"Oh, various things. No, I'd better keep my mouth shut."

"You can be frank with me. But there are many things over which we have no control."

Zipkin went into the kitchen and washed. "Exactly what kind of an animal is man?" he asked himself, and then yawned. "I'm so weak, and yet I take such a burden upon myself. I'll collapse under the load." The night before, he had thought of himself as a giant. Now he rose with his temples throbbing, his legs aching, and a pain in his back. "Am I arthritic? Perhaps I have a bad heart." He put his index finger into his mouth and poked at a molar he knew was loose, meanwhile looking at himself in a mirror that hung above the sink. His hair was already getting thin. "Will I never again be at peace with myself?" he mumbled. "If my parents knew what I've become, they'd die."

Clara entered, dressed in an expensive negligee. With cosmetics on, she once more appeared young and animated. She looked at him searchingly.

"I didn't hear you get up."

"I didn't want to wake you."

Clara became tense. "Alexander, I know that she's your sister and will soon, if you keep your promise, be my sister-in-law. I wish her only good. But now is not the time for us to have a chaperon. The next few weeks we must live alone."

"She doesn't have to travel with us."

"I don't care what she says. I know where her sympathies lie, even though your wife wouldn't even let her into the house."

"Sonya is not my main consideration here."

"Alexander, I don't want to nag you, but it's important that everything be done quickly. You don't have to wait for a divorce. You can send Sabina a bill of divorcement from America."

"No, I can't leave without saying something."

"Why not? You'll only be saving yourself some breath and Sabina unnecessary tears. You consider yourself a Don Juan, but you don't know anything about women. She'll move heaven and earth to keep you. You don't have—if you'll forgive my saying it—the strongest of characters. How much money do you have?"

"Not a groschen."

"Aren't you the cashier?"

"It's my father-in-law's money."

"What about the dowry?"

"I've already told you about that."

"Well, if you want to be a fool, go ahead. You know how impoverished I am. How can a man permit himself to be without a kopeck? Don't get angry, but that's stupidity, not idealism. For whom were you working? The devil? Well, I'll just have to sell the furniture, but I must be certain that you won't have a change of heart. Our decisions must be definite. Neither of us is a child."

"I must have a day or two to think it over."

"What's there to think about? If you intend to back out, let me know now. You either do something like this immediately or not at all. We don't need passports; we'll just slip across the border. Our only baggage will be two suitcases. Once we're out of the country, we have the whole world to choose from."

"Yes, Clara, that's true."

"I have certain matters to put in order before we leave. Unlike you, I can't sit around and brood. First of all, I must go to Jampol and have a good talk with my father. I just can't push the children off on him. I have a few things to say to Celina, too. Besides, her mother is there, and I'd like to see her before I leave. Don't think all of this is such an easy matter for me."

"When do you plan to go?"

"The exact time doesn't matter much. But I must be sure

that when I speak to them I won't be making a fool of myself. I've done too much of that in my life already."

Zipkin swallowed hard. "Go and talk to your father."

"You've made up your mind then? You have no doubts? Remember, I can't trifle with my own father. When I go there, I must be able to give him all the facts."

"You may tell him everything."

"Well, that's what I wanted to hear from you."

29

Calman Jacoby was sixty-five. There had been a time when he
had thought he would be dead by that age. According to the
Talmud, a man who reaches the age when his parents died
should begin to think about his own demise. Besides, he had
worked hard and suffered much. But thank God, he was
healthy. Behind his white beard, his face remained ruddy and
his eyes clear. His back was still as straight as it had ever been.
God had blessed Calman with strength.

Mayer Joel was now in full charge of the estate, and the
lime quarries, which were now almost exhausted. Calman had
turned everything over to his son-in-law, who had enlarged
the mill and installed rollers to grind sifted flour. Calman himself still performed heavy labor, not out of necessity but because he was accustomed to it. He rose, as always, at sunrise,
ate black bread and cottage cheese for breakfast, and drank a
large glass of water. He handled sacks, helped to load the lime,
harnessed horses, even chopped wood. He could not spend all
his time studying the Mishnah or the Talmud. He had lived
for years without a wife; lust seethed in his veins. Without
anything to do, he would lose his mind.

No, Calman had not reckoned with old age. He had once
believed that as the beard grayed, one's thoughts became pure.
But it was not so. Even being a great-grandfather had not

been able to quiet his passion. Yes, he was already a great-grandfather because Jochebed's daughter, Teibela, was a mother. Jochebed, who was eighteen years younger than her father, behaved like an old woman. In a bonnet, with glasses on her nose, she sat most of the day reading *The Lamp of Light* and *The Inheritance of the Deer*. Her father, however, lacked the patience to read for very long.

Even at prayertime, evil thoughts assailed him. At night his imagination seethed with the nonsense he had known in boyhood or when, as a widower, he had coveted Clara. The Jampol matchmakers continued to swarm around him with potential brides; they were even proposing that he marry an eighteen-year-old orphan girl. Calman knew that, according to the Law, he should marry. As it is written in the Scriptures: "In the morning sow thy seed and in the evening withhold not thine hand." Nevertheless, Calman had been unable to come to a decision. When, each year, Daniel Kaminer celebrated a circumcision or had a family feast, Calman was disgusted. Why sire children in one's old age? Why leave orphans?

He now lived alone in one room of the house he had once occupied with Zelda. He had set aside another room for prayer. He had procured a Holy Ark, a Scroll of the Law, a menorah, the volumes of the Mishnah, the Talmud, and other holy books, as well as a lectern, a cantor's pulpit with a candelabrum, and even a copper basin in which to wash one's hands. An eternal light in memory of Zelda's soul burned at the door. He had also provided a guest room for the use of traveling Jews who from time to time visited the estate to solicit subscriptions for books, or to collect money for the support of poor brides. A Jampol woman took care of Calman's house. Calman himself looked after every visitor. He had a bed for everyone. He gave each visitor food, a night's lodging, a few coins, and sometimes even a measure of corn, a pot of groats, millet, or whatever was left over. At times, though infrequently, so many visitors came that a quorum could be formed for prayer. Usually Calman had to pray alone. He walked back and forth in his prayer shawl and phylacteries. He had won and lost a world here. A daughter had been converted. Thank God he had good children as well. Jochebed was an honorable woman, Tsipele a saint.

Calman prayed, reflecting. He kissed the phylacteries worn on the head and on the arm by touching them and then bringing his fingers to his lips. He also kissed the fringes of his prayer shawl. He stationed himself at the Eastern wall for the Eighteen Benedictions. This house of prayer had been his salvation. Here he retired with all his worries and anxieties. He knew well that one must not open the Holy Ark without reason. But occasionally he had a desperate desire to slide back the curtain that protected it, and open the door. The wood within was reddish, wine-colored; wrapped in satin, crowned with bells, and decorated with a tassel and fescue, the Scroll of the Law leaned against the wall of the Ark. It seemed to him that the smells of the spices of the Garden of Eden emanated from it. The Law that Moses had given on Mount Sinai was inscribed on the parchment.

Calman bowed his head and kissed the Scroll. He would die, but this Holy Scroll which he had had inscribed would be passed on from generation to generation. Jews would be called up to it, would kiss it, walk with it, hold it aloft, and dance with it at the Rejoicing of the Law. On the satin mantle, within the Star of David, embroidered in gold was the statement that Calman, son of Sender Jacob, had donated the Torah in memory of his wife Zelda, daughter of Uri Joseph. God willing, when he arrived in the other world, this Torah would count among his good deeds. But who would there be to recite Kaddish for him—Clara's little jewel, Sasha?

11

During the winter Calman could, more or less, forget that he had once had a wife like Clara. But in summertime, when Sasha came to stay with his grandfather Daniel Kaminer and visited Calman, the boy was a constant reminder of his life with Clara. Calman saw before him a son who—may the Evil Eye spare him—grew like yeast. At each of his sudden appearances, Sasha's stature and clothes were so altered that Calman hardly recognized him.

One summer day a grown youth, wearing a jacket with gold buttons, a cap with an emblem, riding breeches and boots almost knee-high, and looking like a Gentile, came to see Calman. More broad-shouldered than tall, healthy, with a shock of shining black hair, he had already begun to use a razor. Speaking a broken Yiddish and laughing with gypsylike eyes, he bewildered Calman for a moment.

"Papa, it's me, Sasha, Senderel!" And Sasha smiled with strong white teeth such as the Jewish boys in Poland did not have.

"How did you get here?"

"By train. Felusia is here too."

Calman pretended not to have heard the name.

"How are you? How is your mother?" Calman asked, and instantly regretted having referred to Clara.

"Everything's fine. I'm giving my teachers a hard time. Mama screams at me."

"Why does she scream?"

"Oh, she screams all the time. I don't learn enough. My marks aren't good. She thinks I should only get five pluses. I don't give a damn. I'd rather have a good time."

"What is having a good time?"

"Everything. Swimming in the Vistula, exercising. Across from our school there is a girls' school and we have fun with the girls. We play tricks on them. Here is my ritual garment!" Sasha suddenly began to search beneath his blouse. "I brought my phylacteries to Jampol, too. I am a Jew."

"Well, thank God."

"Papa, do you still have the gray mare?"

"Does the Hebrew tutor still come to give you lessons?"

Sasha hesitated a moment.

438

"The rabbi with the goatee is gone. A Hebrew teacher was supposed to come, but because of the exams I didn't have time. After vacation, I'll begin again. I have the Pentateuch, and the prayer book and all the rest."

"You can have the mare, but while you're here you'll have to learn a chapter of the Pentateuch, and pray as well."

"I left my phylacteries at Grandfather's."

Sasha was impatient with praying. He would tap his feet and laugh, then grow serious and snatch at a butterfly that flew in through the open window. If it were possible to do so, he would have done everything at once: ride, swim in the pond, eat. He had walked all the way from Jampol. Calman brought in his phylacteries and a prayer book, but Sasha had forgotten everything. He did not remember that phylacteries had leather straps. Calman wrapped them first around the boy's strong arm, and then to form the prescribed letter "Shin" continued them around Sasha's hand and between his fingers. He recited the benediction for him and made him repeat it. Meanwhile, the housekeeper prepared delicacies for the guest. Sasha adored Passover egg cakes and cookies all year round. Pacing back and forth across the prayer room, he gaped at the walls. He stopped for the Eighteen Benedictions but did not beat his breast, or bow to "give thanks." Calman was ashamed and alarmed. Nevertheless, he was fond of the boy. Although he resembled Clara, certain of Sasha's mannerisms reminded Calman of his own father, Sender Jacob, may he rest in Paradise.

Calman made excuses for Sasha. "How was it the poor boy's fault? He was raised among idolaters." In the midst of prayers —he hadn't even removed his phylacteries—the boy approached Calman and, taking him by the shoulders, kissed his forehead. Calman was astonished. That was how Clara used to act. In the midst of anything, she would start kissing.

"Papa, I love you."

"I'd rather you were a Jew."

"What am I—a Gentile? When the priest comes to our

school, the Jewish pupils leave. The Gentiles call us names and we crack their jaws for them. Papa, I'm proud to be a Jew."

"Proud? Why proud?"

"I'm proud . . . They are anti-Semites, but we don't give a damn about them. We can punch, too. The teachers make all sorts of remarks. I answer back. I'm afraid of no one. Once, because I talked back, I got a zero. That's the worst mark. But I didn't care."

"It's best for a Jew to be among Jews," Calman said. "Then he's spared such battles."

"How can I be among Jews? There is no Jewish high school. I want to be an engineer, but the machinery and everything else belongs to the Gentiles. Why don't Jews own land? Why don't they live in Palestine?"

"In the Land of Israel? Because they sinned, and God drove them out."

"The Gentiles sin, too, and they have everything."

"The Jews are God's children, and with his own child a father is strict."

"Some say there is no God."

Calman trembled.

"Who says that? Remove the phylacteries! The phylacteries are God's sign and you speak such nonsense."

Calman helped Sasha remove the phylacteries. In the kitchen he drew a dipperful of water from the barrel for the boy to wash before eating. Sitting at the table, he waited for Sasha to finish and say the benediction. Sasha disposed of one butter-fried pancake after another, washing them down with milk and simultaneously glancing toward the manor house, which was now an officers' club. He had met the officers' wives and daughters the previous year. He had ridden their horses; the officers had taught him to shoot. This year he looked like a full-grown man.

After the benediction, Calman accompanied Sasha to the stable. The gray mare was still fit for riding, though she had aged. The saddle had been mislaid and had to be searched for.

Meanwhile, Sasha went to the river for a swim. Apparently, his mother had not infused him with any sense of modesty. He began to disrobe, exhibiting no bashfulness before his father. Mentally, Calman compared him to Ham, Noah's son.

In addition to disgracing Calman, Sasha reminded him of Clara. He had her face, her eyes, and occasionally even her voice.

III

At night, when Calman was unable to sleep, he would rise and go into his makeshift synagogue. First he would knock, to alert the corpses who pray there after midnight. Lighting the naphtha lamp that hung from a wire above the table, he would open a volume of the Mishnah and study. Sasha, whom he had been seeing every other day, had not appeared for a week. Outside, a mild breeze was blowing. The fields and forests stretched for miles around. Who could estimate how many devils, imps, and hobgoblins congregated there?

Two gilded lions on either side of the Ten Commandments formed the cornice of the Ark. A mezuzah hung on the doorpost; only a real synagogue was exempt from a doorpost amulet. Calman chanted the first Mishnah: "Seven days before the Day of Atonement, the High Priest was taken away from his own house unto the Councillor Chamber and another priest was made ready in his stead, lest aught should befall him to render him ineligible. Rabbi Judah says, 'Also another wife was made ready for him lest his own wife should die, for it is written: He shall make atonement for himself and his house; that is, his wife.' They said to him: 'If so, there would be no end to the matter.' "

Calman chanted the words, tugging at a tangle in his beard. He glanced at the commentary of Rabbi Yom Tov Heller and saw before his eyes the ancient Temple, where in the innermost chamber of the sanctuary, the Holy Ark, the cherubim were all made of gold. Into this Holy of Holies once a year the

441

High Priest would come, dressed in a breastplate and vestment, with a cowl on his head, carrying a pan in which to burn incense. Surrounding the inner sanctum were the various buildings of the Temple. Priests would bring sacrificial animals to the altar, and burn fats and fried meal offerings. Farthest away was the temple court, where all Jews could enter. It was so full that there was no room left for a pin, but when the High Priest intoned the name of Jehovah, the courtyard expanded so that all might bow and kneel.

Calman was filled with longing for the ancient times, when Jews lived in the Land of Israel. Thrice yearly they made a pilgrimage to Jerusalem. They owned their own fields, forests, vineyards, fig trees. A king ruled over the Jews, and men prophesied. All the same, Calman thought, there was sinning, too. Jeroboam placed two golden calves in Bethel and Dan and the Jews worshipped them. How could this have been possible? It was beyond comprehension.

Calman did not even remember when he had learned the chant in which he prayed and studied. It had come down to him through generations of ancestors. The words of the Mishnah were very clear; they dealt with an ox, a jackass, a thief, a murderer, a wedding, a divorce. Yet each word had an indescribable flavor. The Hebrew letters were steeped in holiness, in eternity. They seemed to unite him with the patriarchs, with Joshua, Gamaliel, Eliezer, and with Hillel the Ancient. The tannaim spoke to him like grandfathers. They argued with him as to what was right and what was wrong, what was pure and impure. They made him a kind of partner in sharing the Torah's treasures. Among these shelves of sacred books, Calman felt protected. Over each volume hovered the soul of its author. In this place, God watched over him.